Katie Mettner wears the tit[...] her leg after falling down [...] decorating her prosthetic leg to fit the season. She lives in Northern Wisconsin with her own happily-ever-after and spends the day writing romantic stories with her sweet puppy by her side. Katie has an addiction to coffee and dachshunds and a lessening aversion to Pinterest—now that she's quit trying to make the things she pins.

New York Times and *USA Today* bestselling author **Caridad Piñeiro** is a Jersey girl who just wants to write and is the author of nearly fifty novels and novellas. She loves romance novels, superheroes, TV and cooking. For more information on Caridad and her dark, sexy romantic suspense and paranormal romances, please visit caridad.com

Also by Katie Mettner

Secure One

Going Rogue in Red Rye County
The Perfect Witness
The Red River Slayer
The Silent Setup
The Masquerading Twin
Holiday Under Wraps

Also by Caridad Piñeiro

South Beach Security: K-9 Division

Sabotage Operation
Escape the Everglades
Killer in the Kennel
Danger in Dade

South Beach Security

Brickell Avenue Ambush
Biscayne Bay Breach

Trapping a Terrorist
Decoy Training

Discover more at millsandboon.co.uk

DARK WEB INVESTIGATION

KATIE METTNER

CLIFFSIDE KIDNAPPING

CARIDAD PIÑEIRO

MILLS & BOON

All rights reserved including the right of reproduction in whole or in part in any form. This edition is published by arrangement with Harlequin Enterprises ULC.

This is a work of fiction. Names, characters, places, locations and incidents are purely fictional and bear no relationship to any real life individuals, living or dead, or to any actual places, business establishments, locations, events or incidents. Any resemblance is entirely coincidental.

Without limiting the author's and publisher's exclusive rights, any unauthorised use of this publication to train generative artificial intelligence (AI) technologies is expressly prohibited. HarperCollins also exercise their rights under Article 4(3) of the Digital Single Market Directive 2019/790 and expressly reserve this publication from the text and data mining exception.

® and ™ are trademarks owned and used by the trademark owner and/or its licensee. Trademarks marked with ® are registered with the United Kingdom Patent Office and/or the Office for Harmonisation in the Internal Market and in other countries.

First Published in Great Britain 2025
by Mills & Boon, an imprint of HarperCollins*Publishers* Ltd
1 London Bridge Street, London, SE1 9GF

www.harpercollins.co.uk

HarperCollins*Publishers*
Macken House, 39/40 Mayor Street Upper,
Dublin 1, D01 C9W8, Ireland

Dark Web Investigation © 2025 Katie Mettner
Cliffside Kidnapping © 2025 Caridad Piñeiro Scordato

ISBN: 978-0-263-39715-4

0625

This book contains FSC™ certified paper and other controlled sources to ensure responsible forest management.

For more information visit: www.harpercollins.co.uk/green

Printed and Bound in the UK using 100% Renewable Electricity at
CPI Group (UK) Ltd, Croydon, CR0 4YY

DARK WEB INVESTIGATION

KATIE METTNER

To the unseen and unsung heroes of the digital world
who protect us as we go about our daily lives.

Chapter One

Kenley Bates tugged her stocking cap down lower over her ears and stepped inside the internet café; the sound of sirens and traffic dulled as the door closed behind her. Some might consider Metro Matrix a hangout for the dregs of Milwaukee, but no one better say that to Kenley's face. In her opinion, it was a term that implied everyone who lived in that part of the city was secondary to the rest of the city. Kenley had grown up there and knew the truth was something else entirely. Like any other neighborhood, the people did their best in a world where the deck was stacked against them. She should know—she'd lived it. Most turned their nose up when she mentioned the neighborhood she grew up in but living there had taught her something at an early age that too many people never learned: grab every opportunity that comes your way in life. Kenley worked hard to succeed and then pushed herself to take care of the people who helped her get there. It was important to her to stay true to who she was, no matter where she moved in life.

Knowing she had one way to help, she lived to learn and worked her fingers to the bone until she had a successful business and slept in an apartment overlooking the lake. That didn't make her any better than her friends at the Matrix. She lived in her clients' world so she could work for her people here. What her clients gave her, she could turn around and use to assist those truly in need. She was lucky that her natural-born talent could make a difference for those hurt and victimized by people who saw her clients as nothing more than cogs in a wheel.

Spotting an empty table in the far back corner of the café, she slid her backpack off and settled into the chair. Pretending to read the menu board above the small counter, she took a mental snapshot of the other users in the space. It was relatively empty for a Wednesday night, which she was glad about, but any one person could be the enemy she wasn't expecting. She opened her laptop and signed onto the Wi-Fi without looking away from the space around her.

Metro Matrix was her favorite place to set up shop when her white-hat hacking needed to turn a bit darker. The Matrix, as everyone called it, sold more than an internet connection to its customers. It also sold coffee, soda and snacks, but if you were looking for other services, you could get those, too. All you had to do was knock on the old wooden door three times and wait your turn.

Kenley had never knocked on the door. That wasn't why she took the bus ten miles one way to get here. At The Matrix, she could sit in the corner, run their Wi-Fi through her proxy scrambler and do what she needed to do on the darker side of the web without worrying that someone could track her. She also felt a tethered connection to her people when she sat at one of the tables. The friends and neighbors that she helped whenever she stepped over that white line in the sand. It was a place where she could relax in her work and get the answers someone needed to find justice.

At least that was how she usually felt, but not tonight. Tonight, she was nervous for a reason she couldn't define. High alert was an excellent way to describe it as she tugged her stocking cap down again to be sure her hair was still tucked under it. If she were honest with herself, she'd felt that way for several days now. It was like a hammer was about to fall, and she was in the way.

At thirty-one, some would say she was old enough to know better. Dabbling in the business of the dark web was risky business in and of itself, but Kenley had limited options if she wanted to help the people who had suffered too many atrocities in life. She knew what that felt like. Kenley's desire to fight for those without a voice—or maybe to fight for those drowned out by louder voices—came from life experience.

When she'd discovered in her senior year of high school that she had a natural talent for coding, she'd learned everything there was to know about it. Her quiet skills were loud when a job needed to be done. There were too many people without the skills to prove that they were being railroaded into silence by those with money and power, and Kenley refused to participate in their oppression. Not when she could stop it.

Did she feel dirty that her day job involved working for those who oppressed others? Yes, but it was the means to an end for her. While she spent her days writing code for corporations desperate to protect their business from ransomware and digital theft, she spent her nights sleuthing those same corporations for wrongdoing. She excelled at both jobs. She had more clients than time during the day, and while it afforded her a nice lifestyle, it didn't fulfill her the way her night job did. That was her true passion. Every time she found proof that could hold another big, lying corporation accountable for someone else's pain, it soothed the burn she had suffered. She'd once needed the same help, and when no one was there for her, she'd made it her life's mission to be the person others could turn to when all hope was lost.

After digging out her earbuds from her bag, she popped them in without connecting them to music. They helped her fit in, but music would prevent early warning of someone approaching unexpectedly. With her hands on the keyboard, she was ready to leave Kenley behind and become 51CKL3, her call name on most sites she frequented. Those were the sites where 51CKL3 found those needing help and where she could get a little justice for people who had suffered a tremendous loss.

Sickle was a fitting name for her, as her sole purpose was to cut companies off at the knees when they hurt the innocent. She glanced down at her right leg with a grim smile. She came by that name naturally. Unfortunately, after all these years, she still didn't have answers about her accident, but she refused to give up. Her friend had died for no other reason than greed, and Kenley was determined to prove it.

Her determination to find those answers was why she sat in The Matrix at 11:00 p.m. on a Wednesday in the middle of October. When she didn't have another client to take care of, she used her café time to find proof that her best friend had died due to negligence by the company that made the ATV.

She and Gabriella had been best friends their entire childhood. Gabriella had been a beautiful girl with wavy red hair and freckles across the bridge of her nose. She was tall and loved to play basketball on the JV team. Kenley was the opposite, with long, straight black hair and a skin tone reflective of her Latina mother and Black father. Gabriella had moved in next door when the girls were only four. Since Gabby's mom was single, Kenley's mother had offered to watch Gabriella so her mom could work the night shift as a nurse.

The girls shared Kenley's room five, sometimes six, nights a week growing up and were as close as sisters.

They were ready to start their sophomore year in high school when they'd made the fateful decision to take one last ride on Gabriella's ATV before school started the next day. A final goodbye to summer was said on the back of a four-wheeled machine barreling down a trail, which made them feel invincible. It was something they'd done hundreds of times before, but that day, Kenley had been tossed out of nowhere into the dirt, and her entire world had turned upside down.

Gabriella is dead.

It had been seventeen years, and she could still hear her mother say those three words. When they told her they'd amputated her right foot, it meant nothing to her. Her best friend was dead, and she didn't want to live if Gabriella wasn't by her side. Those were dark days. Days that Kenley tried to forget so she could focus on the one thing that got her through. Building the skills she'd need to prove that the parent company behind the ATV manufacturer was responsible for her best friend's death.

Using those coding skills, she had gotten justice for so many, but she still hadn't found proof that Staun Bril Corporation knew the wheels of their Neo Chase ATVs could shear off at higher speeds. The lack of proof didn't mean they were innocent; it just meant she hadn't looked hard enough.

After checking into a few sites that used the power of the hive mind, she was ready to exit a chat room when she noticed a private message icon. Hope surged in her heart as she clicked it. While she waited for the message to load, she wondered if it was about her inquiries with the ATV manufacturer or a request for help from someone else looking for justice. When the page loaded, what filled the screen wasn't a request for help. It was a childish game that made her angry. She ground her teeth together as she dumped all the 0s and 1s into a text decoder and waited for the message to populate. She hated nothing more than dealing with an inexperienced child who thought secret decoding was necessary on the dark web. It wasn't, but for the sake of her quest, she'd decode the message on the off chance it was helpful. When the short sentence was revealed, she bit back a gasp.

Stop what you're doing before it's too late.

On instinct, Kenley glanced up and searched the nearly empty café. Goose bumps rose on her skin, and she swallowed nervously as her gaze darted around, taking in the other users who were either gaming or, in one case, watching banned anime. No one was paying her any attention, at least not in her physical landscape. Her digital landscape seemed to imply something else entirely.

Rather than buckle to the fear, she thrust her chest out and typed a message into a binary code translator before she copied the 0s and 1s into the text box and hit Send. If this jerk wanted to play, she'd play. It wasn't the first time she'd been challenged on the dark web, and it wouldn't be the last. It was important not to show weakness if she wanted to remain the hunter and not the hunted. It wasn't likely to come to anything more than a battle of wits from behind a screen. She left no identifying information behind, so outing 51CKL3 to the real world was impossible.

Kenley blew out a breath and shook out her shoulders. Maybe it was best to hang it up for the night. She was already jumpy, and that message didn't help matters, but her schedule didn't allow her to get back to The Matrix until the weekend, so she wanted to give the sender a chance to respond. Whoever was behind this was probably jockeying for position in the group—something Kenley couldn't care less about. She wasn't part of the group for the glory or the ego boost. She was there for information and justice. Nothing else.

Speaking of information, while she was waiting, she may as well access the Staun Bril Corporation files. If she were lucky, they'd have updated their research papers, and she'd find proof that they were aware of the axle problem on the older models of the ATV. That was all she needed. Proof that they *knew* the machines had a problem, but they sold them anyway.

Should her parents or Gabriella's mom have been the ones to bring a lawsuit against the ATV company? Yes, but there wasn't enough money for food and rent, much less lawyers. It had taken Kenley years to learn that others had suffered the same fate she had while driving the Neo Chase. Deaths. Amputations. Crush injuries. You name it, and it had been dealt out by the hands that steered the Staun Bril Corporation. Kenley knew that they didn't care about people, only profits. If they cared about people, they would have recalled the machines the moment someone came forward with an injury. Not only did they not recall the machines, but they doubled down on advertising how safe they were and sold thousands more. In her opinion, that was the evil in this world.

The icon alert blinked that she had another message. Frowning, Kenley checked the time. It had only been four minutes. Whoever this was, they were waiting for her. She clicked on the red dot and waited for the 0s and 1s to load again. Once she had them decoded, her fingers faltered on the keyboard.

It doesn't matter who I am. I'm watching you, and you've been a very naughty girl.

Either this guy was a sicko, or he was somehow tracking her. She checked her proxy and shook her head in frustration. It wasn't possible. She never used the same IP twice, and using public Wi-Fi meant there was no way to home in on where or what she was doing online.

Kenley hated to do it, but she had little choice. She'd have to burn that forum and change her digital footprint again. Not that anyone could track her footprints, but changing her online name and persona was occasionally necessary to avoid showing up on radars like the one she'd found herself on. For all she knew, it was a cop behind that keyboard, and the last thing she would do was continue messaging until she walked into a trap.

Furiously clicking her mouse, she deleted everything she'd done on the forum as she backed out, finally deleting herself as a member. Then, she deleted the forum information from her server. Satisfied, she nodded before she signed back into the web. At least the person messaging her could no longer track her if they had figured out a way to do it through that forum. She knew it was impossible to be truly anonymous on the web. Still, without a username and the proxy scrambler mixing up her overseas locations, no one would know she was in a café in downtown Milwaukee, Wisconsin. At least they wouldn't know until she was long gone. As much as she hated to do it, this would be her last visit to The Matrix. Sometimes, you had to know when to fold a losing hand, and Kenley decided she'd just been dealt one.

There were always risks to playing on the internet this way, but the rewards usually outweighed them if you knew what you were doing, and she was confident that she did.

She'd move around a bit and lurk through a few forums she never would have visited as 51CKL3, just in case someone was still looking for her. It was called a diversion digital footprint. Once she laid it down, she would stay off the dark web for a week. It was time to let everything cool off. If no one contacted her through the main web, she could reset all her black-hat profiles and start over.

Bored to death, she trolled through the general forums. Those forums eventually broke off into subjects that depended on your kink for that particular day. Kenley didn't have a kink unless you counted holding people responsible for harming others. She'd spent more than a few nights working with the police to shut down human trafficking sites. It would only be a matter of days before new ones popped back up, but their determination didn't faze her. She kept reporting them because if someone made it difficult enough, maybe they'd give up.

Kenley let out a disenchanted snort. She knew better. That wasn't how human nature worked. Humans were predictable, even her, and rarely could you dissuade a human from doing something on the off chance they might get caught. Case in point—she typed an address into her browser. It was the digital locker where the Staun Bril Corporation held their manuals and research.

She knew the address by heart now, so when she hit Return, she grabbed her water bottle to drink while waiting for the page to load. What loaded wasn't what she was expecting, though. The background was black, with a white spider building a web. Slowly, the spider worked its way across the entire page, covering it in a web before scurrying back to the screen's center. This site was not the Staun Bril Corporation page. Kenley didn't know what it was, but her gut told her she had stumbled across something far more dangerous than ATV manuals. Before the page could disappear, she quickly wrote down the address in her notebook. While the spider continued to do nothing but stare at her, she compared the two lines of code. She had transposed several numbers. Quite unusual for her, but she was tired and working too fast, spooked by the messages she'd been sent.

The spider intrigued her. What would happen if she clicked on it? Like a moth to a flame, her finger hovered over the mouse until she took a deep breath and clicked. It took her to a new screen where tiny spiders with gigantic bulging eyes scurried across the page. Creepy didn't begin to describe it, but Kenley was hooked. She clicked on one of the spiders, and an image popped up. It was the view from a traffic camera. What was going on? After a couple more clicks, she realized each spider on the page went to a static public camera somewhere in America.

Undoubtedly, the dark web had weird games, but this didn't feel like a game. This was bigger. What was it? The next question was, who created it? She clicked on several more spiders, each showing her a view from a traffic or security camera. Leaning in, she realized some were not in the United States. The one she was looking at appeared to be somewhere in Japan.

Before Kenley could do anything, a new screen appeared with twice as many spiders waiting to scurry across the screen. She bit her lip and clicked one in the upper left corner. This time, webs shot from the spider with twelve smaller spiders at the end of each web. She clicked a smaller spider, and another traffic camera popped up. It showed her a familiar intersection. The next spider revealed a warehouse camera. Kenley leaned in as something tickled the back of her brain. She recognized the warehouse. Her eyes were glued to the screen, and she reached for her phone, where she dialed the only person who could help her now.

Chapter Two

Jude Mason was about to call it quits for the night. He'd had a long day of meetings with the team at Secure One and Secure Watch to integrate personal security client lists with their cyber clients. Secure One, a security company out of Northern Minnesota, had been integral in solving some rather harrowing crime cases over the previous few years and had seen the need for increasing cybersecurity. Since they had Mina Jacobs, who was one of the FBI's most talented hackers before she joined Secure One, as their lead cybersecurity expert, building a team around her to strengthen their offerings to clients made sense. Jude was ex-military, as were most people at Secure One, and he'd worked for Secure Watch remotely for almost two years. They kept him busy.

He'd known Mina since her days at the FBI when the military and defense department occasionally worked together. There wasn't much information Mina couldn't get her hands on when lives were on the line. That was the very reason Secure Watch began. Too many businesses and hospitals were falling victim to the evil hackers behind the keyboard. Those businesses needed a team that could stop attacks before they damaged their reputations or bankrupted them. Simply put, Secure One protected the exterior of the businesses while Mina and her crew protected their assets.

Jude had been working as a digital personal investigator for several years after leaving the military but didn't enjoy all the paperwork that came with the job. He'd much rather do the work and move on to the next client while someone else dealt with the business end, so when Mina called him unexpectedly a few years back, he couldn't say yes fast enough. Since he lived in Illinois, keeping him there to work remotely helped them cover the lower Midwest. It was a win-win as far as he was concerned. He could stay home and do the work he loved, but the albatross of paperwork and business advertising was gone.

His phone rang just as he reached for the lamp switch by the bed. With a sigh, he grabbed it and brought it to his ear. "Secure Watch."

"Delilah? It's Kenley." A woman whispered across the line, and while Jude didn't know anything about her, those three words were enough to tell him she was scared. "Wait, this isn't Delilah."

Jude chuckled, the sound low and not womanlike. "No, this isn't Delilah. You've got Jude Mason on the line."

"This is Delilah Hartman's number?" She asked the question as though she suddenly wasn't sure she'd dialed it correctly. "Or, uh, Delilah Porter?"

"It is, but she's on her honeymoon, so I'm taking her calls for Secure Watch while she's gone."

"How—how long will she be gone?" the woman asked, her nerves filling those few words.

"By the sound of your voice, longer than you want to wait. Maybe I can help you?"

"I just... I trust Delilah."

He sat up. Sleep wasn't happening tonight if this woman's voice was any indication. "I understand that, Kenley," he soothed, using the name she'd given him initially. "It's hard to trust someone you don't know on the other end of the line, right?"

"Yeah, I guess," she replied.

"I worked with Delilah in the military. That's why she gave me her phone while she was gone. She trusts me with her phone, which, she hoped, would show her clients that they can trust me too."

"That does make sense," she said, her voice softer the longer they spoke. "I'm a little freaked out and don't know what to do."

"Why don't you start by telling me what's happened?"

"I think I've come across something online that's...um... trouble." She cleared her throat as though she could banish the fear from her voice.

"Trouble for you?"

"Trouble for the entire world."

Those five words had Jude dropping his feet to the floor while he searched for his jeans. "Where are you?"

"At an internet café in Milwaukee," she said, as he flicked on speakerphone and pulled on a shirt. "I've been too afraid to leave."

"Is someone following you?"

Moving quickly, Jude tucked his wallet in his back pocket, tied on his shoes and started to gather his equipment.

"Digitally? Possibly."

"What about physically?"

"Hard to say," she said, and he could tell she was hedging. "I don't think so, but after what I found, I can't say that for sure."

"Give me your current address," he said, grabbing his other phone and typing in the address she rattled off. To say it was in a less-than-safe neighborhood of Milwaukee was being kind. That neighborhood was rough when the sun was out, but walking through it as a single woman at midnight was like playing Russian roulette.

"Is the café open all night?" he asked, pocketing his other phone and keys before he picked up his bags and walked out of the house, locking the door behind him.

"Yes, but I don't know how long I should stay here."

"You're going to stay there another hour and thirty-six minutes," he said, slamming the back door to his SUV closed after he tossed in his bags. "That's how far away I am. Traffic should be light. Hopefully, I can make up some time on the interstate."

"You're coming? Here?"

"You called Delilah for help, right?" he asked, firing up his vehicle and turning on the heater. It may only be October, but at 1:00 a.m., the night had a chill about it.

"Yes, but Delilah is my friend. I'm not sure I can afford to employ Secure Watch to help me with this."

"Don't worry about that right now," he said, the fear in the woman's voice hitting him straight in the gut. As an ex-military man, a woman in need activated his protective side, but there was something different about this woman. He could hear the thread of fear in her voice, but he could also hear something else. Determination? Strength? Both? She needed help, but she didn't need saving. He would do well to remember that when he approached her. "I'll reach out to Secure Watch and let them know I'm just getting you home safely."

Her laughter was relaxed for the first time since he'd answered, so he smiled, relieved that some of the fear had left her voice, if only for a few moments. "What happens if it's more than a ride home?"

"We'll cross that bridge when we get there," he assured her. "While I drive, why don't you tell me what's happened?"

"No," she whispered, her voice low and the fear back in full force. "No. Not a good idea. Terrible idea. Everything has ears, Jude. You know this."

"Okay, you're right. Hang in there. I'm on my way. I don't want you to hang up, but I know you're scared, so how about if we listen to music together?"

"I thought you had to call Secure Watch?"

"That can wait," he assured her, reaching for the radio. "What kind of music do you like? Please tell me you aren't a metalhead."

She laughed again, and while it wasn't as relaxed as before, it wasn't forced either. "No, I'm not a metalhead. My dad always said I was born in the wrong decade regarding my taste in music. My top three are Ella Fitzgerald, Count Basie and Nat King Cole."

"A jazz lover? I can appreciate that," he said, tuning the radio to 90.9 FM. A soft, plaintive piano solo filled the car.

"Billie Holiday," she said, bringing a smile to his face as he merged onto I-94 and pushed the speedometer to 75. She was clearly frightened, and Jude didn't want to dawdle and risk her leaving the café before he got there. He'd keep her talking about anything and everything so she didn't register the passage of time. He had no idea what Kenley had gotten herself into, but he did know one thing: walking out the door of that internet café might put her life at risk, and he couldn't have the death of anyone else on his conscience, no matter the cost to himself.

What was she doing?

Kenley asked herself that question every minute she stayed on the line with Jude. 51CKL3 didn't ask for help. She'd learned how to help herself. Yet, here she was, letting Jude Mason calm her down with jazz history and random stories about his days as a private investigator. She'd shut down her equipment and stowed it in her backpack, but she couldn't find the courage to hang up the phone and leave the café. She was spooked by the messages, but the program she'd accidentally found her way into terrified her. Were they connected? They couldn't be, right? There was no way anyone could predict she would reverse two numbers in a line of code to happen upon their site. It had to be a coincidence. A coincidence that could be deadly if what she saw on that warehouse camera was any indication.

Before she closed out of the system, she'd copied as much information as she could about the Spiderweb program. She'd planned on having Delilah help her map the code once she got back into it, but that was a nonstarter if she was on her honeymoon. Did she trust Secure Watch, the company Delilah now worked for? She did. Explicitly. She needed no more proof that they were on the up-and-up than knowing Delilah worked for them. Adding to their reputation were all the women they'd saved from a trafficking ring, and by catching a serial killer. If Jude Mason worked for them, she didn't doubt that he was the best of the best, too. That wasn't what she was afraid of. She was afraid of dragging someone else into this until they were in over their heads.

Delilah was a master hacker like herself, so Kenley wasn't worried about calling her for help, but she had no idea what kind of skills Jude Mason had. Asking on an open line that anyone could be tapped into was also too big a risk. Since no one had come for her, chances were good no one else was listening in, but it was still better to ask these questions face-to-face.

"Are you still there, Kenley?" Jude asked, his words sharp. They snapped her back to reality, and she nodded as she spoke.

"Yes, yes, sorry, I was getting my things together. Where are you?" Was she seriously considering getting into a car with this guy? The better question was, did she have a choice? In her opinion, considering the situation, she didn't. If he could get her out of this café safely, she could reassess and make a plan. Knowing Delilah had trusted Jude with her phone told Kenley he was trustworthy.

"I'm pulling into the neighborhood now. Do not come out. I'll park and come to you."

"That won't be easy," Kenley said, eyeing the street through the front windows. "It's not exactly paid parking down here."

"I've double-parked a Humvee in Kabul. I think I can handle downtown Milwaukee."

So, he *was* ex-military. That made sense, considering how he jumped into battle with little information. She was already knee-deep in this adventure with him; she may as well play it out.

"I'll be ready," she said, sliding her backpack over her shoulders. "Should I hang up?"

"Yes, I'm pulling up now," he answered. "Toyota 4Runner."

After stowing her phone in her pocket, she casually walked toward the front of the café as if it were any other night. Her gaze was glued to the SUV as a man emerged. Immediately, she assigned tall and dark to the man. He was nearly a foot taller than her five feet, and his dark hair was still cut high and tight. He turned, and she added handsome to her description. It would have been hard not to notice his chiseled jawline accentuated by a goatee, making her wonder what it would feel like brushing against her skin.

Whoa, girl, back up the lustometer, she scolded herself. *He's here to help you, not kiss you.*

A smile tipped her lips at the thought, and as he pulled open the door to the café, she noticed how his muscles bulged under his light jacket. He kept up his military fitness; there was no question.

His gaze locked with hers, and that was when she took in everything else about him in a heartbeat. Hidden behind a pair of silver spectacles were eyes the shade of peridot. She'd heard that green eyes were the rarest color in the world. That made her wonder if the man before her, who assessed the entire café as he waited for her to walk toward him, was equally as rare. When she got closer, she noticed his goatee was dotted with white hair, attesting to his maturity rather than vanity. He tugged her close to his side as soon as she was within reach.

"Head down, straight to the car," he whispered, practically carrying her around the parked car's bumper to get to his. He opened the door for her and took her backpack while she climbed in. He deposited the bag at her feet, closed her door and drove away before she got her seat belt buckled. This man meant business. When she glanced at him, his determination told her she no longer needed to be scared.

Her only worry was that the feeling wouldn't last for long.

Chapter Three

"I'm Jude, by the way," he said, extending his hand for her to shake. The woman in his passenger seat seemed all shaken up and needed a friendly face, even if it was a face she'd never seen before. "I've worked with Delilah on and off for years, first in the service and now with Secure Watch."

She slipped her hand into his and gave it a firm shake, something he wasn't expecting, considering her petite frame. He also didn't expect to feel the snick of connection the moment their skin touched.

"It's nice to meet you, Jude. I'm Kenley Bates. I'm sorry for messing up your plans for the night. I forgot Delilah was on her honeymoon."

"Did you watch the ceremony?" he asked, hoping the small talk would help them relax.

"I did. Saying your vows as the sun sets over Lake Superior might be the most romantic thing I've ever seen."

"I couldn't agree more. I'm just glad they figured out a way to do it that allowed everyone to be part of the wedding without being there in person. That island was special for them?"

"Oh, yeah," she agreed with a nod of her head. "They spent a summer on Madeline Island after being discharged from the army. That was before Delilah had to go on the run to protect Lucas. I'm glad they found their way back to each other. I can't say their honeymoon is super convenient for me, though." The self-deprecating laugh she gave at the end made him smile.

"I promise we will help you out of this jam. Like I said, I worked with Delilah in the service, so I was all in when Mina approached me about working at Secure Watch on her recommendation. Their new cyber division already has more clients than they can handle."

"What branch of the military were you in?" she asked.

"Army, just like the rest of Secure One."

"It seems to be a theme for them, which is understandable, considering Cal feels responsible for everyone getting hurt that day in the war. At least that's the vibe I got from Delilah."

"He did, in the beginning, but with time and love from his wife, Marlise, he sees that he had no better chance of stopping that car bomb than any of the other guys there that day. That's the thing about war. Even if you survive, you don't survive. The person you were before you went into battle does not come back out from it. You're changed on a cellular level, and it takes a long time to accept that."

"Have you?" she asked, her gaze heating his cheek from the intensity of it.

"I'm different," he said tersely. "I went to war from the comfort of a desk chair. I don't get to call myself a warrior like they do."

"Did you see things you wished you'd never seen?"

He nodded rather than answer while he kept his eyes peeled to the rearview mirror for a tail. "Do those things ever wake you up in a cold sweat at night until you remember you're home in bed?" Again, it was easier to nod in acknowledgment than to speak. "Sounds to me like you were also changed on a cellular level. Maybe not the same way as those physically injured in war, but we all know the mind is just as easy to damage as limbs."

"Probably easier," he agreed with a sigh. "That's why Cal always looks for veterans to hire when positions open. There aren't many of us who do this kind of work, so Mina has convinced him we will have to hire from the civilian population. Cal agreed as long as she prioritized people with disabilities, which is a much deeper well to drink from."

"I'm not surprised," she said with a chuckle. "Both about your new well and how many clients you have clamoring for help. I run my own business securing websites from the threat of bricking and ransomware and have more calls than time."

"Secure Watch has the same problem, but then add in the clients who need help when their system is bricked, and they've had to grow faster than they predicted." His gaze darted to the rearview mirror. "No tail yet."

"That's good, right?" she asked, as though he knew the correct answer.

"As long as it stays that way," he agreed. "I don't think returning to your place is safe, though."

"But we have to," she said, slightly frantic. "I need my things."

"I'll stop at a Target once we hit Chicago," he said, signaling left onto the interstate. "That's a safer idea."

"The things I need you can't get at Target," she said as she slowly lifted her right leg and then pulled her pants up.

One fast glance was all he needed. "You're an amputee?"

"Symes," she agreed. "You could say I'm part of your well." He couldn't stop the smile that lifted his lips. "But I'll need my supplies." Before she could say more, she held up a finger. "Wait, if you aren't taking me to my place, where are you taking me?"

"I don't know, but if you're alarmed by what happened tonight, I think we better have Secure One do some surveillance on your place before you go back there."

"Have you talked to them?"

"Not yet. I wanted to get you out safely and then find somewhere to talk openly about the situation. That was going to be my place. I wanted to be home before sunrise but wasn't planning on another stop."

"It's on the way," she promised. "I can be in and out in under five minutes. We'll still make Chicago long before the sun comes up."

"As long as we don't pick up a tail," he said, and she nodded, giving him the address.

While he drove, he glanced at Kenley from the corner of his eye. She was young, or at least younger than him. She was under five-four, and her body was lithe with curves in all the right places, which he'd learned when he put his arm around her waist to help her to the car. She had the perfect heart-shaped face, and her black hair bobbed at her shoulders and framed her cheeks to make her look younger than she certainly was. Her brown eyes were sharp and assessing, and her lips were naturally plump. When he first laid eyes on her, he'd licked his own, his mind immediately wondering what it would feel like to kiss them.

Jude shook his head with a huff and turned right off the interstate, following her directions. Another truck followed them off the exit, and he went on full alert, pushing thoughts of kissing Kenley out of his mind as he committed to memory everything about the truck behind them.

"What's the matter?" she asked, glancing at him as he sped up for a light about to change to red.

"Maybe nothing," he said between clenched teeth. He ran the yellow, and even though it turned red halfway through, the truck stayed on his bumper. "Hell," he groaned. Bright headlights filled his mirrors, preventing him from seeing the driver.

"That truck is following us?" she asked, and he reached out and stopped her from turning around. His hand tingled where their skin connected, but he pushed the reaction aside.

"Yes, but don't look behind you. I don't want them to confirm it's you in the car. We can't go to your house now. They'll know for certain it's you if we do."

"Where are we going, then?"

"I'm going to get us back on the interstate," he said, noticing an entrance ramp ahead.

"We can't go to your place either, then. They'll know you're helping me."

"Well, they already know that, but I'd prefer that whoever they are, they don't know where I live. I'm going to head north until we lose them."

"Do you think we can?"

"Hang on tight," he said with a wink and then yanked the wheel to the right, jumping over the low curb of the turn lane and rocketing down the entrance ramp. The truck overshot and kept going, exactly what he had hoped for. "They missed the turn. They'll find us again, but we've got time to put distance between us."

"Maybe we should get off the interstate?" she asked as he pushed the SUV to eighty. "If they can't find us, they can't follow us."

She was right. It was hard to hide out here when the road was deserted, and they had at most ten minutes before the truck caught up to them.

"That's assuming they were following us," he said, rubbing his chin for a few seconds. "It could have been a coincidence."

"It didn't feel that way to me," she said. "I was watching them in the side mirror. There was no one near us, and then suddenly, that truck was right behind us, and they kept pace."

"That's what my gut says, too," he finally agreed, reading the signs ahead of them. Chances were, they'd encounter the truck after the next exit if he didn't get off the interstate now. If he got off here, he could take the back roads home. It would take longer, but it gave him more options should they pick up another tail. "I don't know what you got yourself into, Kenley Bates, but getting you back out of it will be more involved than I initially thought."

"And you haven't even seen the tip of the iceberg," she muttered.

"Hang on," he warned, and she grabbed the door handle as he turned the wheel to the left, coasted up the ramp, turned right, and then took a two-lane road that was pitch-black on this moonless October night.

As the vehicle rocketed down the road, he couldn't help but think he was the one who needed to hang on now that Kenley Bates was in his passenger seat.

KENLEY WOKE WITH a start, the sun rising over the horizon as the truck slowed for a light. She glanced around frantically until she laid eyes on the man next to her, and it all came flooding back: the café, the desperate call, and the truck that followed them.

"Morning, sleepyhead," he said as he turned right at the light.

"How long have I been out?" she asked, rubbing her face to ensure she wasn't drooling. There was nothing as embarrassing as being in a car with a cute guy and having drool stains on your face. No drool was noticed, so she let out a sigh of relief.

"Not long," he answered. "Only about twenty minutes. You needed it, and all was quiet. We're almost at my place. We can't stay there long, though."

"I figured," she agreed. "They probably got your plate and already know where you live."

"Not yet, but once they break through the information for several shell corporations and businesses that don't exist, they'll know where I live."

"Paranoid much?" she asked, a brow raised.

"By the looks of it, not nearly enough," he answered, briefly lowering a brow at her. "We're a few blocks away. First, I'll do some recon of the streets surrounding the house. I have to be sure no one is waiting in a parked car for us."

"How would you know? Streets in the city are lined with cars."

"Not so much in my neighborhood," he said, his tone chipper as they turned down a street lined with landscaped lawns and perfectly clipped trees. Neat-as-a-pin homes were circled with white picket fences. The only thing missing were the 2.5 kids and the dog. Then again, maybe they were inside getting ready for another day in suburbia.

Kenley whistled as they drove down street after street with houses that all looked identical. "I stand corrected. We don't have much in common."

She noticed his eyes never left the road when he spoke. "Never assume that what you see is what you get, Kenley."

That was fair. It was certainly the case with her. When people met her now, they never imagined that she'd grown up in the inner city. She might not know Jude well, but she didn't see him living in a home like this. He gave off more log cabin vibes than suburbia vibes.

"I don't live here by choice but because it offers safety in numbers. If I had my druthers, I'd live in a cabin in the woods."

Kenley's laughter filled the car. "It's like you can read my mind."

"Your face is rather—" he motioned in the air with his hand "—expressive."

"I've heard that before," she conceded, biting back a smile as he slowed for a driveway. His house was smack-dab in the middle of the block.

"The neighbors are close enough to see anyone trying to break in and to hear my alarm system," he explained, pulling the SUV into the garage. The door slid closed behind them, and he finally let go of his death grip on the wheel. "Everything looked quiet, but we aren't going to push our luck. We'll take ten minutes to get in touch with Secure Watch, grab some extra equipment I didn't know I'd need, and get back on the road."

"Is it safe to drive this again?" she asked when he opened her door.

"Nope. We'll have to take a short walk to pick up a new one. Can you walk half a mile or so?"

"I can walk that far without my prosthesis," she answered. "I won't slow you down."

He closed the door quietly and motioned for her to stay up against the garage wall while he unlocked the door. He made the checking sign with his fingers to his eyes, and she nodded, allowing him to sweep the home. Chances were good that no one had figured out who he was yet, but better safe than sorry. She'd used a burner to call him, and he was smart enough to hide his vehicle registration under a few red herrings, which not everyone thought of when in this business. They couldn't waste time, though. She didn't know who was behind the threats or the Spiderweb site, and until she did, they had to stay on their toes. That was easier said than done when they were both exhausted.

"All clear," he called, and she walked into the house, closing and locking the door behind her.

From her vantage point in the kitchen, Kenley watched him scurry around what should be the living room. Instead of a cozy vibe, it had blackout shades on both windows and enough computer equipment to make her jealous.

"Holy schnikes." She whistled as she walked into his space, her eyes trying to take it all in simultaneously. "You know how to turn a girl on."

He paused in his packing and raised a brow. "Like what you see, darling?" His smirk told her he was joking as she ran a finger across a top-of-the-line server. "Orgasm by computer wasn't what I was going for, but go ahead, I'll wait." He crossed his arms over his chest and leaned back on the table to emphasize his point.

"Har-har," she said, sticking her tongue out at the man she should not be discussing orgasms of any kind with. "You're hilarious. Not. Did you get what you need?"

"Almost," he answered, stuffing a few more things in a bag. "Now it's time to meet Mina Jacobs. She could be the one to save your life."

She would bet anything the man doing the talking was in the running for that title, too, but having an FBI hacker on her team wasn't nothing. Knowing their time was short, all Kenley could think was Delilah had done her a solid by flying off to Hawaii for her honeymoon and leaving Jude Mason in charge of her phone.

Chapter Four

"Do you have any powder?" Kenley asked as he was packing up his equipment.

He paused and turned to her. "What kind of powder?"

"Anything that absorbs sweat would work."

He pointed down the hall to her left. "The third door on the right is the bathroom. There should be some Anti Monkey Butt Powder in the cabinet on the top right shelf. I use it for running."

"You're my hero, Jude Mason," she said in her best Ferris Bueller voice. "Give me five, and I'll be ready to connect with Mina."

"Throw the bottle in your bag," he said as she headed down the hallway. "You might need it."

He was right. She probably would need it if she couldn't return to her place sooner rather than later. Considering the situation, that didn't look promising. She passed a bedroom and paused. It was a guest room, but that wasn't what caught her eye. Through the window, she swore the truck from earlier had just cruised past it. It was an old single-cab truck with thick metal mirrors and strong window tinting. She could count three people inside the vehicle, and while it had been too dark last night, today she noted they were all male.

She shook her head and walked into the bathroom, confident it couldn't be the same truck. Not only was it too soon for them to have found Jude's place, but there were a lot of old white trucks on the road. She couldn't start tilting at windmills every time she saw one. After a quick search for the powder, she found it exactly where he said it would be. Thankfully, the calamine in the powder would keep her limb from itching and absorb the sweat that was to come from walking to his bug-out car.

She quickly pulled the Velcro strips off that held the plate on the back of her prosthesis and pulled her limb from it. After she rolled the special liner sock off, she washed and dried it before covering her limb in powder. The liner sock was a new addition to her prosthesis. Her limb had slowly atrophied to the point that every time her shinbone bumped up against the carbon fiber prosthesis, she was miserable. They'd remedied it using a five-ply sock with an internal gel liner. It took care of the pain but caused a sweating problem she had never had before. At least there were products to help with the sweating issue. It was the lesser of two evils because walking was hard when your leg hurt with every step.

After her leg was back in the prosthesis and the plate was secure again, she washed up and grabbed the powder before returning to the living room. She paused again in the guest room doorway, the hair up on the back of her neck. Stepping into the room, she walked to the window and stood to the side, dropping lower when she noticed the same pickup drive past the house again. Once it passed the room, she darted into the hallway and entered the living room.

"The truck." The two words came out winded but precise.

Jude froze with his finger on a button of some device. "*The* truck?" Her nod had him grabbing the device and sticking that in his bag, too.

"I've seen it twice now. It must be going around the block waiting for us to leave."

"That's going to make leaving a bit more complicated," he said, hoisting the bag over his back. "The fence will buy us time to avoid detection, but eventually, we'll have to step into the open."

"Your backyard has a fence?"

"Yes," he said, motioning her toward the back door again. "Stay low to avoid the kitchen window."

Kenley ducked and followed him to the door, where a half wall gave them cover from the window while he unlocked it.

"It's a tall wooden fence I had put up. You'll understand why when I show you where my surveillance car is. Follow me." With her nod, they left the garage and hurried through the backyard. Kenley listened for tires on the pavement but heard nothing before they reached the end of the fence.

"Do we go over?" she asked in a whisper.

He shook his head and knelt, clicking a button on the bottom of one of the boards, and then a gate swung open.

"I'd say paranoid, but I'm too thankful not to have to scale that fence," she whispered after he cleared the back side and motioned her forward.

"How did they find us so quickly?" he wondered between clenched teeth.

"I wish I could tell you, but I can't. All I know is it was the same truck," she said, her words nothing more than a whisper on the wind. "I saw it when I walked into the bathroom and again on the way out. I haven't heard a vehicle since, so maybe I had it all wrong?"

"No one should have found us this quickly," he muttered as they dipped into the pine forest that edged the neighborhood. With any luck, they'd escape while the truck was doing another round of surveillance.

Kenley could tell Jude was frustrated. She didn't know him that well yet, but his body language told her that much. He was also confused but working hard to control his emotions so she didn't feed off them. Unfortunately, he wore them like a button-up shirt. Cool heads had to prevail if they were to get out of this town before the truck showed up again.

"Mina's an amputee, too," he said as though it would help her connect with someone she had never met or, at the very least, distract her.

"Bet she didn't kill her best friend to become one," she muttered.

"That's oddly pointed, but no, she was beaten by a woman who discovered she was an undercover FBI agent trying to take down her sex trafficking ring. Roman said it was gnarly."

"Who's Roman?"

"Mina's husband. He was her partner in the FBI. Now he works for Secure One. He's Cal's foster brother, and they served together in the army."

"I'm sorry we didn't get to call her before we left," she said, as though it was her fault that some maniac in a truck was hunting her. Then again, maybe it was her fault. She probably should remember she might have started this whole chain reaction.

"I brought my equipment with me, and once we get somewhere safe, we'll call in. Since it's early, no one will expect me to check in until later. If nothing else, the early hour of the morning bought us time. That said, it's almost seven thirty a.m., and the sun is out, leaving us vulnerable to whoever is searching for us."

"Hold up. I'm afraid we aren't going anywhere."

Jude peeked out around the tree until he caught a glimpse of what she had seen.

"There," she whispered, pointing to his left.

Relief filled him. "That's just Boone." He pulled her out from behind the tree and headed for the edge of the forest that butted up to the community soccer field. "He's Mr. Hamel's Maine coon. Boone has been mistaken for a bobcat more than once. He's on the prowl."

"Mr. Hamel will find himself short a kitty if he keeps letting him roam. I've never seen a cat that big. In a neighborhood like this, someone will shoot first and ask questions later."

"Can't disagree," he said, pushing her harder to finish the walk to the garage where he kept his surveillance car. The last thing he wanted was someone to report them to the cops for lurking. He would have done it at a jog but suspected her prosthesis wouldn't allow it. Her entire calf was encased in a carbon fiber socket with the prosthetic foot attached so close to the ground that there was very little clearance for any ankle. Her gait was smooth, but running wasn't easy for her, which he'd learned when he pushed her too hard as they left the house. She was quick on it, but she'd nearly fallen in their haste, and he didn't want her to get hurt. "The garages are coming up on your right," he said, pointing them out through the branches. "Once we leave the trees, we have a lot of open space to cover until we reach them." The hulking buildings he pointed out housed everything from cars to boats to RVs.

"First, if we make it there undetected, which I question, where will we go? If the guys from last night are in that truck, they'll follow us."

"Ultimately, I want to get to Secure Watch."

"Isn't that six or seven hours away?"

"Just about," he agreed, "but when it comes to the danger we're dealing with, at least the little bit you told me, the only safe place is Secure Watch. They have security you aren't going to find anywhere outside of a military base or Taylor Swift's house."

Her snort was audible over the sound of the birds chirping, and it brought a smile to his lips. She enjoyed snark, and he could appreciate that in a woman. He'd just be happy if she bought his story about Secure Watch. That was all it was, though. There wasn't a chance in hell he would bring any of this to their doorstep.

"I just don't think it's smart to drag anyone else into this fiasco," she explained as they prepared to leave the trees and head to the giant metal warehouse. The building was divided into individual climate-controlled garage stalls, and everyone had separate garage doors and openers. It was the perfect place to store his Jeep when he didn't need it for work, but its central location hindered this situation.

"Wait," she said, grabbing his jacket sleeve. "On the left side of the street, what do you see?"

His gaze traveled down the street that led from the dead end. There sat a familiar truck with its nose pointing out.

"They're waiting for us to leave so they can follow us rather than hunt us down and raise suspicion in the neighborhood. What have you gotten yourself involved in, Kenley?" he asked, his gaze darting to her for a heartbeat. "There's no way they should know who I am or where I live yet."

"Let's just say the people I associate with can do much more than break through a couple of LLCs. The ones I don't associate with but who know my name can do even more."

"Do you happen to know which one we're dealing with here?" he asked, trying to decide on their next move.

"Nope," she said, popping the *p*. "But the fact they're waiting to follow us rather than having already killed us is encouraging."

"Well, some good news for once," he said, a shudder racking him as he pulled his Sig from his holster. "It's time to load up the Jeep and get out of town."

"How will we do that when they're blocking our only way out?"

"My surveillance vehicle is an off-road Jeep for a reason. The garage butts up to a trail for ATVs."

"You've thought of everything, Mr. Mason," she whispered. "Except how we're going to get out unheard."

He had thought about that and hadn't found a good answer yet. The Jeep was new and quiet, but if they heard a garage door or an engine catch, they would know it was them.

"We'll address that once we make it across this open space. They'll be watching their rearview, but I don't see any other option here."

"I think the answer is obvious, Jude. The Jeep is not worth the risk."

"Why do I hate it so much that you're right?"

"Probably because it limits our options," she answered with a tip of her lips. "Should we go back for the truck?"

His sigh was heavy when he turned to her and took her shoulders. "No, the truck has already been tagged. I'm afraid our walk will be long if we decide to abandon the Jeep."

"I'll keep up," she promised, shifting the pack's weight on her back.

His nod came with a gentle smile. "I know you will. If we can put some distance between us and the three guys in the truck, we can send an SOS to Secure Watch. When that comes in, they'll know I'm in trouble without an actual call."

"Do it now," she urged, her gaze glued to the truck with three heads visible through the back window.

"It's smarter to wait until we're somewhere they can pick us up without getting tagged."

"That's the frustrating part," she said, shaking her head. "I don't understand how they tagged me to begin with, Jude. My machines are clean. So is my phone."

His gaze traveled the length of her, and he froze for a moment before he reached into his bag and pulled out his wireless signal wand. "Let's make sure before we go any further."

He swept the wand over and around her backpack several times before she grabbed it and held it still. "What are you doing? I'm talking about a program used to track devices."

"I know," he said with a wink. "But they have small trackers, so you might not notice if someone dropped one in your bag."

"I would know if there was a tracker in my bag. I empty it every time I get home."

"Do you shake it out too?"

Her eye roll was enough of an answer. She released the wand, and he checked the seams at the bottom of the bag before running the wand over her coat pockets. "You're clean. I don't understand it."

"I told you that," she said as he dropped the wand to his side. When it went off, he jerked it back to center. "Was that you?"

"It was something," he agreed, running the wand back over his shoes and pockets, but this time, it didn't sound, so he ran it across the ground, wondering if something in the soil was giving them a false positive. He was ready to give up when she moved her foot, and the wand beeped. He glanced up at her and, this time, ran the wand over her prosthesis, slowly moving it down to her shoe, where the wand beeped again. "Is that even possible?" he asked as he stood and stowed the wand in his bag again.

"The foot shell is open, but it would have to be so small, Jude."

"They make small trackers now. Here," he said, taking off his coat and spreading it out on the ground, motioning for her to sit.

The look she gave him was uncertain, but she sat, pulled her shoe off, and then worked at the rubber shell until it popped off the metal foot. Out fell a small round tracker that lay on the ground like a shining specimen of deceit.

"Don't touch it," he said, holding her hand back from picking it up.

"We should look at it. Maybe it will tell us who put it there."

"It won't," Jude assured her, working the rubber shell back over her prosthetic foot once he'd scanned her again to be sure she was clear. "It's a simple one you can buy on the internet in a ten-pack. If I had to guess, they've got one stuck somewhere in your car, too. I'm honestly surprised they didn't go for your bag, but the foot was brilliant. You're never without it."

"Not untrue, but when?" she asked, her confusion real as he tied on her shoe.

"It had to be somewhat recent since the battery is still working on it. We don't have time to worry about that right now, though," he said, helping her up. He shouldered his coat and then his bag. "They're sitting there waiting because the tracker tells them we're moving in their direction, so let's go somewhere else. The faster we get away from it, the bigger head start we get on them. It won't take long before they figure out we found it and left it behind. We'll go right and follow the trees to where they end at the creek. We'll cross there and hike to the next town. We can make decisions once we're clear of the tracker."

Kenley opened her mouth, and he thought she was going to argue, but after staring at him for two beats, she turned to her right and took off through the trees.

Chapter Five

The terrain was rugged, but Kenley refused to ask Jude to slow down or for a break. She would keep pace with him if it killed her. They were in this mess because of her, so she would do anything to keep up with the guy trying to save her life. He was giving her time to figure out what was happening. She had no proof that someone wanted her dead, but she also didn't think the guys in the truck just wanted to talk. She had no idea what this was about, so she couldn't risk assuming it was unrelated to what she'd seen last night on the web.

Jude's arm came out to stop her midstride. "It's a creek. We have to find a way around it."

"Why?" she asked, shouldering her backpack to a different angle. "It's barely ten feet wide. Can't we cross it?"

"Your foot," he answered, motioning at her right leg.

"Is waterproof."

"The shell is open," he countered, and she shrugged.

"It's not a big deal. The water will run out eventually, and then I'll dry it out. I'd rather cross here than go ten miles out of the way to avoid it."

"If you're sure," he said, raising a brow while he waited for her confirmation.

When she nodded, he knelt and untied her left shoe. "Take

that one off. You don't want wet shoes and socks for hours until we can dry them out. Does the right one need to come off?"

"Yes, or I'll be off balance," she explained as she sat down, quickly removing her shoes while he did the same. "I'm taking the prosthesis off. I could get in real trouble if the liner gets wet since it takes so long to dry."

"How will you walk?" he asked, hooking her shoes together for her.

"When they perform a Syme amputation, they retain the heel pad and wrap it around the end of the bones. You can walk on it like you would your foot. It's a bit harder to balance since one leg is shorter, but it can be done. I'll need to hold on to your arm to steady myself since I don't have a cane or crutch."

When she stood and took her first lilting step, he grabbed her elbow and helped her step off the grass and into the gentle creek. The bottom was rocky, so he was patient as she picked her way across to avoid stepping on the jagged rocks. When they reached the other side, he grasped her waist and lifted her onto the grass. Her body tingled from the contact despite the crunch they were in, which told her she might be in trouble when it came to this man. She pulled out shammy towels to distract herself and flipped one to him.

"You carry towels in your bag?"

"I do. They're great for cleaning computer equipment but also come in handy if I sweat in my liner. It's small but will dry your feet so your shoes don't get wet."

"I won't turn that down," he said as he wiped the sand from his feet before he put on his socks. Once they had their socks and shoes on, he tucked the towels into her pack and helped her stand.

"Don't they say that following a river or creek downstream will bring you to a town?" she asked. "Maybe we should follow it."

"It would," he agreed, helping her with her pack. "But that town wouldn't be one we could blend into. I know where we are and where we're going. I'm headed for a bigger city. One where no one will bat an eye at two bedraggled people checking into a hotel. We're almost to an ATV trail that will be easier to walk on, and that will take us to Deer Forest, where we can find food and a place to dial into Secure Watch."

"How long have you been working for Secure Watch?" she asked as they finally broke out of the trees and onto the promised ATV trail. At least it would protect what was left of her stamina after a long night and longer walk through the forest.

At first glance, she thought Jude was thinking about the question, but at second glance, she realized he was keeping a close eye on the edges of the trail. That was probably something she should be doing, too. Just because she didn't think she had more trackers on her didn't mean she was correct.

"Hannah Grace is two, so I guess I've been working there for almost two years."

"Who's Hannah Grace? It's a beautiful name." She sidestepped a rock at the last second before it tripped her up.

"Mina and Roman's little girl. They named her after Cal's longtime girlfriend. Hannah was killed in combat years ago, but she was also the reason Cal started Secure One when he returned from the war. Roman knew Hannah well since they were on the same team in the service."

"A little tip of the hat to someone they both loved?"

"As well as a solid reminder that none of us know the impact we will have on the world until we're gone."

She knew the truth of that statement. Her entire life had

been based on impacting others, even if no one knew she was Sickle.

"Hannah was born shortly after they put some of my former employers in prison, which was two years ago now."

"Military?" she asked, glancing at him in surprise.

"Yep, a major general in the army. He'd been stealing and reselling artifacts and treasures from war-torn countries."

"Wow. Classy and supersmart."

His laughter in response to her comment was loud, and she jumped, which told her she was more affected by the last few hours than she'd let herself believe.

"He may have gotten away with it if Delilah hadn't been able to find Lucas in time. Once they connected again, she could dig deep enough into her old files to pinpoint who had funneled the treasures out of the military pipeline. She thought she was preserving those countries' treasures for them when she was putting them into the hands of a man who planned to sell them for profit."

"Geez," Kenley said with a shake of her head. "I knew something happened when Delilah appeared on the radar again, but I didn't know what. I'm glad they managed to stop him, but something tells me it was at great risk to themselves."

"Not unlike our situation," he agreed, his palm resting on the butt of his gun as though he did it all the time, but she noticed the tension in his fingers, which seemed to indicate he expected to pull it at any moment.

"Do you think we're at great risk?"

"I certainly don't think we're at low risk after what happened last night. I have no idea what's going on, but that much is clear."

They walked in silence for five minutes before she spoke. "I'll tell you everything, but I want to do it when we're somewhere safe. Distracting you now could be dangerous if someone is still tracking us."

"I agree," he said with a nod. "We're almost to Deer Forest, where we can grab a bite to eat and regroup."

"How far is Deer Forest from your house?"

"The way the crow flies? Less than five miles. Over twenty by car, though, to get around the forest. Someone would also have to know which way we went."

"If they find the tracker, they'll know."

"They won't find the tracker."

"We left it in those trees, Jude. Once they find it, they'll know we went one of two ways. We didn't go past them, and they didn't see us in their rearview, so they'll know we went right."

"When you took off running, I grabbed the tracker and dumped it in the storm drain where the street meets the woods. Trust me, if they follow the tracker, they'll be baffled."

Her snicker was loud on the trail. "I'll give you points for thinking on your feet." With a tip of her head, she sighed. "I'm still not going to assume we threw them off our tail."

"Whoever they are," he added with a frown.

"That's the hundred-thousand-dollar question," she agreed, pausing midstep when she heard a sound.

Before she could react, he grabbed her and pulled her into the trees. She knew the sound. It was an ATV rolling down the trail. She remembered the way the machine rumbled under her feet as it roared over the packed dirt, occasionally sliding a bit as it tried to gain purchase on the path worn smooth over the summer.

She tapped Gabriella on the shoulder. "Slow down!" The sound was lost to the wind, even yelling as loud as she could. Kenley motioned with her hands for her to back off the throttle, but Gabriella just laughed and pushed it forward, throwing Kenley back against the seat. She'd have gone sailing through the air if she hadn't grabbed the basket on the back. What was she doing? Gabriella had never been reckless while driving before. This felt reckless. Trail riding was meant to be fun, not terrifying.

Kenley leaned forward again, right into Gabriella's ear. "Slow down! Are you trying to kill—"

Then she was falling, Gabriella's scream filling her ears as she came down, something heavy and hot rolling over her leg right before she hit her head on the path, and everything went black.

"Kenley!" When she returned to the present, Jude was staring at her worriedly. "Into the trees, now."

He'd get no argument from her. They managed to lie flat on the forest floor and wait for the machine to pass them by. Jude had his gun out and pointed at the path, so she could only assume he thought whoever was coming was an adversary.

"Is your head in the game?" he asked without taking his eyes from the path.

"It is now," she answered to his nod just as the front of the ATV came into view. Relief flashed through her when the riders were not the men after them. An older man drove the ATV at the speed of a snail while a boy rode in front, pretending to steer. She couldn't hide the shudder that went through her, and as soon as they disappeared down the trail, she stood and paced the forest for a few minutes until he gently snagged her arm.

"Whatever happened on that ATV can't hurt you now," he whispered into her ear, sending a shiver down her spine. "Stay present with me so we can get ahead of the guys who want to hurt you." Then, as though he understood how difficult that would be, he wrapped his arms around her and held her. She exhaled at how good it felt to be close to another human. Her job was solitary, and she didn't date to avoid entanglements. She'd made that choice, even though it often left her lonely and unfulfilled. Her day job might be innocuous, but her night job wasn't, and she didn't want to get someone innocent wrapped up in it.

Kenley glanced at Jude from the corner of her eye and was sure he could handle himself, no matter the situation. For the first time in years, she relaxed into a hug and accepted the comfort he offered for a situation he didn't understand. That alone told her that Jude Mason might be her savior, but he was a risk to her heart she couldn't afford to take.

Chapter Six

Jude set the bags down on the small table in the hotel room with a sigh. The walk from Target to the hotel hadn't been long, but it had been awkward. He knew his computer and bag were safe, but he couldn't say the same about Kenley's, so he'd insisted she get a new bag and leave the old one in a dumpster behind the big-box store. If there was a tracker in it, their pursuers would know they were in Deer Forest, but that couldn't be helped right now. He had to touch base with Secure Watch and make a game plan before they took another step.

Kenley closed the door behind her and immediately locked it, then pulled the shades across the windows, plunging them into near darkness. Once he flipped the light on, he took in the room. It was a typical, skeevy motel room, but it was also the kind of place that forgot what you looked like the moment you checked in, and he wanted that more than he wanted modern conveniences.

"The first thing we do is call Secure Watch," he said, opening his bag and pulling out his computer and video screen. "The second thing we do is eat the food we picked up so we're ready to move at a moment's notice."

"Maybe we should eat while talking to Secure Watch," she suggested, bringing out the pastries, fruit, juice and hard-boiled eggs for protein. "That way, we can leave as soon as they give us an extraction point."

Jude knew that wouldn't happen but didn't want to tell Kenley. Secure Watch wouldn't pluck them from this situation until they had a better handle on who was looking for her, but he'd let Mina break that news should it come down to it.

"Great idea," he said, plugging everything in and connecting his hot spot to run through the lousy Wi-Fi the motel provided. He hoped it was strong enough to display the video and run his proxy scrambler. Once his computer was running, he dialed into the Secure Watch line and waited for someone to answer.

"Secure Watch, Whiskey."

Relief filled him. Hearing her voice and knowing they weren't alone made him feel better.

"Secure Watch, Jacko," he replied, using his code name to let Mina know it was him. Then he waited while the screen flickered to life.

Their greeting was a security measure in itself. If a team member didn't respond with their code name, the other person had an immediate indicator that there was a problem.

Mina's face filled the screen and while it was grainy, the connection seemed to be holding. "Jude, what's going on? That doesn't look like your living room."

"It sure isn't," he said, sitting down behind the screen and pulling a chair over for Kenley, who joined him with a pastry in one hand and a cup of coffee in the other. He'd never been more thankful that Target had a Starbucks inside it than he was this morning. "Mina, this is Kenley Bates. We've had an interesting night."

"Nice to meet you, Kenley, but I'm thinking maybe I don't

want to hear about your interesting night?" she asked, her lips and nose scrunched up as she stared at them.

Kenley snorted, almost shooting coffee out her nose. "Trust me, it was nothing like that."

"We have a problem," he said, motioning to the woman beside him. "Kenley is a friend of Delilah's and called her phone last night. She needed help, so I responded."

"You didn't call it into Secure Watch before you met up? How come?" Mina asked, typing on a computer off-screen. She was probably running Kenley through every background checker she had.

"I didn't know what I had at the time until I talked to Kenley in person. She didn't want to discuss it over the phone."

"Smart," Mina agreed to Kenley's nod.

"Unfortunately, she was in Milwaukee, so it was a bit of a drive to do that." Mina's brows went up, but Jude ignored that and continued the story. "We were headed for her house when we picked up a tail."

Mina released a word fitting of the situation and Kenley grinned. "That's how I felt about it, too. It turns out I may have seen something I shouldn't have last night."

"It didn't start last night," Jude said, eyeing Kenley, surprised she hadn't picked up on it. Then again, she was exhausted, so that might explain it. "That tracker had been in your leg for at least a few days."

Kenley's eyes widened as the truth dawned on her. "You're so right! I should have thought of that." The sentence ended in a groan he could only describe as distressed, exhausted and frustrated.

Mina waved her hands. "Wait, wait. Tracker? In her leg? What?"

They took turns filling Mina in on the timeline of events until she momentarily leaned out of the camera shot. When she returned, she had a sheet of paper in her hand. "Kenley Bates, age thirty-one, occupation sole proprietor of Cyberlock Solutions Inc." Mina tipped her head back and forth as though she were impressed. "Right lower leg amputee, born and raised in Milwaukee," she read the paper as though it were a grocery list until she glanced up. "Impressive dossier."

Kenley was thirty-one, which made her eight years his junior. Jude should probably consider that way too many years between them, but he couldn't find it within him to care. Kenley carried herself in a way that said she was much more than a number. He couldn't agree more. Their lives might have just collided, but there was a familiarity between them when they shared a quiet space that had nothing to do with what they did for a living. It wasn't a sense of commonality in what they did, but more so *why* they did it.

"It's even more impressive that you got all of that in under four minutes," Kenley said with a tip of her fake hat.

Mina smiled a smile Jude had seen before. She was intrigued. "So, you run an upscale cybersecurity business by day, but you were hanging out in an internet café in a questionable neighborhood in downtown Milwaukee at nearly midnight on a Wednesday."

"That 'questionable' neighborhood," Kenley said, using quotation marks, "is where I grew up, so I respectfully dispute your use of the term. It's not a place for everyone, but for those of us who know it well, it's home."

Mina held up her hands at her chest. "Of course, my apologies. I was looking at it from the point of view of crime rate statistics that came up on my program."

"There's crime, I can't deny that, but good people there also do their best to survive. That's all I'm saying."

"And your family was once one of them. That's respect I can give," Mina said as Jude put his arm around Kenley.

Her anxiety and fear poured into the room, flowing over him until he was compelled to do something, anything, to comfort her. "Were you meeting someone there?"

"No," Kenley answered, shooting him a side-eye and mouthing *sorry* before she finished her answer. "I was running my proxy scrambler through their Wi-Fi while my white hat turned, shall we say, a bit gray."

"You were on the dark web." Mina didn't make it a question. She didn't have to. A white-hat hacker would go gray only if they decided to do a little black-hat hacking somewhere. "Before we go any further, let it be said that we aren't judging you, right, Jude?"

"No judgment, we're just sharing information."

Kenley lowered the coffee cup to her leg with a sigh. "I'm known in the neighborhood as Sickle. When someone needs help proving a company or corporation is at fault for something, they come to me. Sometimes, I don't need the dark web to find the information I want. Sometimes, I do."

Jude suspected she was leaving out half the picture, but he'd let it go for now.

"But something happened last night that made you think you needed Delilah's help?" Mina asked to pull them back to the reason they had called her.

"It started with weird messages from a chat room. The sender wrote everything in binary code."

Mina rolled her eyes. "Such a childish game."

The snort that left Kenley's lips told him she felt the same. "Right, which is why I didn't give them much weight until I came across a program I wasn't meant to see."

"What kind of program?" Jude and Mina asked at the same time.

As Kenley explained the Spiderweb site to them, Jude watched Mina's eyes widen with each word. "There is another site I visit frequently, but I transposed two numbers this time without realizing it. That's how I got to the Spiderweb site. I wrote the new site down, but I don't want to type it out and risk it being intercepted. I also don't want you looking at it from Secure Watch."

"Why did you call Delilah then?" Mina asked, folding her arms over her chest as she leaned back in the chair.

"I wanted to go back in, but I needed someone to help me hide my footprints as I mapped the code."

"What about the program worried you?" Jude asked. "Besides the traffic cameras."

"Each new page not only brought more spiders onto the screen, but it also brought up new cameras even closer to my location. The last spider I clicked on showed me the camera for a warehouse two blocks behind The Matrix. We used to ride bikes past it all summer long."

"Are you saying the program could descramble your proxy and figure out where you were?"

"I don't know what I'm saying other than facts," she answered with a glance at him and then Mina. "I didn't know about the tracker at the time, so it's possible they were using that to freak me out and get me to back out of the program."

"Which worked," Jude agreed. "But that implies the person who put the tracker in your foot somehow knew you would find the program."

"That doesn't make sense," Kenley said, shaking her head. "Landing on the program was an accident."

"I'm going out on a limb here and guessing you've spent a fair amount of time on the dark web," Mina said to Kenley, who nodded. "Have you ever seen anything like this before?"

"Never," Kenley said with a slight shake to her voice at the end of the word.

"I would also guess you don't spook easily, so the fact that this particular program had you calling in outside help tells me you have a gut feeling about it. What is that feeling?"

Kenley glanced at him for a hot second before she turned back to Mina. He suspected he wouldn't like what she was about to say.

"Whatever this program is, it's not an innocent video game. At the very least, it's the misappropriation of public cameras for an unknown reason."

"And at worst?" Jude asked, bracing for the answer.

"At worst, it's a tracking system that could have grave consequences for the entire world."

Chapter Seven

Kenley swallowed back the bile that rose in her throat once she'd uttered those words. She hated even thinking it, much less saying it, but she had to be honest with the team. Keeping the truth from them didn't give them the chance to back away if they didn't want to get involved. She could go it alone, but she hoped she didn't have to, because if those guys found her again, she couldn't outrun them.

Mina was the first one to speak. "Can you get into the program and find its origins?"

"With enough time and someone who can throw them off my trail? Absolutely." That wasn't a lie. It was the reason she'd called Delilah last night. She had to get back into that program and figure out what it was, or she'd never sleep. Her conscience wouldn't let her.

"My thought was we'd come back to Secure Watch, but after being tailed so closely, I'm not so sure that's a good idea," Jude said as Mina shook her head.

"It's not. You know we've got your back, but in this situation, we have no choice but to keep you remote. Coming here could endanger the entire team."

"I was afraid you would say that," he replied.

"Kenley," Mina said, drawing her attention back to the

screen. "How long will you need to get back in and get a better feel for the site?"

"Getting back to the site won't be a problem, but it will take me several hours to better understand the code and who wrote it."

"As long as they didn't see your footprints from the first encounter," Jude interrupted.

"They didn't," Kenley said firmly. "I swept behind myself as I backed out, even though I never played with any of the code. All I did was click the spiders. Honestly, it's on the open dark web. I didn't need to get past a firewall or any security. Mistyping the fifty-two-character link to a different site took me straight there. That means they aren't trying to hide it."

"Which makes me suspect—" Mina said slowly.

"They want people to click those spiders," Kenley agreed.

"Why would they want that?" Jude asked.

"I don't know for sure," Kenley said, leaning in as though she was worried other people were listening. "But I think each time a spider is clicked, the program infiltrates the camera attached to the spider to get data sent back to the program."

"Like a virus?" Mina asked.

Kenley shrugged. "I don't know for sure, but that's my gut feeling. I'll know more once I get inside the code."

"But we still don't know why this program was created or why they want to infiltrate the cameras."

Kenley turned to him and made eye contact. "My gut says terrorists."

"Terrorists?" Mina asked.

Kenley turned back to the video screen. "Of one kind or another. Either foreign or domestic. I'll know more once I get in there, but if they're getting data from cameras all over the world that are telling them traffic patterns, stoplight patterns, pedestrian traffic, and all those data points—"

"It could be utilized to plan the perfect attack," Mina finished, and Kenley shot her a finger gun.

"We need to get moving on this," Jude said, gripping his knees tightly. "Wait, could it be a Homeland Security program?"

"If it were," Mina said with a tip of her hand, "I don't think it would have a dark-net-specific domain suffix. It was dark-net-specific, right?"

"It was," Kenley said. "Which makes the government less likely to have written the program."

"But it's not a zero percent chance," Jude added. "There could be an underlying reason they're using the dark web."

Mina shuffled papers around, wrote something down and then held up the paper. Kenley committed the information to memory and noticed Jude doing the same. When Mina lowered the paper, she nodded at Jude. "You'll find everything you'll need there."

"Kenley, will you need anything for your limb? I have access to the basics like socks and skin protectant."

"A five-ply sock and liquid to dry powder if you have it," Kenley said, folding her hands in the prayer pose. "I brought regular powder with us from Jude's, but it's hard on the silicone in the liner."

With a nod, Mina wrote the items down. "I'll see what I can do. Once you're settled, I want updates as frequently as you can send them via video or text on the Secure Watch phone. If this isn't a government program, we must alert them ASAP."

"Noted," Jude said as Kenley nodded.

"I'll do my best to get in there as fast as possible, but I

also have to be careful so I don't leave a footprint or trail behind. We'll need to do it in phases."

"You'll have everything you need if you give us three hours."

"You're sure Cal is cool with this?" Jude asked.

Mina's gaze narrowed as she drilled him with an aggravated look. "I run Secure Watch, not Cal. So yes, I'm cool with this. When we're done here, I'll loop him in so he knows there may be government officials we'll have to deal with, but other than that, I make the calls."

Jude gave her a cheeky salute and a nod. "We'll take a break here and then move to the next station," he said, not mentioning the address that Mina had shown them. "I'll keep you in the loop once we're set up."

"I suggest you cover any tracks there before you head out," Mina said, her brow raised as though it were a question and not a statement.

"Ten-four," Jude said.

"Secure Watch, out." Mina waved, and the screen went blank.

They stared at each other for a heartbeat, inhaling a breath and letting it out before Kenley spoke. "How long will it take us to get there?" she asked, her eyes darting to the blank screen.

"It's an hour by foot. We need to clean up and fuel up, and then we'll head out."

"She said we'll have everything we need. What did she mean by that?"

"Car, clothes, credit cards, computers and maybe a gun." He took a bite of a doughnut, closing his eyes as he savored food for the first time in hours.

"But it's not a place to stay?" Kenley asked, sipping from her coffee cup again.

"That's unnecessary. There are plenty of hotels we can use once we're out of the area. We'll need to make a game plan for bouncing."

"Bouncing?" she asked, grabbing a hard-boiled egg and taking a bite. "What are we bouncing?"

"Our digital code, so to speak," he said, motioning at the computer. "We can't do this work and stay in one place. We'll need to—"

"Bounce," Kenley finished, and he winked as an answer. "We need public Wi-Fi to make this work. Internet cafés are usually the best and the safest."

"Not when you have Secure Watch covering your back," he said, sitting and wiping off his hands. "Our scrambler will be more than enough if we use Wi-Fi from a hotel. I tossed around libraries or coffee shops, but that makes us visible, and we want to be—"

"Ghosts."

His nod was tight and sharp. "Here's what I'm thinking. We stick to big chain hotels with good Wi-Fi. We move every second night and only at night. That way, we're never on anyone's radar, and we move often enough that no one can home in on us."

Kenley thought it over and held up her finger. "As long as we have a second exit."

"Always a first-floor room with a window or patio door," he agreed.

"Before you dig deeper into this, I want to give you an out, Jude. You've been wonderful, as has Mina, but this may be a fight you don't want any skin in."

He shook his head slowly. "Too late for that, Kenley. The fact that I've spent any time with you at all makes me a target for whoever is after you. Whether that's tied to this situation, they know my address now."

"It is," she insisted, jumping in. "The tracker is confusing me, but I hope more investigation of the program will tell us why someone was watching me."

"Fair point. First, I would never leave you to go this alone when I know how dangerous it is. Second, until this is sorted, I can't return to my normal life either. They already know who I am and where I live. If these people think they can leverage me to get to you, they'll do it."

"Fair point," she said with a smile and a wink. "Partners?" With her hand stuck out, she waited for him to grab it, partly to feel like they were a team and in it together but mostly because she wanted to see if that slip of his skin against hers made her feel the same way it did the first time—charged, connected, protected and, oddly enough, owned.

Jude slid his hand inside hers and squeezed. Not in a handshake-of-partners way either. He squeezed her hand in a way that said he saw through her plan and wanted to feel the same things she did. Her gut reaction told her they weren't all that different after all.

JUDE STUCK HIS arm out to hold Kenley back as he scanned the property across the highway.

"A junkyard?" Kenley whispered from behind him. "Did she give us the wrong address?"

"Mina Jacobs? That would never happen."

"What are we waiting for, then? My dog is barking." He did his best not to smile, but he did, and she punched him lightly on the shoulder. "You can laugh when I'm the one poking fun at myself. That said, let's go."

"Not yet. To answer your question, I'm waiting for a dog."

"I don't see one."

"Doesn't mean there isn't one there."

"Bruh, are you afraid of itty-bitty puppy dogs?"

He turned a side-eye on her. "I've seen what a German shepherd can do to human flesh. If you haven't, then you should consider yourself lucky."

With her hands raised in the "don't shoot" position, she sighed. "Fair, but we can't stand here all day."

Jude took a moment to search around them, coming up with a rock. He pushed her back and lobbed it across the highway until it landed in the gravel entrance of the junkyard. After a sixty-second wait, he grabbed Kenley's hand and helped her over a fallen tree and onto the highway.

"I feel like your military training kicks in once in a while even doing this job," she said as they scurried across the road toward the junkyard. "That was smart. I don't see or hear a Fido anywhere."

"The army taught me a few things about looking before you leap."

"Duly noted," she whispered as she held on to his arm, staying halfway behind him as they walked. "But this place makes me nervous. Why would Mina send us here?"

"Where there's a junkyard, there's—"

"Cars," she finished, slapping herself on the forehead with her palm.

"That's my working theory, at least," he agreed as they approached a tall white fence facing the road. Sliding doors at the center of the fence would open for a car to pass through. However, they were closed. "I don't know for sure, so stay close until we know we're in the right place."

"Any closer, and you'd be giving me a piggyback ride," she mumbled.

The comment made him laugh on the inside, but his concentration was focused on everything around them as they moved toward the white fence with caution. He had his Sig at his waist with his holster unsnapped just in case there was a sneak attack coming.

"I don't see a door," she whispered. "Are we supposed to announce ourselves? Dance? Clap our hand—"

She hadn't finished the word when the large sliding door parted just wide enough for them to enter.

"Camera," he whispered when she jumped in surprise. "They know we're here."

Jude grasped her hand, and they walked through the opening into what could only be described as a place where cars went to die. Every car make, model, brand and age was parked or stacked as far as the eye could see. He noticed an office to the right of them, and he pulled Kenley along by her hand, careful not to walk faster than she could. He feared she'd fall if he didn't take things at her pace. She'd kept up with him for the hike, but he could tell she was tired, sore, and needed a breather. Hopefully, he was about to give her one.

Then he spied it. Next to the office door was a lineup of stickers, including payments they accepted and didn't accept and car brands they sold parts for. Stuck in the middle of the other stickers was an image of two pistols crossed.

Jude tapped it before he opened the office door. "That's why we're here," he told her. "That's the army police insignia. Cal was Special Ops army police. I would guess we're about to meet another."

"It's all making sense now," she whispered as he held the door open for her to enter.

They walked in, both comfortable with the situation now that they knew the person behind the counter was there to help and not hurt. He snapped his holster over the pistol and waited for what felt like an eternity.

"Is there a bell or something to ring?" she finally asked. "Something about this doesn't feel right."

Jude was starting to feel the same way, but this was the address Mina had sent them to. "They have to know we're here. They opened the door for us."

"I know you're here, son," a voice said from the back of the shop.

Jude immediately went for his gun but paused when he saw the man walking toward them. He was eighty if he was a day, wore an eye patch over his left eye, and carried a cane.

"I'm no threat to ya, boy," he said, his laughter alluding to the years of smoking he'd done in his life. "Mina said you're ex-army. I can tell."

"Yes, sir," Jude said, shaking the man's hand when he arrived at the desk. "I was cyber intel."

"Good to meet you. I'm an old friend of Cal's—the name's Archie. I've owned this junkyard longer than you've been alive. I hoped my son would take it over one day, but I never had one, so I guess that's not going to happen."

Archie bent over laughing until he started coughing, his lungs seemingly going to be the death of him. He stood up and dug around in his pocket. "You wouldn't know it by looking, but I have a few clunkers around here that still run." He pulled a key from his pocket and thrust it at Jude. "It will getcha where you need to go."

Jude accepted the key with a grateful smile. "Thanks, Archie. Much appreciated."

Archie motioned them to follow him behind the desk and out the back door of the small office fashioned out of an old metal shed. Parked in the back was a gray Honda Civic hatchback. It was probably the ugliest thing he'd ever seen, but it didn't have to look pretty to run.

"Thanks to our mutual friend, the plates are registered to

someone who only exists on paper. Try not to drive it like you stole it, eh?" He started laughing again, slapping his knee. "But seriously, I wouldn't push this one past sixty-five if you want to stay alive."

"Noted," Jude said, trying to ignore the four tires that didn't match, the missing hubcaps, the downward turn of the bumper, and the piece of duct tape holding the back window up. It was more memorable than he would have preferred, but there was nothing he could do about it. Kenley couldn't continue walking, and they had no time to argue. This would never end if they didn't get back into that program. "Thanks for your help. I'll take good care of it."

"Son, I never want to see this ugly duckling again. Please don't return it. I don't need the kind of trouble that might follow you."

Jude understood his concerns and nodded once. "I'll make sure it finds a good home."

"The bottom of a lake wouldn't be a bad resting place," he said, motioning them around to the back, where he popped the hatch. "I have a few goodies for you. I followed Mina's list to a T."

Jude quickly took stock of the supplies. There were clothes, a second proxy scrambler, and nothing else. "Looks like we're set." He had to admit he was disappointed they wouldn't have a bit more firepower, but he'd have to make do with what he had.

"I hope it gets you to safety," Archie said, slamming the hatch. "Just in case you need an assist, that there blanket on the back seat isn't for keeping warm."

Archie lifted his brows at Jude, and he nodded, understanding. He'd come through with the firepower after all.

"Archie, you've been most helpful," Jude said, shaking his

hand as he held the passenger door open for Kenley. "We'd better be on our way."

Kenley held up her finger and turned to Archie. "Do you have cameras here?"

"Yes, ma'am," Archie said, pointing them out for them. "Can't run a business like this without them. Don't worry, they're 'down for maintenance' right now." He threw some air quotes around in the air. Jude had to bite back a smile.

"I'm glad to hear that, but I have one more question," Kenley said. "Do you use a security company or take care of the recordings yourself?"

"A company takes care of all that for me. I'm an old dog, and those are not the tricks I can learn. Don't worry, they won't come back online until you're long down the road."

Kenley nodded, but Jude could tell that the answer Archie had given them wasn't the one she wanted to hear. "We appreciate that, Archie," she said, sitting in the passenger seat and pulling her legs in. "And we appreciate the help."

Jude shut the door once she was in, and the back-seat blanket caught his eye. He was grateful to Mina for getting them the long gun. He didn't want to shoot anyone, but he also didn't want to be in a firefight with only a handgun.

After a final handshake with Archie, Jude lowered himself into the car and slammed the door. "Here goes nothing," he said to Kenley and turned the key in the ignition.

Chapter Eight

They'd each taken a power nap before leaving the last motel room, but Jude could tell Kenley was still exhausted. They'd walked over an hour to Archie's and had been up for nearly twenty-four hours. He'd decided to stick to the back roads as they made their way into Wisconsin. The hatchback seemed to be in okay shape, but he didn't push the speedometer over sixty. He wanted to ensure the gun in the back seat didn't land on anyone's radar.

Returning to Wisconsin was a risk, but Jude was willing to take it to be closer to the team. If they got in a bind and needed assistance, the closer to Minnesota they were, the better. The plan was to find the biggest chain hotel in a city, check in and get to work. He didn't like the risks that came with a random hotel that he couldn't scout, but they had limited options at this point in the game.

"Kenley," he said, and she finally tore her gaze away from the window to look at him. "Why did you ask Archie about the cameras?" She'd been quiet for the last thirty miles, and while he understood why, he also didn't want her to draw so far into herself that she stopped trusting him to help her out of this situation. "I got the feeling you didn't like his answer."

The woman next to him shifted in her seat and pinned those brown eyes on him. He had to keep his pointed at the road, or he would start thinking about how sweet she would feel under his hands and his lips. It wasn't a good idea to drive distracted, so he forced himself to concentrate on the problem they had to solve.

"Not his answer specifically," she explained. "More the idea of it. I've been thinking about the program and have many questions. If this Spiderweb website gets access to a camera, does it also get access to all the saved data, or can it only get the data from the moment it gets access to it on forward? Does that make sense?"

Jude tossed it around in his head for a moment. "Because it would somehow use the prior data to its advantage?"

"That's my working theory right now," she said. "I'm trying to look at it from all angles, but every time I do, another angle pops up." Kenley rubbed her forehead as though she was frustrated and tired. "Part of me wants this to be a dumb game created by some kid who thinks it's funny. My embarrassment about overreacting would be leaps and bounds less destructive than what a terrorist would do with the information."

"But you can't convince yourself it's a dumb game created by some kid?"

"The tracker in my shoe and the guys in the truck are hard to explain away, but I do a lot of digging on the dark web."

"If you think about it," Jude said, his thoughts following that path, "it has to be a coincidence."

"Because of the tracker," she said, and he nodded. "I thought of that, too. The tracker was in my shoe before I found the site, which means the Spiderweb program has nothing to do with it."

"It also means we're back at square one in figuring out who put the tracker in your shoe and why."

"My brain hurts," she moaned, tossing her head back on

the headrest. "In my opinion, that's less important right now. What's important is figuring out what the Spiderweb program is and why it's there. It could spiral out of control quickly if we don't stop it. What do you think?"

"We're in full agreement. I hope whoever is behind the spiders has no idea anyone found it."

"Oh, they know," she said, holding up a finger. "They know because I was clicking the spiders. Even if all it does is send back data on what cameras came online, they'd know someone clicked them."

"Unless they're already all active," Jude finally said, giving voice to what he'd been thinking for the last few hours.

"Then why make the website?" Kenley asked in confusion.

They both fell silent again as they drove, the car rumbling under them as they made their way toward the Wisconsin border. The exhaust had a hole somewhere, but Jude was grateful for the wheels, no matter the condition.

"For a reason neither of us understand, someone put a tracker in my foot shell," Kenley said, as though she needed to talk it out. "Whether that has to do with my day or night job, I can't be sure."

"Or something else entirely?"

"I don't date, if that's what you're asking," she said, staring straight ahead out the windshield. "My parents are dead, and I have no living family in the area. There would be no other reason to track me."

"Okay, in that case, it has to be work-related and not personal."

"In the end, that's less important than shutting down this camera situation," she said, shifting to get more comfortable on the old seats. This car was probably older than she was, and time hadn't been kind to it. "If we don't, and it gains power underground and off the radar of any governing agency, then we're holding the smoking gun, too."

"We could just go to the authorities, you know," he said with a shrug. "You can turn it over to them to figure out."

"I thought of that for about five seconds last night before I laughed and said nah. Someone sophisticated enough to make that program would see a government hacker on the first keystroke. They might be cyber experts, but I haven't met one yet who is subtle."

"Hey," Jude said with a smile. "I think I take offense at that!"

"There's a reason I'm taking point when we go back in," she said with a wink. "But seriously, this kind of job will be tricky, and I suspect there will be plenty of traps just waiting to snare us. I'd rather do the recon on it myself to see who's behind it. One thing I know for sure is that it's not the government."

"We can't keep it from them forever, though," he said, slowing the car as he noticed the thermometer creeping up toward hot. Great. Just what they needed. He made a mental note to find a gas station where he could grab some coolant in case the radiator was the problem. For all he knew, the gauge was faulty, but he couldn't risk losing their ride due to negligence.

"I'm hoping Secure Watch will facilitate that information once we have hard evidence about who it is or what it's for."

"And if we find out it's a government program?"

"It's not," she said, shaking her head with determination. "You know how the government and the military work. This is not one of their programs. If anything, it's the exact opposite."

"Someone who wants to use the information against them?"

"Possibly. It could be cyberwarfare," she agreed. "It could be anything. That's why I feel like I'm sitting on my hands here. I need more information before deciding what we should do with it."

"To that end, have you decided where we're stopping first?"

"I was thinking Lake Geneva," she answered. "We can drive straight into it from either 47 or 12."

"Not a bad idea since it's enough of a tourist town that they aren't going to remember two new faces. That's only an hour from Milwaukee?" Jude noticed her nod from the corner of his eye. "Not ideal in terms of that pickup truck full of goons, but we have to hope ditching the tracker was enough to throw them off our trail." He pointed at the Secure Watch phone on the console. "Text Mina and have her get us a room at a chain hotel."

"We talked about that," she said, not reaching for the phone. "No calling ahead."

"We did, but then I remembered that since Covid, everyone has contactless check-in. We can check in directly from the phone, and no one will ever see our faces. We can check out the same way. Text Mina and tell her what our parameters are for a room so she knows. She'll have it taken care of long before we get there."

"You make a good point. The fewer people who remember us, the better." She grabbed the phone and punched in the passcode to open it.

He put his hand on hers for a moment. The warmth and softness of her skin seeped into his fingers and warmed him instantly. He hated to admit how much he yearned for the touch of another person. A solitary life was safe, but it wasn't comforting. "To start the conversation, type Secure Watch, Jacko. Then you wait for their reply."

She swiftly did as he said and then glanced at him. "You all have code names? Is that paranoia or purposeful?"

"Both," he answered, his gaze rocketing to all three mirrors to watch for a tail. "Cal, being ex-military, decided when he started Secure One that code names were a good way to protect his team's real identities."

"So, is the way you address each other in the opening sequence also code for something?"

"In a way. When we use that greeting, both sides know no one is being coerced by an outside entity that could put Secure Watch at risk. If you were to text without that greeting or with any other type of greeting, Mina would not respond, burn the phone, and send out the team to help. If I were to get communication from them without the formal greeting, I would ditch the phone and go radio silent."

"I get it now. If someone was in a hostage situation, you'd purposely not answer correctly so they knew you were in trouble. Smart."

Jude tipped his head in agreement while she tapped the phone on her palm. "Want to tell me the site that you visit a lot? The one you transposed the numbers on to find the Spiderweb page."

"If I said no, would I get away with it?"

He laughed loudly in response to her question. "Maybe for right now, but not forever."

"It's a site that holds the unpublished studies that a corporation does on its products. Studies they don't want as public consumption."

"They're using an I2P domain specific?"

"Yep," she agreed. "It's an invisible internet project domain-ending. By keeping it hidden this way, I can only assume they have a greater than ninety-nine percent chance that no one will read it. Without the exact fifty-two-character letter and number sequence, you wouldn't find it. That's about—" she paused and tipped her head back and forth a few times "—forty trillion different combinations of numbers and letters."

"But you found it."

"I did, but I was looking. I didn't accidentally come across it."

"The question I should have asked then was, why were you looking for it?"

"Evidence?" she asked, and Jude cut his gaze to her for a moment.

"The reaction you had on the trail this morning to the sound of the ATV. I've seen that before, always as a PTSD response. You went somewhere. Where did you go?"

The phone beeped, drawing Kenley's attention to the screen where she read the message. "She replied, Secure Watch, Whiskey, go ahead with your message."

"Good. Ask her to stick to hotels that have digital room keys. We want to bypass as many reception desks as possible."

Kenley nodded and typed until the message was sent. "With any luck, we can be inside that site by dinnertime."

"We need food and sleep before we do anything," he said firmly. "After a hot meal and a good night's sleep, we'll commence the work."

"You're forgetting that most hotels have noon or before checkout times."

"We'll be paying for two full nights even though we'll check out at midnight. There's no other way. Then we'll drive a few hours, check into a new place, and repeat the process."

"We might not need to," she argued. "Those guys haven't turned up since we ditched the tracker. Staying put means we find the answers faster."

"You're not wrong," he agreed as they flew by a sign telling them Lake Geneva was exactly two hours away. "But we don't want to be on anyone's Wi-Fi network longer than a day before we move. Secure Watch has strong scramblers, but it's smarter to use a new host as often as possible, considering what we'll be doing."

"Okay," she agreed, turning to him. "But you have to be flexible with the timeline. If we're in the middle of something at midnight, we might have to push leaving back an hour while we finish. Agreed?"

"We can assess our leave times as necessary. Now, you didn't answer my question."

"You didn't ask one," she said, confused when he glanced at her.

"I did. I asked you where you went this morning on that ATV trail."

"Oh, that," she said with a sigh. "It was nothing. It was just an old memory."

"Didn't seem like a good one. You were shaking, and I worried you were going to vomit. You mentioned earlier that you killed your best friend when you became an amputee. Were you driving an ATV?"

Jude watched her cross her arms defiantly over her chest and stare straight ahead as though he didn't exist in the old Honda. Kenley had been a champ and kept up with him for the four-mile walk to pick up the car, but he could tell the lack of sleep was starting to catch up with her. He'd also noticed her shifting in the seat, turning her right leg one way and then the other every few minutes as though she was in pain.

"We still have a long drive ahead of us. If you need to take your prosthesis off to be more comfortable, that's okay."

"I don't think it's smart to be vulnerable, Jude."

She wasn't talking about her leg now. It was the way she said *vulnerable* that made his gut clench. He'd spent the last six years trying to protect the vulnerable. Her words sent a jolt of understanding through him. His entire life was built around this moment. The moment a job became something more. Someone more. That was a scary idea for a guy who had survived the last thirty-nine years alone on this planet for good reasons. Caring about someone made you vulnerable. That was something he couldn't afford to be.

Kenley stared out the window again, and he glanced at her side profile. She was so damn beautiful, but the most beautiful part of her was her brain. The way she cared about protecting others with her skills turned him on more than anything else about her. Watching her walk across that creek this morning on nothing but a tiny pad at the bottom of her leg showed him the strength and determination she had to finish what she started, no matter the cost.

Jude bit back the demand on his tongue. He wanted to know more about her, but she had to be willing to offer it. Demanding information was never the way to go about it, but if he were patient, she'd open up to him in her own time. If there was one thing the military had taught him, it was patience.

Chapter Nine

The car had gotten them across the border into Wisconsin before it started to overheat, and it required another hour to cool off enough for him to fix it. They'd taken advantage of the break, bought food from a small diner, and eaten it at a picnic table under a tree. Kenley had convinced Jude that it was safer than a booth in the diner. They needed to avoid as many cameras as possible, considering what they were up against. She'd even gone so far as to wear a mask into the diner to grab the food.

Thankfully, Mina had found a hotel with digital keys and got them a room with two beds. They could check in without making contact with anyone, and once they had, Jude insisted they clean up and take a nap before they started working. While she'd wanted to argue with him, her eyes betrayed her by drooping while he was showering, and that was the last thing she remembered until she woke a few minutes ago. The room was dark, and the clock read 9:00 p.m.

"You needed the sleep," Jude said from the other bed.

Surprised, she sat up. "I didn't know you were awake."

"I heard you stirring. How's your leg?" he asked, sitting up and stretching.

They'd found two backpacks in the old hatchback, and the clothes he'd included for Jude were dry tech shirts that hugged every ridge of his well-defined chest. He might work with computers for a living, but if what lay under that shirt was any indication, he still visited the gym regularly.

Her bag held several changes of clothes, the powder and socks she requested, and a stocked first aid kit. She'd never been more grateful for the bottle of Tylenol than she had been when she shook two into her hand and swallowed them. Her leg was aching from the hours over rough terrain in a prosthesis made for city living. Jude was intuitive and, without being told her limitations, was able to help her navigate through the forest. He had saved her life. There was no question in her mind. If he hadn't answered the phone, she would already be in the hands of the people who wanted her—even if she didn't know why.

"How's your leg?" he asked again, scooting to the end of the bed to pull on his shoes. His jeans looked buttery soft and hugged his muscular thighs with every movement. Something told her Jude liked to run or bike when he wasn't lifting weights at the gym.

"No problems." She was going for sunny and unbothered, but the truth was something else. Her leg was sore, but that was to be expected. The Syme socket she was wearing wasn't the best for long-distance walking.

"You may as well know that I can already tell when you're lying to me," he said, strapping on his watch and sliding his glasses onto his face. "A little twitch at the corner of your right eye gives you away every time."

Instinctively, she raised her hand to caress the corner of her eye. "If you want the truth, it's sore but won't hold us up."

"I'm not worried about it holding us up," he said, sitting on the edge of the bed, holding her powder and liner. "I'm worried about you being in pain and ignoring a problem."

"It's sore from the uneven terrain, that's all," she assured him. "A Syme foot has low clearance because our limbs are long. That means we get very little dynamic return from the prosthetic foot. Amputees with shorter limbs have more clearance and can use sockets and feet that offer a better response to uneven ground."

"I didn't know that. Would it have been better for them to have amputated higher?"

"Absolutely, and I wish they had, but the situation called for a Syme, so that's what they did. I wish they'd gone below the knee, as that would have offered me better prosthetic options. It is what it is, but in these situations, I feel my disability more than I do in the city." She couldn't bring herself to look at him and see pity in his eyes, so she motioned at his hands instead. "Where did you find my liner?"

"You must have worked it off in your sleep. When I came out, I found it on the bed, so I asked Mina how to clean it so it was ready. She also explained how to inspect your limb for any blisters and how to treat them."

"You don't need to do that." Her immediate hand-waving indicated how uncomfortable the idea made her. "I checked it over last night. It's fine."

"Mina said you would say that, but she also pointed out you're likely to give it a quick glance and nothing more because you're used to it. I'm not, so I'll likely see something you might miss. I'll get your lotion on while I'm doing it."

"Can't say I'm super comfortable with that idea, kind sir," she said haughtily, glad the blanket covered her legs.

"Then it's time to get real comfortable, real fast, Kenley." He said those words in a no-questions-asked way. "We're a team, and if we're going to be a team, then I have to know your baseline. If I don't know your baseline, I can't watch for a developing problem. Our situation is precarious and an injury to your limb could put us in extreme danger."

"Are you using your military voodoo on me now or something?"

"No, I'm using my *common-sense voodoo* on you now. Is it working?"

A frustrated sigh escaped her lips as she pulled the blankets off. "You don't want to see this, Jude. It's gnarly."

"I'm thirty-nine years old, Kenley. This isn't my first rodeo." That was his only reply, aside from his fingers waving in the air for her to give him her leg.

"Probably not like this one," she muttered before she scooted up to the headboard. Did she want to show Jude her leg? No, not even a little bit, but he was correct that an injury to her limb would slow them down too much and maybe put their lives at risk. That said, showing a cute guy your amputated limb was vulnerable on a level that she hated. Without much choice, she sighed and pulled her pant leg up. There was her leg in all its glory—or rather, what was left of it. "I can't shave my leg, which makes inspecting the skin harder."

"Why is that?" he asked, inspecting the limb as though none of the scars that crisscrossed it, nor the matchstick thin bones nor the bulbous pad of displaced skin and muscle at the bottom bothered him in the least. Instead, he held her limb gently, glancing up to make eye contact with her before returning to the leg to check for skin breakdown. She wasn't used to anyone else touching her leg, much less caressing it with such tenderness. How he held it and ran his fingers over the heel pad was a sensation she'd remember for the rest of her life. The look in his eyes said he wanted to heal her with his touch. There was something else there, too. A look of longing to connect? A desire to know someone deeper than he knew himself?

It took her a moment to remember the question and answer it. "Uh, um, it can block hair follicles, which leads to infection."

"I had no idea that was a thing," he admitted, rubbing his finger over a spot just below her knee. She shivered as his skin brushed against hers and raised goose bumps across her arms. "There's no hair here, though."

"My prosthesis rubs it off," she explained to his raised brow. "The socket designs for my type of amputation are limited. I hear there are some new ones out there, but I don't have coverage for prostheses, so I have to use what I can afford."

"You didn't get a settlement from the accident?"

"I lived in a questionable neighborhood, remember?" she asked, unable to stop the eye roll that followed.

"Mina didn't mean anything by that, Kenley." He cradled her leg in both hands, and his warmth seeped into her. Slowly, she relaxed her hip until the weight of her leg, and maybe some of the world, was in his hands. "She's not that kind of person."

Kenley leaned her head back against the pillow and sighed. "I know, and the neighborhood has changed since I lived there, but growing up, I didn't know that. It was home, you know?"

He nodded as he lowered her leg to rest on a pillow. "I get that. We all have different childhood experiences, and they shape who we are as adults. From what I've seen, your childhood experiences taught you perseverance and a never-give-up attitude that still serves you well. Never apologize for that, okay?" He leaned on the bed and made eye contact until she nodded. It took her a moment because she found herself lost in his eyes. They were shining green this morning, but they told her how too many of his adult experiences had shaped who he was now. "You have a blister on the outside bottom of the leg."

"Really?"

He motioned for her to sit up, and she looked down at the heel pad. She was more than surprised to see he was right. "I didn't even see that."

"Probably because you didn't check, right?" he asked, grabbing the first aid kit Mina had sent along and walking back to the bed. "Tell me what to do."

"I can do it." She held her hand out for the kit, but he didn't move until she sighed and leaned back against the headboard again.

"Wipe it down, dry it, and cover it with the clear bandage you'll find in there. Make sure there aren't any wrinkles in the bandage, or that will cause more skin breakdown as I walk on it."

"When did the neighborhood change?" He followed her directions, and the swipe of the antiseptic wipe on her skin made her hiss. "Sorry." He offered her a wink, and she glanced away, embarrassed by the situation, even though he was more than cool with it.

"It was always a poor neighborhood, but it wasn't until the drugs moved in that it developed that reputation. I grew up in a small house with neighbors of mixed ethnicities. My mom was Latina, and my dad was Black. I was their only child. My best friend, Gabriella, lived with her mom, who was a nurse. Her mom and dad were from Guatemala, but her dad died when she was just a baby. Her mom worked nights, so Gabriella slept at our house, and my mom got us ready for school."

"Which explains the best friends part." He waved a piece of paper over the wound to dry it as he prepared the bandage with the other hand.

"We were for a decade." Was she going to tell him what happened? Could she lay herself bare in a room where only the two of them existed? Did she have the strength to tell him how she got her best friend killed without crying? The answer was no. She never could, but she could see the determination in his eyes. He was going to keep hounding her about it until she told him.

"The summer before we started our freshmen year, Gabriella's mom bought her a used four-wheeler. There was a trail that ran behind our houses, so we'd go riding almost every day. It was the day before school started, and I begged her to take it out one last time. A final goodbye to summer." Kenley's voice broke, and she cleared her throat, forcing herself to concentrate on the way he smoothed the bandage over her leg and not on the memory of her best friend's final moments.

"What happened when she agreed?" he asked, as though he knew she needed help to tell him the rest of the story.

"Gabriella loved riding, but she didn't want to go. I begged her until she finally agreed, so we took off down the trail, with her driving and me behind her. She kept pushing the machine faster and faster, cackling and jumping up and down like a maniac."

"She wasn't normally that way?"

"No. She was never reckless. I mean, we were barely old enough to drive one, so we always kept it below thirty on the trail."

"But not that day?"

"Nope." She sighed and shook her head. "All these years, I've wondered if she acted that way because she was mad that I'd begged her to go until she gave in. I kept leaning in and motioning for her to slow down. It was so loud, and there was so much dust flying around it was almost impossible to communicate. Instead, she hit the gas and threw me back into the seat so hard it took me a minute to reorient myself. The next thing I know, I'm flying through the air. I land hard on the trail, and the machine rolls over me before my world goes black."

His long fingers had wrapped around the bottom of her limb, cupping it gently and massaging it as he listened. "Did she miss a turn because of the speed?"

"The trail was straight, so that wasn't a problem. All we know is that a front wheel sheared off, and when it went off, so did we. Gabriella was crushed by the machine when it came down on her chest and head. I was the lucky one." Kenley motioned at her leg and then closed her eyes, willing the tears to stay away since she had too many hours left to spend with this man.

"I'm sorry, Kenley. You feel guilty for begging her to take the ATV out, right?"

"Wouldn't you?" The question was defensive, and she sucked in a breath to dial it back. It wasn't his fault she'd made bad choices as a kid.

"Survivor's guilt is a real thing, sweet pea."

Sweet pea? That was new. Maybe he wasn't a babe kind of dude, but sweet pea?

Or maybe he's trying to comfort you, and you should stop obsessing over it.

She rolled her eyes at internal Kenley while she stared over his shoulder. Maybe he'd think she was engaged in the discussion even though it was the last place she wanted to be. "Especially when you're guilty of murder."

He squeezed her leg while he shook his head. "No. You aren't responsible for what happened to Gabriella. You may have asked her to take the ATV out, but she drove it recklessly. ATVs will flip on a dime, but losing a wheel is a catastrophic situation you couldn't predict. Not to mention, you were fourteen."

Kenley forced her face to remain expressionless. She still didn't have proof that the company knew the wheels sheared off at high speed, but once she did, they'd pay for her catastrophic situation and a whole lot more.

"Some say I was old enough to know better but young enough not to care."

"Do you think that's true?" he asked, smoothing the lotion over her limb, making sure all her skin was covered.

"What I think is, we need to get to work."

His hands paused on her limb, and he lifted a brow. Jude asked the question again, this time in a way that demanded an answer. "Do you think that's true?"

"The one thing I can say about the whole thing was I did care. There's never been a reckless bone in my body, Jude. Gabriella, not so much. She loved to push the limits on everything, but she was bigger than me—bolder, stronger, braver."

"Not true," he said, handing her the special liner to roll on over her limb. She did it without thinking but did notice that he watched her closely. He followed each step she took as though he would one day do it for her. She almost laughed aloud at the thought. As if a guy like Jude Mason would stick around once they were out of this pickle. He was eight years her senior, and while she didn't have a problem with the age gap, his life experience would surely lead him to a much older woman. "You were strong and brave enough to stand up and tell her she was being reckless. Now, you do a job that requires you to be bold, strong and brave. Don't underestimate yourself, Kenley. That would be a huge mistake on your part."

"Do you have a girlfriend, Jude?" She asked the question

without thinking but didn't apologize for doing so. The answer was important to her for some reason.

"I'm single. Why?"

She shrugged nonchalantly as though her heart hadn't skipped a beat when he said he was single. Jude carried her prosthesis over and removed the plate so she could slip her limb into the socket.

"I was thinking if you had a girlfriend, she would be a lucky woman to have someone as supportive and caring as you. I hope the woman you end up with knows what a gem you are."

"I'm not all that, Kenley," he assured her. "I have ghosts I live with every day."

"Maybe, but don't we all? What I know is no man has ever cared for my limb the way you just did. Most won't even look at it, so touching it, patching it up and preparing it for the day is above and beyond."

"That's caring about a friend." He reached out to steady her as she stood and seated her limb into place in the socket before she pulled her pants down over it. "The last thing I want to happen is you get hurt over all this, Kenley. Despite the tracker and everything else, I believe you're an innocent player. I may not know why yet, but my gut tells me it has more to do with you being good and them being evil than anything else. What do you say we start figuring out who they are?"

He squeezed her hands before she could escape the close confines of the beds. His smile was easy and relaxed, yet it carried heat that caught her off guard. The man before her didn't see her as a burden. What he saw her as she didn't know, but she did know she could trust him with her life, and he wouldn't let her down.

"Remember, Kenley, you're not fighting this battle alone

anymore. I've got you. Together, we can find them and stop them."

He stepped back to allow her to pass, and all she could think was she sure hoped so because if they couldn't, the world was in serious trouble.

ELECTRICITY FLOWED THROUGH Kenley's fingers as she prepared for battle. It had taken them far too long to return to this program, but Jude was correct—there had been little choice. The rest and food were necessary, or they'd be too tired to keep their wits about them and avoid detection. She checked the clock on her computer. It was 11:00 p.m. If they worked all night, they might get a good handle on what this program was for and who was behind it. A niggling sense of doom reminded her that the person behind it was skilled, and it may take everything she had just to stay ahead of detection.

"Are you ready?" she asked, watching Jude prepare himself on the other side of the room. He would click the spiders while she ran the code. She hoped the code would tell her what was happening each time a spider was clicked. Once they knew that, she'd better understand why the website existed. She could leave it alone without a guilty conscience if it were an innocent game. But if it were something more, as she suspected, she'd hopefully be able to corrupt the code long enough to report it to authorities. "Before we start, I want you to know something." He glanced over and met her gaze with a nod. "Sometimes I wear a dark hat, but it's always for the good of the people. I'll make sure that's the case this time, too."

"I respect that, Kenley. It's also the only reason I'm here. I may not know why you turn dark sometimes, and while that needs to be discussed, I know that it has no purpose other than good. Now," he said, grabbing his notepad and a pen, "let's do this. I've decided to write down any identifying information I can see for every camera that comes online when I click it. You want me to pan the camera around like I'm playing with it, right?"

Her heart melted when he agreed that she was a good person, even though she didn't feel she deserved his confidence. She would accept his help and respect but put off telling him why she turned to the dark net for as long as possible. Sure, he knew about the accident and that she was on the dark web looking at research, but he didn't know the lengths she'd gone to over the years to convince big corporations to pay for their mistakes. Maybe she'd never have to tell him if they could sort out this site quickly. Something about the idea of losing Jude's respect didn't sit right with her.

"Yes, but don't stop specifically on a building or street sign to write it down. That would make it obvious."

"Right. I can use the arrow keys to work the camera while I write. Do you want me to call out the location for each one?"

"No, that would be too distracting—unless something is concerning. With any luck, the coding will tell me its location as soon as the camera comes online. I don't want to be distracted if that's the case. We want this to be a random game of whack-a-spider, making the cameras that pop up equally random. If it doesn't show in the code, it will be up to you to get as much information from each camera as possible. I'll call out if I can see the camera in the code, so you know."

"Ready when you are, Sickle," he said with a wink, his hands poised on his keyboard.

They'd already typed the address into their anonymous web browser so they could go in together, making it harder for one person to tail them both and splitting the focus of anyone watching the site.

"The sense of doom I have is strong, so stay alert," she said and then nodded for him to hit enter.

The Secure Watch router that replaced the hotel's router was robust and would likely suck a large part of the hotel dry when it came to Wi-Fi, but there was nothing she could do about it. It was late enough in the evening that they had to hope everyone else was bedded down for the night. It was hard to wrap her mind around the idea that people were going to bed tonight, utterly unaware that a program like Spiderweb existed. They went about their daily lives thinking they were safe, but the truth was the opposite. Safety was an illusion created by the idea that we control our own destiny. Nothing could be further from the truth.

She'd learned that lesson the hard way at fourteen. The accident had taught her that control of her life was not hers but fate's. The forces around you reacted to your decisions to determine the outcome of any given action. Then there were the things far outside your control, like the decisions other humans made in their lives that trickle down to yours. A prime example was the person who'd built this program. If their end goal was to wreak havoc and chaos in the world, it would trickle down into the lives of everyone in this hotel, town, state, country and world.

Before her eyes, the giant spider appeared, and she dug in, waiting for the code to load while Jude kept the spiders busy. If this was a kids' game, she expected the code to be easily read and changed, but that wasn't happening. With her fingers flying, she made attempt after attempt to pinpoint code specifics, but each time he clicked a spider, the program blocked her from mapping or changing the code.

"Are we getting anything?" Jude asked without taking his eyes off the screen. "We're fifteen minutes into this."

"Nothing," she answered between clenched teeth. "Whoever coded this is blocking me at every turn. I haven't figured out how yet."

"You're saying it's definitely not a video game for weirdos?"

She couldn't help it; she laughed. "Nope, I can say without a doubt it's not a video game. It's weird, but not a game. What are the cameras giving you?" Kenley continued to type, trying to beat her way through the code but hitting a brick wall every time. Whoever wrote this program was skilled.

"From what I can see, the spiders are set up in groups," he explained, concentrating on the screen. "If you jump around between spiders, you get random cameras. Some are US, and some are foreign, but if you stay within one spider pod, all the cameras on that pod are within one region or country. When you finish the cameras on one pod, another pod of smaller spiders pops out again, if that makes sense."

"It does," she said, pausing long enough to read the code scrolling across the screen. "What doesn't make sense is how they're hiding the camera information when it comes online." Kenley was frustrated with her lack of progress, but it was early yet, and she couldn't let the frustration consume her. She had to consider this a matter of life or death and couldn't risk missing something because her frustration took her out of the game for even a beat. With a deep breath in, she forced herself to stay calm and calculated.

"It's there," he said, his mouse still clicking. "You just haven't found it yet."

They fell silent then, both of them concentrating on their respective jobs. She'd broken through the first line of defense and could finally start mapping the code. "Some strings here resemble something you'd see in government coding."

"Are you saying we're messing in a government program right now?" he asked.

"No, I'm saying some of the coding resembles it. That doesn't mean it is. I'm going to send some of these strings of code to Mina. She can run it down for us while we keep working."

"What's your gut telling you?"

"That it's there to throw people off," she answered, still typing. "The rest is like nothing I've seen before regarding the government programs I've worked on."

Kenley quickly copied and pasted some of the code into a secure message and sent it to Mina with an explanation. Her suspicions were on high alert as she kept plowing through the code. If she was right, and she prayed she wasn't, she might know who wrote this program. If it was who she thought it was, then this game was going to be long, complicated and dangerous.

She heard Jude suck in a surprised breath.

"What's wrong?" Kenley asked, glancing up to see him frozen in place as he stared at his screen.

"I don't know how, but this thing found us," he said, his voice calm but his back straight. "I didn't realize it at first, but now I see that each spider pod has been moving closer to Lake Geneva. The one I just clicked is a parking lot camera across from Lake Geneva City Hall."

Kenley's fingers faltered on the keyboard. "That's impossible," she said. "How? We're blocked every which way from Sunday."

"I can only tell you what I'm seeing, Kenley. What I see says we get out now."

Their fingers started flying as they backed out of all their operations and cleared their computers.

"Get our bags together while I pack the equipment." Jude started unplugging the router and packing the equipment bag.

"We're leaving?"

"As fast as we can." He grabbed her machine and stuck it in the bag as she gathered everything else. "If they've pinpointed us to the city in the hour we've been on the site, I don't want to be here if that truck shows up again by morning."

"Fair point," she agreed. "But I can't figure out how the program is doing it!"

"That doesn't matter right now. What matters is that we know it can. We also know that with any other program, we would be phantoms, so this is a next-level situation."

"I would think it was my machine, but you were using yours to click the spiders," Kenley said, slinging her backpack on her shoulders and grabbing one of the equipment bags.

"While that's true, your machine was in the room. If it happens again, we're going to burn your machine."

"Absolutely not," she said, sticking her finger in his chest. "That machine is well over seven thousand dollars and holds my entire life."

"Isn't that a small price to pay if it means we're alive at the end of this?"

He stared her down, and after a few seconds, she backed away. Let him think what he wanted. She wasn't burning her machine. They left the room and headed for the parking lot, where the Honda sat like a giant metal blob. It was an '87, which meant the only thing older than it was Jude, and not by much. It smelled like cigarettes and bad decisions and was so ugly it was easy to remember. They needed to get out in the dark of night if they would escape unnoticed.

With the bags stashed in the back, she climbed into the passenger seat, surprised when Jude handed her the long rifle Archie had hidden under the blanket.

"Just in case," he said as he slammed her door and ran around to his side of the car.

"Wait." She grasped his arm before he started the car. "You said the camera was in the parking lot across from City Hall?"

"Yes, why?"

"Do we know where City Hall is? We know that the camera is active, which means others could also be. How do we drive out of town and avoid the cameras?"

He tossed his hand into his hair as he let loose with a moaned cuss word. "I was concentrating on getting out and didn't even think about that. You're right. We know one camera is active, but there could be others. The only answer is you go incognito." He grabbed the blanket from the back seat and held it up.

Kenley sighed and nodded before she climbed out of the car again and got into the back seat, stretching out on the floor as best she could before he covered her with the blanket.

"As soon as we're safely out of town, you can rejoin the land of the living," he promised. Blob the Slob's engine sputtered to life, and it jostled her as he put it in Drive.

"I don't know what you've gotten us into, Kenley, but that website is no video game."

If nothing else, they'd established that before they had to cut and run, but the heavy pit that settled in Kenley's gut said she might have to negotiate with terrorists, and that could go real bad real quick.

Chapter Ten

The fuel pump clicked off, so Jude stuck the nozzle back into the pump and screwed on the gas cap. He glanced around the truck stop outside Madison, searching for any threat that might be waiting for them. His nerves were frayed after the last few days of running on nothing but adrenaline and fear. Not only had the program figured out where they were, but it had done it in such a short time that he was scared if they went into the program again, they'd never get ahead of it before whoever was after Kenley found them. She had fallen asleep within twenty minutes of climbing back into the passenger seat once they were out of Lake Geneva. While he could have used her as a lookout for a tail, he couldn't find the heart to wake her until he had to pull into the station for gas.

They were anonymous here just by the sheer number of people who came and went from a truck stop this large. They'd blended into the sea of faces while using the restrooms and stocking up on food and necessities. He had grabbed a couple of burner phones as well. Once activated, they could at least use them to locate hotels and use Google Maps. He was flying blind right now other than following road signs, which wasn't always the best way to escape a villain disguised as a computer programmer. At least, that was what Jude considered to be the situation. He also wanted some burner phones in case they had to ditch the Secure Watch phone and their equipment. Did he think that was going to happen? No. But two nights ago, he hadn't thought he would be in a car as old as this one, while on the run with a gray-hat hacker.

The driver's-side door creaked eerily when he pulled it open. It was nearing 3:00 a.m., and fatigue was starting to set in. He lowered himself with a groan and pulled the door shut.

"I should drive the next stretch so you can rest," Kenley said, unbuckling her seat belt.

Jude glanced at her and noted the look of trepidation in her eyes. "Before I tell you no, I want to say this has nothing to do with me being a man or ableist."

She lifted a brow at him slowly. "What's left?"

"Warrant officer of the US Army." She motioned at him to speak. "This is a four-speed manual transmission. While I don't doubt your ability to drive, I do doubt your ability to drive a manual in a car older than you are in the dark on the interstate with the prosthesis you're wearing."

"I could do it." She threw a little defense into her tone, but from what he could tell, there wasn't much pushback. "It wouldn't be easy, but I could."

"And if we picked up a tail?"

She held up her hands and then buckled her seat belt again. "You win, but I feel bad that you have to do all the driving when you're exhausted."

"They train that into us in the military," he said, pulling away from the pumps and back toward the interstate. "I can do it for a few days when necessary. Did Mina respond?" He'd left her in charge of updating the team and checking out of the hotel that they had run out on.

"No, but someone named Riker did?"

"Reece," he clarified as he flipped his signal light on to merge onto the mostly empty interstate at this time of the morning. "Reece Palmer. He's a core member of the team."

"Okay. He'll update Mina in the morning unless we have an absolute emergency and need the team immediately."

"Agreed. We don't know that anyone is tailing us, just that they can somehow see where we are when inside that program."

"I don't know how to shut that site down if we can't break the code," she pointed out. "I don't want Mina messing with it either, because if it does have tracking capabilities, it will lead whoever this is to Secure Watch."

"True. That said, we could still turn it over to the authorities. There's a real possibility it's their program, and we're messing with something that's a matter of national security."

"Oh, no, it's not them," she said, shaking her head. "I would have smashed their code in a matter of twenty minutes. The fact that I couldn't break through that code tells me whoever is behind this has intentions that don't align with the government's modus operandi. How long were we in the program before it started moving the cameras closer and closer to you?"

He pointed into the back seat. "I wrote time stamps on my notebook."

She unbuckled her belt and knelt on the seat, digging around in the bags. Jude forced himself to keep his eyes on the road, even though he wanted them all over her. She was the first woman in years who kept him constantly intrigued. Did she have a compelling backstory? Absolutely, and it was a heartbreaking one, but that wasn't it. Whatever this attraction was, it had something to do with the part of her she never let others see. Her internal struggles that she didn't tell anyone about were what made him want to be the one she shared them with.

He'd gotten a glimpse into her soul at the hotel as he held her leg in his hands. She hadn't wanted him to see her limb yet still she'd trusted him enough to show it to him. Knowing that nearly brought tears to his eyes. When she let him bandage the blister, he'd felt the change in the tide of her trust levels. She could have done the bandaging herself, but she'd allowed him to, all while baring her soul to him about how she'd lost her foot. His visceral reaction to seeing her leg told him he might be in trouble when it came to this woman. His protective side wanted to wrap her up in a blanket and lock her in a room where she could rest while he fought all her battles. That was a dangerous way to think about any woman, much less someone like Kenley. She was intelligent, driven, beautifully damaged, and far better at her job than he could ever hope to be. His insight into who she was had been appreciated, but he still didn't know why she did what she did on the dark web, and that was a mystery he wanted to unravel. It would have to wait for another day, though. Maybe a day when they weren't trying to outrun an invisible spiderweb.

"Found it," she said, flipping back around and buckling her belt. With his penlight pointed at the book, she paged through it and ran her finger down each note he'd made, finally tapping the last entry. "It looks like we'd been working about forty-six minutes when the first group of cameras turned toward the Midwest. We were in the program about fifty-five minutes when it landed on Lake Geneva."

"It only took them nine minutes to turn the regional cameras into city-specific ones."

"I bet it would have been another four or five minutes, and a camera would have popped up around the hotel."

They were both silent for several miles as they thought about the implications.

"Even if someone on their side of the program was changing the code every time you clicked a camera, there's no way they could pinpoint locations that fast. Especially when we've got our VPNs covered so tightly."

"No, you're right," he agreed, a bad feeling filling his gut. "But you know what could?"

"Artificial intelligence?" she asked, and he nodded.

"This feels like machine learning to me the deeper we get into it."

Kenley tapped out a rhythm on her lap for a moment and then grabbed their phone and started punching in a text. The phone buzzed back and forth a couple of times before she spoke. "I asked Reece to find us an internet café that's open right now. He sent me directions to Unchained Night Owl just outside Madison."

"I don't think messing with that program again so soon is a good idea, Kenley. Especially somewhere in public that we're not familiar with."

"We don't have a choice, Jude. We have to test our theory about the timeline. We have to stay long enough for it to put us in Madison. If it can't, then what happened earlier at the hotel was a coincidence and not a rule."

"And if it's a rule?"

"Then we run like hell."

UNCHAINED NIGHT OWL was like night and day when compared to Metro Matrix. Their clientele was urban college kids, which Kenley could glean just by reading the drinks menu on the small bar in the corner. There were also a few tables of college-age boys gaming together where, occasionally, one would yell out in victory, breaking the silence of the otherwise quiet night.

Kenley knew Jude thought this was a bad idea, but an internet café they could drive away from was better than a hotel where they had to sleep. She'd spend only enough time in the program to see if the cameras started moving in their direction immediately. They'd get out long before the cameras could zero in on them, or at least that was her plan. If they were dealing with AI, then every time she went into the program, it might make it easier for it to find her. While that would tell them that machine learning fueled the site, it would put their entire plan at risk. If only she could figure out how it was tracking them with such precision.

"Do you have anything?" Jude asked as he continued clicking spiders.

"No. Well, yes and no. I can read the code, but it's not letting me add anything to corrupt it. Every time I try, it immediately changes the original code."

"Which tells you what?"

"They're definitely using machine learning."

The sentence hung between them as they worked, keeping an eye on the stopwatch they'd set to ensure they didn't bypass that forty-six-minute rule. Her only goal was to see if the cameras could find them just by their presence in the program. She continued to try to corrupt the code while they waited, but that wasn't happening, so she turned her focus to the program's author. She had six minutes to figure it out, but there was no doubt it would take a lot longer than that.

"The author is using machine learning to hide themselves," she finally said, glancing up at Jude. "If the machine can change the code on the fly, then I'll never get ahead of it to break into it."

"Should we shut it down for this go-round?"

Kenley pointed at his laptop. "Did any of the cameras get close to us?"

"The last one," he said. "It was a restaurant camera about two hours east of here."

"That could still be random, though. Where was the one before that located?"

He checked his notebook before he answered. "Davenport, Iowa. That was a rather large shift if you ask me."

With her lip trapped between her teeth, she considered the leap. "Maybe, but were they the same pod?"

"Yes, want me to finish it?" Her nod had him clicking another smaller spider; this time, a traffic camera opened and revealed the intersection of State Street in Madison. That was only a few miles from them by way of the crow.

"Shut it all down," Kenley said immediately, backing her way out and shutting off her computer. "We need to get far away from here, grab some sleep, and then I want to bounce some things off Mina."

"Agreed. I think that was proof it knows where we are," he said, jamming everything in his bag before they left the café and headed back toward the Honda. He'd had to park a few blocks away, which he wasn't happy about, but Kenley could see the benefit of not having the ugly blob parked directly in front of the café, which likely had cameras.

"Do you think it can do that without someone clicking the spiders?"

"I don't know," he admitted with a shrug. "But I don't want to be there to find out. Anything is possible in this situation, and all we can do is stay ahead of them by anticipating what they *might* do, not what they *will* do."

"It's funny how we walk around every day of our lives being tracked by cameras without a care in the world until we realize someone could turn them into weapons."

"I couldn't have said it better myself," Jude said, opening the car door for her. She noticed he did that every time, and she had to admit that she liked it. Not that she needed him to, but because he wanted to. That small, consistent gesture told her who Jude Mason was more than anything else. He was a protector, and as much as she hated to admit it, she needed one of those right now.

Chapter Eleven

The sky had that predawn look as they plowed through the night, but Jude wasn't feeling the new day vibe. He was exhausted. He needed to lie down for a bit if they were to keep one step ahead of this situation. Once they rested, he'd call Secure Watch. He hoped the team had some ideas on the best way to proceed. If he thought it would help, he'd turn it over to Homeland Security right now, but not while Kenley was involved. He had to protect her until she was clear of whoever was hunting her before he could even consider turning the project over to someone else.

Speaking of Kenley, she had been quiet since they left the café a few hours ago. Unsure of the right decision and unable to bounce anything off Mina, he'd decided to head west toward Iowa. It was the wrong direction for Secure Watch, but he didn't want to lead anyone to their door. He hoped Iowa had more cornfields than cameras.

"Geofencing!"

"What about it?" he asked, glancing over at her. The moonlight showed him the bags under her sweet eyes and the fatigue that tugged at her shoulders. She was strong, but he wasn't sure anyone was strong enough to shoulder a burden like Spiderweb. It was time for both of them to get a solid six hours of sleep before they did anything more. Doing a job like this while tired would only put them at risk of making a mistake and revealing themselves to the wrong person.

"That's how they're tracking me. It's the only answer."

Jude was silent momentarily before he tipped his head to the right. "Theoretically, it would work."

He knew geofencing was a technique used by marketers to track devices within a defined area. If a tagged device moved into that area, the marketer might text about a business near the person's location. The technique snowballed in terms of applications, and it was now used by many others, including law enforcement. If the police were looking for a suspect or a victim, they delineated points on Google Maps and then searched within that area for the device connected to that suspect or victim. Jude had seen the police use it for good, but there were those out there willing to exploit the technology and use it for evil. Many people didn't understand how easy it was to be tracked when you had a homing signal in your back pocket. It made sense that if someone could build out a program like Spiderweb, they could certainly set up a geofence for Kenley's phone.

"It's the only answer. There's no other way they could know where I was after we ditched the tracker."

"Geofencing works, but it's not as precise as a tracker, Kenley. They have to pick an area to fence, so there's no way they could drill down that fast on the cameras."

"But think about it, Jude," she said, turning to lean against the door. "Once they knew I'd lost the tracker, all they had to do was geofence the entire state of Wisconsin. Hell, they could geofence the entire Midwest. Once my device appeared on the fence, they could easily assign the AI to home in on me."

"If that's what they did, Kenley, we're screwed. It's going to be impossible to hide."

"Not impossible, just inconvenient."

"Unless they're tracking you from inside the computer," he suggested, cutting his gaze to her for a moment. Her brows went up, and she motioned for him to continue. "We know that with the advancement of AI, hackers can send a virus via an email that you don't even have to click. Just the act of it arriving in your inbox allows it to infiltrate your computer."

"Agreed, which is why my machine has no email service installed," she said with a wink. "My emails come in on a different computer."

"You weren't kidding when you said there was no way for anyone to track you."

"At least not through my machine, or so I thought. Geofencing wasn't on my radar because I didn't know anyone who would want to track me. Now that I know someone is, that's the only answer."

"Is there a way to prove it?"

She held up her finger and grabbed the Secure Watch phone, which would not come up on any geofence since it hadn't been tagged by the person setting up the fence. "How far are we from Prairie du Chien?"

"The last sign I saw said twenty miles, but that was easily ten miles ago. Why?"

"I would bet there's a post office there. We're going to mail my phone and computer. Then, as it moves through the mail system, it will keep showing up on the geofence. Essentially, it will send them on a wild-goose chase."

"We don't have to do that." Jude glanced at her. "If we stop and remove the devices' batteries, they won't show on the geofence." She must be tired to have forgotten that simple hack.

"You're correct, but if we mail them, it will draw them

away from the direction we're going. That buys us time to figure out who's behind this program."

"We'll be down to one computer, though. That's going to make it difficult."

He noticed her shrug from the corner of his eye. "We'd be down one anyway. If we put the battery back in and fire it up, they'll get an immediate alert. That machine is dead to us other than as a distraction for our little friends."

"I must be tired not to have thought of that," he mumbled, rubbing his forehead.

Her laughter sent a shiver down his spine. A shiver of anticipation more than anything. He wanted to hear that laugh for years to come, so he'd better get his head in the game.

"Do you have a way to make purchases in this situation? I can't use any of my cards right now."

"I do. Are you thinking what I'm thinking?"

"Probably," she said with a lip tilt. "When we finish mailing the machines, we go buy a laptop. It doesn't have to be fancy as long as it has enough power to run the VPNs and scrambler. That's all I need to dig in and finally root out Spiderweb's creator."

"There has to be a big box store in the next town." He stopped speaking and stared straight ahead, his thumbs tapping on the steering wheel as he ran the last few days' events through his head. Who was tracking her to start with, and why?

"Tell me what you're thinking," she said, resting her hand on his arm. The warmth it offered dragged his tired mind back to the present.

"I keep returning to who was tracking you in the first place. What do you know that is so damning that they need to trace your whereabouts at all times? It can't be the creator of Spiderweb since they didn't know you would happen upon it."

He noticed her grimace, and it set in stone his determination to get to the bottom of Kenley's antics on the dark web. First, they'd get some sleep. Then he'd grill her for the answers he needed to keep her safe and bring this to a close.

"I will set that aside for now because it's a waste of energy, like a hamster running on a wheel," Jude said after a few moments of silence. At this point, he had no choice but to work with her if he wanted answers. "I like the idea of not being tailed, but when we stop at the post office, we'll mail my machine too. It's been in the same room as yours, so it's possible they were able to geotag it as well. It's better to mail them both and pick up two new computers than keep using an already tagged machine. Technically, the Secure Watch phone is dead to us now as well. That was also in the room."

"Hadn't thought of that, but you're right," she said. "It's better to be safe than sorry."

"I want to have them off our persons before we cross the state line into Iowa. That way, they have no idea what direction we went from the last place they could track us."

"The question is, what direction will they think we went?"

"My gut says if they know who I work for, they'll figure we went up through Iowa into Minnesota."

"I have to agree with you. And let's not fool ourselves. They know everything about you by now."

With a nod, he tipped his head in assent. "All right, that's the plan then. We'll mail the equipment and head to Iowa. Who are you going to mail them to? You can't send them home, or they'll know it's a trick sooner rather than later. I don't want you to send them to Secure Watch. That's going to lead them to their door."

"I'm sending them to my business post office box. We

know this will only buy us forty-eight hours at best, no matter where I send them. They'll catch on and know they were duped, but it will tie their hands just long enough for us to find safety and hack into that program without them knowing it's me. With any luck, by the time they realize I'm not with the machines, we've got their number."

A smile lifted Jude's lips for the first time in too many hours. "You think like a hacker. I can't say that I love it, but in this case, I love it."

"I am a hacker, and for the most part, my hat is white. I might dabble in the underbelly of the internet, but it's for a good reason."

Jude wanted to ask her what that reason was, but the lights of Prairie du Chien were on the horizon. He suspected the answer to his question would take longer than they had at present. "I'll pull over long enough for you to grab the equipment bag. We'll get the batteries out of the devices for now. That will allow us to move around the city untethered for a bit. Hide that gun, too. I'd rather we weren't arrested. Once we're ready to ship the devices, we'll return the battery to the phone so they can follow its journey. Where is your post office box?"

"Eau Claire, Wisconsin."

"Really? Why isn't it in Milwaukee? How do you deal with mail?"

"It's a virtual business address box," she explained as he found a side road to turn off the highway. "I didn't want to use my home address or any of the addresses around Milwaukee. It has to be a Wisconsin address, but the state of Wisconsin does not require it to be near my home address. I get very little mail at it, but it will accept packages. They'll hold the machines until this nightmare ends, and then I can forward them anywhere. Secure Watch won't be happy about you sending their equipment through the mail, but it can't be helped."

"It's the only way." His shrug said he wasn't bothered by the idea. "They all have to go together, or the ruse won't work. There's very little on that laptop, so it's not a huge worry."

After he slowed the car enough, he pulled it over onto the shoulder of an old country road. "Eau Claire isn't far from here, but it is the direction we want them to think we're going, so let's do it."

With a nod, Kenley hopped out and hid the gun in the back seat on the floor under the blanket. Then she grabbed the devices from the hatchback and slammed it shut. Jude had a handle on a plan that would allow them to eat, shower and sleep, then drive to their next destination before they messed with Spiderweb again. He wasn't sure if Kenley was tired or in denial, but she had to know the creator would know it was them the second they went back into that program. He'd use the next twenty-four hours to set up a safe zone—both to do the work and to find out what Kenley was hiding. Whatever it was might be more critical to solving this case than she thought.

Kenley climbed back in and handed him his machine. He'd no sooner flipped it over to remove the battery when Kenley sighed. "My brain isn't firing on all cylinders."

"Why?" he asked, glancing at her.

"The battery doesn't come out of this phone." She held it up as the logo appeared on the screen.

"That's why Secure Watch uses only older technology," he explained, holding up his phone. "The batteries come out easily. Also, if we have to ditch one, it doesn't kill the bottom line."

"Now what?" she asked, waving the phone at the laptop.

"The battery comes out of my computer, but it's internal and requires tools."

"Which I have," he said with a nod at his computer. "But, if we can't take the batteries out of one, there's no sense in taking them out of any. When we get to town, we'll park the car at a restaurant nowhere near the store or the post office and go on foot to get what we need. As long as the devices are stationary, our cover is maintained. They'll know the last place we stopped, but they'll think we stopped for breakfast and nothing else."

"Fair enough," she said, turning the phone over again. This time, her brows went up. "I have a message."

"From?" He leaned over to see the screen after she put in her passcode. "It's in binary code?" Jude noticed her hand trembling as she held the phone.

"The messages on the forum the other night were all in binary code," she whispered. "How did they find me?"

"First, decode the message. Maybe it's someone else."

She nodded and set about copying the message to transfer into a decoder. Was this message from someone else? Absolutely not, but Jude would do anything to wipe away the fear she wore, even if it only lasted a moment. Kenley had him coming and going, which wasn't good. He'd made it a point to never get close to anyone. He had a job to do. He had a singular goal to save as many people from harm as he could before his days on earth were done. He'd participated in enough heinous situations in the service to know he had amends to make to humanity. He couldn't let the beautiful, sexy, intelligent, brave woman beside him keep him from accomplishing his goal.

Maybe she could be the one to heal that broken part inside that keeps you from living. Did you think of that?

He shook his head at that voice. It was dangerous to think,

much less believe, that Kenley could be part of his life after this was over. You didn't always get what you wanted, and in this case, Kenley Bates would be the one who got away.

Chapter Twelve

Kenley took a deep breath as she waited for the binary to decode. Jude had put his arm around her shoulder, which, if she were honest with herself, made her feel safe in a way she hadn't since this whole thing started. Whatever showed up on the screen couldn't hurt her as long as she trusted in her skills and those of the man next to her.

When it decoded, she read it aloud. "Are we having fun yet? I know I am, Sickle. I do enjoy imagining your reaction when you found the tracker. Shame. Shame. You should pay better attention when you're in line at Starbucks. No matter, technology has been my friend since I was old enough to hold a phone. You may have bested me for a moment, but I will best you for all time when I shut down your side business once and for all. Ta-ta for now, bestie. 54V4N7." She dropped the phone to her leg and let out a long breath.

"Do you know 54V4N7?"

"That's his hacker handle. It means savant, and he is if I've ever met one. Not that I've met him in person, but we've tangled online plenty of times."

"You've been on his radar before?"

"Since the first time we crossed paths. I haven't been off it since."

"And now he's stalking you," Jude said, his words clipped.

"He put the tracker in your shoe. Do you remember being in line at Starbucks?"

"Only nearly every morning, Jude. You said the batteries on those trackers only last a few days?"

"A week tops," he agreed with a nod.

"I was in Milwaukee for the last month, but if he put it in there, he had to know who I was. I never reveal myself online, Jude. Especially not on the dark web."

"When did that message come in?"

Kenley checked the time stamp before she answered. "Early this morning after we closed out of the Spiderweb site."

"Is it possible that Savant is the mastermind behind Spiderweb?"

"Anything is possible, Jude, and after digging into the code, I've had that fear in the back of my mind. I don't know why or what his motive would be other than to say he isn't afraid to work for people with a lot of money and zero morals. If a terrorist asked him to set up a site like Spiderweb, he'd say as long as your money is green."

"A gun for hire, just in a different way."

She tipped her head in agreement at the apt description of a man for whom she had no respect. Her reasons were the opposite of Savant's: she wanted to help people, and he wanted to hurt them. That made for a battle of wills that would never be won.

"We need to get out of here," he said, taking the phone from her and powering it down.

"You don't want me to respond to him?"

"Oh, no," he said with a shake of his head and a little smile. "Let him sweat a bit. Do you know how to find him on the dark web?"

"We've run into each other online many, many times. He's never hard to find."

He shoved all the devices back into the bag at her feet, reached over, buckled her seat belt, and then turned the car around on the country road. "Then I say, we stick to our original plan. We mail the devices, pick up new ones, and find a place to stay. Once I've had a reasonable amount of sleep, you'll tell me what your side business is and why Savant wants to shut it down."

Headed back into town, Kenley focused on how she would tell him that story without incriminating herself to the man she was starting to care about a little too much. However, she wasn't worried about being arrested for her work on the dark web. She was worried that the man sitting next to her would abandon her once he knew the lengths she'd go to in order to get justice for others. The saddest part was that she wouldn't blame him if he did.

KENLEY LISTENED TO Jude talk up the Walmart associate as he checked out two computers, peripherals, and two more burner phones. He was smooth; she had to give him that. Jude was regaling the man with the story of how their apartment burned down, leaving them not only homeless but without any way to contact the outside world.

Tugging her hat down a bit more, she bit back a snort as she perused the book section next to the electronics, not wanting to be caught up close on the cameras. Knowing Savant had been near enough to get a tracker in her shoe told her he knew who she was without her having the same advantage. He was a ghost in more ways than one and not one that she wanted to confront face-to-face.

A woman with a shopping cart pulled up close, a little one in the front banging keys on the metal and making quite a racket, drowning out what Jude was saying. Kenley plucked a romance novel off the shelf, a guilty little pleasure she told no one about. She'd been reading the stories since she was nine, having found the first one on the table beside the couch at Gabriella's house. It had been about a private detective protecting a woman on the run from her husband's boss, who wanted her dead. She was hooked. She'd read every old suspense novel they had before she started on the new ones. Holding this one to her chest, she recalled all the years she spent with Gabby, giggling over their next book boyfriend and whispering late into the night, trying to decide who was the guilty party in the story. Kenley often wondered if these books were why she was the way she was. Using the dark web might not be the safest way to accomplish her goals, but it was effective.

"I just love those books," the woman said as she browsed the shelf, her toddler carrying on with the keys while singing a song to which only he knew the words. "I always keep one in my purse to read in the car during school pickup. It's the only time there's silence," she said, but she shot her little boy the sweetest smile. "The princes and sheikhs are my favorite. You look like a suspense girl."

With laughter on her lips, she held the book out. "Guilty as charged."

The toddler threw the keys on the floor as a finale, and the woman turned to pick them up, giving Kenley the perfect opportunity to escape. She met Jude at the edge of the electronics department, their new equipment nestled in the cart. She would have to find a way to pay Secure Watch back for all of this, though she had no idea where to start.

"Make a new friend?" he asked, slinging his arm around her as he pushed the cart one-handed.

"Just bonding over romance novels," she said, forgetting she was still holding it. "Shoot. Let me put this back."

He stopped pushing the cart long enough to pluck it from her hand. "Cowboys. Cute."

"Cowboy lawmen," she corrected, reaching for it. "It's a great series. I didn't realize the new one was out."

"You have been a bit distracted." Jude tossed the book into the cart as Kenley tried to grab it. "You deserve some me time."

"Jude." She hissed his name as he started walking again. "We're not buying that. I already owe Secure Watch wages for the next few years!"

"Then another few dollars won't break the bank, sweet pea. Next up, stationery and packing supplies."

"Excuse me?" she asked, grabbing the cart until it stopped between home and sporting goods. "This isn't romper room time at the store. There are cameras everywhere!"

"I know, and if you keep acting like you've got something to hide, they're gonna notice you," he stage-whispered. "Seriously, Kenley, no one watching those cameras is after you. Take a deep breath." He inhaled, expecting her to follow him, so she did, holding it until he let his out, too. "Now, let's pick up the few things we need to mail our precious cargo safely once the post office opens." He tucked a piece of hair behind her ear, still covered by the hat, and patted her cheek with a smile. "Relax. You'll be far less noticeable that way."

With her nod, he started off again toward the boxes and packing supplies. She hated to admit that he was probably correct about it all, but at the same time, this was nerve-racking. Chances were good that Savant was nowhere near Prairie du Chien, but stranger things had happened in her life. She wasn't willing to lower her guard the way Jude had.

She followed him, pretending to check out different items

on the ends of each aisle as they made their way to the one they wanted. He looked relaxed with that swagger only accentuated by his backside wrapped in a tight pair of Levis. No matter how often she scolded them, her eyes wouldn't stop watching his every move. A little part of her prayed the boxes were on the bottom shelf, so he had to bend over to grab one. Her snort was audible, and he glanced back at her, wearing a smile that said he knew exactly what she was doing and fully supported it.

Once they'd gathered all the packing supplies they needed, he motioned her toward health and beauty aids. "What are we doing?"

"You'll see."

His wink told her she might not want to know, but she trailed after him as he weaved up and down a few aisles, stopping in front of the family planning section. He eyed the condom selection with a critical eye, scanning each package.

The awkwardness was killing her, and she had to say something. "Uh, this feels a bit forward of you, Mr. Mason."

He side-eyed her as a grin worked its way to his face. "It would be if I planned to use them for their primary purpose, but I don't."

Relief filled her for a moment before indignation set in. "Are you saying you're not looking for a fast fling with a one-legged woman while on the run? I can't decide if I should be hurt or angry!"

He turned and pulled her to him by her jacket until he could rest his forehead against hers. "I'm not looking for a fast fling. However, a slow, comfortable screw up against the wall with a one-legged woman cannot be ruled out."

"What's stopping you?" she asked, eyeing his lips. It would be so easy to press hers to his, but they were in the middle of the condom aisle at Walmart, so that maybe wasn't the best idea she'd ever had.

"Sheer will, and I'm hanging on by my fingertips, so don't push me, or I just might grab you on the way down."

His gaze drifted to her lips for a moment, and she waited, wondering if he'd take the chance of PDA in Walmart, but at the last moment, he stepped back, grabbed a pack of condoms from the shelf and tossed them into the cart.

"Every Secure Watch bag has a supply of condoms in it for uses other than the one you're thinking," he explained, walking up and down the aisles until he found the first aid supplies. "They're useful for all kinds of things, including protecting phones from moisture, which is the reason I'm buying them. We'll secure each phone inside one before we mail them. The rest I'll keep in the bag for emergencies."

It was the way that he said emergencies that sent a shiver down her spine. She knew she had to say something, but she wasn't trained in sexual innuendos while in Walmart. Before she could say anything, he did. "We need to get more of that covering I put on your blister last night. I noticed you're limping again."

"When we left Blob the Slob at that restaurant, I didn't know there would be a three-mile walk to the store. I may have to wait here while you mail the packages and then come back to pick me up." Kenley grabbed the right supplies and dumped them into the cart along with everything else. "Besides, there's no way we can carry all this."

"I've got us covered," he promised, pushing the cart toward the front of the store. "We need to check out, but we have to avoid the self-checkouts since they're covered in cameras. Then, I've got a ride coming to take us to the car."

"A ride?"

"It turns out, my friend back in electronics, Sam," he said, hooking his finger behind them as he searched for a checkout. "His mom drives a cab here in town. She'll be waiting for us when we finish to zip us back to the car for a little less than five bucks."

"What a deal," she said dryly as he started unloading the cart. Kenley moved in closer to his ear. "I don't think that's a good idea. We don't want anyone to know what we're driving, nor do we want to drag anyone else into this."

He cut his gaze to her for a beat before he finished unloading the cart. "If I thought we had a choice, I'd avoid it, but we don't." Then he turned to pay for the items, chatting with the older woman at the cash register.

Kenley felt terrible that they had to drag someone else into this game when she was the reason they had to play it at all. If she had kept her nose out of other people's business, she'd be at home taking care of her clients. Her heart skipped a beat at the thought. With the fear and anxiety over the last few days, she'd forgotten all about her business obligations. Would she even have a business left to go back to? Fear rocketed through her, and she bit back a moan. If Savant wanted to ruin her life, he may have found the way.

Chapter Thirteen

As far as seedy motels went, this was one of the better ones in Jude's experience. It was clean, quiet, and had a small kitchenette. He was glad he'd picked up some necessities at the store, and he'd promised Kenley when she finished in the shower that he'd have hot tea ready so they could call Mina for a chat.

She'd been unusually quiet since they left Prairie du Chien. They'd crossed the border into Iowa and stopped about an hour later at this motel. It was clean and seemed to be a biker hangout, which hopefully worked in their favor by hiding Blob the Slob. Kenley had taken to calling the old Honda that, and he couldn't disagree. It was a blob, but it got them where they needed to go every time, so he couldn't complain about Archie's choice.

Jude poured hot water into two mugs and dropped an herbal tea bag into each. He was beyond tired, but adding caffeine to the mix wouldn't help in any way other than keep him from sleeping once he did lie down, which he planned to do as soon as they talked to Secure Watch. The message from Savant ran through his mind, and he groaned. He wished he hadn't had to mail her phone this morning. Part of him wanted to hang on to it, hoping Savant would send another message, but that would be a mistake.

They'd talked it over, but Kenley assured him it was the best and only move. She promised that she had all the tools at her disposal to reach Savant once they were connected to the web again. He could tell she didn't want to, though. Something about this faceless guy scared her, but from what he'd read in that message last night, that fear was well-placed.

The bathroom door opened, and Kenley walked out carrying her prosthesis and gingerly putting weight on her right leg. She was wearing the lounge clothes they'd picked up that were fleece and warm, something Kenley never seemed to be. She'd bucked him at every suggestion he made this morning at the store, not wanting to spend money she didn't have. He respected that to a degree, but they were in a situation they couldn't have predicted, and little spots of comfort were necessary when stressed. A warm pair of pajamas, a cup of tea, a good book. Those were the only things he could offer her right now. They wouldn't help her mental stress, but if they made her a smidgen more comfortable physically, then he would pay for them all day long.

She accepted his help when he put his arm around her waist and helped her to the desk to sit. "You look warm and comfortable for the first time in days." He knelt and took her tiny limb in his. "Except for this." He inspected the spot where the blister was, disheartened to see it had popped and was raw despite the protective bandage. "Good thing we bought more supplies. We're going to need them. Can we take this bandage off and let it get some air while we're talking to Mina?"

Kenley nervously glanced at the window and back to him. "Do you think we're safe here? If we take the bandage off, I can't wear the prosthesis. That means moving quickly is out of the question."

"I believe we're safe here, Kenley." And he wasn't lying. Now that they'd shed the machines and weren't carrying an electronic trail anymore, he figured they had at least two days before they could land on Savant's radar again. As long as she stayed out of the chat rooms that he frequented, there was no way for him to tag their new machines. "We're no longer carrying an electronic chain that was holding us down. We'll call Mina, sleep and then get to work."

"I'm not as confident as you are, but there's no choice. We'll let it get air while we fill Mina in and then bandage it again before we sleep. If I had an ice pack, I'd ice it while sleeping." She laid the towel on the floor and lowered her limb.

"Would that help the pain?"

"Some, but mostly, it would bring the swelling down, so it didn't rub inside the prosthesis."

He held up his finger, walked to the freezer and grabbed the bucket. "I happened to see an ice machine in the lobby, so while you were showering, I ran down and got some since we bought pop." He tied the bag full of ice closed and carried it back over. "There's plenty more where this came from."

"Thanks, Jude. You are a lifesaver."

After removing the bandage, wiping it down and propping the limb on the bag of ice, Jude sat next to her and dialed into Secure Watch.

"Secure Watch, Whiskey." The screen stayed black until Jude replied, and then Mina's face flickered onto the screen. "It's so good to see you guys," she said, leaning back in her chair. "We've been worried."

"Nothing to worry about, boss," Jude said with a wink.

"A large purchase request came through on the card this morning. I approved it, knowing there was a good reason."

Jude noticed Kenley grimace and rubbed her back with an encouraging smile. "Thanks, boss. We've made some discoveries, which is why we're calling. It's time to fill you in."

"Namely, how we were being tracked and by whom," Kenley added, taking over the conversation. "Or one of the whoms, at least."

"Did you break through the Spiderweb code?" Mina asked, but Kenley shook her head.

"Not yet. Every time I got close to corrupting the code, it changed."

"And while the program was doing that to her, it was tracking me," Jude said, rubbing Kenley's back to keep her calm.

"Tracking you how?" Mina asked, her head tipped in confusion.

He explained to her that the spiders were directing the cameras closer and closer to them. "She realized we might be in a geofence."

Kenley took over. "That's the reason for the large purchase this morning. We had to mail our machines and the Secure Watch phone to my post office box."

"Especially after she got another message in binary code on her phone this morning," Jude added.

"Smart idea. That will make them think you're moving around," Mina agreed. "That also explains the new computer purchase. The binary code player again? Still no identity on him?"

"Oh, I know who he is," Kenley said. "His dark web name is 54VAN7. Savant." Mina sucked in a breath, and that surprised Jude.

"You know of him?"

"I worked for the FBI. Of course, I know of him. How on earth are you tangled up with that rotten apple, Kenley?"

Jude listened while Kenley told his boss how she met Savant. "According to the message, he's the one who put the tracker in my shoe."

"Did the message say why?" Mina asked, and they both shook their heads.

"Nope, but that's nothing new with Savant," Kenley said with a shrug.

"What concerns me is that he or someone he employed was close enough to Kenley to drop a tracker in her shoe," Jude said between gritted teeth. "Someone like that is unpredictable, and even if we sort out the Spiderweb program, she will still be vulnerable to that maniac."

Mina held up her hand. "Let's take one thing at a time. Kenley, I hope you don't mind, but I patched into your business server so Reece could cover your current clients. We also contacted those you had set up for intake to let them know you had been in an accident but would contact them as soon as possible within the week. Everyone was more than sympathetic."

With her hand on her chest, Kenley let out a breath. "Thank you," she whispered, her shoulders falling forward. "It hit me in the middle of the store today that my business could fall apart because of this, which is probably what Savant wants. I spent the last three hours trying to figure out what to do but hadn't come up with anything. I owe you, big-time."

"It's no problem," Mina reassured her. "Delilah and Lucas will be back tomorrow, and she can cover your clients until you return, which I'm hoping won't be much longer."

Jude shrugged. "I can't make any promises, but I hope the new computers will allow us to stay in the program longer before they realize it's us."

"That's going to be a good trick," Kenley said.

"Okay, they'll know it's us but won't be able to track us."

"How do you plan to keep them from tracking these devices?"

"I've deleted all the apps, turned off the location-sharing settings, and we'll use a VPN that stays overseas. Whoever made the program will know we're in it, but they won't be able to track us since the computers won't be tagged by the geofence."

"Mina, would you put some feelers out to see if the Spiderweb program is something the government is working on?" Kenley asked, leaning forward. "Some of the coding was reminiscent of what I encountered when helping a government agency with some bricking. I'm not at liberty to say who, but I also don't have the channels you do to ask questions and get answers."

"After you sent me those code samples, I did some digging. I could hear no chatter about it in any of my usual haunts. I did a deeper breakdown of the lines of code you sent, and while it's close, I think the same thing you do. It's reminiscent but not the real thing."

"Thanks for your candidness and professional opinion. I didn't want to be an island in that belief, but I've done enough with the government to know their code. That's not it."

Jude held one hand out. "So, we know Savant put the tracker in her shoe for his own sick games." He held out the other hand. "We don't know who put the geofence out for her devices and why."

"If I were a betting woman, I'd say it was when she landed on the spider site," Mina said with a shrug. "I've seen dark web programs do this before. It's likely as soon as Kenley clicked on the first spider, her machine was tagged."

"It still doesn't make sense," Jude pondered. "She uses a VPN for everything she does at The Matrix. There's no way they could continue to track her computer once she signed off."

"We all know that's not true," Mina said. "We are never completely anonymous on the web. When dealing with guys like Savant regularly, you can bet you're always at risk of picking up a bug and not knowing until it's too late."

Kenley turned to him. "Think about it, Jude. We used your computer to click the spiders in the hotel room, and they found us in fifty-five minutes. The spiders are putting us on a geofence, but I'm starting to think it's a completely different kind than we're used to."

"Can you explain?" Mina asked.

"You think it's more of a geofence that only works when you're in the program?" It dawned on him then what Kenley was thinking. She could be right.

"Yes!" Kenley agreed. "That's why the AI slowly starts to home in on you as you click the spiders. The spiders are there to keep you clicking while the AI works to break through your VPN to reveal your real location."

"It's the only answer," Mina agreed. "Without the AI, it wouldn't be possible, but anything is possible with that in the mix now."

"My biggest fear is that every time we do that, a large swath of cameras in one region comes online for the program." Kenley was silent for a second before she waved her hands. "Okay, so we don't click the spiders. It didn't help us last time other than to tell us how quickly the cameras could find us. They aren't showing up in the code when they activate, so there's no sense in continuing to click. I'll have to find a new way to bust through the code."

"Wiping and reinstalling the operating system will clear any geofence. Does that also work for tracking systems like what you're talking about?" Jude asked. "We couldn't do that with our other computers since they hold important information that we couldn't back up on the fly, but we can wipe these new ones ten times if necessary."

"Wiping and reinstalling your operating system will clear any tracking system on the computer. I think it's only tagging you while you're in the program, but you're better safe than sorry. Also, when you restart it, you know the machine is infected if the system bricks," Mina explained.

Bricking a computer could be done in several ways, but Jude was often surprised at how frequently and incorrectly people used the term "bricking" when it came to phones and computers. If a device wasn't working right, but you could install a new operating system, it wasn't bricked since it was recoverable. If you couldn't turn it on, or once you did, the system was so corrupted that you couldn't install any operating system, the device was considered a brick. An expensive paperweight. Sometimes, it was a user error—someone might power down or unplug a computer while installing a firmware update. However, more often than not, the cause was malware. When big corporations had their system bricked, it could usually be traced back to a malicious BMC firmware—baseboard management controller—uploaded remotely to their server. Once that happened, getting them back online could take days, weeks, or even months, which was catastrophic for hospitals and other public entities.

"I'm on it, boss," Jude agreed. "But first, we sleep."

"You sleep, I'll work." Kenley practically rubbed her hands together in glee until Jude shut her down.

"Back me up, Mina. She has a blister on her limb, and it's swollen. Ice and elevate, right?" he asked, his brow raised at the screen while he waited for his friend to agree with him.

"He's right, Kenley. You know how quickly a limb issue

can get you into big trouble. I don't have a way to get you antibiotics either, so you need to let your body rest and heal."

"Every minute we aren't in that program, those cameras gather more information. We need to shut it down." Her insistence filled the room, but Jude wasn't having it. They both needed to sleep before fatigue caused them to do something they'd regret.

"We don't even know what it is yet," Jude pointed out. "We know it's not a video game, but we don't know anything beyond that."

"We also have no idea how long that program has been there," Mina pointed out.

"I do," Kenley said, pushing herself back up in the chair. "I got the date from the code. I haven't thought much of it until now. The program went live on July 4th."

"Okay, it's been up for three months. Another three hours won't hurt anything," Mina insisted. "Sleep, eat, and then attack. In the meantime, I'll dig into the government connection. Do you have a number where I can contact you? You said you mailed the Secure Watch phone."

Jude grabbed one of the burner phones and held up the number for her to copy. When he lowered the number, he glanced between the screen and Kenley. "Do you think that date is significant?"

"July 4th?" Mina asked, her head cocked in confusion.

"Independence Day," Kenley said with a breath.

"Whose independence is the question," Jude said, glancing at Mina. "Thinking about it for a hot second, it feels pointed to me."

"I was so busy trying to stay ahead of the code that I didn't even think about the significance of the date, but I agree with Jude," Kenley said.

"I don't disagree," Mina nodded, making a note on the pad

next to her. "It could be the government making a point, or it could be someone who wants to use this country's birthday to make a different kind of point. Give me a few hours. I'll get back to you."

"Thanks, Mina," Jude said as she waved, and the screen went black.

"I should have realized that clicking the spiders activated the geofence," Jude said, leaning back in the chair.

"Don't beat yourself up, Jude. We assumed we were being followed because the cameras kept finding us after we found the tracker in my shoe. I'm relieved to know that's not the case. They only know where we are when we're in the program. As soon as we leave it, the tracking stops. That's good news. It means we can stay here for a few days without anyone knowing where we are."

"Until you go back into the program. Then you'll be back on its radar."

"I'll do it in shifts," she explained. "A little at a time. No longer than thirty minutes in the program since we know it took forty-six minutes last time before they found us in Madison. At the thirty-minute mark, you reset one computer while I fire up the second one. Right now, we're both tired. Let's get some sleep and then make a plan when we're rested and sharp again."

They both turned toward the giant elephant in the room. A king bed. One. Singular. Unfortunately, some biker event was happening, and this was the last room for the night. The bed was big, but it would still pose a problem for Jude. He didn't have the willpower to share a bed with Kenley and not hold her all night. She needed comfort, which was one thing he knew for sure, but that didn't mean she wanted it, and he had to respect those boundaries.

"I'll take the floor," he said, holding his hand out to help her up. "I can sleep anywhere."

He walked her to the bed and pulled back the covers. Once she sat, he lifted her limb onto the bed and stuffed a pillow under her knee.

"This bed is big enough for the both of us, Jude." He handed her a mug of warm tea and then grabbed the first aid kit to fix the blister before they went to sleep.

"Here's the thing, sweet pea. If I'm in this bed, I can't promise that my arms won't end up wrapped around you by the night's end."

"That's a bad thing?" Her sharp intake of breath, when he swiped the antiseptic over the blister, told him they'd done some damage to it today. Grabbing his flashlight, he inspected it closely, looking for any signs of infection. It was raw and bleeding around the edges, but otherwise, it was okay.

"It's a bad thing if you're not looking for that. Respect and trust are important in this game we're playing. I don't want to break yours by doing something unwanted."

"If I say I want you to wrap your arms around me, would that help?"

"Only if you meant it." He added a wink and lip tilt to let her know he was teasing but also not teasing. "I'm going to put antibiotic ointment on a bandage and cover the blister so you can ice it during the night. Once you're up and need to put the prosthesis back on, we can clean it again and use the clear bandage."

"That would be fine. I'm sure after some time out of the prosthesis, it will start to heal quickly. And Jude?" she said, and he glanced up from where he was opening the bandage. "I meant it."

Chapter Fourteen

Kenley wondered what time it was, but she couldn't turn to look at the clock without disturbing Jude, whose chest was pressed tightly against her, with one arm thrown over her hip to hold her there. She'd woken up that way about twenty minutes ago but wasn't ready to give up the comfort his arms offered, so she stayed still. The deep darkness of the room told her it was well after five, and the sun had already set. Considering they didn't climb into bed until after noon, it could be even later.

Now that she was rested, she was ready to tackle this monster monkey on her back. She had no hope of stopping Spiderweb until she could figure out who was behind it. Her biggest fear was that whoever coded Spiderweb had turned it over completely to machine learning, which would allow it to spiral out of control once more people knew the website existed. If others were clicking spiders on the site, and each click trained the program to grab more cameras in each area, it was only a matter of time until the Spiderweb program controlled every camera on every corner in every city. There were too many terrorist organizations in the world that would jump into a bidding war to own the data and control of all the cameras in the world. They could use the information to cause carnage at yet unseen proportions or incite another world war. They couldn't allow that to happen, no matter the cost to her. Somehow, she'd protect Jude, even if that meant they eventually parted ways.

Jude was the kind of man she could see herself sharing her life with if that kind of life was in the cards for her. She wasn't sure it was, not when she brought situations like this down on her head by doing something she knew was inherently dangerous. It wasn't right to drag others in only to make them fight a battle that wasn't theirs to fight.

When is it going to stop being your war to fight?

"How'd you sleep?" Jude's voice was soft and sleepy as he tightened his arm around her waist. "I dreamt that I was holding a beautiful woman only to wake up and realize I was."

She slid her hand down his arm until hers was over his on her waist. "It was nice to be held by someone who cares, Jude. I don't have those kinds of relationships in my life."

"Ever?" He instinctively pulled her closer even though there was already no space between them.

"My life doesn't allow for solid connections, Jude."

"And that has something to do with the dark web and Savant, right?"

She rolled over to her back, hoping he'd drop his arm, but he didn't. He just rotated it around to lay it across her belly. "My work is my penance. I don't expect you to understand that, but I've lived this way for seventeen years."

"Your penance? Do you mean for the accident that killed Gabriella?"

"Yes. She died, but I lived. Now it's my job to prove the accident wasn't Gabby's fault."

"The accident wasn't your fault either, sweet pea. Has no one ever told you that?"

"Of course, they have. Part of it is my fault. I begged her to take it out that day! When she said no the first time, I should have walked away. She wasn't in the mood and proved that once we got on the trail. I don't know why she acted the way she did, but I know if we'd been on any other brand of ATV, she wouldn't be dead. With her gone, it's my responsibility to prove what I already know."

"Tell me what you already know, Kenley."

She bit her lip and shook her head. It had been seventeen years, and she still hadn't voiced what she'd been doing to hold Staun Bril accountable to another living being. That was her battle to fight, not his.

"Let me ask this a different way. It's been seventeen years. How are you going to find evidence?"

"That's what I do on the dark web, Jude. I talk to people and seek information proving what I already know."

"What do you already know, Kenley?" He whispered the question this time with his mouth near her ear, sending a shiver through her. It felt like understanding, anticipation and seduction, as it traveled from her head to her heart and then lower to the parts of her that hadn't opened themselves to a man in too many years. Why did he have to be so damn determined to know the truth? If she told him, she ran the chance of him thinking she'd lost it, but if she didn't tell him, he'd find fifty different ways to ask the same question until she answered.

"I have a database of owners with the same brand ATV as we were driving that day who also had accidents. Everyone was told that the wheel had sheared off the front axle. Every single one of them was going over thirty on the machine. There has been every imaginable injury you can think of as a result."

"And you're investigating with the working theory that the company knew what?"

"They knew the wheels would shear off the axle at higher

rates of speed. And even after they found out, they continued to make and sell the machines without fixing the problem."

"That's a pretty big accusation, Kenley."

"That's why I haven't gone public with it. I'll be vulnerable and admit you're the first person I've ever told. While I know that people are still being hurt and killed by the Neo Chase, if I can't find evidence that the company knows about it, then there's no way to start a class action lawsuit."

"But there is," he said, turning slightly to make eye contact. "That's the lawyer's job to find the evidence. The legal way."

"This isn't my first rodeo, Jude. When my white hat goes dark, I get things done. I've found evidence on over thirty cases to bring people, my people, closure and justice."

Jude sat up and rubbed the sleep from his eyes. "Wait, you use the dark web to hack into companies' private files?"

"Not always," she answered, and his shoulders relaxed slightly. "Sometimes I do it on the regular web."

"Kenley!" His voice was exasperated, and she sensed a bit of disappointment. "That's vigilantism!"

"That's right!" she exclaimed, sitting up and sticking a finger in his chest. "And it gets the job done, so don't tell me it's wrong. I do it for the right reasons, and that's what matters!"

Jude sat shaking his head as she flopped onto the pillow, anger vibrating through her tightly as she forced her hands out of the fists she'd made. "I understand why you do it, Kenley. I understand you want to right the wrongs you think you've made, but you can't keep putting yourself at risk like this. Not to mention, your life isn't your own if you spend all your time in the past."

"Gabby's life passed her by, too, didn't it, Jude? She was gone before she could live! I do this for her. Every person I get justice for is also a little bit of justice for Gabby! Can't you understand that?"

"What about you? Haven't you paid a heavy enough price for a decision you didn't make? Sure, you asked her to go out, but you weren't the one running the throttle full bore. You weren't the one not listening to someone telling you to slow down. That was all her, and you can't take responsibility for her actions."

"Have you ever lost someone, Jude?" It was the only question she could think to ask that he might understand.

"Many people, Kenley. I was in the service. I'm responsible for people losing their lives."

"How do you cope with that? I'd sure like to know."

He sat in silence, his jaw ticking as he held her gaze, refusing to let it go but also refusing to answer her question. "How did you really find the Spiderweb site? Were you snooping through case files?"

"I didn't lie about that, Jude. Staun Bril, the company that makes the Neo Chase ATV, has a log of case information regarding their machines on the dark web. The only way to get to it is by typing in the fifty-two-character address. I mixed up two numbers, and the Spiderweb site popped up."

"A company has documents with dot-onion suffixes?"

"No, it's an I2P domain suffix."

"An invisible internet project? That means they're sharing it back and forth between people."

"Yep," she agreed, turning to her other side. "Since I intended to go to a different I2P domain but landed on the Spiderweb site, it makes me wonder if it also shares info between people. If that's the case, we must shut it down before it gets out of hand."

"Unless it's a government site."

"It reads like government coding, but something is off. I

can't put my finger on it, but I will as soon as we get going." She glanced at the clock and blew out a breath. "It's eight p.m. We need to make some headway tonight." She sat up and stretched, dropping her arms back to the bed with a sigh. "After we eat. I'm starving."

"Me, too," he whispered right before he grabbed the front of her shirt and dragged her to him, his lips landing on hers. The emotion behind it shocked her, and she jolted. He paused the kiss until he was sure she wanted it. Rather than pull away, she tipped her head to the side and dropped her jaw, inviting him to take the kiss as far as he wanted.

Jude's kiss was hot, sweet, plaintive and moan-worthy, all in the first three seconds. Time warped, and her other senses dulled while she was under the skilled lips, tongue and hands of this man who was eight years her senior but made her feel like he was her other half. The half she'd been missing her whole life. That was a bold statement, but this was a bold kiss, and she needed to be honest with herself. She was developing feelings for Jude Mason that had nothing to do with the case and everything to do with the virile man that he was. This kiss was an accumulation of desire, need and want that had built up over the last few days. They needed an outlet for the sexually charged environment they'd been sharing.

When he ended the kiss and drew back, Kenley immediately felt lonely and filled with pain again. His lips had stolen those feelings and allowed her to feel something else for the first time in seventeen years. Something other than guilt that she lived, shame that she didn't want to, and unrelenting pain in her leg that reminded her every moment of the day she had made her bed and the knowledge that she would lie in it forever. She was torn between two worlds, the past and the present, but no matter what choice she made, someone lost.

That made it an impossible choice. If there was one thing she knew for sure, it was that. She'd spent the last seventeen years trying to make the choice by not making the choice.

"Kenley," he whispered, her head in his hands as he smoothed her hair away from her face. "Why am I so drawn to you?"

"If I knew, I'd share that answer with myself," she said with a lopsided grin. "But that kiss was wow."

"Trust me, I wanted it to be so much more, but you need to hit the keys." He let his hands slide down her arms to take her hands in his. "Promise me when this is over, you'll think about finding a way to live again?"

"I can't stop helping people, Jude. That's just who I am, like it or not."

"I like it, Kenley. Don't think for a moment that I'm not impressed with your fortitude, kindness and desire to right wrongs. All I want is for you to be safe while doing it. This isn't safe."

Moved by his plea, she trailed a finger down his cheek. The shrouded room made her brave enough to open her soul to the man before her. "How many people, Jude?"

"Unfathomable numbers, sweet pea." His answer, while short, was honest to her ears.

"Is this work you do to avenge them or yourself?"

"Oh, sweet pea, it can always be both." Before she could respond, he stood and turned on the bedside lamp. "Wait there. I want to check your limb and bandage the blister before you get up. Then I'll fix some food while you get ready to work."

And like that, Jude, the man who had kissed her with an uncompromised passion, was gone, replaced by the Secure Watch operative who was ready to slay dragons for her and all of humanity. As he tenderly bandaged her limb to prepare her for the workday, she couldn't help but wish they were locked in this hotel room for a different reason at a different time with a different objective. When his eyes softened, and his hand caressed her face, she could almost convince herself they could be more someday. But wishing never got a girl anywhere. Relying on someone never got the job done in the end, either. She had to save herself and prove she wasn't a damsel in distress.

When this job is done, will your penance be paid?

Kenley shifted on the bed and shook her head at that voice. Never.

Chapter Fifteen

The room was small, but Jude needed an outlet for his nervous energy, so he paced the short distance between the walls with his notebook in hand in case she called anything out for him to write down. Was he nervous? Yes. He was nervous that the new machine would be tracked and that they wouldn't be able to find the answers before Spiderweb went viral and took over every camera in the nation. Hell, maybe even the world. They had no idea how deep the web was woven, and he was considering a new plan. If Kenley couldn't get anything tonight, he'd burn the machines, leave them in the room and get her to Secure Watch ASAP. Once there, she could work with the team where the machines could be monitored, and more hackers could be trying to break the code simultaneously. He had no other move but that right now.

Kenley would hate that plan, but somehow, he'd have to convince her. As long as they were isolated, not only were they sitting ducks, but close contact with Secure Watch was nearly impossible. Even using the video linkup was a waiting game as Mina worked things out in the background to help them get answers. The picture, in general, was one he wanted off his wall, but to do that, he had to trust Kenley, even knowing her motivation. His steps faltered. Were her motivations significantly different than his own?

He had become a digital private investigator to do the same thing. The only difference was in how they did it. He stayed above the line while she dipped below it, at risk to herself, but to ease someone else's pain. Did that make him better than her because he kept his hat pristine? The other question he had to ask himself was, were her tactics legal? Technically, they weren't illegal, even if they were in the gray area. She wasn't breaking the law using the dark web, and from what she told him, she worked with law enforcement and the government, presumably Homeland Security, to do her part in keeping ahead of traffickers of humans and drugs. For every action, there was an equal and opposite reaction. She was thrusting her feelings of guilt onto those who truly deserved it, and the result was feeling free for a brief moment in time. At least, that was the best he could deduce from what she'd shared with him.

Telling her she shouldn't feel guilty for surviving the accident was wasted breath, he knew. He still did it as a gentle reminder that others recognized it wasn't her fault. She'd lived with this guilt for so many years it wasn't guilt anymore. It was PTSD. He'd seen it many times over in soldiers who returned from war. Hell, Lucas Porter, Delilah's new husband, struggled with the same kind of guilt. He'd been in a Humvee when it hit an IED; men on each side of him had died while he survived. There was never any rhyme or reason to death, at least not one that the living could discern. Gabby had died while Kenley lost her foot, but the tables could have been easily turned if just one factor had been different that day. If they had been in a different place on the trail, if Kenley had been sitting differently, or Gabby had hit the brakes instead of the gas, their entire life paths would have changed.

Jude crossed his arms and stared at the woman furiously typing on the laptop. What if she'd died that day? Would Gabby be doing the same thing Kenley was to try to save the world? Would Gabby try to save soul after soul after soul to atone for the loss of her friend? He couldn't know for sure, but he suspected the answer was no. Not in the way Kenley had, because everyone reacted to trauma differently. Watching Kenley so absorbed in her work that nothing else mattered did tell him more about her than her words. She cared. She loved. She hurt. She wanted to change the world. Her way of doing it just looked different than his.

It was his job to protect her, and there was a gnawing fear in his stomach that if he failed and she disappeared from his life, he would never be the same. They were here in this hotel room for a reason that had begun—

He paused as he did the math in his head. Hell, her accident had happened the same week he walked into cybersecurity school. A shiver racked him at the thought. Had he been preparing for this moment since that day? Had his career trajectory and life been aimed at 11:00 p.m. on Wednesday, October 24? Were his blood, sweat and tears over the past seventeen years all for her? Suddenly, all those choices he'd made over the years when he wasn't sure they were right came into focus, and the bigger picture was revealed. Kenley was the finished masterpiece.

"Write this down," Kenley called, and Jude snapped to attention. "If the file ends with open parentheses, open quotation dot txt close quotation close parentheses."

Her fingers flew across the keyboard, but she stopped talking, so he looked at what he wrote. "That's Python."

"Yep," she said, still typing as though her hands were independent of the rest of her body. "Send that to Mina. Ask if I'm correct that it's a prompt to search for dot txt extensions."

"On it," he promised, grabbing the phone and sending Mina an opening message. She responded immediately, and he sent the message he'd written. "Mina says, that's correct. She wants to know if that's in the program."

"Tell her yes. I've seen many of them, which tells me two things."

"Do you want me to type this to Mina?" he asked, and she nodded as she continued to work.

"Python is an AI language, so they've set the program up to work in the background anytime someone stumbles upon it. It also tells me they set it up to check directories. If it can check directories, it can infiltrate them with malware, giving them control of the camera without the owner knowing."

Frustrated with how quickly things were changing, he deleted the beginning of the message and instead sent, Will be in contact shortly. Too much to type.

"Are you saying the camera owner doesn't realize malware has been installed?"

"Essentially," she agreed with a nod of her head. "The program doesn't need to move the camera. It just needs the data it's sending back to the server mainframe."

"That's a good point." Jude let a curse word fly when the implications settled across his shoulders. "They'll use all of that information to keep training the machine so it can use it at a later date."

"Bingo," she said, still typing. "And the first thing they did was train it to block out hackers. I've busted my way through to the code without clicking any spiders, but it wasn't easy or for the faint of heart."

"I don't know many hackers this dedicated to breaking into a program." Jude only knew one, and she was sitting at an old cigarette-burned table on a subpar computer, still getting the job done.

The room went silent again, and she continued typing as code scrolled across the screen. Jude texted Mina back that she was still working. Then, he went to the kitchen and grabbed a can of Diet Coke. He was glad he'd insisted they buy snacks and drinks at the store so they didn't have to leave the room more than necessary. His mind drifted back to the moment in the condom aisle when her eyes grew to the size of saucers as he sorted through the options. He smiled. Then he remembered how she felt in his arms as he held her. Soft, sweet and perfectly fit to his body so he could protect her from harm.

Admitting that was scary. He wasn't the kind of person who needed anyone, or even desperately wanted anyone. He had to ask himself if that was because he hadn't found the right someone yet. When he and Kenley were together, the years between them melted away, and they were equals. They played off each other's strengths when the moment mattered and compensated for each other's weaknesses when time was short. He was used to a solitary work environment and life, and spending so much time with her should have felt off, but it didn't.

It felt right.

Those were the three words he'd been trying to avoid agreeing to in his head. No matter how right it felt, they had jobs in different states when they finished with Spiderweb. The distance wasn't far, but it was far enough that a long-distance relationship wouldn't last. Then, there was the age gap to consider. Was an eight-year difference too much? Did he care? He'd enter his forties when she was still firmly planted in her thirties. Would they want different things at different times of their lives? He knew what he wanted, and that was someone to come home to every night. Someone to spend quiet nights with and share endless summer days on the lake with him. When he thought about those days, Kenley appeared beside him in every scenario. She was there saying *I do*, playing in the surf on their honeymoon and holding his baby. Kenley was there for all of it.

She had eroded his long-held belief about his life in a matter of days.

That kind of life wasn't right for a man like him.

Kenley had walked into his life and challenged a belief he'd held dear for over eighteen years. Was it maturity that had turned the tables on him, or was it the woman? Maybe it was a bit of both, but before he could even consider making Kenley a more permanent part of his life, he had to get her through this crisis. Once they were safe, he'd have to explore her feelings on the matter. She sensed the draw between them; there was no question, but that didn't mean she was looking for any kind of relationship. She didn't seem to want anything other than to be a vigilante for justice, however misguided that may be.

Sighing, he set the drink down and walked over to Kenley. "How's it going?" He massaged her tight shoulders, which resulted from hours spent on the keyboard.

"Still haven't gotten much more out of it. I saved a couple of lines of code to send to Mina to get her take on it."

"You're nearing the thirty-minute mark. Maybe you should back out now?"

"I hate to, but I think you're right. I want to wipe and restart the machine to see if it bricks."

"Do you think the program is going to install malware?"

"I hope not, but everything is on the table when dealing with machine learning."

Jude pulled up a chair and sat. "Before you sign off the

dark side, are there any forums Savant visits regularly? Is there any place he might message you if you aren't responding on your phone?"

"Savant is everywhere and nowhere. I tend to stay incognito unless I'm working on a case. I burned the forum from the other night where he contacted me—at least, I'm assuming it was him, so I can't go back there. There's only one forum where I have any presence at all times. I've never seen him there, but I can check." She clicked the mouse and typed in an address, then hit Enter.

"You're a moderator of this forum?" His brow was raised to his hairline. He was not only surprised but a little bit disappointed.

"Yes, because I started it," she said with a shrug. "It's the only way to discuss some of these companies without the information being leaked."

"This is where you find your cases to solve, so to speak?"

"No, this forum is only for people who have been hurt or lost loved ones to a Staun Bril ATV."

He flicked his gaze to the number of members in the forum and sucked in a breath of surprise. "There are over four thousand people in this forum."

"Yep," she agreed as though that was common knowledge.

"Kenley, a class action lawsuit of this size would be a no-brainer for any lawyer. Why aren't you convincing these people that's the way to get a settlement?"

The way she turned slowly in her chair said he was about to be schooled. "We don't want a settlement, Jude. That's not why we're here. We want action. We want them to stop making these ATVs. We want to avenge our loved ones and hold them responsible for our injuries. None of this is about money, don't you see that?"

He tucked a loose lock of hair back behind her ear before

he spoke. "I understand that, sweet pea. This is about justice and holding the guilty parties responsible. A class action suit would do that. They'd be found guilty, but you'd also get money to take care of your prosthetic needs for years to come. It's noble that you want to shoulder this burden yourself, but you don't have to. Don't you see that?"

Rather than respond, she clicked around on the screen until she was inside a chat room, scrolling through the messages so quickly he couldn't even catch more than a word here and there. Finally, at the bottom was a private message tab. There was a notification that said 3.

"I just checked this the other night," she said with a frown before she clicked the inbox. After a quick scroll, she shook her head. "They're all from Savant."

"Is that the same account that messaged you Wednesday night?" Jude asked, and she nodded. "Which means he knows where you are."

"As I said, Savant is everywhere."

Her teeth ground together as she spoke, and he stroked her jaw tenderly. "Relax, Kenley. We aren't going to let him get the best of us. It's two against one now."

She relaxed her jaw the longer he stroked it. Her eyes closed, and she sucked in a deep breath before she clicked the first message. Once again, it was filled with 0s and 1s. "This is going to take forever."

He smiled at her grumpiness as she called up a decoder. As far as he was concerned, they had all the time in the world, and he was here for every second he could get before she disappeared from his life for good. He grabbed the phone and opened the camera.

"What are you doing?" she asked, pasting in the first message to the decoder.

"I'm saving you time. I'll take a picture of the messages so we can send them to Mina. Ready?"

With a nod, she hit Enter and the message that popped up told him they were in for a long haul. "Kenley, Kenley, Kenley. You've been a naughty girl. I think it's time I expose what you're doing and let the world pass judgment. What say you?" Jude read.

Slowly, Kenley stood, walked into the bathroom and slammed the door. When she didn't return, he slid over and got to work.

Chapter Sixteen

There was a knock on the door. "Kenley. You can't stay in there all day."

Sighing, she pushed herself up and opened the door. "Can't a girl have an existential crisis alone?"

"Not when I'm around."

"Clearly." She said the word with total and utter frustration as she walked past him into the main room.

"I decoded the other two messages, wiped the computer and rebooted it," Jude said as he grabbed a pop from the fridge and handed it to her. "Sorry, I don't have anything stronger."

She popped the top and took a long swallow. "That's okay. I don't drink. Never been my thing."

"Mine either," he agreed, lowering himself to the chair by the table while she perched on the bed. "Anyway, the computer didn't brick, which is good. I was able to do a clean install of the operating system."

"What did the other messages say?" she asked, tapping the can with her finger.

Jude grabbed the phone and opened the photo app. "The one said, Hey, bestie. Did I scare you with my last message? Yes? Good. I'm coming for you, and you won't see me until it's already done."

"What's already done?" Kenley asked, tipping her head to the side.

"I can only assume he means destroying your business, as he mentioned in the text he sent to your phone."

"Let him," she said with a shrug. "I don't even care anymore. There are far bigger problems in the world than what happens to my business. Like some terrorist having control of every camera in the world."

"Agreed," Jude said. "That's one of the reasons I shut my business down and went to work for Secure Watch—security in numbers."

"Not to mention the power of the hive mind. Okay, hit me with the third message."

"The third one was sent not long before you started working today. All it said was, Come out and play, Kenley! This is getting boring. I think he's angry that you're not engaging."

"Good. Let him focus on that. I want to get to the bottom of Spiderweb before he rears his ugly head again. I'll go back into the program while you search to see if Savant has outed me yet."

"Why do you want to go back in? It's only been an hour."

"Exactly the reason," she said, pushing herself off the bed and walking to the table. "If this is machine learning, then I would expect the path I used to get in last time to be blocked."

"The machine is anticipating the next *attack*," he said, using air quotes around attack.

"Essentially. If that bears out, then we can contact Mina and give her an update."

"Tell me more about the search you want me to do. Do you expect him to out you, and if he were to do that, how would I search for it?"

"I don't know if he'll out me for sure, but something tells

me if I make him wait too long before I engage with him again, he will. Or at least he'll try. While in the bathroom, trying not to crawl out of my skin with anger, I realized that he found the forum I had started. That means he got the address somehow, and that's why he thinks I've been a 'naughty girl.'"

Jude nodded along as she spoke. "You want me to do a dive and see if you're showing up on aboveground forums about vigilantes or a sudden flood of negative reviews for your business?"

A finger gun and a wink revealed her agreement. "My hope is he has a bit more patience in him. Just enough for me to sort the Spiderweb program and then turn it over to the cops. I'll deal with him when that's done."

"You won't be dealing with him without me," Jude said, grabbing the laptop. "Fair warning. I won't leave you alone when you're at risk for an attack. He's already been too close to you as far as I'm concerned, and he will not get close to you again."

"Jude," she said, but he held up his hand.

"Don't tell me that you're not my responsibility. I know that. You are so much more than my responsibility, so until the threats cease, or Savant shows himself, you're never alone. Understood?" When she nodded, he smiled and softened his intensity as he grabbed the phone again. "Mina is on standby right now. I'll text her to say you're conducting an experiment, and then we'll contact her."

"Thanks, Jude," she said, smiling at him. "Without you, I'd be in serious trouble. I don't like to be a damsel, but if I have to be one, I'm glad you're rescuing me."

"No, sweet pea," he said, setting the laptop down and walking over to her. "You're not a damsel, and I'm not rescuing you. You're a brilliant, beautiful brainiac who wants to save the world. I'm here to do any heavy lifting, that's all. This is all you."

Then he leaned down and kissed her so gently her heart thumped hard in her chest. This man was doing things to her that no man ever had before. It terrified and energized her at the same time. She wanted Spiderweb and Savant out of her life, but the last thing she wanted was to lose Jude, too. He ended the kiss with a caress to her cheek, and she vowed to dig deep and not stop until she found the answers they needed to cut down the spiderweb and be free.

KENLEY WASN'T SURPRISED when she couldn't hack into the Spiderweb program like she had just hours before. But she was anticipating it, so it only took half as long as the last time before she waltzed through that door to inspect the code again. Mina had texted them back that while the code looked like the government created it, it was written that way to throw people off on purpose, as they all expected. Kenley wanted to find the code's weakness and rid the world of this nonsense. The problem was that she would never be as fast as the machine, so trying to bust the code was impossible.

"This is just not working," she moaned, trying to keep up with the scrolling code. She finally dropped her hands to her lap to take a break. "If anything, I'm training the damn machine to be smarter and faster." Rather than give up, she put her hands back on the keyboard and clicked out of her text box, letting the code run freely across the screen, reading it as it went. "Maybe the key is finding the right place to put the code to corrupt it," she pondered.

"Is it possible you can't corrupt it from the outside?" Jude asked from across the table.

"I've never seen a program that can't be corrupted with a virus or malware."

"Have you ever seen a program like this before?"

That question didn't justify an answer since he already knew she hadn't. This program was something out of science fiction. If she had to guess, it had taken years to write the code. A 5 caught her eye, and then she realized six lines later there was another 5. She quickly took a screenshot of a code block, scanning it repeatedly for a pattern that went with the 5. Then she saw it.

"No, no," she whispered, clicking the box out and grabbing another portion of the code farther down. This time, the name screamed its presence from the page. "It can't be. It's just not possible." Her whispered denials brought Jude around the table to see what she was looking at.

Her finger shaking, she pointed out what had been there all along. "5, 4, V, 4, N, T," she read, turning to look up at the man she had come to care too much about in too short a time.

"Savant." He said the word with a finality that sat heavily in her gut. "This is Savant's work? Is he trying to prove his prowess?"

"I don't know what he's doing, Jude. He hates the government with a burning passion, though. If you go on any forum that deals with anything government-related, he'll be there shouting about the corrupt and immoral leadership in our government at every level."

"Is the government aware of this?"

"Absolutely. They've been trying to figure out where he is, but he disappears every time they get close. When he feels safe again, he pops back up."

"You mean the government doesn't know who he is?"

"Nope, at least not as of my last government job a few months ago."

"What kind of work do you do for the government, or am I not allowed to ask?"

"Let's just say I'm always on the side of the good guys, and it usually involves trafficking or drugs. We'll leave it at that." He put his hands up as if to say, *Good enough*. "This is bad, Jude." She turned back to the program and started clicking out of it. "If Savant wrote this program, there's no hope of breaking it. I'm good, but I'm not that good. There's no one that good other than Savant."

"Do you think he knows it's you in the program?"

She shook her head back and forth a few times and finally gave him the palms up. "I can't say yes, but the fact that he made the website so close to the one I visited all the time makes me wonder if he wanted me to see it. If he hoped that eventually, I'd type something wrong and land on the page."

"Which is exactly what happened. I think you should message him," Jude said, pulling his chair over and sitting.

"Message Savant? Why?"

"He's messaged you, and you haven't responded yet, so let's give him a little attention. Make him think you're worried about your reputation, so you're distracted and scrambling."

"And unaware that he's behind Spiderweb?"

"For now, yes."

"And for later?" she asked, clicking open a tab to go to her survivors' forum.

"Later, we'll have a plan put together by one Mina Jacobs and hit him when he least expects it."

With a grin, she opened a binary code writer and prepared to type. "I like the way you think, Mr. Mason. Let's do this."

As she typed the message into the box, her head spun. Had Savant figured out a way to take control of every camera in the world? They were in serious trouble if he had, and it would be up to her and Secure Watch to stop him. Her biggest fear was that it was already too late.

Chapter Seventeen

"This guy is on every government watch list," Cal said as he walked behind Mina. "How do we find him?"

"We don't," Kenley answered. "He's been a ghost for years. I only know he's in the country because of the tracker in my shoe. For all I know, he was one of the guys in that truck tailing us. I picture him as the anonymous dude with the mask and the black robe in a dark room, staring at the camera. He may be a savant, but it's not with social skills. On the other hand, his hacking and coding skills make him the best in the world."

"Why did you decide to tangle with him?" Mina asked as she typed on her computer.

"I didn't even know who he was in the beginning," she admitted, glancing at Jude, who nodded with a smile. It felt foreign to her that, in such a short time, he was the one she looked to for strength now. Strength to keep going and the strength to say aloud the things she'd kept hidden for so many years. "I was seventeen when I started dabbling on the dark web."

"What were you looking for?" Cal asked, leaning on the back of Mina's chair. He'd joined their meeting once they knew who was behind Spiderweb. "Trouble?"

"You don't need to look for that on the dark web," Kenley said with a lip tilt. "No, I was looking for evidence that my friend's death wasn't an accident. It didn't take long to discover I was right, and thousands of people were hurt by the Neo Chase ATV, which was what my friend and I were riding that day. One second, we were flying down the trail, and the next second, we were in the dirt. She was dead, and my foot was mutilated. Over the years, I've searched for evidence to prove the company knew the wheels sheared off the axle at high speed."

"That's all you were doing there?" Mina asked, her brow tugged down to her nose in disbelief. As a former FBI agent, she knew what went down on the dark web.

"Not all," Kenley admitted, shifting in her chair. Jude put his arm around her waist and snugged her against his hip.

"Tell them everything so we can make a plan to get Savant out of our lives," Jude encouraged her.

"What he said," Mina added with a smile.

"We're not judging you, Kenley," Cal said as he pulled out a chair and sat down. "Both Mina and I have done some pretty sketchy things in the name of helping people. If that's all you were doing, you have nothing to fear."

"Not exactly true," she disagreed. "I mean, all my interactions there were for good, but I do have something to fear, and that something is someone. When Savant got wind of what I was doing, it put me on his radar."

"And what were you doing?" Cal asked, leaving the question open-ended for her to fill in.

"I worked with Mina's former employer a time or two, along with the CIA, Homeland Security, and some smaller government organizations, to help facilitate the downfall of some trafficking rings and the like. I can't say much more than that."

"And when you weren't helping mankind?" Cal asked, clearly unimpressed by her good deeds.

"I still helped mankind, but I used different techniques. I worked for individuals who were injured or had lost loved ones because of failures by large corporations. Using the dark web to find the information is the means to an end for me. Some wouldn't consider it honorable, but it's important to hold these companies accountable for their failures. It wasn't all on the dark web. A lot of that was done in the light."

"When did Savant become a problem for you?" Mina asked. "How long has he been a problem?"

"We've been sparring probably close to ten years now. He seems to have an odd fascination with me. It's like I'm his nemesis because I'm using the dark web for good and reporting those who are breaking the law."

"I'm just happy to hear that your heart was in the right place," Cal said with a wink. "I can respect someone who wants to help others even if they're motivated by their own pain."

"That sums it up pretty well," Kenley agreed. "Unfortunately, I picked up a rather unsavory character along the way, which has led us here."

"Do you think he intended for you to find the Spiderweb site?" Mina asked, folding her hands on the table and leaning in. "Otherwise, it seems like a massive coincidence."

"Agreed," Jude said as Kenley nodded.

"Now that I know he wrote the program, I can assure you, he wanted me to find it," Kenley said. "The site was set up with the same URL as the I2P page I frequented for a Staun Bril document. If he knew that, which, as the world's best hacker, he did, then all he had to do was make his URL something close and wait for me to mistype and land on it."

"Feels like there are easier ways to get you to click on

his site," Jude said. "Forums and sites like that live for that kind of stuff."

"True, but I don't think he wanted anyone else to find it," Kenley said.

"You think he wanted only you to find it? To what end?"

Kenley's shrug was lazy. "My guess would be to prove he was better than me. To prove I couldn't hack his program or play with his coding. At the same time, he didn't want to take a chance that someone else might come along and report it."

"You're saying he built that entire website to prove to a woman he's better than her?" Cal asked with a hint of shock in his voice.

"Come on, Cal. You can't be surprised by that," Jude said, shaking his head. "You were in the military."

"Fair point. But now that we know this, how do we stop it?"

"I sent him a message before we called you," Kenley explained. "I told him we figured out he was the one who coded the site, and then I told him to take it down so it didn't fall into the wrong hands. I promised to leave the dark web and never return if he did."

"Do you think he's going to?" Mina asked with surprise written all over her face.

"Absolutely not," Jude jumped in. "There's no way he spent all that time on a website with the potential to give him all this power to take it down now. I don't think this was ever really a game for him. It was, in a way, but he wanted one of the best hackers in the world to find it and try to bring it down. Savant knew he had a winning hand if Kenley couldn't take out Spiderweb. Considering how much he seems to hate the government, this entire situation was a setup to assure him he'd found a way to bring it to its knees."

"I don't disagree," Cal said, glancing at Mina, who nodded.

"I don't either," Kenley said, ignoring Jude for interrupting her. "My gut says he will return with another game. He'll give me some hints on how to get back into the program and change the code, but I won't bother. The program uses machine learning, and that's not something a human mind can ever get ahead of or beat."

"We're at a crossroads then," Cal said. "What's left to try?"

"Finding the server that holds Spiderweb." Kenley dropped the bomb without glancing at Jude. She'd purposely pretended she didn't know what to do so he couldn't talk her out of it before she got Mina and Cal on board. "If I can get to that server and install malicious firmware to the normal updating tools, then when I reboot it, it will brick the entire system."

Cal glanced at Mina. "Would that work?"

"Absolutely," Mina said, wearing a grin. "I'm sure he has the entire program backed up somewhere, but it would buy the government time to find him and stop him for good."

"Has there been any chatter about this program anywhere, Mina?" Jude asked, and she shook her head.

"Nothing. No one in my government channels had heard of a program with that ability, but they were all freaked out by the concept."

"I'm more than freaked out," Kenley said. "After being inside the program, I'm terrified of what could happen if this fell into the wrong hands. I've seen enough of the code that when this is all said and done, I want to help write a firmware update that can be sent to the cameras' operating systems. That way, even if he gets the program back online, he can't get back into them."

"I can get you in touch with the right people," Mina said with a nod. "That is if your contacts can't help." She added a wink, and Kenley realized it had just dawned on them all that she wasn't just a cybersecurity professional running a business from her home.

"First, we have to stop Savant," Jude said. "How do we find that server? It could be anywhere—it could be in his mother's basement, for all we know."

Mina cracked a smile, which made Kenley chuckle.

"That's fair, but it's not. This program needs a large server—far bigger than anything he can keep in his house, much less maintain. It needs serious power with its capabilities to keep changing and building in real time."

"We're back to how do we find that server," Cal said.

"We get him talking," Kenley mused. "I've started the conversation, and now he won't be able to stop bragging. Once he thinks he's defeated me, he'll give me all the information I need."

"How can we help?" Mina asked.

"Get a security team together," Jude answered without pause. "If she's going in somewhere, she's not going in alone."

"Agreed," Cal said. "Once you know where the server is located, I'll dispatch a team to cover you. I'll also alert the proper authorities."

"No!" Kenley exclaimed.

Cal shook his head. "That has to be part of the deal, Kenley. We won't notify them until you're nearly done with the installation. We don't need the authorities mucking up the job, but we also have to cover ourselves legally."

Kenley let out a breath and nodded. "Okay, I can accept that. I'm glad we're on the same page. Unfortunately, it's a waiting game now. We'll give Savant time to get comfortable with my admission that I can't break his code, which will require more messages back and forth before that happens. Once it does, things should unfold quickly."

"In the meantime, we're going to eat and rest," Jude said, putting his arm around her again.

"We'll be ready when the time comes, and we'll be in touch. Secure Watch, out," Mina said, and the screen went black.

Kenley blew out a breath and stood, rolling her shoulders to ease the strain and fatigue. After pacing for a bit, she sat on the edge of the bed. "I hate the waiting game."

"Me, too, but we'll ue it to our advantage this time. I also want to check that blister in case we need a different plan."

"It's better. I'll leave the bandage on it, and in a few days, it will be nothing but a memory."

"As long as we can avoid too much walking, which might be hard depending on where the server is."

"We'll meet that challenge when we come to it. You were working on looking to see if Savant outed me before Mina called, right?" He nodded. "Has he?"

"Not from the quick search I did of the regular web. I can't say what he did on the dark web. I'm not a pro at navigating it."

"The way I am, you mean." She didn't intend the sentence to be snarky, but it was there and chock-full of sarcasm. "You think what I do there is wrong. I suppose the rest of the world will, too."

"The more I've thought about it, the more I see why you do it," he said with a shrug. "In a way, we aren't that different. I took digital private investigation cases for the sole reason of rescuing someone in a bad situation. I can't judge what you do or how you do it if the information you need is located in a different place. If I thought for a second you were doing something that put others in danger, I wouldn't condone it, but that's not what's happening. If anything, the only person in danger is you. I wouldn't say I like that, but you're a big girl. You make your own decisions."

"Thank you for saying that, Jude." She folded her hands in a prayer pose. "I don't think it's wrong to help people any way you can, but I'm tired. I'm tired of running, hiding and playing games. I've been doing this for years, but Savant has opened my eyes to the danger I put myself in every time I go down that dark hole."

Jude stood and walked over to her, taking her hands in his. "It's good that you've come to that realization. We might take down Savant, but someone else will replace him. Fighting for justice is noble, but doing it in a way that protects you is the smartest option."

"That's what you do, right? You protect damsels in distress?" Once again, her tone was snarky while not meant to be. He was too close, too potent, and too kind, caring and handsome for her not to want to pull him to her. At the same time, the other half wanted to push him away. The battle within her was raging, and she had no idea who would win.

"Not always," he said, kneeling before her now. "At least not since I started working for Secure Watch. When I was a digital private investigator, there were many times that I was fighting for a woman who had been victimized by her husband or boyfriend. It wasn't about saving damsels in distress. It was about using my skills to right wrongs."

"You're saying we're not that different?" The question was asked with high skepticism because, in her book, Jude was far wiser about the world than she would ever be. That came with experience, and boy, did he have it. He'd lived through wars and made decisions that may have helped determine the fate of the nation.

"In most ways, we're the same, Kenley. You'll tell yourself

that's impossible because we've lived different lives, which is true, but in the end, here we are with the same skills, both trying to rescue people whose lives have fallen apart."

She tipped her head to the side as she thought about the message he was trying to give her. He didn't think she was wrong because she used the dark web to dig up dirt on big corporations. He was scared that doing that would put her in danger. If that were the case, then the only reason he would worry about her being in danger was because he cared about her.

He pushed himself up to take her lips. "I care about you, Kenley." The words were whispered against her lips before he kissed her again. Her soft mewl of happiness at the connection fueled him, and he ran his tongue across her closed lips, asking for entrance.

When she allowed it, he slipped his warm tongue alongside hers and rested there for a moment, wrapping her in his arms as he did so. Then he turned to sit on the bed, pulling her onto his lap.

"Kenley," he whispered, his breath warm against her neck as he kissed the hollow there. "I want you more than I want air."

"Same." She threw her head back when he started to kiss his way back up her neck to her ear, where he nipped the lobe.

"The age gap," he whispered into her ear.

"Doesn't matter," she moaned as he slid his hand up her ribs. "Not to me anyway. Does it matter to you?"

"Not even a little bit." Then his hand slipped under her shirt to run across her ribs and up her back, where he relieved her of her bra in one fluid motion.

"Is it just the forced proximity making us feel this way?"

she asked, sliding her hands into his hair as he kissed across both collarbones.

His gentle laughter tickled her neck before he spoke. "Are you trying to talk me out of this?"

"I'm trying to make sure you don't have any regrets, Jude."

"My only regret would be not taking this chance to be with you, sweet pea." He leaned back and grasped her chin gently. "Do you know when I knew you were different than any other woman I'd met?" She barely shook her head, so he smiled and kissed her lips before he answered. "The moment I heard your voice. This feeling came over me that said you would change my life, and there was an unseen force saying, get to her. Help her. Protect her. Then I laid eyes on you and wondered if I could draw the next breath. I've always believed I'd rather carry a little bit of regret for what I did do than a whole lot of it for what I didn't do."

"So you are going to regret this?"

He dipped his head and took her lips again as he rested her back against the pillows and then knelt over her, slowly unbuttoning her top. When the buttons were undone, he left her lips to kiss down her neck to the dip between her breasts. He laid his lips there for a beat before he gazed at her from his position on her chest. "The only thing I'll regret about this is that, eventually, I'll have to wrap you up again and take you back out into that cold world. For now, just for now, let's pretend we don't."

Before she could speak, he pushed aside her bra and lavished her breasts with the attention they'd been begging for. His warm hands kneaded and caressed them while his hot tongue teased her nipples into hard buds in the chilly room. With his hands still on her breasts, he kissed his way down her belly, dipping his hot tongue in her navel and pulling an unexpected gasp from her lips. She slid her hands back into his hair and pulled him up to kiss her while she worked at the buttons of his shirt. She wanted to see, touch and feel his heat and energy against her skin.

"Let me take off your prosthesis," he whispered as she ran her hands over his hard chest, the soft hair tickling her fingers. Her hands froze, and she glanced up at him, grabbing his hand as it went for her leg.

"Leave it on. It won't hurt anything."

He shrugged the rest of the way out of his shirt before he leaned in to press himself to her chest, matching their hearts together. "Absolutely not. It pains me to know you want to leave it on to protect yourself. I desire all of you, Kenley. Your leg has no bearing on that. If any other man thought your leg wasn't worthy of the same kind of attention and care as the rest of you, then he wasn't the right man."

"You mean every man, then?" she asked with her smart-aleck tone back in force. She wished she could find a place to be less defensive about her leg, but she hadn't lied when she said every man she'd been with took issue with it in one way or another. They all thought she was a little less beautiful, a little less talented, and maybe a little less everything because of it.

"All the wrong men," he said, taking her hand and kissing her knuckles. He walked to the end of the bed, his belt open, and the snap on his jeans popped. She could see the outline of his maleness and yearned to touch him, but he was a man on a mission.

Jude lifted her prosthesis and took his time removing the back plate so she could slip her limb out. He set it aside and then rolled the liner sock down, obviously having paid attention to the way she did it, and then stowed it in the prosthesis.

With unhurried tenderness, he held the end of her limb in one hand while running the other over her skin, raising goose bumps. When he lowered his lips to kiss his way up the limb to her knee, she had to swipe away a tear. His gentle caress and tender kisses did everything to heal the part of her heart that believed she was damaged and unlovable or needed to prove herself because of what was missing, not what she still had.

When his fingers grasped the waistband of her lounge pants, she lifted her bottom, allowing him to strip them off in one motion. In the blink of an eye, she was bare and open to the man who, just a few days ago, was a stranger. Not anymore. He'd become so much more the moment their eyes met, and as she watched him gaze at her body as though she was priceless art, she understood why. He was made for her.

"Beyond beautiful," he whispered, running his hand up the inside of her right thigh to her groin. "I've ached for someone like you, sweet pea, for years." The sentence was barely complete before he lowered his lips to her thigh and kissed his way to her center, teasing and sucking until she wanted to come apart from the power of his lovemaking.

"Jude," she cried, grasping his belt loop and pulling him to her. "Let me see you." Her words were laced with passion, but as he lowered his boxers, she came to understand her desire for him fully. "Let me touch you."

With a smile, he took her hand and taught her how he liked to be held, touched and tasted. When he could take no more, he climbed onto the bed and grabbed a silver packet from the drawer by the bed.

Her brow went up. "You did have plans." She snatched the packet from his hand and waved it in the air.

When he laughed, it was dirty and delicious. "I'll admit I bought a bigger box than necessary, just in case."

"Always prepared," she said, ripping open the package. "Kind of like a Boy Scout."

"Oh, sweet pea, I am the furthest thing from a Boy Scout you'll ever find."

"Good, because I like a bad boy, and I like him dirty." Before he could respond, she popped the condom between her lips and rolled it over him slowly and with precision. A moan ripped from his chest, indicating exactly how he felt about her actions.

"The good girl is about to learn how dirty this bad boy likes it," he whispered as he poised at her juncture. "And then, we'll have to review for the test."

She inhaled as he thrust forward, filling her with nothing but good sensations. When he pulled back and thrust forward again, she was struck with the need to be with this man until the end of time. His legs shook from the effort it took to hold back, so she wrapped her legs around his waist and lifted her hips. He slipped deeper, and when their eyes met, she watched him fall for the good girl, her name on his lips.

Chapter Eighteen

Jude woke to the clacking of keys, though he could tell she was trying to be quiet. The woman he'd made love to just an hour ago was wearing his T-shirt while sitting at the table, typing a message. He was taken by her before, but after sharing such intimacy, he was a goner. His only goal was to not let that show once they left this room. He couldn't risk allowing her sweet body or the idea that she could be his to distract him when he was the only one there to protect her.

Did he think Savant was still stalking them? He'd told Kenley he'd pulled back his friends, which was supposedly all in good fun, but it didn't feel like fun when they were trying to avoid that pickup truck. As for digitally, it was unlikely he had a pin on them yet. The VPN provider and scrambler they used changed their location so quickly that it was next to impossible to break through and find their actual location. Even if he knew where they were, let him come. Savant was nothing more than a bully made of flesh. Jude had dealt with plenty of them.

"Savant responded," she said without turning as though she knew he was awake. "He's hedging on my conceding the game already."

"Did he expect you to beat your head on the wall for a few more days?"

"That's what I just asked," she said, finally turning to smile at him. Her hair was mussed from his fingers, and her lips were still plump from his kisses. "I told him I'm persistent, but I'm not dumb. There's no way for me to get ahead of a machine that can compute ten times faster than I can."

"Now we're back to waiting?" he asked as she turned off the computer and stood. "Do you think he's still tracking us?"

"That was the other half of his message. He congratulated me on figuring out he was tracking the phone but was frustrated that he couldn't find the new device I was using."

The mere idea lifted Jude's lips. "Excellent. The last thing we want is to run into his goons again. He said he called them off, but there's no telling what he might do if he feels threatened and has our location."

"Agreed," Kenley said.

She walked over to him, standing between his legs where he sat on the bed. He hadn't dressed, and while his nakedness would typically make him feel vulnerable, just the opposite was true. He was confident, which was never something he felt with any other woman after sex.

Maybe the difference is you made love to Kenley.

Though that *was* probably the difference, it didn't fix any of the other circumstances they found themselves in. If anything, emotions could do more harm than good in a life-or-death situation. The problem was the emotions were there, which meant he had two choices. He could use them to his benefit or let them get the better of him. The military worked to instill the idea that emotions didn't belong on the battlefield. If that were true, thousands of men who were saved by the sheer will and determination of another human being over the course of history would have died rather than been rescued, patched up or protected. Sometimes, you could fight evil with love. That might be what he'd have to do here if Savant came at them.

Jude grasped her hips and snugged her into him. He wanted to slide his hands under the T-shirt to connect with her tender skin. "How do you feel?"

"Satisfied. Happy. Surprised," she whispered, leaning in to kiss him as he cupped her bottom, loving the feeling of her warm skin under his hands again.

"Surprised?"

With her lips near his ear, she answered. "You're the first man who has ever been comfortable with my leg or willing to touch it, much less kiss it the way you did."

Jude suspected that was the case, but it broke his heart to have it confirmed. "Maybe those other men saw your leg as a weakness but I see it as strength. Physically and morally. It's often painful and difficult, but you keep going because you're determined to turn that pain and loss into something good that will benefit others. It takes a strong mind and body to do that, Kenley. I'm sure there were times you wanted to give up or give in, right?" She nodded against his neck, where her lips had made their way. She was kissing her way back to his ear, raising goose bumps on his skin and a more visible reaction from his groin. "But you didn't give up. You kept going through all the pain and all the grief to stand for something you believe in."

"I thought you didn't agree with my vigilantism."

"After some reflection, I understand why you do it. Though the how may not be to my liking, if you're changing lives and not breaking any laws, then I have no right to judge you. All I want is for you to be safe, and I feel like right now, you're not."

"Right now," she said, gazing into his eyes as her pupils dilated. "I've never been safer. When I'm in your arms, nothing can hurt me. I know you'll keep me safe, Jude, both physically and emotionally. Right?"

A growled yes was all he got out before she grasped him in her hand. On his surprised intake of breath, she laid a kiss on him that said emotion was in play for her, too. She might not know where they were going, but she knew they would get there together. He thrust against her hand, and a moan fell from his lips when she pulled away from the kiss. She reached into the drawer and grabbed another silver packet.

"Will you prove it?" she asked in a whisper, rolling the condom down and pushing him backward on the bed. She climbed up and straddled him, pressing her lips to his again in a desperate attempt to have as little space between them as possible.

"I'll prove it over and over and over," he promised against her lips as she lowered herself over him inch by inch until she was fully seated on his lap, his hardness throbbing at the heat and pleasure she offered but also at the trust she had put in him. The mere thought had him thrusting upward to close all the gaps of reality between them. In one fluid motion, he stripped the shirt from her tiny body and reveled in the beauty before him. "You're so damn beautiful, Kenley Bates. Don't ever take that away from me."

Before she could say anything, he grasped her nipple between his lips and suckled, bucking his hips against hers in a race to the finish line that would have them falling into each other's arms as winners. He didn't want to think about anything outside this room or this woman. He didn't want to think. He just wanted to feel, so for now, he'd pretend they were any other couple stealing away for a tryst before returning to reality.

"Jude," she moaned, her head thrown back as she stilled against him.

His name on her lips was all he needed, and he drove them across the finish line in a short thrust. She called his name one last time and fell against him, spent and sated. He wrapped his arms around her and pulled the blankets over them, loving how she settled into his chest and dropped off to sleep. After a kiss to the top of her head, he let his eyes droop closed, too, taking advantage of what little quiet time they had before the storm intensified and they were swept up into a tornado that might eat them alive.

JUDE TUCKED THE blanket around Kenley and grabbed the phone before he slid outside to stand against the door. After having her sweet body over him, he needed some fresh air to get his head back in the game. It wasn't just that they'd made love again. It was that she'd given herself to him in a way he wasn't expecting or prepared for when she straddled him. There were no declarations of feelings, but they both sensed it was more than sex between two people trapped in a situation not of their making. It was the coming together of two hearts that had finally found each other.

With a breath out, he hit the button and waited while the phone rang. "Secure Watch, Whiskey."

"Secure Watch, Jacko," he responded, and Mina's face popped up on the small screen. "Hey, Min."

"Jude, good to see you. I was hoping you'd be in touch and update me."

"About an hour ago, Kenley got a message from Savant. He's suspicious that she's thrown in the towel already. She assured him she had better things to do than try to go head-to-head with a machine that could compute ten times faster than she could. We're awaiting his response."

"Give me your opinion, Jude. What do we have here?"

"We have a dude whose brain is like a computer, but

he has zero social skills that tell him when something isn't acceptable."

"Agreed. His name is fitting. He's a savant who has skills that should be harnessed by the government, not having him working against them. What do you think his endgame with the Spiderweb program is?"

"At first, I thought it was a way for him to mess with Kenley because he has so much hatred for her and what she does on the dark web."

"That's never been very clear on our end," Mina admitted.

Jude took a moment to explain in more detail what Kenley did and why. "She admits that sometimes she's looking at documents she shouldn't be, but feels like if a company is lying about a product that is hurting people, it's her job to expose them."

"And the government jobs she does?"

"To ease her guilt about the rest of it," Jude answered. "She hasn't come right out and said that, but it's the vibe I got as we talked. When she sees something, she says something. Whether it's a sex trafficking ring, drugs or murder plot, she always lets the authorities know where to look. Sometimes, she does the looking for them."

Mina shrugged with a smile. "Maybe this makes me a bad person, but I have zero qualms with what Kenley is doing with these companies. So many of them are telling bald-faced lies to sell products that harm people. I'll take her tactics all day long if she can stop just one person from getting hurt. That said, and as I'm sure she's learned, the dark web is a dangerous place to play. I hope this event has proven that to her."

"Oh, it has," Jude agreed with a nod. "She wants to find Savant and then return to the business that makes her money and nothing else. She decided that vigilantism can only go so far."

"Too bad. Cal and I considered offering her a job at Secure Watch."

Jude raised a brow at that bomb. "Really? I didn't think Cal would condone what she does enough to trust her."

"Cal? My dude, he's spent half his life as a vigilante. He's never met her, but he feels a commonality he can respect."

"True. It's easy to forget what Cal did before Secure One grew to be so successful."

"We also see a commonality between you and Kenley."

Jude rubbed his forehead as he took in the area around him. The same bikes that had been there earlier were still parked in a row along the doors. There weren't any pickup trucks or other cars besides Blob the Slob, who was still hunkered in the spot where they parked him at the very edge of the lot. He'd decided it was better not to point the genius directly to their door if he were to show up. Jude prayed that Blob started again when they needed to leave, because there would be a showdown, even if he didn't know when or where yet.

"Jude? Care to respond?"

"If I say no, can that be the end of the discussion?"

Mina's laughter traveled through the phone and into the space around him. He couldn't help but smile even if he was extremely uncomfortable. "You should know me better than that by now, Jude Mason."

"It was worth a shot," he said with a shrug and a lip tilt. "I should get back inside and check messages. Kenley finally gave in to sleep, so I'll take this shift while she rests."

"How's her limb?"

"Healing," he answered, letting a breath out in relief that she wasn't going to keep grilling him about his feelings for the woman asleep behind the door. He might say something he shouldn't. "The last time I bandaged it, I saw new skin over the blister, and the swelling was down. She can wear her prosthesis now without pain. We must keep her off her feet as much as possible, though."

"You bandaged it?" Mina asked, surprise filling her tone.

"I did. Kenley has bad judgment when it comes to whether something is fine or in need of help. I don't have that bias."

"Fair," she agreed. "I'm just surprised she lets you touch her limb. I couldn't bring myself to let Roman touch mine for months after the amputation."

"The vulnerability was real, but we got past it and are better for it. I needed to understand her limitations in that prosthesis, so I didn't push her past them again. She says there are better ones, but she can't afford them. She never got a settlement from the accident and has to pay for everything herself."

"That's unfortunate. I hoped that wasn't the case, but I'm not surprised. So few insurances pay for prostheses. It's something that needs to change. Maybe that's my ace in the hole. She could get whatever she wanted if she worked at Secure Watch." Mina threw him a wink. He smiled at the idea that maybe there was a better, healthier path forward for Kenley.

"Do you know that she has over four thousand people on a forum who have been hurt by the same ATV that caused her accident? I've been slowly prodding her into filing a class action lawsuit. If what she says is true, a lawyer would certainly find evidence that the company knew about the problem."

"That's a lot of people. I'm surprised no one has brought a suit against them already."

"Some have, apparently, but have given up after hitting constant roadblocks. That's why they turn to Kenley. Well, anyway, you should go be with your family."

"You care about her, don't you?" Mina asked, completely ignoring his statement.

"She needs someone in this life to care about her, Mina." That was a safe answer to all the questions swirling around in his brain.

Mina's laughter was softer this time as she shook her head. "Very military diplomat of you, Jude. Here's what I'll say about the look on your face and the spark in your eye when I say her name. Over the next few days, as we try to stop Savant, use it. Don't be afraid of it. Use it to keep her safe and make the right decisions about your future."

"Use what, Mina?" Did she want him to admit he loved Kenley? It had only been a few days since they met.

"That love you feel for her." He opened his mouth to speak, but Mina held up her hand. "Don't come at me, bro. I'm simply telling you what I see. You look like a well-loved man tonight, and I'm here for it. If there's one thing I've learned in this life, it's that if you fight evil with love, you'll win every single time. You may take a few hard hits, but love will always win, so use it to your advantage to keep that woman safe. The team is ready to help, but right now, you're the only thing standing between her and Savant, so be the pillar she needs and show her how much you care even if you can't put that into words now."

"The fact that I can put it into words at this moment scares me. It's only been three days, Min. It takes me three days to decide to put away my laundry."

"Oh, Jude," Mina said with a chuckle. "You do make me laugh. Love isn't always a matter of time. Sometimes time is what brings us love."

"Change the narrative," he said.

"And change your life," she said with a wink. "I'm going to get back to digging into the government's knowledge of this program and whether they already have someone on it.

Right now, all signs point to no, but I'd be surprised since Savant is very much on their radar."

"You have to remember how the dark web works, Mina. That's where you go when you don't want the government to discover what you're doing. Savant has used that to his full advantage. If he could put malware on cameras without leaving a trace, no one would be the wiser until he sells the program or uses the information for evil. Only then would they realize something was wrong."

"And by then, it would be too late." She sighed.

"We have to stop him in any way possible. That said, bringing the authorities in too early will hinder our ability to do that, no matter what Cal says. According to Kenley, Savant hates the government with the heat of ten thousand suns, which means he will continue to push back with bigger and bolder programs unless he's stopped for good."

"We agree there. Please message me as soon as you hear something from Savant. The security team is on standby until we have a plan."

"Heard and understood," he said. "Thanks, Mina. For all the advice, too."

"No thanks needed as long as you take some of it. Whiskey out."

Jude hung up the phone and let out a sigh. Was he going to take any of her advice? He unlocked the door and slid back inside, not surprised to see Kenley still asleep as the clock ticked toward midnight. The longer he gazed at her, the more he understood that Mina was right. Sometimes, time brought love. He had to agree as he walked over to the bed and caressed Kenley's cheek, bringing a smile to her lips as she slept. Now, he just had to keep that love safe until he could share it.

Chapter Nineteen

Kenley watched Jude work from her position on the bed. Funny, it was only a few hours ago that he had done the same to her, as though they were sizing each other up for how big a heartache they'd cause each other. Was it weird that she didn't want to be the cause of his heartache and just be his heart? Less than seventy-two hours wasn't a long time to get to know someone, but it had only taken the first time she saw him step out of his SUV to know she was about to meet her destiny. Maybe that sounded ridiculous, but it was the image lodged in her heart. Not because he was coming to save her either. Because he was coming at all. He could have said to take a cab home and call in the morning, but he hadn't done that. He'd driven almost two hours in the middle of the night to extract her from a place that had suddenly become dangerous.

His fingers flew across the keyboard as the adrenaline in the air caught up to her. "Jude, what's going on?"

Once she'd strapped her prosthesis back on, she grabbed her lounge clothes, slipping into them before she walked over to him. The last thing they could do was get distracted by each other again.

"Savant responded to your message," he answered quickly as he typed in a program she didn't recognize.

"We've been conversing, and he had some interesting things to say to you."

"Why didn't you wake me up?"

"You needed the sleep. It never occurred to him that it wasn't you who was answering. He was responding quickly, so I just kept the ruse up."

"Does he believe I've given up on breaking the code?"

"Oh, yeah," Jude said with a lilt of laughter at the two words. "Now he thinks he's bulletproof, and that's exactly where we want him."

"That's when he'll slip up, right?"

"He already did, sweet pea," he said, hitting Enter on the keyboard and waiting for the information to hit his screen. Jude turned to her and took her face in his hands, kissing her with a hard smack of excitement. "Pretending to be you, I asked him where Spiderweb sleeps, and he said it was a secret we'd never uncover. He also kept referring to Spiderweb as a cyclone. One that would sweep the entire world right into his hands."

"A cyclone? That's weird. We don't have cyclones in the Midwest. We have tornadoes."

"Exactly!" Jude exclaimed, turning back to the computer screen. "But Iowa State University's football team is the Cyclones."

"Are you saying he knows we're here?"

"Nope, I'm saying I think Spiderweb sleeps in Iowa. I just have to find it."

"How?"

"Well, he mentioned this professor he once had. According to him, when he was twelve, he attended college at Iowa State, and she taught him advanced coding techniques. Her name was Professor Dracker."

"Hero worship?"

"It felt a little like that. Whether that was his point or not, I can't say, but it was an odd last name. I searched Mina's databases, and there's no Professor Dracker at Iowa State, but it did bring up a former Iowa State professor who now works on Dracker Drive in Ames."

"I'm not connecting the dots."

He held up his finger and waited for the computer to finish spinning. When it did, they both sucked in a breath. "I knew it," he said, shaking his head with a smile. "He couldn't resist thinking he was so smart."

"That Spiderweb sleeps on Dracker Drive in Ames, Iowa?" She leaned in to see the screen a bit better. "Pauline Hardy is now a cybersecurity specialist for hire?"

"And it looks like she's not afraid of the underbelly of that kind of cybersecurity." He pointed out some information on the screen for her to read.

"She's listing her expertise in all things dark web scraping. That sounds like the kind of company Savant would keep. Can you bring the address up on maps?"

After opening a browser and typing in the address, they waited until the pin grabbed the location. Jude hit the street view and zoomed in to check it out. "Looks like an office building. She must rent space there."

"Does it give a suite number or anything?" He flipped back to the other tab, and she searched the page, but nothing was listed. "That's inconvenient. Do you think she owns the entire building?"

"Anything is possible. It could also be on a directory in the building."

"What if it's a trick?"

Jude tossed his head from side to side. "I considered that. It would be easy for a guy like Savant to plant a fake name on the internet, but something tells me everything he said was true. Is he leading us to the building? That's what I believe, but maybe it's the only way this will ever end. All we can do is not take anything at face value, and both be on the same page before making a move. If something feels off, we fall back and regroup."

With a nod, she took his hand. "I agree with everything you said. If he's giving us these 'clues'—" she used air quotes "—then he wants us to find this building and whatever is inside. If we're lucky, it will be the home of Spiderweb, and we can finally exterminate it. What do you say, partner? Are you up for a short road trip?"

"I wouldn't have it any other way," he promised, kissing her firmly. "Let me call Mina while you pack. We have a date with data and destiny in Ames."

Jude grabbed the phone, and Kenley hurried to the bathroom to change her clothes and pack. When she closed the bathroom door, she realized she had never questioned Jude's deductions and didn't ask to see the messages. Jude Mason had all her trust. Now, she had to hope he didn't break it.

JUDE UPDATED CAL on their location while Kenley stood with her back against the building, waiting. The office building on Dracker Drive was much larger than she expected, and their research on it was minimal. Unfortunately, they couldn't approach the front door to look for a directory, as it faced the street and several large cameras. They'd found a door at the back that had one small camera and a keypad. Jude pulled out a can of black spray paint and contorted his arm, giving the lens a shot of the paint. It would buy them time and not much else. Then again, there was a good chance the building didn't have anyone running security inside, and the cameras went to a security company's central hub. Kenley prayed that was the case. They needed enough time to get inside and find a server large enough to hold Spiderweb.

When they climbed into Blob the Slob to leave the hotel, Kenley had sucked in a breath on a hope and prayer that it would start. As she stood staring at the door to what could hold her destiny, she realized she hadn't let it out yet. This was far from over. They were just getting started, but fortunately, the car had started on the first try. Since Ames was less than an hour from the hotel, they made record time getting to the building.

"We have to wait for the rest of the team to arrive," Jude whispered. "They need to run interference for us. Not to mention, we can't get the door open without the right PIN. We also don't know what's inside, if there are servers, or which would be his."

"It's simple," she replied as they scooted along the building toward the keypad. If her theory were correct, she'd get the door open after one or two attempts. "He goes by 54V4N7 online. He's also arrogant and has a God complex, so I'm pretty sure I can bust his code."

"We're not supposed to go in until Cal and the team get here."

Kenley checked her watch. "They're easily another hour out, Jude. Savant could kill the program or move it off this server to a different one if we wait. He could be doing that now for all we know!"

He grasped her elbow to calm her. "If we go in and get caught, Secure Watch can't help us."

"I'll take my chances," she said, pulling the hood up on the black hoodie she'd found in her bag. "Are you with me, Warrant Officer Mason?"

"I've got your back. You get two tries. If you can't get in, we'll wait for Cal."

"Agreed," she said, sliding toward the keypad while trying to avoid the camera. He'd given it a shot of paint, but they had no way to know if a hidden camera was inside the keypad. The best she could do was shield her face with the hoodie and pray. Before she stepped up to the keypad, she checked her pocket for the flash drive she'd tucked in it before they left the car. She'd written the code for the malware while at the hotel and had it ready to install in Savant's server once they found it. A little click-clack and Spiderweb would be demolished.

After a deep breath in, Kenley inspected the keypad. She wasn't surprised it was low-end technology. It was doubtful too many people tried breaking into a random office building. While she knew it was wise to wait for the team, it was also a considerable risk that Savant would tire of the game, pack up his toys and go home. Jude might think the evil genius was being coy by dropping hints, but Kenley knew better. Savant had orchestrated this entire game. He wanted an epic showdown with her, so he made Spiderweb's address so close to the one she had always visited. He'd never made it a secret to anyone who would listen that he took offense at what she did on the dark web and wanted to bring her down. In his opinion, the dark web should never be used for good, but that wasn't an opinion they shared.

Savant must have wanted her to find the server. What would be waiting for her when she got there was impossible to predict, but she knew the time was now if she was going to beat him at his own game. All she could do was cross her fingers that he was still behind a keyboard somewhere, not behind this door. Her flash drive would solve the problem, but first, she had to find where Spiderweb slumbered.

Chapter Twenty

Kenley inhaled a breath and typed 5447 on the keypad, then waited for the door to click. When it didn't, she cleared the pad and typed in 5135. With a snap, the lock disengaged, and she pulled it open, waiting for Jude to join her.

Once inside, he pulled her against a wall and leaned into her ear. "How did you do that?"

"I suspected the code would be a combination of our call letters. It wasn't even hard, but he's cocky, so I'm not surprised."

"We are in the middle of nowhere. He probably thought he was safe from anyone bothering to try and break the code to get in," Jude said as they made their way down empty corridors. "That also means that this woman he's talking about may not exist, and this building is his."

Jude's words made her trip on her own feet. She pulled up against the wall and took a deep breath. "You're right. I didn't think of that. Why would a code specific to him open the door if someone else owned this building? Of course, he is the world's best hacker. He could have changed the pad code in anticipation of our arrival."

"He could have, but my gut says he's the owner. We need to wait for backup from Secure One, Kenley. This guy means business. You say he's a harmless nerd, but I don't feel that way. The hair on the back of my neck is standing up."

"Mine, too, but we don't have time to wait. It's been three hours since you chatted with Savant. If we don't make a move, he will."

"That's what I'm afraid of," Jude mumbled, following her as she scooted forward. She pointed at a directory listing near a set of double glass doors.

They read the list of businesses, and Kenley immediately started to sweat. "They're all names of spiders," she whispered, pointing at the directory. "Tarantula, Black Widow and Brown Recluse." When she finished reading, she stepped back and took it all in. "This one." Her finger pointed at the fifth one up.

"Sydney Funnel-Web?" Jude asked, and she nodded.

"It's the most poisonous spider in the world, and it has 'web' right in its name. It's also on the fifth floor."

"That means?"

"His name on the web starts with a 5," she clarified.

"I'll bite, no pun intended." He gave her a wink that instantly lowered her heart rate as they moved closer to their own Black Widow. "What's your plan?"

"Find an elevator," she responded, and he raised a brow. "Where there's an elevator, there are stairs."

"Fair point, but I feel like we're going deeper into the underbelly of this place."

"We are, but if we use service stairs, we're less likely to get caught on camera right away."

They walked down several more corridors before they found the elevator. Sure enough, there was also a set of stairs. As they took each flight, Jude allowed her to set the pace, and she did her best to keep from grimacing. The stairs were rough in her prosthesis but worse when she had a blister to protect. Not doing this wasn't an option. If she ever wanted to be free without looking over her shoulder, she had to stop Savant.

At the top of each flight of stairs was a heavy steel door. Jude grasped her arm and held her still halfway up the last steps to floor 5. "Catch your breath before we go any further. How's the leg doing?"

Before saying it was fine, she stopped and took stock of everything. "We're good. Your bandage is holding up." Admitting that almost choked her up. Earlier, he'd insisted they weren't leaving the hotel room until he'd assessed and rebandaged the blister on her limb. Thankfully, the last few days of lying low had helped heal it quickly and without infection. She'd get away with nothing but a memory as long as the swelling stayed down. She just had to hope all these stairs didn't worsen the problem. Then again, everything was about to come to a head, which meant their days of hiding out would be over, and she could go to the doctor if needed.

Sadness filled her at the thought of giving Jude up for good. He had a life in Illinois working for Secure Watch. She had a business in Milwaukee. The miles between them weren't insurmountable, but assuming he wanted to be part of her life after all this was an assumption she couldn't let her heart entertain. They were good together at the keyboard and in bed, but did that translate to life? She couldn't answer that question, but her gut told her the moment she lost Jude, she'd feel it in her soul forever. Did it scare her that she could see a future as a couple for them in only three days? Yes, but not in the terrifyingly scary kind of way. More in the anticipation kind of scary.

"That's a relief. Let's keep it that way," he whispered, kissing her softly. "Stay right where you are." He pulled the phone from his pocket. "I have to update Cal."

"How far out are they?" she asked, trying to read the message over his shoulder.

"About ten minutes. It turns out he brought the chopper. Mina is waiting in a secure location with a computer. Once you install the malware, she'll log on to the program to see if it implodes. I'm giving Cal the credential information now because this feels like a setup to us."

Kenley bit her lip for a moment. "I was just thinking everything was a bit too easy."

He sent the message and glanced at her. "I think we should wait for the team. I have hand-to-hand skills, but that's nothing against a knife or a gun."

"I thought you had a gun?"

"I do, but the last thing I want is for bullets to start flying. If there's nowhere to hide, you could get hit."

Kenley turned and grabbed his shirt in her fists. "I care about you too, Jude. The last thing I want is for anyone to get hurt. I can go in alone. It'll take less than five minutes to plant the malware and leave."

"You are absolutely not going in there alone. We don't know who or what is waiting for us. We don't even know what we're looking for!" His voice was barely audible, but she heard the frustration and fear loud and clear.

"Savant is too smart to be dangerous to our bodies, Jude. I know him."

"I'm less worried about the evil genius and more worried about the person he hired as his muscle. If you don't believe he did, you're naive, Kenley Bates."

She shook her head momentarily before unzipping her pocket and readying the flash drive. "I believe this game of cat and mouse needs to end, Jude. For me, for you, and the world. Whatever we find in there can be weaponized to destroy countries. That's not something I want hanging over my head because I was too afraid to stop it." She shook the flash drive in her hand. "Am I scared to death? Yes. But sometimes you have to live scared, Jude, so let's do it. Let's live scared."

Before she could turn, he grasped the back of her neck and pulled her into him. When his lips landed on hers in a passionate kiss that was fast and dirty, she memorized every second of it so she wouldn't forget. "You want me to live scared? Fine, I'm frozen with fear, knowing I could lose you in the next five minutes. I'm terrified knowing that if we live through whatever is about to happen, I'll lose you when our world stops spinning on an axis created by Savant. I'm even more terrified that I'll never have a chance to tell you that I lo—"

Kenley put her finger against his lips. "Shh." It was no more than a hiss. "Do not say those three words, Jude Mason. Save them. Save them until they can mean something more than a hurried confession in a stairwell. If you say those three words, I'll take your hand and run away from all of this to be with you."

"Let's do it. Let's run away," he begged, holding her elbow. "We can let the authorities and Secure Watch deal with Savant."

"And they will, but for all we know, Savant is launching an attack with Spiderweb as we speak. Since the day I logged on to the dark web, this was my destiny. I have to finish it. You have to trust me."

She waited while Jude stared her down, his jaw ticking as he made whatever decision he had to make. She fell even more in love with him with every moment he stayed by her side. He could turn around and walk down those stairs to wait for Cal, but she knew he wouldn't do that—not if he loved her.

"All right, but if I see one thing I don't like, we back off and wait for the team."

With a nod, she turned and finished walking up the stairs, peering through the window in the door into floor 5. "It just looks like another hallway," she said.

"I hate hallways," Jude muttered as she opened the door. They slipped through, following the long, dark corridor.

Kenley noticed it branch off to the left ahead, and she motioned Jude against the wall so she could peek around the corner. Then she leaned into his ear to fill him in. "Offices filled with nothing but servers. This is where Spiderweb is."

"How do we find the right server?"

Kenley had already considered this, and if her luck or Savant's ego held true, she knew the answer: "Fourth office, fourth rack, seventh shelf."

"His name numbers again?" When she nodded, he shrugged as though he didn't have a care in the world. "Let's try it. Maybe there will be other markings on it to tell us for certain. I don't want to crash someone else's program."

"This malware is geared to shut down Spiderweb only. As long as no one else is trying to target all the cameras in the world, my malware wouldn't harm their program."

"Brilliant," Jude whispered, and she noticed a grin on his face.

"It's a stopgap measure until we can get the patch out to everyone with security cameras. I'm not convinced he doesn't have a backup somewhere."

"Beat him from the inside out. There's no other answer when fighting someone we can't see. Are you ready?"

He squeezed her hand, and they slid around the corner, staying tight to the wall to avoid detection as much as possible. It was dark, but the servers put off a fair amount of blue light to guide them. She mentally counted off the offices until they reached office four at the back of the building. With a nod from Jude, they slid across the hallway and into the room. Jude pushed her up against the wall and held up his finger. He drew his gun and walked around the large server cabinets, checking between each one with his gun pointed forward.

"It's clear. Fast and ugly, right?"

She nodded while he took up a shooter's stance at the door. Kenley counted seven data racks in total, so she counted four over and then seven servers down. There was a translucent spiderweb sticker over the front of the display.

"Found it," she whispered. "But the rack is locked."

"Wire cutters left side pouch," Jude said without turning to her. "Cut the cage and reach your hand in to open it."

"Well, look at you," Kenley said, grinning as she pulled the cutters out of his belt. She lifted herself on her toes and kissed his cheek. "Always the Boy Scout."

She registered his amused snort as she cut into the cabinet. After a few frantic minutes, she had a hole big enough for her arm to slip through and unlock the cabinet. She finally had access to Savant's game.

Kenley knelt and worked the server out of its slot, needing access to the back of it for the flash drive. Once she had it inserted, she needed to reboot the system, which would implode the system as a whole. While he might have a backup somewhere, she couldn't worry about that now. That was a problem for an older, more mature Kenley, who would pass her information to the government and let them deal with the evil genius.

The flash drive was cold in her palm as she gripped it, contorting herself enough to find the slot on the back of the server. Almost giddy, she slid the drive into the slot and smiled at Jude. Almost there. Savant used a headless server, meaning no monitor, keyboard, or mouse was in play. She had a keyboard in her backpack, but she hoped that if she unplugged the server, it would be enough to reboot it and bring it back online. She needed to plant this and get out, so Mina would have to tell them if the internal server destruction worked.

Kenley found the power cord and the backup power cord and pulled them both. When she pulled them, a bright light lit up the office in front of theirs. Since the rooms were glass boxes, the light was blinding. Kenley threw her arm up to her face as Jude did the same.

"You are in a tricky position, aren't you, Sickle," a voice said from the other office.

In one motion, Jude stepped in front of Kenley, who was still on the floor. He aimed the gun at the glass in front of them. "Who are you, and what do you want?"

"Let's ask Kenley who I am."

"Savant." The word dripped like poison from her lips. "Why all the games?"

"Because I like to win, Sickle."

"You're not going to win this time, Savant. People know."

"The people who know can do nothing to Spiderweb. The government couldn't work together long enough to tie a shoe, much less break the web I've built. I want to thank you for engaging with the program. You brought over seven hundred new cameras online for me. A drop in the bucket compared to the number of cameras worldwide, but I take satisfaction in knowing you'll beat yourself up over all seven hundred day after day."

Kenley grimaced, thankful Savant couldn't see that he was right. "Another few minutes and none of that will matter, Savant. I'll break the web while my friend kills the spider."

Savant's laughter ran a shudder down her spine.

"Why can't we see this guy?" Jude whispered.

"He likes to play games, but he's about to lose this one."

"I always wondered what it was like for a spider to watch its prey struggle in the web before it died. Watching you is giving me an insight into why they leave their victims there for a few days. As you swing in the wind, doing anything to break free and run is delightful to watch, but you may as well stop. You can't go anywhere. It's sad to think you can't run because of the people you've tried to stop all these years. How does it feel, Kenley, to know no matter how hard you try, the bad guys always win?"

"Shoot him. He deserves worse," Kenley growled at Jude, who didn't pull the trigger. She grasped the power cords to reattach to the server. She could almost see the lights flash from yellow to green and back to yellow.

"I wouldn't do that if I were you," a voice said from behind her just as the light in the other office went out.

Jude spun and angled his gun at the voice just as Kenley jammed the cords back into the server. There was a bright flash of light again. That was the last thing Kenley remembered as her world went dark.

Chapter Twenty-One

The monitors beside the bed beeped a steady rhythm, reassuring Jude more than annoying him. The sound was better than the rapid, irregular and scary rhythm he'd first heard when they got Kenley to the ER. She'd been out cold for hours now, and he was starting to worry that he might never see those sweet brown eyes again. She had to open them soon. He had so much he wanted to share with her about how wonderful their life could be together.

"You've got to wake up, Kenley," he whispered, stroking her forehead as the machines clicked and ticked around them. "I've spent my entire life making impossible choices, but this choice, the one I have to make about you, will be the easiest one I've ever made."

"Hey, Jude."

The words brought a smile to his lips, and he leaned forward, surprised to see her eyes open. He expected them to be dull and cloudy, but her brown eyes shone with clarity and honesty.

He rubbed her forehead with his thumb in a slow, steady rhythm. "Hey, sweet pea. I've never been happier to see those brown eyes pinned on me."

"What happened?" she asked, her voice hoarse. The

doctors had warned him her voice may come and go for a few days.

"You don't remember?"

Her eyes closed again momentarily, and she took a heavy breath when they reopened. "Savant."

Jude's lips tightened at the name, but he continued to stroke her forehead. "He set you up, sweet pea. We walked right into it."

"All I remember is the bright light in the office and him telling me I would lose." She stopped talking and moved her lips around as though her mouth was parched. He grabbed the cup from the stand and held the straw so she could take a drink. "Thanks. Did you stop him?"

"He was never there, Kenley."

"What? No. He was. We talked to him. He was behind the light, hiding like a coward."

"It was nothing more than smoke and mirrors," he said with a shake of his head. "Cal showed up within seconds of you being electrocuted and cleared the office. There was no one there. He used a spotlight to blind us and was patched into the coms system from somewhere remote."

"Electrocuted?"

Jude nodded as he gazed at the woman he'd fallen head over heels for in a matter of days. "He somehow electrified the server, and when you plugged the cords back in, you took a jolt."

"The server?"

"It was destroyed, but it wasn't the right server. Before he disappeared, he regaled me with the story about how you picked your ego over me, but you fell to his cunningness. Spiderweb remains."

"Electrocuted?" She lifted her hands to her face, turning

the white gauze mittens left and right in a dance of disbelief. "My hands!"

"Shh," he soothed her, his heart breaking as a tear leaked from her eye. "It's not as bad as it looks. You have second-degree burns on the palms and several fingers, but they don't think they'll need skin grafts. The dressings will be changed frequently to prevent infection."

"I'll still be able to work?"

"Yes," he promised. "But you'll need some time off to let them heal. We can worry about all of that tomorrow. Today, I want you to rest."

"I didn't pick my ego over you, Jude," Kenley whispered, her eyes fluttering closed for a moment before they snapped open to meet his gaze. "I did it *for* you."

She stressed the word so hard that he tipped his head in confusion. "For me?"

"For the chance to be with you. Our future was too uncertain if I didn't stop Spiderweb from growing. The only way to start a new life with you was to finish my old life and let it disappear. That's what I was trying to do."

"Because if Savant controls all the cameras, he can sell that to the highest bidder, and then we're all at risk?"

Her nod was slight against the pillow with its stark white pillowcase. Her bronze skin was a startling contrast to how full of life she still was just a few hours after nearly dying from electrocution.

"We might be an unconventional couple, but I still wanted a chance to be together," she whispered. "I wanted to experience the kind of love that people talk about, the kind my parents had before they died. I experienced it for the few days we were together, and selfishly, I wanted more. I wanted a life of that kind of love. I love you, Jude Mason. If I didn't believe in love at first sight, I do now. Maybe I was greedy in doing what I did, but I did it for us, not my ego."

"Shh," Jude whispered, wiping her tears with a tissue from the bedside. "I love you, too, sweet pea. You had me from the moment I heard your voice on the line. When you fell to the floor in that office, I turned my back to a monster to breathe for you until help arrived. I would have traded places with you if I could have, but all I could do was scream for help until Cal pulled me away so the EMTs could take over. I wanted the same chance you did but knew I'd blown it by not insisting we wait for backup."

"No, that was on me," she said with a weak smile. "I should have known Savant would do something dramatic to up the ante. That's how he rolls. He electrified the cabinet on demand?"

"It appears so. The police are still working the scene, but the last I heard, he was able to activate it remotely. The evidence response team said you were lucky. The server below the one you were working on took the biggest hit. You got a residual electrocution, but the one below it would have killed you."

A smile spread across Kenley's face as she lifted her gaze to his. "That's because he didn't want to destroy Spiderweb."

"I don't understand."

The doctors told him she might be confused or even have limited amnesia when she woke up. It appeared they were right, so he reminded himself to be patient with her.

"He wanted me to think the last server, number 7, was his. There was a spiderweb sticker across the front, so all signs pointed to it. He made it too obvious, Jude."

"You were working on the one above it…" The light had come on, and she smiled with a nod.

"I didn't know if that was right, but I took a chance. Did Mina try to get onto the site?"

"No, as soon as they told her you'd been electrocuted, she grabbed an Uber to the hospital. The team just left about an hour ago to head back to Secure Watch."

"Can you text her? Ask her to check the site. See if it loads."

"I will, but you need to rest."

"Once I know," she promised, biting her lip while he texted Mina and waited for her reply. "Savant has a copy of the program somewhere, but he'll have to lay low for a bit now. I hope we bought the government time to get a malware patch in place."

While he waited for Mina to reply, he stroked her forehead and gazed into her tired but bright and alive eyes. "I'll thank God you didn't fall for his ploy every day until I die, Kenley Bates. Everything about you is beautiful, and I want a second chance to protect you for the rest of your life."

"You don't need a second chance. If it weren't for you, I would be God knows where in Savant's lair. This whole thing has taught me the importance of not ignoring our personal safety. I was so focused on my digital safety that I forgot to protect my person, which was my downfall."

His phone beeped, and when he saw the customary greeting, he replied with their question. The response was immediate. "Mina is on it."

Kenley scooted to the edge of the bed. "Lay with me."

She didn't have to ask him twice. He kicked his shoes off and carefully climbed onto the bed, making sure not to jostle any of the wires or tubes that were monitoring the heart and lungs of the woman he loved. Jude just wanted her healthy, and he'd do anything to ensure that happened.

Settled with the blanket over her, he pulled her to him and

kissed the top of her head, his eyes going closed as he inhaled the scent of her, even if it was tempered with antiseptic. The phone beeped, and he couldn't help but feel like the next moment would dictate the course of his life from here forward. He lifted it to see a picture response. When he enlarged it, a smile spread across his face. A grim reaper stood against a black screen, a prosthesis on her right leg and a sickle over her shoulder as she was half turned to walk away. Jude showed her the picture, and her giggle of glee healed the fractured portion of his heart to make it whole again.

"I did it," she whispered, relief filling her voice. "Spiderweb is gone. Maybe not for good, but hopefully long enough to find him and destroy the program at its core."

"I love you, sweet pea," he whispered, wrapping his arms around her.

"I love you, too," she said, glancing up into his eyes. "Will you stay with me?"

"I wouldn't be anywhere else," he promised as her lids closed. As he lay there, the truth he had been unable to see all these years was evident. He didn't need to protect all the women in the world; he only needed to protect one. Now that she was in his arms, he was never letting go.

KENLEY EXITED THE conference room, and Jude stood, stretching his hand out for hers. As soon as she was close enough, she slipped hers into his, her soul calm again. It had been two weeks since her showdown with Savant. The burns on her hands had improved significantly, but she still wore fingerless compression gloves to protect the new skin as it grew in.

"How did it go?" he asked, helping her into his SUV before he jogged around to the driver's side.

"As expected."

"The FBI asked you to work for them?"

Her nod was immediate, but she laughed at the memory. "In at least six different ways and two different languages."

"What did you tell them?"

"No, in two different languages multiple different times."

"You're kidding, right? They didn't ask in two different languages?"

"I'm not kidding." Her laughter filled the car, and he joined in. "They legitimately asked me in English and Spanish—jokingly, I think, after I turned them down in English."

"You didn't have to turn them down on my account," Jude said as he pulled into a spot in front of a pizzeria.

"I didn't turn them down on your account. I turned them down on my account, Jude. I'm done tangling with Savant. He's no longer my problem. If they want to root this guy out of his hole, that's on them. I agreed to help them with situations where my skills can benefit them in exchange for one thing."

"Not working on the task force to find Savant?"

"No." She turned to him and took his hand. "They understood why I didn't want to be on the task force. I agreed to help their coders formulate a camera patch so his program can't control them if he brings it back online."

"Is there a patch that can do that if he's using machine learning?"

"I believe there is. The machine learning aspect has more to do with how the program finds the next camera after one spider is clicked. If we can write a firmware patch for the cameras that confuses the program on where to turn for its next target, eventually it will—" She made a bomb-exploding motion with her hands. "But writing that patch and convincing everyone to install it will take some time. Then again, maybe it won't once Homeland Security contacts the right people. The security world needs to know this was a legitimate threat that is still out there, at least until they can arrest Savant. I got the vibe that they'll do anything to get him into custody, so I suspect it won't be long before that happens."

"Good, he's a dangerous loose end they can't leave hanging. Especially as volatile as he is."

"Agreed. If they can find him, he'll face a whole host of charges, but Savant had nothing to do with my agreement to help them on the dark web. Instead, in exchange for my help, I asked them to investigate Staun Bril Corporation for negligence." Jude's eyes widened, and Kenley grimaced. "Sorry for just dropping that on you, but I didn't know how to tell you I planned to ask them."

"So you just didn't tell me?" Jude asked, clearly hurt. "I'm not sure how I feel about that."

"Don't be upset," Kenley begged. "I was going back and forth on whether I should even ask them. I almost didn't, but when they wanted my help, I decided to go for a give-and-take exchange. Rather than take payment, I want Staun Bril to be investigated. If their crimes are egregious enough, the feds can shut them down."

"If they shut them down, it will be harder to get a settlement, right?"

"Not from what they told me. They said it can go two different ways. They can shut them down and liquidate their assets to pay any lawsuits if they find evidence of negligence. On the other hand, the company can agree to pay any lawsuits, plead guilty to negligence if that can be proven, and remain in business if they fix the problems."

"But it all hinges on proving they're negligent," Jude said, and Kenley nodded. "I promised to give them all the information I have, including access to the forum where all the victims are." She held up her hand. "I'll be transparent about why I'm doing it and move the forum to the World Wide Web where everything is on the up-and-up. That way, anyone on the forum who isn't comfortable talking to the feds doesn't have to join the new forum. It will be a place where anyone else injured by one of their machines can join if a class action lawsuit is filed."

"I must admit, I like the idea of you not being on the dark web where Savant can find you."

"I'll be easier to find on the World Wide Web, but it's riskier for Savant to touch me there. If the FBI has a job for me that I have to work underground, I'll have a new name and persona each time, even if they catch Savant."

"I feel much better about that," he said, kissing her knuckles. "Come on, let's go get dinner. You've had a long day."

She waited for him to come around and open her door, feeling that long day settle into her bones. Her meeting with the government entities had started at 8:00 a.m., and now it was nearly 6:00 p.m. All in all, she was glad it was over. She'd been dreading it since she got out of the hospital and made her way back to her little town house in Milwaukee. Jude had stayed with her, working remotely for Secure Watch from her house while she tried to pick up the pieces of her business part-time while letting her hands heal. Now that this meeting was over, they would have to decide about their future. As Jude opened the door and took her hand, she knew she didn't care what they did as long as they were together.

"I should have asked if you wanted pizza," Jude said as he held the door open for her.

"Pizza is great," Kenley assured him, leaning into his shoulder. "I know you've been craving it since you've been at my place. 'No one makes pizza the way Chicago makes pizza' has never been said more by anyone in the last two weeks." She winked jokingly, and he dropped a kiss on her lips.

"But it's true, though. I'll have to figure out how to get my fix now that I won't live here."

"You're moving?" The surprise had her pulling back on his hand as they entered the restaurant. "You didn't mention that."

"I guess we've both been keeping some secrets from each other," he said, his eyebrow raised. "I'm moving to Minnesota."

Kenley's heart sank, but a familiar voice spoke before she could say more. "It's about time you got here."

"Mina!" Kenley exclaimed, coming face-to-face with the woman who had become a friend over the last few weeks. "I can't believe you're here!"

"We decided it was time to meet the woman who saved the world."

"We saved the world together," Kenley said, her smile bright. "Wait. We?"

"The whole gang," Mina said with a wink.

Kenley threw her arms around Mina and embraced her. "Thank you for everything. For the record, I couldn't have done it without Jude, you and the rest of the team."

Mina motioned them to follow her, and Jude put his hand on Kenley's back as they walked into a small banquet room full of people she'd never met. A giant sign hanging over a buffet table said, WELCOME KENLEY.

"Welcome Kenley?" she asked, turning to Jude, who was grinning like the Cheshire cat as the man she knew as Cal stepped forward.

"It's so good to see you up and moving, Kenley," he said, squeezing her shoulder rather than shaking her hand.

"It's nice to meet you in person finally, Cal. Well, all of

you!" The group, which, on quick headcount, was over a dozen people, laughed and nodded as they waved from their positions around the room. Her friend Delilah stepped forward, and Kenley squealed and hurried to her. "You're here!"

"Of course! After all, you did call me. I'd apologize for not answering, but I think things turned out exactly how they were supposed to."

Kenley glanced at Jude, who was still standing in the same place, but all his attention was on her. "I know you're right all the way to my core." After a quick hug, Kenley stepped back and took Delilah's hand. "You look happier than I've ever seen you. I can't wait to catch up and hear all about your honeymoon. First, it seems, we have some pizza to eat."

"Actually," Cal said, motioning to Mina. "We brought you here for a reason."

Mina nodded and motioned at the people standing around the room. Some she'd met, and others she hadn't, but they all wore a Secure Watch or Secure One polo shirt, so she could only assume they all worked together. "I spoke with some of my former colleagues while you were on your way over, and they informed me, much to their chagrin, that you had turned down all of their job offers."

"Yes, ma'am," she said with a nod. "The last thing I want to do is work for the government."

"Good. Then I'm hoping you'll come to work for us," Mina said with a smile.

"I don't know if I'll have time to do contract work along with my business," Kenley said, her heart sinking. Jude said he was moving to Minnesota, and she realized that meant he would be working at Secure Watch.

"She means instead of your business, sweet pea," Jude said from behind her.

When she turned, she nearly ran straight into him. "Like sell my business and work at Secure Watch exclusively?"

"It's not so bad," Cal said, probably hearing the surprise in her voice. "We had five new cabins built on the property this past year. There's room for everyone."

When she glanced back at Jude, he had gotten down on one knee. "I was hoping you might want to share one with me." He pulled out a black box from his pocket and cracked it open. Inside was a teardrop diamond solitaire. "Sorry, sweet pea, it's only a carat," he winked.

Kenley put her hands to her mouth in shock. Was he proposing less than a month from the first time they met? "Are you serious?"

"As I've ever been about anything." He smiled, but she heard the nerves in his voice. "Has it only been three weeks since we met? Yes. Does that matter when I know you're the woman I want to spend the rest of my life with? No. So, I'm down here on one knee asking you to marry me because my gut said you might feel the same way. If you don't want to leave your business, we'll figure it out. All I want is for you to be my wife."

"I put my business up for sale last Friday. I planned to move to Chicago to be closer to you."

"Sounds like you two need to work on communicating better," Lucas said from behind her.

"They were communicating, just not with words," Roman said, dragging groans and laughter from everyone.

Carefully, Kenley knelt and pressed her forehead to Jude's. The laughter and good-natured ribbing around them were drowned out by the beat of their hearts together. "You're sure? You really want to marry the hot mess that is me?"

"Every last burning ember," he answered.

"Then you better put that ring on it and make it official,"

she said. "Let's make it a short engagement. What's your schedule look like tomorrow?"

His laughter filled her to overflowing as he slid the ring on her finger and planted his lips on hers. Their friends clapped and cheered when he helped her up. When she flashed her finger in the air, the ring twinkled under the lights and threw rainbows across the faces of the people she would now call family.

"It looks like we'll be putting in an application for one of those cabins, Cal," Kenley said as Jude slid his arms around her waist.

"Application accepted and approved!" Cal exclaimed. "Let's eat!" Several servers were loading pizza on the buffet, and with whoops of excitement, everyone streamed toward the table to grab plates of the gooey masterpieces.

Kenley turned in Jude's arms and smiled. "I love you, Mr. Mason."

"Not a smidgen as much as I love you, sweet pea," he whispered, lowering his nose to touch hers. "Are you ready for a fresh start?"

"As long as I'm with you, I'm ready for anything. I couldn't be more excited about a new adventure or living a lighter and happier life with you."

"I'll spend every day from here forward making you happy. I'll start by kissing you right before feeding you a slice of Chicago's best pizza. It's better than wedding cake."

"Well, that's yet to be determined," Kenley whispered. "I'll have to have the wedding cake to make that kind of life decision."

"Set the date, and I'll be there."

"November 21st sounds like the perfect day," she said, leaning closer.

His brow went up as he stared down at her. "That's next week."

"Just enough time to get a license, dress, cake and a justice of the peace. I don't see any reason to wait, do you?"

"Not one," he agreed, lowering his lips to hers. "Tonight, I promise you'll have everything you'll ever want in this life, Kenley Bates."

She had no doubt, because the only thing she'd ever want was him.

* * * * *

CLIFFSIDE KIDNAPPING

CARIDAD PIÑEIRO

To dearest Axel, the new member of our family.
May you grow up with a love of reading
and always have a book in your hand!

Chapter One

Mercedes Gonzalez Whitaker relaxed in the passenger seat, appreciating the fresh pine scent wafting through the open window and the kaleidoscope of greens in the fields and mountains along the highway. The deep jewellike colors of the evergreens and lighter almost silvery gray of the aspens dotted the Colorado landscape. As dusk descended, the chill of night replaced the warmth of the day. So different from the heat and humidity of a Washington, DC, June or the weather she'd experienced growing up in Miami.

It was why she loved coming out here for the annual gatherings with the Whitaker clan and why she and her husband, Robert, would sneak out in the fall to watch the changing of the foliage, especially the aspens, as large stands of the poplars painted the hillsides with streaks of gold. Robert had once told her how aspens grew via their roots, creating glades of clones that were all one living organism, sometimes acres in size.

Much like her Cuban Miami family had spread their roots and grown, the patriarchs standing tall in the center while their children and grandchildren became ever stronger and likewise prospered. She missed being around her sprawling and loving Gonzalez family. Robert loved spending time with them as well and maybe it was time to visit them soon.

Robert, she thought with a loving sigh and gazed at her husband as he drove.

The years have been kind to him. There were the barest hints of silver at his temples and the faintest smile lines at the corners of his bright hazel eyes. Handsome and he still stole her breath away.

Smiling, she reached over to brush the back of her hand across his cheek. It was sandpapery rough with the start of an evening beard.

He shot her a quick look from the corner of his eye. "Everything okay?"

"I was just thinking that when this is over, we should visit the family in Miami. Lately, I feel like we don't spend enough time with them and with your family here in Colorado."

Peering at her again, he said, "Maybe it's time to consider retiring. It'll give us more time with both families. We have enough years put in at the NSA, and those DC winters…"

He didn't need to finish because they both hated the northeast cold and damp. Despite the fact they'd been living in the DC area and working for the National Security Agency for nearly thirty years, she often missed the warmth of Miami in wintertime and the palm trees decorated with Christmas lights.

"Maybe," she said, closing her eyes and smiling as she imagined sitting poolside in December and, more importantly, spending time with her children and the rest of the Gonzalez family.

A hard jolt and the sudden swerve of their sedan jerked her from that pleasant daydream.

"What the—" Robert muttered and fought to keep the car under control as another more powerful blow threatened to drive them off the road.

Mercedes braced her hands on the dashboard and console as another shot against their rear bumper sent the nose of the vehicle toward a small ditch on the side of the highway.

Robert yanked the steering wheel hard, knuckles white with pressure. Miraculously, he kept the car from tumbling off the road.

She whirled in her seat to see a large black pickup behind them increase its speed and ram the back of their sedan again. Metal groaned and crunched as the pickup shoved the car toward the ditch.

"Rob?" she said. Fear gripped her as her husband frantically fought the wheel and accelerated away from the pickup.

The engine roared as he created a fragile distance, but then their assailant raced past them and clipped their front fender.

They said those last moments of your life passed in slow motion and Mercedes understood it now. Images of her children, husband and family slipped across her mind as the sedan flew off the edge of the road, seemingly floating in space for long minutes until the hood of the car smashed into the ditch.

CBI AGENT RYDER HUNT wasn't supposed to meet with the Whitakers until morning. But when his friend and Regina police chief, Jackson Whitaker, had called to say his aunt and uncle hadn't arrived as expected, the Colorado Bureau of Investigation agent had stuffed necessities into a bag, leashed his corgi, Delilah, and packed both for the trip to Regina.

He had been on his way when the report had come across the police scanner.

Doubling back to the road where an abandoned car had been found after a Good Samaritan phoned it in, he prayed his gut was wrong about it being the Whitakers' car. The road wasn't commonly used to go from the airport to Regina, but someone familiar with the area might use the bypass to avoid traffic.

Robert Whitaker was familiar with the area.

A sick feeling filled Ryder's stomach as he pulled up behind the squad car on the edge of the highway. Flashing lights shot streams of red and blue across the night sky, warning of danger.

After a quick command to Delilah to stay put, Ryder hurried to where one of the officers stood staring at the sedan precariously positioned in a ditch. A quick look at the red-and-white license plate confirmed it was a rental car and his blood ran cold.

The Whitakers would have been driving a rental car.

The state patrol officer faced him as he approached, and he flashed his badge to identify himself. "CBI Agent Hunt."

"Officer Sanchez," she said and motioned to the car. "Looks like it was forced off the road. See the damage to the rear bumper and front fender? I called Denver PD so they could send a CSI unit and detectives."

"Smart move, Officer Sanchez," he said and shifted closer to examine the damage. Much like the young officer had noted, angry gouges, dents and crumpled metal marred the back bumper and the front driver's-side fender.

"My partner is running the plate so we can determine which rental company it belongs to," Sanchez advised.

Ryder nodded. "Do you have an evidence collection kit?"

"I do. I'll go get it." The officer hurried to the trunk of the squad car. He followed but hung back slightly to get a better view of the crime scene because he had no doubt that's what it was.

Hunkering down on his haunches, he scrutinized the roadway, trying to pick out anything unusual. There were some indentations a few feet ahead of the rental car. He walked over and bent down again to peer at the road. Tire tracks and, from this angle, he detected drag marks from the open driver's-side door to the roadway.

Whoever had been driving had been pulled from the car and moved to a second vehicle.

Walking back to the squad car, he paused to glance toward the passenger's-side door, but it was darker there and hard to see. As he returned to the squad car, Officer Sanchez handed him the evidence kit and latex gloves.

Smiling, he said, "Thank you. Could you do me a favor and walk up about ten feet from the front of the rental car? You'll see tire tracks on the road. Please make sure CSI stays clear of them when they arrive."

The officer headed that way and, as if on cue, an unmarked car as well as a CSI van slowly drove past the squad car.

As requested, Officer Sanchez waved them well beyond the front of the rental car and any evidence.

A second later, her partner walked up to him and introduced himself. "Officer Ryan," the young patrol officer said.

"CBI Agent Ryder Hunt," he said and flashed his badge.

"I got a hit on the license plate. It's from a rental car company at the airport," Officer Ryan said.

"Good work. Why don't you give them a call and find out who rented it while I work with the detectives and CSI team?"

With a nod, the officer stepped away and Ryder hurried toward the officers who had just arrived. Within minutes, he pointed out his initial findings and they got busy taking photos and preserving evidence along the roadway.

Officer Ryan returned with the news Ryder had feared from the moment he'd pulled up to the scene. The officer flipped through his notepad and said, "The vehicle was rented to a Robert Whitaker, who checked it out of the lot a couple of hours ago."

"Thank you, Officer Ryan. If you'll excuse me," he said and walked away to make the dreaded call.

His friend answered after only one ring. "Jackson. I have some bad news."

"Good morning and welcome to Flight 3758 to Denver. If you're not going to Denver, you're going to have a really bad day," the flight attendant chirped with a bright smile and then launched into her spiel about the plane's safety features.

The woman's cheeriness made Sophie Whitaker's head throb. She slipped on her headphones to avoid the drivel and get some rest. After the call from her cousin Jackson, Sophie hadn't been able to sleep more than a few fitful minutes at a time. Her mind had been too busy replaying the video call from her parents the day before.

"We'll only be gone for about a week," Mercedes Gonzalez Whitaker had said.

Her father, Robert, had tacked on, "We just wanted to get some time alone with Jackson before the new baby arrives."

Sophie had worried something was wrong with her cousin Jackson, who had recently become chief of police in Regina, or his newlywed wife, Rhea, who was expecting their first child in only a few weeks. But her parents had reassured her that everything was fine.

Yet Sophie had sensed dangerous undercurrents in their demeanor from the deep furrow plowing across her mother's forehead to their forced smiles, as brittle as eggshells.

Her brother, Robbie, had tried to reassure her that everything was okay, but that sense of impending doom had lingered throughout the day as she and Robbie had worked on a new investigation at the family's South Beach Security Agency in Miami.

Jackson's call the night before that her parents were missing had only confirmed that she'd been right to worry. Especially when Jackson had admitted that her parents had been coming to Regina to help him with a case he was working with Ryder Hunt, an agent with the Colorado Bureau of Investigation.

She'd tried to pry more out of her cousin, but he'd been reticent to discuss anything over the phone or to send her any materials since he suspected they had either a leak or some kind of hack in his police department. That was the only explanation for why someone had known about her parents' involvement in the case and when they'd be arriving in Denver.

Unable to shut off her thoughts, she turned to her brother and noticed that Robbie had dozed off. She suspected that he hadn't gotten much sleep either and was using the plane ride for a catnap.

She closed her eyes again, trying to rest. She'd need to be sharp when they finally met with Jackson and Agent Ryder Hunt.

Ryder Hunt. She'd found a picture of him and several other agents on the CBI's Facebook page. They'd been receiving honors for their work on various investigations.

In her mind's eye, she recalled the photo of the glowering man who might be handsome if he smiled. He'd been dressed in a suit and tie but something about the photo had made her think that he'd be more comfortable in a cowboy hat and boots. He had that rough-and-tumble look, as if the suit was barely restraining him.

She didn't doubt that once on a case, nothing could hold back CBI Agent Hunt.

Sophie was sure the investigation was the reason for her parents' disappearance. It had to be, she told herself over and over until the soft bump and increasing whoosh of the engines dragged her awake.

The flight attendant's voice crackled across the loudspeakers. "Welcome to Denver. The temperature is currently seventy degrees but have a jacket ready for the evening when the temps will dip to the forties with the possibility of snow. We'll be at the Jetway shortly, so make sure to gather all your belongings."

Sophie snagged her knapsack from beneath the seat and Robbie grabbed his bag. A second later, he stepped into the aisle to bring down their carry-ons. They had traveled light to save time and Jackson was waiting for them at the pickup area.

Sophie nearly jumped out of her skin during what seemed like an interminable wait until they were able to deplane. Once her feet hit the tiled floor of the terminal, she raced to the exits, Robbie at her side.

She spotted her cousin the moment she stepped out of the terminal. Jackson stood at the curb, wearing a white Stetson, his police uniform and the shiny gold badge that said "Chief" on his chest. She was about to race into his arms when a man wearing a rumpled dark blue suit joined Jackson.

Agent Ryder Hunt. She recognized him immediately from the CBI Facebook photo. He was even more dangerously handsome in person. Fighting back an unwanted reaction, she waited for Jackson to introduce him.

RYDER SUCKED IN a breath as his gaze locked with the beautiful woman's tired and icy-blue stare.

Jackson's cousins, he presumed, as she and a man who had to be her brother walked up to them. There was too much resemblance between the two with their similar Roman noses, dimpled chins and engaging blue eyes.

Jackson hugged her, shook the man's hand and then introduced him.

"Ryder, these are my cousins Josefina and Robert. Sophie and Robbie to family," he said with a wave of his hand in their direction.

"Sophie. Robbie," he said with a dip of his head.

"Agent Hunt," Sophie said, the unexpected chill in her voice matching the ice in her eyes and her curt nod.

Robbie held out his hand and smiled. "Nice to meet you, Ryder. I wish it was under different circumstances."

"I do as well. Jax asked me to come with him so I could fill you in on the case while we drive to Regina," Ryder explained, popping open the door of the black SUV emblazoned with the Regina police emblem.

"Is that where you found my parents' rental car?" Sophie asked as she paused by the door.

Ryder shook his head. "No. The sedan was located just on the outskirts of Denver. We'll be coordinating with Denver PD on any evidence or leads they get. We'll find them, Sophie. I promise you."

Sophie nodded and her gaze warmed slightly with his words. "We will," she said and stepped into the SUV.

Ryder slipped into the front passenger seat and, once they were all settled, Jackson pulled away to start the hour-long drive to Regina. That would give him time to brief them on the investigation.

He half turned in the seat so that he could see them, especially Sophie. He'd have to be dead not to acknowledge not only what a beautiful woman she was but the intelligence in her aqua-colored eyes. "Jackson reached out to me when he realized evidence had been stolen from the Regina Police Department and the corresponding CBI digital records were also gone."

Sophie narrowed her gaze and said, "Let me make sure I'm getting this right. Someone stole physical evidence and hacked your database to remove any trace of it?"

"That's right. Jackson was investigating the physical theft and asked me to find out what I could about the loss of the digital records. When I realized there had likely been a hack and advised Jax, he suggested I reach out to your parents," Ryder confirmed.

"Because our parents are experts with the NSA," Robbie interjected.

Jackson nodded. "I never expected something like this might happen. If I had, I wouldn't have placed them in such danger."

"What did happen? You found the car. What did it tell you?" Sophie asked, her mind racing to gather information.

Ryder coughed uneasily, worried about sharing what they'd found, but Robbie said, "We can handle it, Ryder. We deal with this kind of thing all the time."

Ryder knew Jackson's cousins worked for some fancy investigative and security agency in Miami, but this case involved family. That made it way more complicated.

Sophie seemed to read his mind. "We've had to handle investigations involving attacks on our family. We can deal."

The way she said it was almost too clinical, which worried him that she wasn't handling this well at all. Despite that, he answered her prior questions. "The vehicle had been forced off the road. The airbags had deployed and..." He hesitated, but Sophie pressed him to continue.

"Go on, Ryder," she said, her tone almost pleading now.

"There was blood on both airbags. It's not uncommon for

people to have minor injuries when airbags deploy, and it was a small amount of blood."

"Probably a nosebleed or minor cut," Jackson chimed in and shot a quick look at them in the rearview mirror.

"You're sure it was just that?" Robbie pressed and grabbed hold of Sophie's hand.

"We're sure. You don't need to worry that they were seriously injured," Ryder said.

"Only that someone was deadly serious about kidnapping them," Sophie replied, voice tight with fear.

Jackson peered at him for the barest second, as if begging him to keep silent, but Ryder thought his cousins demanded complete honesty. "Someone is serious about keeping them from investigating this case. We believe it's State Senator Connell Oliver. He was being prosecuted for an alleged rape that occurred within Regina PD jurisdiction."

Jackson added, "A woman claimed that Oliver had raped her. They met at a popular ski resort not far from Oliver's vacation home. They started chatting, had a drink or two, and he invited her back to his home where the rape occurred."

"And you had physical evidence of this?" Sophie pressed.

Jackson nodded. "We did. When she made the allegation, we took steps to preserve evidence and sent it to the CBI for processing along with Oliver's DNA when we obtained it. We had enough evidence to prosecute, but now…without the DNA evidence, the case will be much harder to prove."

"Which is why you called in Ryder and our parents? To find out how the evidence was stolen from your office and the records destroyed at the CBI?" Robbie asked, clearly wanting to dot every i and cross every t.

"It is," Ryder confirmed. "We also feared that if someone had figured out how to wipe records from the CBI, they could do it for other cases and maybe even—"

"Find out how to hack CODIS or AFIS. That's why my parents said yes to helping out, isn't it?" Sophie said.

"It's why they came to help. They wanted to make sure all those databases were protected. They're too important to law enforcement to be compromised," Ryder said.

A long silence followed as Jackson's cousins digested that, but then Sophie said, "Whoever it is, whether Oliver or someone else, they want to stop that at all costs, including kidnapping our parents. Why not just kill them? Wouldn't that have been easier?" Her voice was hoarse, emotion nearly overwhelming her as she tried to stay in investigator mode.

"The fact that they took them means they need them for something. Maybe it's to hide their tracks," Ryder said.

"Or crack the other databases and your backup files. What is your backup procedure at either location?" Robbie asked.

An embarrassed flush worked across Jackson's face. "I hate to say our backup procedures weren't up to snuff. We're a small police force and this kind of thing was…unexpected," he admitted.

"So, no backup. What about you, Agent Hunt?" Sophie queried.

"I'm told we have a 3-2-1 strategy. Two backups were on-site, one on tape and the other on a hard disk. The last copy was at our IT company's off-site server," he advised.

"'Was'? So it's gone?" she pressed.

Ryder nodded. "It's gone from there and our servers. We've located backups from last month and are examining them to see if the evidence can be restored."

"Someone wants it disappeared, and maybe other data as well. Do you know if Oliver is connected to any criminal elements?" Robbie asked.

With a dip of his head, Jackson said, "It's been rumored that Oliver has ties to the wrong kinds of people. We think they might have been the ones to help him get rid of the evidence."

"And get rid of our parents when they're done with them," Sophie said softly.

"That's not going to happen, Sophie. We will get to the bottom of this," Ryder said, strong conviction in his tone.

Sophie nodded but bit her full bottom lip with worry for a second before she said, "We will find them. We have to find them."

There was nothing else Ryder could say to reassure her. He only nodded and turned his attention to the road. They'd be in Regina in less than an hour and once they arrived…

He wanted to believe they could solve this before anything else happened to the Whitakers. Only it seemed that for every step forward, they were forced to take two steps back, and he was tired of always being behind.

Once they got to Regina, he intended to find a way to change all that.

Chapter Two

After the car crash, Mercedes had been slightly dazed and confused. Hard hands had pulled her from the vehicle, yanked a hood over her head and zip-tied her hands.

She remembered being tossed into a van and, seconds later, the floor vibrating beneath her as something landed beside her with a thud and a groan.

Rob, she had realized.

Robert and she had ripped off their hoods and checked for injuries.

Luckily, the blood on Rob's face was just from a broken nose and she had only a small cut on her eyebrow courtesy of the airbag. She was sure they'd be achy in the morning, but nothing seemed broken.

The back of the van was dark and all they could do was huddle there, wondering how to get free. Wondering why someone had grabbed them, and when their nephew Jackson would realize they had been taken.

The van had driven for at least an hour before it stopped. Whether they had gone in the direction of Regina, she couldn't tell. But as the back door opened, she caught a glimpse of familiar mountains before their abductors jerked the masks over their heads again and forced them from the rear of the van.

Their captors had donned ski masks to hide their faces, which she took as a good sign. If they couldn't be identified, they might not kill Robert and her. Or at least that's what she hoped.

"What do you want with us?" Mercedes said as the men pushed them forward and she stumbled on uneven ground.

"Shut up," the man beside her said, grabbing hold of her arm and dragging her upright.

"They're going to be looking for us," Robert said, which earned him a backhanded slap.

"We said shut up," the other man said and shoved Robert, who knocked into her.

Rough hands hauled her onto a padded seat and buckled her tight. Rob was buckled in beside her and, a minute later, they started to move.

Cold air whipped around them during a noisy, bumpy and bone-jarring ride. Over and over, she flew up and came down hard or got jostled from side to side on uneven ground.

The chill worked into her bones, and she shivered, praying for the ride to end.

When it did and their captors shut off the engine for what she suspected was an ATV, blessed silence filled the night.

Footsteps, soft as if on pine needles, sounded for a second before one of the men unbuckled her and dragged her from the seat and onto the ground.

With a shove, he pushed her forward but then wrenched her to a sudden stop. The squeak and groan of a door opening told her they'd reached some kind of structure. Between the dark of the night and the mask, it was hard to see anything, but the larger shape in front of her seemed to be a building of some sort.

Her captor tugged her inside and, seconds later, she heard another creak. With a forceful shove, the man thrust her into the space. Robert stumbled in, knocking against her back before the heavy clang of the door registered.

"Scream all you want. No one will hear you. As for escaping, good luck with that," one of the men said. The sound of their footsteps moving away and the squeak and groan of another door warned that they'd left.

With their captors gone, they pulled off their hoods.

Mercedes peered at the space where they'd been imprisoned. An old jail of some kind. They had been locked into the sole cell.

"First things first," she said and stared down at her zip-tied hands. Even in her dazed state after the crash, she'd remembered some of the NSA-required SERE training that had taught them how to survive, evade, resist and escape. She had clenched her fists and positioned her palms downward so that the bindings were not as tight. Working her hands back and forth, she managed to get one thumb free. That made it possible to slip her hands from the zip ties.

"Good work," Robert said. He tried to free himself, but his bindings were tighter. She searched the dark for anything she could use to cut his ties. Nearby, there were markings on the stone walls of the cell. Someone had been scratching lines onto the stone as if keeping track of days. Peering downward, she noticed a hand-sized rock with one pointy end that had likely been used to etch the wall.

She grabbed it, approached her husband and motioned for him to hold his hands up. Wedging the sharp end beneath the zip tie, she rubbed back and forth, pleased as the stone bit into the plastic until the binding fell free.

Robert embraced her tightly. "We'll get out of here somehow," he said as they walked to the door of their cell.

Together, they jerked and yanked on the heavy metal bars. They were thick with rust and she'd hoped age had weakened them, but they held fast. They stepped away and looked around for another avenue of escape.

A window sat high up in their cell wall but it, too, had heavy metal bars and was too small for either of them to slip through. But it could give them a clue as to where they might be.

"Help me up," she said, and Robert gave her a boost so she could take a look. As she had thought before, familiar mountains. Possibly a ski trail not all that far away, she assumed from the break in the tree line. They weren't at the top of the mountain, but close.

When she dropped back down, she said, "I think we're near the ski resort just outside town."

Robert shook his head in disbelief. "Why bring us here? Why so close to Jackson and Agent Hunt?"

"And close to Connell Oliver. His vacation home is nearby too. He's got to have something to do with this, but why escalate from a rape to kidnapping? What do they want with us?" she said and shivered.

The temperature had dropped dramatically, and cold air swept in through the broken glass of the window.

Robert took her into his arms again. Relief and warmth flooded her with his gentle touch and his calm words. "We do whatever they want until we can figure out how to get free," Robert said and cradled her face with his hands.

She forced a smile and laid her forehead against his. "We will survive this."

"We will, my love." He kissed her and his love gave her hope as it always did.

They were alive and, for now, that was all that mattered.

SOPHIE HAD ALWAYS loved visiting Regina to see the Whitaker side of the family. The July visits helped them get away from the heat and humidity of DC and Miami summers and, in mid-February, they enjoyed the ski slopes and hiking trails around town.

Regina was a postcard-perfect town with a charming downtown. An assortment of shops served the locals as well as the tourists who came to hike or ski the mountains, or visit the nearby lake for fishing and water sports.

The police station was much as she remembered and looked like something on a movie set. The building had the same enchanting style as the other structures along Main Street. Wide steps leading to the front door were flanked by terraced gardens filled with the blues, yellows and pinks of hyacinths, daffodils and tulips.

Their cheeriness was in stark contrast to the turmoil they were all feeling as they walked into the station. A young female sergeant welcomed them back and came around the desk to hand Ryder the leash to a stubby, short corgi, who barked happily at the sight of him.

Ryder smiled—she had been right about how handsome he was when he smiled—and bent to rub the dog's chubby sides.

"Yes, I'm back, Delilah," he said with a chuckle, standing and smiling at the desk sergeant. "Thanks for watching her, Milly."

"My pleasure, Ryder," the woman said, a flirtatious gleam in her eye that unexpectedly annoyed Sophie. "I don't mind watching her for longer if you need me to."

Ryder grinned, handed her back the leash and said, "That would be great. She gets a little rambunctious around crowds."

Milly returned to her desk, buzzed them through, and they hurried to a conference room at the back of the station.

"Make yourself at home," Jackson said and waved to the conference room table.

Sophie and Robbie walked over, set down their knapsacks and pulled out their laptops.

Ryder closed the door, leaned against it and crossed well-muscled arms against his broad chest. He shot an uneasy glower at Jackson and coughed before he said, "Jax and I are worried that the systems here are compromised, but we haven't had a chance to confirm that."

"Understandable. They knew when our parents were coming in," Robbie said.

Sophie held out her hand and wiggled her fingers. "Let's start with your phones."

Ryder shared a questioning look with Jackson but then acquiesced, as did Jackson.

Robbie and she immediately got to work loading protection programs and scanning for malware. While they waited for the searches to finish, she pulled out a radiofrequency detector from her knapsack.

"Trey lent us this to check for any hidden bugs in the office," Sophie explained.

"Trey? Who's Trey?" Ryder asked, dark brows crinkling over his puzzled cocoa gaze.

"So sorry. Our cousin Ramon Gonzalez the Third, which is why we call him Trey. He's assumed leadership of South Beach Security," Robbie said.

"Your family's agency," Ryder said just to confirm.

Sophie nodded. "It's where we work in Miami with our Gonzalez cousins."

"Jax speaks highly of them and of you." Ryder visibly relaxed.

"We think highly of Jax as well," Sophie replied and quickly tacked on, "As soon as the scans on the phones are done, we'll have to power them down as well as any other cell phones in the building. We need to do the same to your Wi-Fi so that we can detect any signals from a hidden camera or microphone."

"I'll ask people to shut off their phones and then I guess you can check them out as well. As soon as you're ready, let me know and I'll have Milly the desk sergeant call IT to cut off the Wi-Fi," Jackson said and walked out of the room.

"Do you think that will be necessary at my CBI location?" Ryder asked and gestured to the device she held.

Sophie shrugged and shook her head. "I'm not sure. It's more likely that your leak is here, and it may be the same person who stole the physical evidence."

"They've probably been compromised by Oliver or his people," Ryder suggested.

Robbie nodded. "Do you know if Jackson has surveillance video of the evidence room area?"

With a dip of his head, Ryder said, "He does. Jax insisted on installing CCTV and making some other changes around here when he became chief, but there was a blip in the video and the digital log for who checked in and out of the area is also gone."

Sophie let out a low whistle. "They tampered with that also. We'll have to check the firewalls as well as any other security systems on the servers."

"Sometimes I wonder if Jax shouldn't have kept to the old-fashioned way of signing in and out of the evidence room," Ryder said with a shake of his head before plowing on. "My IT people checked our CBI servers and found an open port, which might have allowed the hack, and closed it."

"Hopefully that's enough, but if you'd like, we can make some suggestions on additional steps you can take," Robbie said and opened his laptop.

"That would be appreciated." Ryder glanced at Sophie. "Do you need passwords and the like to log on?"

Sophie pursed her lips, hesitated, and shook her head. "We're going to try and hack in. It'll help us shore up any holes, but it may also give us some clues about the hacker."

Ryder's mahogany-brown brows shot up in surprise. "Clues? Really? Like what?"

"Like how talented they are," Robbie said from his spot at his laptop.

Jackson walked back into the room. "Phones are off. Let me know when to shut off the Wi-Fi."

RYDER WATCHED AS Sophie took a quick look at their smartphones to see if the scans had finished and smiled. "Done. Both phones are clean."

She gave his phone back, but as her hand brushed his, a blast of heat shot up his arm. When she pulled away shakily and a flush of color erupted across her cheeks, he realized she had been affected by that simple touch as well.

"Please ask IT to cut the Wi-Fi," Sophie said with an elegant wave of her hand at her cousin.

Jackson grabbed the conference room phone and called the front desk. "It's time, Milly."

Sophie nodded and the men followed her as she walked through the station house, passing the detector over assorted areas and watching for any signs of a signal. Based on her behavior, it seemed to Ryder that she wasn't finding anything in the central area where there were half a dozen desks for the Regina police officers. She continued to a duo of nearby interview rooms, three cells for holding prisoners, the conference room and an adjacent break room. From there she went to an office for Jackson's second-in-command and then finally to Jackson's new office.

But after sweeping Jackson's office, she shook her head, blew out a frustrated breath and murmured, "Nothing."

"Nothing?" Jackson said, surprise in his tone.

Sophie nodded. "But that doesn't mean someone wasn't spying on you."

Ryder closed the door to Jackson's office, understanding what Sophie was implying. He'd almost hoped that she had found something because that might have meant it was possibly someone other than one of Jackson's officers. "They probably did it the old-fashioned way. They either eavesdropped or searched your office," Ryder said.

With a determined nod, Sophie said, "Exactly. Did you write the information down anywhere?"

Jackson shook his head. "I didn't, which means they must have been nearby and overheard it." With a rougher shake of his head, he asked, "You think one of my officers is involved? That they're dirty?"

Ryder understood what his friend was feeling. You trusted your fellow officers. You relied on them to watch your back. "I know it's tough for you to imagine that, Jax."

"It is. I've been with most of these officers for some time. I'd trust most of them with my life," he said.

"Or my parents' lives," Sophie said in a too-calm voice, making Jackson instantly regret his words.

"I'm sorry, Sophie. As hard as it will be, we will follow any leads including to any of my officers," Jackson said with a rueful nod of his head.

"I'm sorry, too, Jax. I can't even begin to imagine how hard this must be for you," Sophie said, which raised her a lot in Ryder's estimation. He appreciated that, as hard as it was for her, she was willing to support her cousin in his moment of pain and betrayal.

"Where do we go from here, Sophie?" Ryder was prepared to let Robbie and her take the lead. For the moment at least.

"We find whatever hole let this rat in and we plug it. Then we identify who might be the leak—"

"And feed them what we want them to think," Ryder interjected.

"Exactly. It may help identify them and also lead us to Oliver or whoever is behind this hack and theft," she confirmed and offered him a smile, her earlier chill melting away.

She is stunning when she smiles, he thought, and it dragged a grin from him.

That had her staring at his mouth, way too intently because it made him imagine having those smiling lips against his. That she was uncomfortable with her perusal, as well, was evidenced by the way she blushed and said, "Let's get to work."

Sophie jerked the door open and raced out, Robbie close behind, but Jackson and he hung back.

His friend eyeballed him and said, "She's my cuz, bro."

Ryder nodded. "I know, Jax. Believe me, I know."

On his way out the door, Jax tapped Ryder's chest with his finger and whispered, "Treat her right."

Chapter Three

The rough, rusty metal of the bars scraped against her skin as she tried to open the lock on the cell door with the metal picks they had fashioned from her bra underwires. Over and over, she tried to trip the lock, but the wires weren't strong enough and kept bending from the pressure on the tumbler.

"I can't get it. The underwires are too weak," she said and retracted the L-shaped pick she had fashioned.

Robert held out his hand to display what looked like some old springs from a bed or cot. "I found these in the back of the cell. Maybe we can pound them out to use."

The springs were thick, inflexible and, like most of the metal around them, rusted. "It'll take time to pound them out if they can even hold up to that," she said, worried the metal would be too brittle from age and rust.

"Do you have a better idea?" Robert said with an arch of a salt-and-pepper eyebrow.

"No," she said and handed him the stone they'd used to break free of the zip ties.

Robert took the stone and searched the jail cell for anything flat he could use as an anvil surface. He finally found a stone block that had come loose from a corner, laid it flat and began pounding the bedspring.

The sound of stone striking metal was loud, echoing against the jail cell walls.

Mercedes worried it would attract the attention of their captors, and listened intently for their return, but there were no signs of activity from outside.

Dirt and rust flew off with each strike of stone against the spring, finally revealing stronger metal beneath the abused surface.

Robert hammered away, creating an L shape at one end and leaving enough of the bedspring at the other end to use as a handle.

He repeated the actions with the second spring, working the metal until he had another L-shaped key.

"Do you think you can use these?" he asked and handed them to her.

They were heavy and the corkscrew handles made them a little awkward, but Robert's arms were too big to pass through the bars near the lock area. Echoing his earlier statement but with some levity, she said, "What choice do we have?"

He chuckled, as she'd intended, and walked with her to the jail cell door, vigilant for signs of their captors as she slipped her hands past the bars and inserted the picks into the lock.

The metal of the springs was rough against her hands as she used the L-shaped hooks to work past the wards in the lock and pull back the bolt, much like a key would do.

Sweat dripped down her back as she worked, fumbling with the metal hooks until she suddenly felt something give beneath her fingers.

To her surprise, the lock opened.

"It worked," she said, her tone a mix of glee and disbelief.

"Let's go," Robert urged and shoved the door open.

They rushed through the small remaining jail space to another door, which was luckily unlocked. But as they opened it, they were unprepared for the sight. Snow had fallen, dusting the ground and trees all around them with an icing of white like powdered sugar on donuts.

The snow had already covered the narrow dirt road in front of the jail, obscuring any earlier tracks from their captor's vehicle. Looking around, the mountains that had seemed familiar had disappeared beneath a heavy cloud cover brought on by the snow. The trees around them were thick, making it impossible to see if any nearby structures might cue them on how to reach Regina. But the road was a first step.

"We should follow it down," she said, worried that even though it was the logical thing to do, it also risked exposing them to whomever had kidnapped them.

"We keep to the edges and out of sight," Robert said, clearly in tune with her thoughts.

She took the first step toward freedom but a strong blast of wind whipped the snow around and penetrated the lightweight jacket she'd worn on the plane, reminding her that spring weather in Colorado could be temperamental.

It also warned that if they didn't find civilization soon, they could die of exposure.

Looking at Robert, she realized he had the same concerns. Like her, he had only a spring-weight jacket.

"Maybe we should wait out this weather," she said, reconsidering their earlier plan.

Robert shook his head. "We both know what'll happen if we stay. Better we choose our way to go. Together," he said, slipping his hand into hers and giving it a reassuring squeeze.

"Together," she said and pushed ahead.

"Let me run through this again," Sophie said, wanting to make sure she had all the details straight before they did a deep dive into their investigation.

She grabbed the marker and wrote down what she understood of their current networks, where all the data had been stored and backed up, and what controlled access to various areas in the police station and at the CBI.

"We believe that the hacker entered the CBI network through an open port, but they may have broken in through some other way also. Have your people run any scans to look for unusual activity?" she asked.

"They're running diagnostics to see if it might have been a denial-of-service attack that let them in," Ryder told her as he also took notes.

"Great," Sophie said and glanced toward her brother, Robbie. "You're checking the same things here, right?"

"I am, and at first glance, I can see there were jumps in activity for the last month or so," Robbie confirmed.

"Right. Let's take a step back and check the timeline," Sophie responded as Jackson moved to write out the info on a whiteboard.

When he finished, Sophie rose and considered the details. Pointing to one spot on Jackson's timeline, she said, "So the district attorney wanted to see the evidence and it was missing. Is it normal to want to see it at this time?"

Jackson nodded, rose and grabbed another marker in a different color. "The DA wanted to refresh her memory because the trial was supposed to start in three weeks," he said and jotted that info on the board.

"But the evidence was being stored for at least three months before that, which means it might have vanished well before you noticed that the digital data was also gone," she said.

With a reluctant nod, Jackson confirmed it. "It's very possible it happened some time ago."

"But we know the DA had reviewed the digital files about

a month ago and they were intact," Ryder advised, and Sophie walked over and wrote that on the timeline.

"That might explain the recent activity on your network logs," Robbie advised and tacked on, "Was anyone complaining about the network being slow?"

"Some of the officers working the night shift," Jackson said.

Sophie wrote that info on the board and gestured to it. "So the hacker likely worked at night. Our first clue."

"Maybe they have some other job that keeps them busy during the day," Ryder said while he wrote in his notebook.

Sophie nodded and said, "That could mean several things but, for starters, maybe they're not full-time hackers. They also didn't phlash your systems—"

"'Phlash'?" Jackson questioned, brow furrowed as he tried to understand the term.

"It means the hacker didn't destroy all your systems by replacing the firmware on your devices with corrupt firmware. Based on that, we can assume the person isn't some kind of hacktivist," Ryder explained to his friend.

"I agree," Sophie said, impressed with Ryder's knowledge, but then again, if he worked for the CBI, he was likely a cut above your run-of-the-mill investigator.

She wrote that information on the board and said, "Our hacker is likely a cyber mercenary—"

"Or part of an organized crime network since we suspect the senator has connections to some unsavory types," Ryder elaborated.

"Are you certain of that?" Sophie pressed, worry tightening her gut because of who might have kidnapped her parents.

Ryder shook his head. "Not sure at all, but think about the scale of this operation." He ticked off each element on a finger as he continued. "They stole the physical evidence, hacked two systems and kidnapped your parents. Seems to be a lot for one person to accomplish on their own."

"But Oliver has beaucoup bucks," Jackson countered and rubbed his fingers together in emphasis.

"Let's keep it at cyber mercenary for now. Works at night, so possibly not a full-time actor. Not a hacktivist. Skill level could be anywhere from beginner to expert," Sophie said.

"You think a beginner did this?" Jackson challenged, eyebrows raised in question.

"Using an open port to enter a system is basic beginner stuff. So is a denial-of-service attack," Robbie offered.

"There's also the possibility that whoever stole the physical evidence gave them their password," Sophie pointed out.

Jackson waved his hands in the air. "I know we're not as fancy as South Beach Security, but we do limit what our users can access."

Sophie raised a palm in apology. "I didn't mean to imply that you don't use appropriate measures. It could be as simple as stealing an administrator's password. Is that possible?"

With a rough sigh and shake of his head, Jackson said, "Of course it is."

RYDER UNDERSTOOD HIS friend's frustration. You trusted the officers in your squad to watch your back and have the same high ethical standards. Clearly, that hadn't happened in this case and, as important as it was to find the hacker, it was even more important to find out which officer had breached their duties.

"Do you think you have enough to go on to find the hacker?" Ryder asked, not wanting to usurp Sophie's role as the lead at the moment.

Sophie glanced at Robbie, who gave a little shrug and communicated something in a silent sibling way.

"I think we do," Sophie said, and Robbie nodded in agreement.

"Good, so let's focus on who had access to the physical evidence and passwords." Ryder ignored Jackson's scowl and flush of embarrassed color. As the new chief, the breach would not reflect well on his leadership.

Despite that, Jackson didn't hesitate to provide the information. He flipped open a file on the tabletop and removed some papers that he passed around. "This is a list of every officer and employee who has access to this building. Those that are highlighted are individuals whose badges could grant access to the evidence room."

"I know you hate to do this, but is there anyone on this list who either might owe something to Oliver or is subject to being compromised?" Ryder prompted.

"Oliver had been on the town council and was mayor at one time. He had a lot of power over local politics. Things like who got hired or got a permit or license they needed for a business," Jackson said as he grabbed his papers and on another portion of the whiteboard added a list of names.

When he was done, he pointed to the whiteboard as he explained his rationale for placing each person on the list.

"Mark Dillon is one of our youngest officers. His father owns a restaurant in town that needed a permit to expand into a nearby lot."

Sophie narrowed her eyes and tapped her index finger to her full lips thoughtfully before she asked, "Wasn't Mark the officer who helped us find Rhea's twin sister?"

Jackson nodded. "He did. He's an avid hiker and environmentalist, and now in training for our new K-9 unit, which brings us to Diego Rodriguez," he said, pointing to his name on the list.

"Diego served with you in Afghanistan," Ryder added, familiar with the fellow Marine with whom he had spent time when they'd all get together to go skiing, snowboarding or hiking.

"He did. I trusted him with my life in Afghanistan and would do it again," Jackson said without hesitation.

"But you put him on the list?" Sophie and Robbie spoke at virtually the same time.

"Diego is heading up our K-9 unit and there was a lot of dissension on the town council about officially adding it to our force. In the past, we relied on Mark's dogs, but they weren't officially trained. Oliver was instrumental in pushing through the approvals for the expansion to add that K-9 unit," Jackson admitted, his hesitation obvious.

Ryder understood. Brothers in arms had each other's backs and putting Diego on the list had to be difficult. Wanting to move on to ease his friend's discomfort, he said, "Anyone else?"

With a shrug of broad shoulders that seemed heavy with guilt, Jackson said, "Roger Cromwell."

Sophie flipped through her papers quickly, as if double-checking something, and then quickly said, "He's relatively new, isn't he?"

Jackson nodded. "He is, and before you ask, there's nothing that I can put a finger on. I've just gotten some funny vibes and actions from him lately."

"Like?" Sophie pressed while Robbie typed away on his laptop.

Jackson added his comments below Cromwell's name as he spoke. "He missed a shift and was late for another. Made it up without coordinating with me. In a small PD like ours, that causes all kinds of problems."

"Seems like he missed more than just one, according to your payroll system," Robbie said, flipping his laptop around so they could all see the screen.

"Let's put that up on the monitor." Jackson grabbed a remote and turned on the large screen at one side of the room.

With a few keystrokes, Robbie fed his laptop image to the large monitor, and it was immediately clear that Cromwell's attendance had become slightly erratic over the last month or so.

"I didn't realize," Jackson muttered, cursing beneath his breath and running his hand through his hair in frustration. "Rhea's had some doctor's appointments because of her pregnancy and I took time off. I didn't want us to be short-staffed, so retired police chief Bill Robinson worked some hours for me."

"Any worries about Robinson?" Ryder asked, well aware that Jackson admired the old chief and had thought of him as his work dad. They'd been on the force together for several years and it was thanks to Robinson's recommendation that Jackson was now the police chief.

"No doubts," Jackson said, no reluctance in his voice.

"Would Robinson be willing to chat about Cromwell or any of the others?" Sophie asked, her tone conciliatory, realizing how difficult this was for her cousin.

Jackson shot a quick look at his watch and shook his head. "Bill was always an early-to-bed, early-to-rise kind of guy. He's probably halfway through his dinner and getting ready for an hour of being a couch potato before hitting the sack."

Almost in response, Robbie's stomach gave a loud grumble. He splayed a hand across his midsection and said, "Sorry. I guess Robinson isn't the only one who might be hungry."

Raising his hands in apology, Jackson said, "No, I'm sorry. Between picking you up and getting started on this investigation, I lost all track of time. I'm sure you all want to grab a bite and maybe get some rest."

"A bite sounds nice. After, Robbie and I can work remotely on some things," Sophie said.

"I'm sure you'd like to get home to Rhea, so why don't I take Sophie and Robbie out for dinner?" Ryder offered, not wanting to pull away Jackson from his very pregnant wife.

"That would be great. I'll call Bill in the morning to arrange a chat." Jackson grabbed the remote and snapped off the monitor.

The room became a flurry of activity as laptops were closed and stowed away, and papers were gathered for their departure. Once they'd left the room, Jackson locked it up to keep any prying eyes away from their investigation.

As they reached the front desk, Ryder walked over to Milly and said, "I hope Delilah hasn't been too much of a bother."

Milly laughed and gestured to the corgi, who was lying on her back, short legs pointing upward and tongue lolling out of her mouth. As Milly bent and rubbed her belly, Delilah scrunched up, looking like a pill bug curling into a ball. "She's been fine. Do you want to take her now?"

"We can find a restaurant that will let us sit outside with her," Ryder said, earning a sharp laugh from Milly, who motioned to the windows along the front wall of the police station.

The sun and warmth of the afternoon had fled. Darkness had descended early and fat, heavy flakes of snow whirled around, turning the quaint street outside into a scene from a snow globe.

Sophie muttered a curse and Robbie laid a hand on her shoulder. "It's going to be okay, Soph."

Sophie violently shook her head, and her voice cracked with emotion as she said, "Mami and Papi are out there. In that."

Chapter Four

"They're going to be fine. You've got to believe that," Robbie assured her.

Jackson repeated the sentiment. "They'll be fine," he said, but as Sophie met her cousin's gaze, there was no denying his fear.

"We need to get going," she said, intent on having dinner even though she wasn't hungry and, more importantly, settling in for the night to work some more.

"I hate to impose, again, but do you mind watching Delilah for a little longer?" Ryder asked Milly.

"Not at all. She's a doll," Milly said and once again bent to rub the dog's belly.

"She's a K-9 school dropout," Ryder said with a laugh, drawing Sophie's attention to the rotund corgi splayed at Milly's feet behind the sergeant's desk.

When Sophie looked down, the corgi popped to its feet and peered up at her, a jaunty grin on her face. It somehow managed to drag a fractured laugh from her. "Someone actually thought she could be part of a K-9 unit?"

Ryder stood beside her and, this close, his pine-fresh scent enveloped Sophie, calling to her to peer at him. As she did so, she realized that stern look from his photos and first meeting with them was gone, replaced again by an indulgent and welcoming smile that made her heart trip a beat.

"Yeah, they did. I mean, corgis are great herders and smart. The officer had read an article that some police force in Asia was using one and thought he'd give it a shot."

Sophie laughed again. "A *long* shot."

His smile broadened and his dark, mahogany eyes twinkled with humor, causing another little skip of her heart. The warmth of his body, so close to hers, ignited heat in her core, all things so out of place considering their current situation.

She stepped away from him and said, "We should go. Robbie and I still have a lot of work to do tonight."

That smile and twinkle disappeared to be replaced by that no-nonsense face. "I'll swing the car around. You're not dressed for this weather."

"You're not either," she said, but he just rushed out of the station in his suit jacket.

"Intense," Robbie breathed, dragging a chuckle from Jackson.

"He is, but you can count on him for anything. I'm glad he's on our side," Jackson said.

"Good to know. Are you coming to dinner?" Sophie asked.

Jackson shook his head. "Rhea's sister, Selene, is visiting for a few days. I thought it would be good for her to be around since I knew we'd be busy. I've also made arrangements for you at a nearby bed-and-breakfast. In the meantime, CBI provided a list of black pickups in the area, and I have my officers checking for any that are damaged."

"Things are moving along," Robbie said unconvincingly.

"I know you'd like it to move faster, but we have to assume your parents are wanted alive for some reason and are safe and sound for the moment," Jackson urged, his gaze skipping from Robbie to her and then toward the front door as a snow-crusted Ryder walked in.

"Ready when you are," Ryder said, brushing fat flakes from his rumpled blue suit jacket.

"We're ready," Sophie said, wondering how quickly they could be done with dinner so she and Robbie could work on locating the hacker and, in turn, her parents.

MERCEDES HUDDLED NEXT to Robert as a strong blast of wintry wind created a cyclone of snowflakes around them.

"Maybe we should have stayed in that jail cell," she whispered against his ear as he tucked her ever tighter.

"It might be too late to turn back," he said and shifted away from her to peer around for any kind of shelter.

He pointed to an outcropping of rocks with an indentation that could provide minimal protection from the snow and wind. "Not a cave but it might do."

"Some pine branches would help insulate us," she said.

Together they broke off half a dozen or more boughs from some nearby trees. They dragged them to the indentation, set some on the ground for bedding and lay chest-to-chest to keep their vitals warm. After, they covered themselves with the rest of the branches.

Her hand was sticky with resin as she cradled Robert's bruised face and noticed the smudges of black beneath his eyes from his broken nose. "We will survive this, mi amor."

He smiled weakly and copied her gesture, skimming a thumb across her cheekbone. "We will. I'm sure Jax and Ryder are trying to find us. Probably the rest of SBS as well. There's no way Jax wouldn't have called family to help."

"You're right," she said just as a sharp gust rushed over them, bringing the clean scent of snow and freshly cut pine. Surprisingly, their makeshift shelter was providing some protection. Her core was warm as she burrowed her hands beneath Robert's jacket and cradled his back. Her hands were finally free of the chill she'd experienced as they'd hiked across the mountain on the rough, narrow road.

He did the same, splaying his hands across her back to draw her as close as possible, conserving their body heat.

"Come the morning, they'll find us," she said, and as her eyes drifted closed, she repeated that mantra, certain that her family would stop at nothing to locate them.

DINNER HAD BEEN PLEASANT and helped to take her mind off the danger threatening their parents. But the second Robbie and she were settled in their rooms, they'd be back to work, tracking down whatever information they could on who had hacked Jackson's systems and Ryder's Colorado Bureau of Investigation.

The inn that Jackson had chosen for them was a short two-block walk from the police station. Ryder pulled up in front of the carefully restored Victorian. Even with the dark of night and whirling snow, the bright yellow of the siding and touches of pink and purple on the gingerbread made the place seem happy.

"It's very pretty," she said as Ryder pulled their bags out of the back of his Jeep.

Ryder glanced toward the building, snow collecting quickly on his dark hair and the shoulders of his suit jacket. "Mrs. Avery does a great job of keeping it up," he said and, not a second later, the front door of the bed-and-breakfast opened, spilling light onto the freshly shoveled path.

"I heard you pull up," an older woman called out as they wheeled their bags to the front door.

"Thank you for waiting up for them, Mrs. Avery," Ryder said and hugged the woman, who offered him a bright smile and swept an age-spotted hand across his shoulders to brush off the snow.

"Anything for you and Jax's family," she said then introduced herself. "Maggie Avery. I'm sorry that your stay isn't for happy reasons."

Sophie shook the woman's hand. "We are too. You have a lovely place," she said and looked all around at the period antiques that filled the lobby area and parlors beyond.

"Breakfast is available in the morning from six to nine. Wi-Fi info is posted in each of the rooms. You have number one, and your brother is in two, across the hall from you," Mrs. Avery said with a wave up the stairs after shaking hands with Robbie.

She pulled out two brass keys from a pocket in the apron tied around her waist and handed them over. The key was slightly cold to the touch and heavy. Slipping it into her jeans pocket, Sophie walked to the stairs but, as she got there, Ryder jumped in and said, "Let me."

Without waiting for her reply, he grabbed her suitcase and hauled it up the stairs to the hallway. At her door, he held out his hand for the key.

She arched a brow. "I think I can do this myself, thanks."

Ryder shook his head. "I'd like to make sure it's safe, if you don't mind."

"I do mind. I mean, I appreciate the chivalry and all that, but I can take care of myself," she said, tightly clutching the key in her hand.

Ryder laughed and shook his head again, ruefully this time. "Not chivalry. Self-preservation. Jax would tear me apart if anything happened to you on my watch."

Even as a teenager, Jackson had always been overly protective of his cousins, especially the women. Ingrained in him by his military father, she appreciated it at times. Why it rankled her when Ryder did it, Sophie didn't know, but she relented, handing him the key as Robbie unlocked his room door and walked in.

Ryder opened the door and did a quick inspection of the room, checking the bathroom area and closets to make sure all was in order.

Stepping back out to the hallway, where she had been impatiently waiting, he handed her the key, now warm from the contact with his hand. That warmth transferred itself to her, chasing away the chills of the night and the lingering fear for her parents.

"Thank you," she said grudgingly.

"You're welcome. I can pick you up in the morning, if you'd like," he said, shooting a quick look at Robbie, who had returned to the door of his room.

Sophie glanced from him to her brother and then back to Ryder. "It's just a short walk and I checked the weather forecast. Snow should be done and melting by then."

"I guess I'll see you in the morning. Good night," Ryder said and, with a tip of his head, hurried down the stairs.

"He gets to you," Robbie teased once Ryder was out of earshot.

"He's too…" she began but couldn't find the right word.

"Alpha?" Robbie offered with an arch of a dark brow and twinkling humor in his aqua eyes, so like her own.

"You think I can't handle alphas, what with Jax, Trey and all the new K-9 handlers we have at SBS?" Sophie said with a rough chuckle and shake of her head.

Robbie brushed past her, laptop in hand, and plopped himself on the small settee in her room. "You do better with betas like me," he said and opened his laptop.

"You only think you're a beta. We both know you could kick ass if you had to, but not tonight. I need to clear my head." She walked over, pushed his laptop closed and pointed to the door.

"See? Me, being beta," he joked as he hurried out.

She closed the door behind him and then leaned against it, considering what he'd said about Ryder.

Definitely alpha, but as she'd reminded her brother, she'd dealt with that kind of man all the time. Maybe it was his broody darkness. She'd always been a sucker for broody as a teen. But she wasn't a teen anymore, she considered, hauling up her backpack to pull out her laptop.

She kicked off her damp hiking boots, grateful she had worn them in anticipation of having to do a lot of running around. Her feet would have been freezing without them thanks to the unexpected April snow, not to mention the fact that she was more used to the warmth of Miami days. She wasn't sure she could ever get used to the cold and sometimes erratic Colorado weather.

Opening her laptop, she had several e-mails from the SBS team back in Miami. They had been doing investigations at their end and had found a wealth of additional information on Oliver, including many suspect business deals and possible connections to unsavory actors.

She skimmed the messages, leaving them for a deep dive later. First, she wanted to find anything that might lead to their hacker. Robbie was likely doing the same, but sometimes working apart let them see different things. And she had weird abilities that she kept from anyone except those closest to her. Not even Jackson knew of her unique skills.

Because of that, she got to work, examining the network system reports that showed increased activity over the last few weeks. As they had noted before, the traffic was always at the same time and after a typical nine-to-five day, hinting at the fact that whoever it was possibly wasn't a full-time hacker. It reinforced that this wasn't a professional cyber mercenary, since they would have done a better job at hiding their intrusions.

She was deep in thought, running that info around in her head, when a notice popped up that she had a new e-mail.

Narrowing her gaze, she considered the sender's odd address. She almost dismissed it as spam and deleted it, but something made her open it.

I didn't sign up for this. I need your help, the message began and went on to provide an address not all that far from the inn.

Come alone. No one else, not even your brother, the sender warned.

Clearly, whoever it was had done some digging around to not only find her e-mail address but to learn who Robbie was and that he was there with her.

The hacker? she wondered even as she replied that she would meet them.

Setting aside her laptop, she dragged on her damp boots, grabbed her jacket and key, and crept down the stairs as silently as she could, not wanting to alert either her brother or Mrs. Avery that she was on a mission.

Opening the front door, she was grateful that in the short time since they'd arrived, the snow had grown lighter and the winds that had whipped the damp chill through her body had dimmed. She zipped up her jacket and rushed out, determined to uncover a vital clue to where her parents might be.

"Thanks so much for watching her, Milly," he said and took the leash from the desk sergeant.

"My pleasure. Delilah's lots of fun," Milly replied. "Hopefully my replacement will be here soon, not that I mind the overtime."

Ryder glanced around the station. In the back, two officers sat at their desks, processing some paperwork. He recognized Mark Dillon, one of their possible suspects. The other officer was unfamiliar.

"Is your replacement late? I can watch the desk if you have to go," he offered.

Milly waved him off. "No need. Like I said, the overtime is welcome. It's just that Cromwell has been a little unreliable lately. He's supposed to be working the desk to make up for the time he's missed," she said with a grimace at the mention of the other officer.

Not a second later, an officer rushed through the door, apologizing as he did so. "Sorry, Milly. Had to shovel," he said and stopped short at the sight of him and Delilah.

"This is CBI Agent Hunt and Delilah," Milly explained, tossing her hand in their direction.

"Roger Cromwell," the man said and offered his hand.

Ryder shook it. Slightly clammy and cold, maybe from the shoveling. *Or maybe from something else*, he thought as the man's eyes narrowed and his color faded a bit.

"Nice to meet you," he said, but didn't offer any other info as he dipped his head at Milly. "Thanks again."

"Anytime," Milly said and slipped from around the desk to allow Cromwell to take over.

After a sharp nod and intense stare at Cromwell, which had the other man looking away and fidgeting with something on the desk, Ryder turned and clicked his tongue to command Delilah to follow him out of the police station for the short drive to his small lake cottage on the edge of the Regina town limits. He kept it for weekend visits for fishing, hiking or skiing.

But as he unlocked the SUV doors and opened one to let

the short-legged corgi hop into the passenger seat, he caught sight of Sophie rushing out the door of the inn.

Her head tucked deep into the collar of her lightweight jacket, she wrapped her arms around herself to combat the cold.

She walked briskly down the block, away from the police station and downtown, toward a more residential area and a complex where a high school sat within a short distance of some athletic fields and a rec center.

Interesting and worrisome, he thought as he gave Delilah a hand command to hop down from the seat.

Softly closing the SUV door, he followed Sophie, keeping well back so as not to capture her attention. Hoping that whatever or whoever had drawn her out of the inn at such a late hour wouldn't be dangerous.

Delilah padded beside him, enjoying the walk. She had surprised him when he had first gotten her by being very active. When she pulled ahead of him, he reined her in, keeping her close so Sophie wouldn't notice them as she turned onto the athletic grounds and headed straight for the first set of bleachers by the football field.

As he scoped out the area, he realized that there was no easy way to follow her without being seen. But he tried, hugging tight to the fence line.

When Sophie was about halfway to the bleachers, he spotted someone moving beneath the structure. The person had on a dark-colored ski vest over a black hoodie. The hood was pulled up to hide their features. The person's hands were jammed deep into the pockets of their black jeans, but Ryder still worried that whoever it was might be armed.

He hurried forward and, as he did so, he stepped on a branch that snapped, the sound as loud as a gunshot in the quiet of the spring night.

Immediately, both Sophie and the unidentified person glanced in his direction. A heartbeat later, the hooded someone raced back beneath the bleachers.

Sophie gave chase, speeding after her suspect.

Ryder muttered a curse and rushed in the same direction along the opposite side of the fence, hoping to intercept the suspect and Sophie at the other end of the football field before they reached the high school.

Delilah loped along beside him, falling behind with her shorter legs. He had no choice but to drop her leash and speed forward without her. But it wasn't fast enough.

As he reached the end of the fence, their suspect hopped up and over a shorter gate by the concession booth for the football field and disappeared behind the high school building. He raced to the spot, but there was no sign of the person who had melded into the warren of paths students used to enter the school. Searching the ground for footsteps he might follow, he noticed the cement path must have been salted since all the new snow had melted. There were no traces of where the suspect might have gone.

A second later, Sophie caught up to him, breathing heavily from dashing after their suspect. She jammed her hands on her hips and sucked in a deep inhale before releasing angry words in a sharp stream.

"What did you think you were doing? You chased them away!"

Chapter Five

Sophie sucked in another breath and held it, trying to quell her anger at Ryder's interference, but also to stop her heart from racing after the short sprint across the field. She definitely had to get out from behind her desk more.

"I thought I was following someone who was doing something ridiculously stupid," he shot back, obviously as annoyed as she was.

"I wasn't being stupid. I was following a lead," she said as the corgi finally caught up to them and sat at Ryder's feet, that silly grin on its face that somehow tamped down the heat of her anger a little. *But only a little.*

"Didn't it occur to you that they might want to kidnap you as well?" he challenged, one dark brow arched in emphasis.

"Their e-mail didn't sound threatening. It sounded pleading, and I told you, I can take care of myself," she said, poking his chest with her finger to emphasize her point.

A mistake.

He snagged her finger and in one swift unexpected move, he had her arm twisted behind her back and her front plastered against him.

Another mistake, she realized. Being that close to him caused all kinds of feelings to rush through her as he hardened against her softness.

He immediately released her from his grasp and took a step back.

Reluctantly, or maybe in apology, he said, "I know you're a capable agent. I've heard enough about what you've done with SBS. But it wouldn't hurt to have backup."

Because he had seemingly given ground, she swallowed her pride and said, "You might be right. But he specifically said to come alone."

"How do you know it was a 'he'?" Ryder asked and gestured for her to walk back toward the inn.

"The quick glimpse before he ran away. Broad shoulders and small hips. And his sneakers looked way too big to be a woman's size."

"Women can have that same shape, and the vest would have hidden other features," he said. Then quickly added, "The ground might be soft near the bleachers. Maybe we can find a footprint."

She nodded. "Sounds good."

They hurried back in that direction, Delilah loping along behind them, the padding of her footsteps loud in the night.

At the spot where they had seen their suspect, the fading remnants of a footprint in the snow marked the grassy area along the edge of the bleacher. Ryder reached into his pocket, drew out a quarter and placed it at the end of the heel print to use as a size reference.

Sophie whipped her phone from her pocket and snapped a series of photos as the falling snow quickly obliterated the edges of the print.

"Hopefully, we can use these to gauge what his shoe size is," she said and waved her phone back and forth.

Ryder retrieved his quarter, rose and, as Sophie shivered against the cold, ripped off his suit jacket and tucked it around her.

"You didn't need to do that," she said while savoring his lingering body heat on the inside of the jacket and the warmth it was providing.

"I'm used to the cold. I suspect with your Miami blood, you're freezing."

He wasn't wrong so she didn't argue. Instead, she began a brisk walk back toward the bed-and-breakfast. "Thanks."

"No problema. You won't do anyone any good if you get sick," he replied with a shrug of his impossibly broad shoulders.

Sophie wanted to argue that she wasn't that delicate, although, in truth, the cold had seeped into her bones. He just made her want to argue. She wondered if it wasn't some kind of dance they were doing, and her uncertainty reminded her it had been too long since she'd been in any kind of relationship.

Helping her cousins with the agency kept her way too busy.

"Penny for your thoughts," he said almost awkwardly. They had walked nearly two blocks without a word passing between them.

"Not sure you want to know," she said, unsure how he'd react to the fact that something about him was drawing her in ways she didn't want. To head off the next most logical questions, because if she was anything, it was logical, she said, "Just thinking about why our suspect would regret his actions and ask for help."

"Maybe what's happened is more than they bargained for," he suggested for consideration.

She nodded. "I think so. They said, 'I didn't sign up for this.'"

"'Sign up' means they agreed to do something, probably for money, much like you had already suspected. This is some kind of cyber mercenary but likely not an experienced one," Ryder said, connecting all the dots they had already uncovered.

Tossing a thumb in the direction of the athletic field and high school, she said, "And my money is on it being someone local. They knew just where to run to escape."

"And based on their knowledge of the area and their speed, maybe even someone young who went to that school—"

"Or still goes there," she said and peered at him to see if he agreed. Snow dusted his hair and his shoulders, making her feel guilty that he had sacrificed his comfort for hers.

He mulled it over for only a hot second and nodded. "I agree. But would a high school kid have the skills for the hack?"

Shrugging, she dipped her head from side to side, mulling over what she knew so far. "Possibly. Finding an open port and using that vulnerability is pretty standard. Creating an effective attack is a little more complicated. What I want to see is how they accessed the database to steal the info and then hid their tracks."

"Is that what you were going to work on tonight?" he said as they reached the inn.

She hesitated at the front door, as if unsure if she could enter, and he said, "The door isn't locked until nine and Mrs. Avery will be in the parlor to keep an eye on things."

Not the kind of thing that happened in a big city like Miami, but in a small town like Regina, she supposed it was easier to be trustful of your visitors and neighbors.

She grabbed the handle, pushed through and spied Mrs. Avery sitting in the parlor by a fireplace, reading.

The innkeeper glanced their way as they entered and immediately popped up to greet them. "Oh my, you must be freezing." She brushed the snow from Ryder's shoulders.

"Let me bring some hot chocolate up to your room," she added and rushed away for the promised beverage.

Sophie raised her eyebrows in both surprise and question. "I guess you're staying?"

"If you don't mind. Hot chocolate sounds good." He dragged his fingers across the top strands of his hair to remove the last of the snow. He bent and rubbed Delilah's fur and when he was done, she shook her short, squat body to rid herself of the last of the flakes.

"It's the least I can do for the loan of this," she said, slipping his jacket from her shoulders and returning it.

DEFINITELY THE LEAST, Ryder thought as he followed her up the stairs, because she both infuriated and intrigued him at the same time.

With a click of his tongue, he commanded Delilah to follow them, not that she would stay behind without him. Since he'd rescued her from his colleague's misguided attempt to turn her into a K-9 agent, she rarely left his side and he had to admit that he didn't mind it. His life had been far too empty, and the corgi's presence had made his house seem more like a home.

At her room, Sophie pulled the heavy brass key from her pocket, unlocked her door and, with a wave of her hand, invited them to enter.

He sauntered in, giving her space because he already knew how risky it was to be close. It was too confusing for both of them.

The room had a small sitting area next to a gas fireplace that guests must love to chase away a Colorado chill like the one that had descended that day.

Sophie immediately walked to the fireplace, flipped it on

and stood there, rubbing her hands up and down her arms to brush away the cold.

The heat from the fireplace was immediate, the warmth reaching even to where he stood a few feet away.

"That feels good," he said, unclipping Delilah's leash. The corgi immediately rushed over to lie at Sophie's feet by the fireplace.

She bent and stroked Delilah's fur and the dog immediately rolled over to present her belly for a rub, stubby legs waving in the air.

Sophie laughed, the sound almost musical. It stirred something inside him. His research had hinted at the fact that she wasn't someone who had the luxury of moments as simple as this one. The South Beach Security Agency seemed to always be involved in time-consuming and dangerous investigations.

Much like this one and, worse, this time it was personal.

"She's a doll," Sophie said with an almost wistful smile. "I always wanted a dog."

"I never thought I'd own one," he said and walked over to likewise pet the corgi who was in doggy heaven with all the attention she was getting.

"So, if she's Delilah, you're the Samson she took down?" Sophie teased, her aqua-colored eyes alight with humor.

He couldn't deny it. "For sure. Delilah stole my heart."

"But no one else?" she asked, eyes narrowing to consider him but a welcoming smile on her face.

Was she flirting with him?

"Are you asking for yourself?"

Some women might have backed off with his response. Sophie wasn't that kind of woman.

"Maybe," she said, rising at the sound of a knock on the

door, the moment shattered. "Excuse me." Sophie opened the door.

Mrs. Avery bustled in, holding a tray with marshmallow-topped mugs of hot chocolate and a small dish piled with several cookies. She rushed over to the sitting area and set the tray down on the marble top of the antique coffee table. Returning to the door, she stopped and said, "If you need to come and go after nine, the code for the digital front door lock is 8-2-7-8-9. Each guest gets their own code, in case you're worried about that."

"Thank you, Mrs. Avery. That does relieve some concerns," Sophie said with a smile before closing the door behind the innkeeper, locking it and returning to the sitting area.

Ryder gingerly sat on the delicate settee, worrying whether it could hold his weight as it creaked slightly as he settled at the spot farthest from the fire, leaving the warmer seat for Sophie.

Sophie walked over and stood before the table and settee, hands clasped in front of her. She rocked back and forth on her feet, possibly hesitant at joining him on the narrow space of the couch.

He patted the space beside him and, because she seemed to draw out the bad boy in him, said, "You wanted to know if there was anyone else. Now's your chance to find out."

She shifted on her feet again but then joined him. The settee did another little creak with her additional weight. She was curvy in all the right places, like the soft thigh pressed to his thanks to the size of the small couch.

"Thanks. The fire feels nice," she said as she bent and snared a mug from the table. She held it in her hands, using the heat of the hot chocolate to warm her.

"It does and luckily, you won't need it for long. It's supposed to warm up into the sixties tomorrow." He snagged his hot chocolate and a cookie as well, savoring the butteriness of the shortbread.

"¡Gracias a Dios!" she muttered and sipped her drink.

"Yes, thank God. I like the snow, but I'm ready for spring and maybe some fishing and kayaking," he said, likewise grateful that warmer weather was on the way.

She did a quick little side-glance, her hands wrapped around the mug so tightly they were white from the pressure. "Do you fish and kayak alone?"

Sophie was obviously taking him up on his earlier challenge. "No," he said, and a frown spread across her lips until he added in a teasing tone, "Sometimes Jax comes with me."

A wry smile graced her lips before she schooled her emotions and reached for a cookie. As she did so, her shoulder and the side of her breast innocently brushed across him.

"Sorry," she said with a little almost-embarrassed jump.

He set his mug on the tabletop and shifted slightly on the settee, determined to see her face. "Are we going to keep on dancing around the eight-hundred-pound elephant in the room?"

She likewise set her mug down and did a half turn to face him. "And what would that elephant be?"

He gestured between them with an index finger. "I don't think I'm misreading the signals even though neither of us might want this—"

"What's *this*?" she challenged, mimicking his action with a perfectly manicured index finger.

He snagged her finger, pulled her closer until their lips were barely an inch apart and whispered, "This."

HIS LIPS WERE AS LIGHT as a soft summer breeze against her lips. They tempted and enticed. Urged her to join him in that first simple dance of introduction and exploration.

She sighed at the gentleness of it, at the way he pressed his lips to her, teasing her lips to open. He cupped her cheek, urging her closer, and she moaned with need. It had been way too long since she'd allowed herself such pleasure.

A sharp, insistent series of raps on her door jerked them apart.

"If it's Robbie, I'm going to kill him," she said as she shot off the couch and rushed to the door.

She yanked it open, and Robbie stood there, holding his laptop. He looked from her to where Ryder sat on the settee, a napkin now strategically placed on his lap. A bright flush of color erupted on his cheeks, and he stammered out, "S-sorry. I thought you might want to know that I broke through one of the spoofed IP addresses."

With a wave of her arm to welcome him into her room, she said, "Let me guess. It's at the local high school?"

"How did you know?" he said and proceeded to the settee, where he plopped into her spot by the fire. "Feels good. Can I have one?" He grabbed a cookie before either Ryder or she could reply.

He popped the cookie into his mouth and, while he chewed, said, "Actually, we need to isolate the exact location, but it's definitely for an IP address in that area. How did you know?"

She looked at Ryder, who raised a hand, deferring to her.

"I got a message from who I assume is the hacker."

Robbie almost jumped out of his seat with her revelation. "Really? Have you analyzed the message headers? Tried tracing them?"

"No, I haven't done that yet," she reluctantly admitted.

"Why not?" he pressed.

Ryder jumped into the discussion. "Because your sister decided it made more sense to go find the hacker."

"And Ryder followed me and interrupted the meet, so the attacker ran," she shot back in challenge, her earlier annoyance returning.

Robbie skipped his gaze between the two of them. Shaking his head, he pointed at her and said, "It was foolish to go. You could have been kidnapped like Mami and Papi."

"That's what I told her," Ryder said with a satisfied kind of harrumph at the end.

That earned him a condemning glare from Robbie and another point of his finger. "And you need to understand that Sophie can take care of herself. She's a black belt who can probably kick your butt," he said, his pride obvious.

"Gracias, Robbie. Ryder and I have reached a…truce of sorts," she said, and heat rushed to her face with the lie. She hoped it wasn't too obvious, not that it had to be with Robbie. They were as close as two siblings could be, almost as if they were twins.

"Well, if the truce is working, don't you think it's time you got to work on analyzing that message?" he said.

RYDER DIDN'T KNOW whether to strangle or bless him. *All things considered, probably bless him*, he thought and said, "I should let you get to work. It'll be nice to be able to tell Jax you've made some progress."

Sophie marched over and crossed her arms against her chest, almost angrily. "And what are you going to do?"

Ryder slowly rose to his full height and walked to stand in front of her. "I'm going to my place, take Delilah for her last walk of the night and then call my contact in Denver to see what info their CSI unit may have gathered from the crash site."

A visible release of her anger came as she relaxed the hold she had on herself, nodded and offered an apologetic smile.

She brushed a hand down his arm. "You'll keep us posted if you hear anything?"

He cupped her cheek and ran his thumb across her lips, wishing it could be a kiss instead but not with Robbie sitting there, watching their every interaction. "Of course. I'll be back in the morning, and we can walk to the police station. It should have warmed up by then."

"Sounds good," she said with a welcoming smile.

He made a hand command to call Delilah over, leashed her and walked with Sophie to the door, where he hesitated, wanting that final kiss before he left. Risking it, he brushed a fleeting kiss across her lips and whispered, "Don't work too late."

She nodded and lingered at the door as he walked away. He told himself not to look back, but he did, satisfied to see she was still there, her features a tempting mix of innocent and sensual.

He drove that thought from his brain because he still had work to do and couldn't afford the distraction she presented.

Rushing out of the inn, he harnessed Delilah into the front seat of his SUV and called his contact at the Denver police department.

"Good evening, Ryder. How are you doing?" Detective Sam Adams asked.

"We've made some progress in identifying the possible location of the hacker. How about you?" Ryder said and pulled out of his parking spot to head to his nearby weekend place.

"We're eliminating people in the Denver area from that list of black pickup owners. We've also confirmed the make of the tires based on those tracks you noticed. I'll send you that info in a second," Adams said.

"Have you located any CCTV cameras or witnesses who

might have seen the incident?" he pressed, doubtful given that the Whitakers had been on a road that wasn't well-traveled.

"Nothing yet, but we'll keep on trying," the detective said and quickly added, "Do you think you could send one of your IT geniuses to help us locate any CCTVs along the route and also double-check what our people have done to make sure we don't have any intruders in our system?"

The thought of losing Sophie so quickly after meeting her caused a sudden and unexpected ache in his gut. He hoped that when he proposed the Denver visit Robbie would volunteer. "I'll check in the morning and let you know."

"I appreciate that, Ryder. Keep us posted." Adams signed off.

As Ryder drove, he ran through everything they knew so far, sorting the info to decide what would be the next steps to recommend to Jackson. Once he was confident about it, he dialed his friend, although he hated pulling him away from Rhea at this time of night.

"I hope you've got news," Jackson immediately said.

"I do," Ryder confirmed and advised him on everything that had happened that night, what it had revealed and the news from his Denver contact.

"Progress," Jackson said, but Ryder didn't fail to notice the reluctance in his friend's voice.

"I know this is personal because it's your aunt and uncle, in addition to jeopardizing the case against Oliver, but we will make it happen, sooner rather than later."

"Agreed. I can hear you're still driving, so get home and get some rest. I'll see you in the morning," Jackson said and ended the call.

It didn't take much longer for Ryder to reach the lake cottage. Located on the banks of the mountain lake at the far end of town, it provided a nice change of pace from his condo in Denver.

He parked, freed Delilah and took her for a walk along the rocky shores of the lake. A full moon kissed the surface of the waters, making them shimmer beneath the gentle light. At the end of the lake that was farthest from his home and town, water cascaded over a dam that held back runs from heavy rains or a spring thaw. In the distance, mountains surged into the night sky. Clouds obscured some of the peaks, but others were still frosted with the remnants of winter snow and today's unseasonable spate of flakes.

As he walked Delilah, he wondered if Sophie and Robbie's parents were up in those mountains. If they were safe.

He wasn't a gambling man, but if he had to put his money on it, he suspected they were there somewhere, and alive, since someone wanted them for a reason. Otherwise, they would have just eliminated them at the Denver crash site.

And, much like Jackson, he thought it was because Oliver or some of his more dangerous associates wanted them to do something with the Regina PD and CBI databases or even possibly the national databases like AFIS and CODIS. If they were able to do that, who knew what havoc they might wreak?

They had to stop that at any cost.

He just hoped the cost wouldn't be the lives of the Whitakers.

POWERFUL HANDS SNATCHED her away from her husband's comforting warmth.

Mercedes landed with a rough thud on the hard ground and, a second later, a sharp knee in the middle of her back drove her into the cold snow. Her attacker jerked back her arms, and the bite of plastic dug into her wrists as she was restrained again.

The snow chilled her skin as she looked toward their makeshift shelter. Robert was being held down by another man. He struggled to free himself but the man who had easily controlled her joined the fray and, within a few minutes, Robert was likewise bound with zip ties.

Her captor carelessly hauled her to her feet. A shove sent her stumbling forward on uneven ground until she regained her balance. She picked her way across the underbrush on the road and the bright moonlight illuminated the snow on the ground, highlighting the way.

"You've cost us a lot of time," her attacker said, delivering another punishing shove as they trudged along.

They had been walking a little over fifteen minutes when the ground beneath her feet grew smoother and became a wide swath of just snow.

The road. They were back on the road, she sensed and looked around.

A large black ATV sat just yards ahead.

Another careless shove sent her tumbling forward.

She landed hard, the impact driving her breath away. But that didn't deter her attacker. He hauled her to unsteady feet and almost tossed her onto the ATV's padded back seat.

As she plopped down, Robert lurched into the space, propelled by a goad from his captor. When he sat beside her, a darker, wet-looking stain on his face warned that he was injured.

She leaned close and whispered, "Are you okay?"

"You both won't be okay if you try another escape," replied the attacker who had slipped into the driver's seat.

Robert tipped his head close and, in a low tone only she could hear, said, "I'm sorry. I should have fought harder."

She laid her forehead against his and kissed his face. "No, you shouldn't have. I want you alive. I want *us* to get out of this alive, mi amor."

"We will. We will," he said, earning a loud guffaw from the driver.

"How sweet. Sickly sweet."

That earned the driver an elbow from the man in the passenger seat, who said, "Get going."

He turned and faced them, his mask obscuring his features but not the annoyance in his tone. "Don't do any more stupid things and you might just get out of this alive."

Mercedes tucked her head against Robert's and fought back tears, taking hope from the attacker's words that their imprisonment would be temporary. After all, their captors still hadn't revealed themselves, staying masked the entire time.

And, despite their rough treatment, even with the escape, they were unharmed for the most part.

All good, she thought as the ATV bumped along the snow-covered road. A road that looked relatively new based on the visibly bright ends of branches and trees that appeared recently cut.

Cold air swept across the open ATV, chilling her and making her shiver until the ATV shuddered to a halt in front of a larger mound of snow.

Straightening, she stared at the mound, puzzled as their attackers hopped out of the cab and swung around to haul them off the back seat.

She didn't fight them, mindful of their earlier words that cooperation would ensure their safety.

They trudged around one side of the mound along a narrow path to a cement pad in front of what she could now see was a cinder-block structure, reminiscent of an old Cold War bomb shelter. She had seen photos of bunkers like that in several history books.

One of the men pushed her toward the door but she delayed, wanting a look around before they were imprisoned.

Bingo.

The earlier cloud cover had cleared, and an immense contemporary-looking home peeked from the surrounding trees halfway down the slope. On an adjacent mountain, another group of homes, very symmetrical in size and shape and close to a series of trails through the forest, hinted that it might be the ski resort.

"Move," her captor commanded, shoving her through the door into a dimly lit room.

Once Robert was through the door also, one of the attackers positioned himself at the entrance, arms tucked against a broad chest. The second attacker cut her zip ties off and then did the same to Robert's.

He walked to the door and hit a switch.

Bright light nearly blinded her after the dark of night.

The door to the bunker clanged noisily, reminding her of the old jail cell where they'd been held earlier.

But this new space was light-years away from that rusty and decrepit cell and looked relatively new. The shadows of things here and there on the floor hinted at the fact the space may have been used for something else at one time.

Now it was clearly intended to be their prison. Two cots lined one side of the room while a large worktable with state-of-the-art computers sat on the other. A refrigerator and water dispenser stood beside a cabinet topped with a coffee maker and microwave in the middle of the sidewall. A door on that wall hopefully led to a toilet.

Robert walked to the fridge and opened it, revealing what looked like several premade meals, milk and other essentials.

He glanced her way and lifted a bloodied brow. "Looks like they intend for this to be a long haul."

She nodded, walked over, skimmed a hand along his jaw and applied gentle pressure until she could see the gash by his brow. "Go sit on that cot while I find something to clean that cut."

Rummaging through the cabinet, she located some paper towels and adhesive bandages but nothing else. *It will have to do*, she thought, wetting the towels with water from the cooler and walking over to Robert.

She sat beside him and gently wiped away the dried blood. Blotting the cut, she winced at the sight of it and the bruising already forming. Drying the area carefully with a fresh paper towel, she then ripped open the bandages. A butterfly bandage would be better to seal the cut but there were no scissors anywhere, which made sense.

She'd have no hesitation plunging it into her attackers.

Instead, she did the best she could to draw the wound closed with the regular bandages and, satisfied with her handiwork, she slapped her thighs and said, "There. That should be good."

Robert nodded. "Thanks." He peered around the room. Gesturing to a few cameras set high on the ceiling corners and on the computers, he added, "What do you think they want with us?"

Mercedes had no doubt about what they wanted. "To finish what the hacker started."

Chapter Six

"Did you get a good night's sleep?" Robbie asked as he grabbed a cup of overnight oats and then piled his plate with pastries that Mrs. Avery had set out for the inn's guests. Besides them, there was a young couple who had come to do some hiking, based on what she'd overheard at a nearby table.

With a shrug, she said, "Good enough." After all, she couldn't spill to her brother that she'd had a series of steamy dreams about Ryder Hunt and what might have happened if Robbie hadn't interrupted the night before.

But Robbie knew her too well. He lifted a dark brow and said, "Really? Seems to me that broody CBI agent is just your type."

"Just a work colleague," she insisted as she snagged a cranberry-orange scone and some whipped butter off the breakfast buffet and added a yogurt parfait as well. She wanted to power up in case they didn't have time to eat later in the day.

Back at their table, Mrs. Avery had poured them large mugs of coffee and left an assortment of sweeteners and cream.

"Not a Cuban coffee, but it will do," Robbie said and dug into his plate of food.

A Cuban coffee would have had way more caffeine and

sugar. *But we aren't in Miami anymore*, she thought, feeling like Dorothy in Oz even though they regularly visited their Whitaker cousins in Regina.

But the other visits had all been for fun and nothing like what they were facing now.

It made her lose her appetite even though everything that Mrs. Avery had laid out looked and smelled amazing.

Robbie had no such problem, she mused as he scarfed down a blueberry muffin from his pile of pastries. He gestured to her still-full plate and said, "I know you're not hungry, but you need to eat. It's going to be a long day, and you'll need the energy."

"And how do you know it's going to be a long day?" she pressed, breaking off a piece of her scone and smoothing the soft whipped butter on it.

"Because we have a lead on the hacker's computer and he reached out to you, which says to me that they want to come in from the cold. Now we have to get them to open that dialogue again after Ryder messed things up," Robbie said nonchalantly.

"You make it sound so easy," she said as she popped a piece of scone into her mouth and nearly moaned at the tastiness of the slightly salted butter, the sweetness of the pastry and the bright flavors of orange and cranberry.

Robbie wagged his head from side to side thoughtfully. "They're already running scared. A promise that they won't be prosecuted might be enough for them to cross the finish line."

She chuckled. "You're just full of metaphors this morning, aren't you?"

With a shrug and laugh, he said, "Trying to stay optimistic. I worry that the longer Mami and Papi are held, the lower the odds of bringing them home alive."

His words knotted her stomach, but she forced herself to take another bite of buttered scone before she said, "We'll find them. Soon."

The slight squeak of the front door dragged her attention toward the entry where Ryder and Delilah had just entered the inn.

The knot in her stomach relaxed and turned into a skittering mess like hundreds of butterflies attacking her insides.

She splayed a hand across her midsection, hoping to quiet them, and failed miserably as his normally stoic and dark features broke into a smile as their gazes locked.

RYDER COULDN'T HOLD BACK his grin at the sight of her sitting on one of Mrs. Avery's dainty Victorian chairs.

He had told himself the night before that getting involved with Sophie would only complicate an already complicated situation. Jackson was one of his best friends and wouldn't appreciate him messing around with his cousin. Not that he was the kind to mess around with women.

Her parents had been kidnapped and she was part of the investigative crew. All things that could affect her emotions and maybe color what they were both feeling.

But despite all those admonitions to himself, there was just something that pulled at his gut and had him taking ground-eating strides to reach her.

"Good morning," he said, voice husky with unexpected emotion.

"G'morning," Sophie replied, and Robbie echoed her greeting with a laugh.

He'd ignored her brother and quickly made up for it. "Sorry, Robbie. Good morning. Are you ready to head over to the station? Jackson said he'd be there at eight."

Sophie glanced over at Robbie, who nodded and shot to

his feet. "I need my laptop. Should I get yours as well?" he asked and, without waiting for her reply, held his hand out for her key.

"Sí, gracias," she said, rising and drawing the key from her jeans pocket to give to him.

As he walked away, Ryder said, "Do you always use Spanish when you get flustered?"

A bright flush worked its way across her cheeks and spread down her neck to her...

He stopped from looking ever more downward as his body reacted to that innocent blush, and her soft cough drew his attention back to her face.

"Robbie and I often speak Spanish with each other and family, but yes, sometimes when I'm...flustered. I also curse a blue streak in Spanish when I'm mad," she said and eyeballed him in a way that said not to dare her to prove it.

"I'll keep that in mind." He motioned with his head toward the front door as Robbie bounded down the stairs with two backpacks as well as a jacket for her.

Ryder helped her ease on the jacket and picked up the backpack, since his mother had raised him to be a gentleman, but recalling her words of the day before, he handed it to her to carry.

"I know you can take care of yourself," he said to confirm that he'd honor what she'd said.

"Gracias," she said with a warm smile.

They hurried out of the inn and quickly made the short walk to the police station.

Milly was back at the front desk as they entered. She buzzed them through and said, "Do you need me to watch Delilah?"

"I think I'll keep her with me for now. She missed me

yesterday," he said, bent slightly and rubbed Delilah's head before going to their war room.

Jackson was just coming out of his office to join them. He unlocked the door and they entered.

Ryder unleashed Delilah, who promptly waddled to one side of the room, lay down and rolled onto her back, assuming her dead bug pose in the hope of earning a belly rub.

That she got from Sophie before she took a spot at the table.

Ryder sat beside her and opened his notebook while Sophie and Robbie powered up their laptops.

Jackson walked to their investigation board and jotted down some notes before facing them. With an angry jab in Sophie's direction, he said, "That wasn't a smart thing to do last night."

Angry color flooded her face and she muttered something in Spanish. A curse, he suspected from their earlier discussion.

To head off even more dissension between the cousins, he said, "As dangerous as it was, it gave us information. For starters, we know that whoever it was—"

"Probably the hacker," Sophie interrupted.

Ryder nodded and continued. "Probably the hacker. We know they want out, so we should focus on finding them immediately as they might be the key to finding your parents."

"We've got an IP address. We should work that," Robbie said with a wave in the direction of his laptop.

"Do you think you can isolate the location of that address?" Jackson asked from his spot near the board.

Robbie nodded. "I may be able to identify the ISP with that IP address. It all depends on whether they were also using a VPN in addition to the spoofed IP address."

Jackson's eyes opened wide and he shook his head. "Whatever that means, go ahead with it. Sophie, what about you?"

Sophie emitted a little chuckle. "More geek speak for you. I'm going to analyze the message headers and track where it came from."

With a wave of his hand, he said, "Have at it." His friend glanced in his direction and said, "What do you say about some old-school-style investigations?"

"I'm game."

Reveille sounded and bright lights snapped on, jerking Mercedes awake after a fitful night of sleep.

Robert likewise shot upright in the cot opposite hers, his salt-and-pepper hair in erratic spikes that he finger-brushed smooth.

She ran her fingers through her hair, trying to put it into some semblance of order, although she didn't know why she cared what her captors might think.

"Good morning, y'all. I hope you slept well," said a digitally modulated voice that didn't mask the slow honeyed tone of the Deep South.

She shared a look with Robert, and he nodded, keeping silent as she did.

"I'll take that as a yes," said the disembodied voice and plowed on. "We need your help with a few things. You can find it on the computer screens that are now active."

They rose as if one and walked to inspect the screens.

Her eyes widened at what they were being tasked to do. Most of the items involved removing evidence and database entries for a couple of prominent underworld figures as well as accessing the cloud backups for Senator Oliver's investigation.

She glanced at her husband, eyes questioning even though

she understood how damaging it would be to any pending cases. She had no doubt what the punishment would be if they disobeyed. But if they did do as asked…

"We do this, and you let us go?" she asked.

A small hesitation created fear before the voice said, "That would only seem fair."

Somehow, she didn't think *fair* factored into what was happening and Robert clearly felt the same way.

"That doesn't seem very definite. We need definite," Robert warned.

The laughter came immediately. "How definite is this for you? Do it or die."

RYDER SAT ON a chintz-covered sofa across from retired police chief Bill Robinson, who lazed in a well-worn leather recliner.

The chief had a bull chest and broad midsection straining a light blue shirt that was a remnant of his time on the force. The right breast was empty of the police chief's badge, which now sat on Jackson's chest, while the left had an embroidered patch with Regina's emblem. White, blue and gold colors on the badge-shaped patch showed the mountains in the background, skiers on a slope to the left and a swimmer in waves to the right.

"Thank you for chatting with us today," Ryder said and pulled his notepad from his jacket pocket.

"I wish I could say it was my pleasure, but not with you thinking one of our men is dirty," Robinson said and shot a hairy eyeball at Jackson as he sat beside Ryder on the soft sofa cushions.

"We have to consider every possible scenario. Believe me, I don't want to think friends like Mark or Diego might be involved," Jackson assured him, earning a reluctant nod from Bill.

"I noticed you didn't include Cromwell," Bill challenged with another arch of a thick, bushy brow.

"I don't know Cromwell enough to call him a friend yet," Jackson admitted.

"I don't either. Not sure I'd call him a friend even if I did," Bill said with a pained grunt and shrug of meaty shoulders.

"Why is that?" Ryder asked, picking up on the old chief's discomfort.

Gazing upward, as if weighing his words before he spoke, Bill finally said, "Something rubbed me wrong from the start about him, but we were so short-staffed that I couldn't turn away an experienced officer."

Ryder took a quick look at Jackson, who nodded and added, "He was one of Bill's last hires before he retired."

"You oversaw him on some shifts while Jax was on Selene's case with Rhea. Did that change your initial impression of him?" Ryder prodded.

Robinson immediately and emphatically shook his head. "Not really. He was late for a few shifts and his incident reports were often sloppy and incomplete."

Ryder squinted at Jackson, who added, "I thought so, too, but worried I was being too much of a stickler because I had just become chief."

"Not at all," Robinson quickly chimed in. "I know you've been strapped for time between Rhea and working extra shifts since we lost an officer to another force, but I think if you weren't, you'd axe Cromwell."

"I would. I've actually been thinking about promoting Milly if she'd accept it," Jackson said.

"Milly would love it, I think, and you could hire a civilian to work the front desk," Robinson suggested.

"Great minds," Jackson said with a smile at his old mentor.

While Ryder appreciated the rapport between the two men, he had a more pressing mission than the staffing at the station.

"Do you think Cromwell is capable of removing evidence from the station?"

Robinson pursed his lips as he considered the question. "Like I said, I don't want to think any of my men are dirty, but if anyone would, it might be him. And I don't think it would be difficult for Cromwell to do. No offense, Jax. Cromwell was working many of the late shifts and had access. It might not be hard to hide his actions while other officers were out on calls."

"What about motive?" Ryder asked.

Another shrug of meaty shoulders came before Robinson said, "Isn't money always a great motivator?"

"Because he owes others?" Jackson challenged with eyes wide in emphasis.

"Or because he's greedy," Robinson said, shifting in his seat, which creaked from the weight of him.

"Fair enough. Thank you for your time," Ryder said and shot to his feet, sensing he'd gotten all he could from the old chief and eager to reach out to others about Cromwell.

Jackson also rose, walked over to Robinson and shook his hand. "Thanks for your thoughts, Bill. They're much appreciated."

Ryder likewise shook the old man's hand and again offered his thanks. "We appreciate your time. If there's anything else you think of—"

"I'll be sure to let you know, Agent Hunt," the man finished for him.

They'd left the chief's house and had just stepped out into

the street when the hackles on Ryder's neck rose in warning at the squeal of tires.

Ryder threw his arm out in front of Jackson and yanked them both back toward the sidewalk.

A classic Camaro SS, bright red, with heavily tinted windows and license plates obscured by dark gray covers, sped by, dangerously close. Wheels screeched against the pavement and the muscle car fishtailed as it turned onto Main Street a few blocks away.

Jackson immediately grabbed his radio. "All officers be on the lookout for a 1970s red Camaro SS with white racing stripes. Approach with caution."

"Do you think that was a warning?" Ryder asked, double-checking the street this time before walking across.

"Seems too coincidental to not be," Jackson said as he opened the driver's-side door.

Once they were seated, a report burst from the radio as Jackson reached for his Mobile Data Terminal.

"Lost him on the highway heading east toward Denver. He clipped my front end and sent me off the road into a ditch," Diego advised and then muttered a curse.

"Are you and Poppy okay?" Jackson asked, concern for his officers the most important thing.

A sharp bark drifted across the line before Diego said, "Poppy and I are fine."

"I'll call Denver and have them issue a BOLO for the Camaro as well. Call for a tow and head back to the station. We'll see if we can't get some paint samples for evidence," Jackson advised, an angry flush across his face.

"Roger that." Diego signed off.

"This is another escalation. Whoever is behind this isn't easily dissuaded," Ryder said, a sick feeling in his stomach that the odds of getting the Whitakers back alive were dropping by the second.

With a quick bob of his head, Jackson said, "I agree and I'm tired of being on the receiving end. It's time to put the screws to Oliver."

SOPHIE STRETCHED IN her chair and when that wasn't enough, she rose, placed her hands on her hips and bent backward to work out the kinks.

Robbie glanced in her direction. "Stiff?"

Sophie nodded. "Been sitting for too long," she said and shot a quick look at her watch. "We've been at this for nearly three hours."

"I knew it was almost time for lunch." Robbie smiled.

She shook her head because Robbie and his stomach were like clockwork, but she didn't know how he could eat with all that was happening.

"I don't know how you do it," she said, about to sit again when a knock came at the door.

She opened it to find two identical women holding bags and boxes. Jackson's wife, Rhea, and her twin sister, Selene, who had been visiting when her parents had been taken.

Hugging Rhea as best she could thanks to her large baby belly, Sophie then embraced Selene. "It's good to see you again."

"It is. I just wish it wasn't under these circumstances," Selene said in a voice with an almost melodic lilt, possibly a result of her new career as a musician.

Robbie had hopped to his feet with the entry of the two women and he likewise hugged them, but as he stepped back to his laptop, his gaze lingered lovingly on Selene, surprising Sophie. She'd never seen quite that look on her brother's face, but she could understand why.

Like her sister, Rhea, Selene was a beautiful woman with electric-blue eyes that were bright against her pale creamy skin and nearly black hair. She had a lithe but curvy body that her loose boho-style clothing couldn't hide. Musical bracelets danced on her wrists and several rings adorned long, elegant fingers.

"We're just dropping off some lunch since Jackson texted to say he'd be back at the station soon," Rhea said as she and Selene started to empty an assortment of bags and sodas onto the conference room table.

"Let me help," Robbie said and joined the two women in spreading out lunch.

A second later, another knock came at the door and Sophie again opened it to reveal Jackson and Ryder standing there. The two men entered and she shut the door to avoid anyone glimpsing the notes on their whiteboard.

From the looks on the men's faces, it was obvious they weren't happy.

"What's happened?" she asked, praying that it wasn't bad news about her parents.

"We visited my old chief, and someone sent us a warning on the way out of his house," Jackson said and then relayed the information about Diego and his K-9, Poppy. He finished with, "They should be back at the station shortly so we can collect some evidence from the cruiser. Denver PD is also on the lookout for the vehicle."

"What about Oliver? You said you went to see him?" Sophie asked, worried that they didn't seem to be making much progress.

Jackson's lips thinned into a tight slash. "He said to call his lawyer and shut the door in our faces."

Sophie peered at Ryder. "Is that it? There's nothing else we can do?"

Ryder jammed his hands on his hips and nodded. "Oliver is entitled to counsel. But we'll keep up the pressure and work on his associates to find a crack. Once we have that, we'll get him in the box and sweat him. Have you made any progress?"

"We've found the source of the hack and message. The IP address is definitely at the high school," Robbie said.

"Any way to ID who sent the message?" Ryder asked, his gaze drifting from Robbie to rest on her.

She shook her head. "No, but we know what time it was sent. He must have gone from sending the message to waiting for us at the meeting spot at the school."

"Which explains how he knew to make his escape. Just to confirm—it's a 'he' because most hackers are male?" Ryder asked.

Sophie bobbed her head to confirm. "Less than two percent of hackers are female."

"So you're an exception," he said, eyeballing her in a way that made her heart skip a beat.

"I am," she replied and then looked at Jackson and said, "You mentioned your contacts in Denver. Anything there?"

"Still searching for the pickup and now for this vintage Camaro," he advised.

"Can't be too hard to find such a unique car," Robbie said, brow crumpled in thought.

"Not if the car is registered. They've started database searches at their end, and we can help out. Which reminds me. They'd love to have one of you check their systems to confirm they don't have any possible vulnerabilities," Ryder said, once again glancing from her to Robbie.

"Whoever is going back to Denver can hitch a ride with me. I'm going back tomorrow," Selene offered.

Sophie met Robbie's gaze, hers questioning, and his answer was clear.

"The hacker reached out to Sophie, so I think she should stay here," Robbie said, his response plausible even though Sophie suspected he had other reasons for going to Denver.

"You're welcome to stay with me. Rhea's old place has more than enough room," Selene said with the faintest splash of color on her cheeks.

Was love in the air at such a difficult time? Sophie sneaked a peek at Robbie, whose gaze had never left Selene.

"That seems to make the most sense. Hopefully, the hacker will reach out again," she said, echoing Robbie's rationale.

"Hope isn't a plan," Jackson chastised, seemingly frustrated by the state of the investigation.

"You want to create a crack? Let's visit the high school and see if they have any CCTV footage they'll share. Then we'll go to their computer lab to put some pressure on this hacker," Sophie said.

Chapter Seven

Ryder sat beside Sophie and the high school's head of security, and across from Mary Peterson, the high school principal, whose face was pinched with annoyance.

"What do you mean the file was deleted?" Mary said, eyes boring a hole into her head of security.

The man shifted his hands uneasily on his pant legs and sent a quick look in their direction before he said, "We were hacked. I'm assuming by whoever CBI Agent Hunt and Ms. Whitaker are trying to find."

If the state of the principal's attire and office was any indication of her basic nature, this kind of deviation was thoroughly unacceptable, Ryder considered thoughtfully. She wore a pristine white shirt and an impeccably tailored dark blue suit. Books were neatly arranged on shelves beside some strategically placed bric-a-brac and awards commemorating the school's success.

"You're telling me that one of our students possibly broke into our systems?" she said, ice coating her words.

Ryder decided it was time to make an ally of the security chief. "Whoever he is, he's a gifted hacker. It would be hard to keep him out, but I believe Sophie might be able to help recover the files. Am I right?" he said and glanced at Sophie in the matching chair beside him.

Sophie nodded and offered an encouraging smile to the school officials. "Yes, you're right, Agent Hunt. This is an experienced hacker. But we should be able to restore the video file and possibly offer some suggestions on plugging any vulnerabilities in your system."

"That would be greatly appreciated. Would you mind assisting them, Max?" the principal said and visibly relaxed, losing her ramrod-stiff posture to sink into the cushions of her leather executive chair.

Max, the head of security, nodded and lumbered out of his chair. "I'll take them to our office and call our IT head also."

"That would be great, and please keep me posted on whatever you discover," Mary said as she rose from her chair and shook their hands. Her grip was strong, her nails perfectly manicured, reinforcing Ryder's earlier perception of how controlled she was and what she expected of her people.

His assessment was confirmed as they walked out of her office and Max said, "Mary's tough but fair. I hope we can resolve this issue without it getting out of control."

"I'm sure we can," Ryder said as Max led them down the hall.

As they walked, students' heads swiveled and murmurs erupted since Ryder had made it a point to prominently drape his badge from his shirt pocket.

Sophie took a quick peek in his direction and whispered for his ears only, "Pressure."

He smiled and nodded but his gaze noted every student who walked by, including one young man who tucked his head down into the folds of his hoodie and averted his face. The hoodie was black with a stylized image of a grizzly bear in white on the back, but several teens were wearing similar clothing. *A school mascot*, he thought.

The person last night had worn a hoodie but the dark ski

vest tossed over it would have hidden the team insignia on the back.

"See something interesting?" Sophie asked as she noticed his attention had been snared.

"Young man. Black hoodie. Sandy-haired and average height. Black knapsack with chains. He's way down the hall."

Sophie slowed her walk and scrutinized the direction he'd mentioned. Narrowing her gaze, she said, "Body shape and height aren't far off from last night's suspect."

"Right. We'll have to ask around to see who he is," Ryder said as they resumed their walk to the security office.

In no time, they slipped into a room at the end of the hall where another security officer was keeping an eye on several monitors. He glanced their way as they entered and Max said, "Could you please get Mr. Snyder?"

The man immediately hopped to his feet and exited, and Max held his hand out in the direction of the table where the other officer had been sitting.

It was a serviceable workstation with a couple of keyboards as well as a bank of monitors displaying grainy black-and-white images from several areas in and around the school.

After Sophie sat at the table, Max quickly explained what the various images represented. "We have eyes on every doorway into the school as well as a few in outside areas that we feel need additional security, like the athletic fields and bleachers, and wooded areas to one side of the school."

"And the videos from all of these camera feeds were deleted sometime last night?" Ryder asked just to confirm.

Max blew out a rough breath and dragged a hand through his thinning hair. "They were. We didn't realize it until Chief Whitaker called and asked if we could give him the videos.

Honestly, we never had this kind of problem before," he said in apology.

Ryder clapped him on the back. "Don't blame yourself, Max. It's not the kind of thing you expect and, like we said, this is an experienced hacker."

"A pro, huh?" Max said with a sigh of relief.

IT TOOK ALL of Sophie's willpower not to admit that it was likely a student behind the hack. Of course, the fact that it was a student didn't mean that he wasn't a pro and so, to alleviate Max's concerns, she said, "Whoever did this is highly skilled."

Without waiting for Max, she went to work on the keyboard, which was still live even though the officer sitting there had departed. "You should set each computer to lock after a minute or so. It will increase security and conserve power as well."

"Will do," Max said.

Sophie took out a portfolio and pen to make notes as she began a search through the files, getting a sense of the network architecture that a normal user might have. Much like she expected, access to certain network files and settings was restricted and likely limited to someone who had administrator clearance.

With a few keystrokes, she noted the IP address and was about to try to hack deeper when the other security officer returned with whom she suspected was Mr. Snyder, the head of IT.

He was a tall man with a pronounced forward stoop, probably from spending too much time on his computer. She pegged him to be in his midforties and nervous as he wrung his hands over and over after he entered the room.

"I understand you need some information," he said, his gaze darting back and forth between her and Ryder.

She rose and held out her hand to relieve some of his anxiety. "Sophie Whitaker. I'm Chief Whitaker's cousin and part of the South Beach Security Agency in Miami. Jax asked us to help with a case he's working on."

Snyder's hand was damp and slightly chilly as she shook it.

"Roger Snyder. I teach a few technology classes and double as the head of IT. We're a small school district, so many of us do double duty," he offered by way of apology and shook Ryder's hand.

"I coach the football and baseball teams," Max said.

Sophie could picture him as a jock. Despite the salt and pepper in his close-cropped hair, his muscular body was still in shape beneath the khaki uniform he wore.

"The Regina Grizzlies, I assume?" Ryder asked, one brow arched in question.

"Yes, that's our team mascot," Max confirmed.

"Do you have lots of fans? Sell a lot of Grizzlies gear?" Ryder prompted.

Both Max and Roger nodded emphatically. "Our teams are very successful, so we have a lot of fans, both in school and in town. You'll see a lot of Grizzlies gear."

With a tight smile that said he'd hoped it was otherwise because it just increased the number of possible suspects, Ryder said, "Thanks for that info."

Wanting to get back to the reason she was there, Sophie faced Roger. "I was about to try and hack into your network, if that's okay with you?"

Roger shifted to and fro on his feet, reluctant, but after a glance at Max, he nodded and invited her to return to the keyboard.

Ryder stood next to Max as Sophie went to work, fingers flying across the keys while she explained to Roger what she was doing and gave tips to improve security.

Her tone was patient and noncondemning, which surprised him. He'd dealt with more than one tech geek at work and had sometimes found them lacking in people skills.

Sophie had people skills in spades and, despite her highlighting several gaps in security on the school's network, Roger never seemed put off. If anything, he leaned forward, eagerly accepting every nugget of info she fed him as if it was manna from heaven.

"Got it," she said brightly and with a broad smile as one of the monitors suddenly displayed the video of the athletic fields and bleachers from the night before.

Sophie came into view as she was halfway to the bleachers, and someone stepped from behind them. Mostly in black from his Chuck Taylors to his jeans to the vest and hoodie pulled forward to keep his face in shadow.

Ryder leaned closer and said, "Can you freeze it there?"

Sophie immediately did as he asked, and they both scrutinized the photo. But it was grainy, and whoever it was had made a point to hide themselves well. The hoodie did a good job of keeping his face dark and so did the shadow cast by the bleachers.

"He knew exactly where to stand to stay hidden," he said.

Sophie nodded. "He did, but he's close enough to the bleachers that we can use them to estimate his height," she said and, after a quick search, added, "Average rise for the steps is between seven and three-quarters and eight inches. Using that formula would put our suspect at about five feet six inches in height."

"Like the young man we spotted earlier," Ryder mused, recalling the teen who had grabbed his attention in the hall.

"You noticed someone?" Max asked as he, too, examined the video.

"We did. Does he look familiar to you at all?" Sophie asked the two men.

They both shook their heads, almost in unison. "It's too dark to see much," Roger said.

"If you don't mind me making copies of these files, we'll try to enhance the images," Sophie said and slipped a USB drive into the nearby desktop. "Also, you should disable USB access on the computers that your students and teachers use. They probably used a thumb drive to load malware that enabled their hack."

"Like the Stuxnet virus?" Roger said, keeping a vigilant eye on Sophie as she copied over the files.

"Just like Stuxnet," she confirmed and removed her USB from the desktop.

"You mentioned seeing someone," Max repeated, pulling them back to their earlier comment.

Ryder nodded. "Young man. About five foot six or so. Longish sandy hair. Black knapsack with chains. Black Grizzlies hoodie, but as you said, there are a lot of those."

Max and Roger shared a concerned look before Roger hesitantly said, "It sounds like Matt Clark. He's one of my best students."

"And one of my best pitchers. He's a senior and we keep on hoping he'll be able to land a baseball scholarship at one of the local universities, but it hasn't happened so far," Max added.

And might not with only months to go before graduation time, Ryder thought. "If he doesn't get a scholarship, will he still go to college?"

Once again, Max and Roger peered at each other, reluctant. "Possibly not," Roger eventually conceded.

"Single mom. Dad's nowhere in sight. Younger brother. Matt's a good kid. Does what he can to help out his family," Max said, and his admiration for the young man was evident.

Ryder dipped his head to the side, considering their comments. "You said he is one of your best students. Good enough to help someone with an IT problem?"

Roger shifted uncomfortably in his chair and nodded. "He's done work for some of the smaller businesses in town as part of an internship program we started last year."

"Would you mind sharing the names of those businesses?" Sophie asked.

Another conspiratorial look passed between the two men. "We'll have to clear that with Principal Peterson," Max said.

"And the Family Educational Rights and Privacy Act may require that you get a warrant and that we let Matt's family know that you've asked for that information," Roger added. After sharing another look with the head of security, he said, "We've probably already said too much."

Ryder held his hands up in a not-to-worry gesture. "We'll keep whatever you shared with us confidential and ask Chief Whitaker to see about getting that warrant."

"We'd appreciate that. Like we said, Matt's a good kid. I can't imagine that he's involved in anything like this," Max said.

Except for the fact that his family needed money, college would be out of the question without said money, and time was running short for any kind of help.

As far as Ryder was concerned, that made good kid Matt Clark their No. 1 hacker suspect.

Chapter Eight

The laser focus of the cop's gaze had burned twin holes into his back.

He still felt the heat as he hurried out the side door and ducked into the wooded area bordering the high school.

A quick peek revealed he wasn't being followed, but for how long?

He had no doubt the cop had stared at him as he'd passed him and the pretty woman in the hallway. Those eyes had stayed on him, propelling him toward the side exit even though he had one more class for the day.

Mrs. Watson would be mad that he'd cut out…again. He'd missed her English class a few times in the last month since they'd needed him at the local grocery store where he clerked when he wasn't doing an odd IT job or two.

Or did that hack for Oliver, the little voice in his head reminded, no matter how much he wanted to forget what he'd done.

But he'd had little choice. He'd needed the money to help his family and maybe have enough set aside to pay for a semester of community college.

He hopped over a small log and pushed on, constantly looking backward to make sure he wasn't being followed.

It wasn't until he'd popped out on the far end of Main

Street that he doubled back to head toward the center of town and the grocery store.

He hadn't gone far when he noticed the cop and pretty hacker strolling off the school grounds and moving in the direction of the inn and police station.

Staying back, the hunted became the hunter as he followed them.

Their heads were bent together, almost touching, since the woman was on the taller side.

He didn't doubt that he was the topic of their discussion and wondered how much information they'd been able to glean in the security office.

While he'd deleted the video files, unless he'd run a BleachBit to shred every bit of data, the woman could have recovered them if she knew her stuff. And based on what he'd read about her on the South Beach Security website, she knew her stuff.

As worried as he was about being discovered, he'd also been excited at first about outwitting her and her brother, both respected white hat hackers.

Until Oliver had gone totally berserk and kidnapped their parents.

It was why he'd reached out. He wanted no part of what was happening now, he supposed, but a second later the burner phone in his back pocket vibrated, reminding him that he was still stuck in the mess.

Dropping farther back from the couple, he answered.

"YOU SAW HIM?" Sophie asked while walking beside Ryder, tucked so close their shoulders brushed, rousing all kinds of emotions.

"I did. Same teen from the hall," he said without peering back.

"Matt Clark?" she pressed, forcing herself not to look over her shoulder and clue the young man that he had been seen.

"Presumably. He's old enough to drive. We'll have Jackson pull up his license and check the DMV to see if any cars are registered in his name."

While Jackson was doing that, Sophie intended to search social media and other websites to get a sense of who Matt Clark might be while Robbie worked on enhancing the images on the videos she had recovered. Hopefully, it would be enough to haul the teen in for questioning that might help locate her parents.

It had already been over forty-eight hours since they'd been kidnapped.

Were they badly injured? More than just nosebleeds? She recalled Jackson's words about the blood in the rental car.

Were they somewhere warm? Yesterday's unseasonable snow still frosted the grass and bushes beside the sidewalk.

"You okay?" Ryder asked and shot her a side-eyed glance.

She nodded. "Just thinking about my parents. Worried about how they're doing. If they're still alive," she said, finally voicing her most serious concern.

Ryder wrapped an arm around her shoulders and gave a reassuring squeeze. "They were taken for a reason—"

"To breach those other databases," she finished for him and met his gaze.

"Probably for that. FBI and others are monitoring them for any attacks. CBI is on the lookout as well. As long as it hasn't happened, they're safe."

"But what about when they do it or if they can't?" she pressed.

Ryder's gaze darkened, grew intense. "We will find them well before then."

He didn't strike her as the kind of man who made promises he didn't keep. Because of that, she echoed his words.

"We will find them before then."

MERCEDES AND ROBERT huddled together over the quick lunch they'd assembled from the contents of the refrigerator and cabinets along the one wall of their jail.

The canned tomato soup seemed like a gourmet feast, and it warmed her insides and hands nicely as she cupped the large soup mug. Even though there was a heater pumping warm air into the space, the cinder block seemed to eat up all the heat. Plus, a chill had settled into her center, the chill of fear that hadn't left her since the moment of the crash.

"My love, stop worrying. It's going to be okay," Robert insisted, tucking her tight to him and rubbing his hand up and down her arm in an attempt to warm her.

"Mi amor, they're not going to let us go, no matter what they say," she whispered close to his ear in the hope that whatever mikes were in the room wouldn't pick up her words. She had no doubt the room was bugged.

Robert, ever the optimist, said, "We haven't seen their faces. He's modulated his voice. Seems like a lot of trouble if they're not going to let us go."

He had a point, and she embraced that thought. Coupled with the hot soup, it melted some of the chill in her center.

They had finished the soup and a tuna fish sandwich when the disembodied voice erupted from the speakers again.

"I hope y'all enjoyed your meal. I know you must be plumb tired, but it's time to get back to work. My friends are getting impatient."

"These things take time," Robert declared and held his hand out to help her from the cot where they'd sat for lunch.

"It's taking too much time and, I'll tell you what… Y'all have to deal with the names on the list," the voice warned.

Mercedes had never been one to be pushed around. She tilted her chin up a defiant inch and asked, "And what if we can't?"

A harsh laugh erupted before the voice said, "I like a woman with fight, but don't doubt me. You don't want to know what will happen if you fail."

A click signaled the connection had ended.

Mercedes looked at Robert and, despite any misgivings about what they were being asked to do, said, "The authorities are watching for our attack. They may have already noticed increased network traffic."

"Maybe. We'll have to take that chance if we're going to hack in before that deadline."

Mercedes nodded and sat down at the desktop, wishing she had the hacking tools on the laptops their captors wouldn't let them access. It was part of the reason this was taking so much time. They'd had to rebuild the programs they normally used to test and stop hacks. They'd only finished recoding them that morning after an all-nighter of work.

But she'd also left behind little breadcrumbs that would be a message Sophie or Robbie might uncover if they picked up on the hack they were about to perform.

Especially Sophie with her unique abilities. If anyone could locate the message, it would be Sophie, and Mercedes hoped that she and Robbie were already working on this investigation.

RYDER STOOD BESIDE Jackson as he knocked on the door of the Clark home.

The door whipped open and a boy stood there, a younger,

smaller version of the teen Ryder had seen at the high school. Same sandy hair and slight build. Blue eyes that were similar to those he had noticed on the teen's driver's license.

Those blue eyes widened in surprise at the sight of Jackson and popped open even more as the young boy took in Ryder's badge.

"M-m-may I help you?" he stammered, flustered.

"Who is it, Danny?" a woman called out from deep in the simple Craftsman-style house.

"The p-p-police," Danny shouted back, which brought the woman rushing forward, wiping her hands on a kitchen towel.

Much like her son, her blue eyes widened at the sight of them on her doorstep. "May I help you?"

"May we come in? We'd like to chat with Matt, if that's okay with you?" Jackson said.

She hesitated for a long moment then nodded, apparently deciding it was better to cooperate than to put up a stink. "Matt's not home right now. He's at work down at the grocery store," she said but waved them to come in.

They stepped into a house that was well-kept and tidy even though the furniture seemed to be a hodgepodge of styles and a little worn in spots. If Ryder had to guess, he suspected some of it had been salvaged from the curb or picked up at yard sales. But it was all clean and orderly.

"Thank you for inviting us into your home. Would you mind answering a few questions?" Jackson asked, his tone smooth and welcoming to put the mother at ease.

The woman eyed him, still nervously wringing the kitchen towel in her hands. "That depends. What's this about?"

Ryder and Jackson shared a look and Ryder took over the questioning, adopting a more formal stance. "We're investigating State Senator Oliver. You may have seen in the news that—"

"What does that have to do with my son?" she immediately challenged, her mama bear rising in defense.

"There's nothing to worry about, Mrs. Clark," Jackson said, hands held up in pleading, trying to ease her worry.

"Seems like there's a lot to worry about when I have two cops standing in my home," she said and quickly added, "And it's Ms. Williams now. I don't use my ex's name anymore."

Not an uncommon occurrence but Ryder sensed there was more there. "What was the reason for the divorce?"

A gusty breath erupted from her and she glanced in the direction of her younger son, who still stood there shocked but listening intently. "Don't you have homework to do, Danny?"

She didn't have to say more. The boy rushed off. Seconds later, the squeak of a door hinge followed by a soft thud said it had closed.

Ms. Williams relaxed slightly and finally answered. "Danny was too young to remember the violence, but not Matt. I put up with it for years when it was only me, but the day he turned his fists on my Matt, it was time to go. I packed up the boys and never looked back."

"It must have been hard for you," Jackson said, his voice consoling.

"It wasn't easy. It hasn't been easy. Money is tight, but we make ends meet, especially with Matt working at the grocery and taking on some odd jobs here and there," she said and gestured to the two chairs in front of a couch whose brightly colored flowers had faded long ago, much like the woman before them.

She had been pretty at one time, with a girl-next-door look. But dark smudges that seemed permanent made her blue eyes sunken and those eyes dull and lifeless. Deep lines etched the sides of her eyes and frowns had gouged brackets beside her mouth. The domestic violence and what had followed had taken a toll on her.

Ryder hated returning to his hard-investigator stance since he understood what it was like to live with such violence more than most, but he had no choice. "Do those odd jobs include working for Senator Oliver?"

She hesitated but then nodded. "Mr. Snyder was nice enough to get Matt an internship with Oliver. I think it had something to do with the social media for his last campaign."

"And is Matt still working for him?" Ryder pressed, lifting a brow in challenge.

"No." She pounced, nearly hopping out of her seat before pulling back and whispering more softly, "At least, I don't think so."

Sympathetic to her plight, Jackson said, "It's okay, Ms. Williams. Whatever is happening, we will take care of Matt."

Her lips pressed into a rough line and she bobbed her head up and down, like one of those drinking bird toys, all the time strangling the kitchen towel in her hands.

It made him remember his suffering mother, always waiting for either another blow or news about her alcoholic husband. Because of that, he softened and said, "Sheriff Whitaker is telling you the truth. If Matt's in trouble, we will do what we can for him."

The change in his demeanor helped relax her and she fell back onto the couch cushions. "Thank you. Matt's a good kid. He really is."

He understood because he'd once been like Matt.

Rising to his feet, he said, "Don't worry, Ms. Williams. We will do what we can to help Matt if he is in any kind of trouble."

Jackson followed his lead, standing and offering comfort. "We'll watch out for him."

They let themselves out, but not before catching a glimpse of Matt's mother sitting on the couch with his younger brother huddled close to her.

It once again roused painful memories, and his friend noticed.

"I know it wasn't easy for you either," Jackson said.

"No, it wasn't. I understand where Matt is coming from and how hard it is for him," he said, sympathetic to the boy's plight.

"But that doesn't excuse him becoming a black hat," Jackson reminded as they hurried to the police SUV for their drive to the grocery store located just off Regina's business district and not far from the high school.

Ryder didn't doubt that Matt's mom might have called to warn him and if Matt was like any other teenager, he'd likely have his phone on him at all times. That meant he might already be on the run.

"I'll take the back," Ryder said as soon as they parked, certain they'd have to chase down the young man.

Jackson nodded, stepped out of the SUV and slipped on his white Stetson. "I'll speak to the manager and locate Matt," Jackson said and hurried in the direction of the grocery store entrance.

Ryder marched toward the side of the store and nearly jogged around to the back.

There were several loading bays where workers were transferring boxes and crates of grocery items to carts for movement into the store.

A delivery truck for a local farm was parked in the farthest bay and workers were off-loading boxes of lettuce and other vegetables onto the dock.

He immediately recognized Matt Clark.

Hurrying toward the dock, he had almost reached it when Jackson popped out of a nearby door with the woman he assumed was the store manager.

Matt's head whipped in the direction of Jackson and the manager and, a heartbeat later, he jumped off the loading dock and ran around the truck to escape.

Never good to run, Ryder thought as he gave chase. He'd run more than once from his father until the day he'd finally stood his ground and found freedom.

He raced around the truck, up the side of the store and into the parking lot. Matt was just yards ahead, well within reach, and Jackson was just behind him, hot on his heels.

Ryder never saw the car that hit him.

All he saw was the world whirling all around him as he flew through the air before landing hard against the pavement.

Pain filled his body and dark circles danced in his gaze.

Suddenly, Jackson was there, looming above him.

"Hang on, Ryder," Jackson said.

He opened his mouth to speak, only it didn't seem to be working.

Nothing seemed to be working as darkness drifted into his vision and claimed him.

Chapter Nine

Sophie sat by Ryder's bedside, quietly working on her laptop while also keeping an eye on the sleeping CBI agent.

He'd been awake and conscious when they'd first arrived at the hospital and luckily he'd suffered only minor injuries. No breaks, but he definitely had a concussion and the doctors had insisted on holding him overnight despite his determined denials.

From the corner of her eye, she saw his eyelids tardily drift open and closed her laptop.

"How are you feeling?" she asked as his dark gaze settled on her.

"Sore. Heck of a headache," he said as he adjusted the bed to an upright position and massaged his temples with his fingers.

"It's the concussion," she said, and her phone's alarm started chirping. She shut it off and, at his questioning glance, told him, "I was supposed to wake you up and see how you're doing."

"I'd be doing better if I was at the station, working on the investigation."

"Jackson is there with Robbie," she said and slipped her laptop into her bag.

"Were you working?" he asked and gestured to her knapsack.

"I was and I think I have something," she said, excitement coloring her voice.

"Did you identify the hacker?" His tone was hopeful.

She shook her head. "No, although it seems we're not off in thinking it's Matt. Why would he run if he's innocent?"

He shrugged and immediately grimaced in pain from his injuries before schooling his emotions. "People run for all kinds of reasons."

She eyed him, curious. "It sounds like you have experience with that. With Matt's history," she said since Jackson had given them some background on the boy.

With another pained shift of his shoulders, he said, "My dad was an alcoholic. He also liked to use his fists."

"I'm sorry," she said and laid her hand on his, offering support in the only way she could.

He smiled weakly and took hold of her hand, surprising her, and yet she liked the weight of his hand in hers. Took comfort from it while also giving comfort.

"I'm not sorry. It made me the man I am," he said and squeezed her hand.

She wanted to ask what kind of man that was since, up until now, he'd sometimes been hard to read. Despite that, he'd called to her, maybe because she'd always been drawn to wounded animals. Brooding men, Robbie would have reminded her, and maybe it was because brooding often hid injury.

Instead of asking outright, she said, "Is that why you went into law enforcement?"

A harsh laugh escaped him and had him grasping at his ribs with a pained grunt. "Not at all. Hated cops for a long time since they never helped us. Luckily, my dad left after I stood up to him and he realized he couldn't terrorize us anymore. Life got about as normal as it could after that. Since I couldn't afford college, I joined the Marines."

"And met Jackson?" she asked, wondering if that was how the two men had become friends.

"And met Jackson. When we finished our tours, we came home and, with our backgrounds, it seemed natural to go into law enforcement."

"My cousin Trey did the same thing," she said, thinking of the man who had followed his family's legacy of service and was now the head of their security agency.

He narrowed his gaze, considering her as he asked, "So why did you become involved in sort-of law enforcement?"

"You mean my work at the agency?" At his nod, she continued. "My brother and I were white hats in high school and college. Gave us lots of experience that we used to develop popular programs to help protect networks. Also created some successful gaming applications and, since money was no longer an issue, it seemed like we should do more with our talents. We decided to join the family business and help others. Much like you."

HIS FAMILY CONSISTED of his mom and brother, so having an extended family like the combined Gonzalez-Whitaker clan was foreign to him.

"A big family must be nice," he said wistfully, which surprised him. He'd thought he was long past any desire for the normal things he'd seen in his friends' households.

"It is, although it can be a little overwhelming at times, especially as it grows bigger and bigger as cousins marry and have babies, like Trey, Jackson and now Mia," she said and, despite some hesitation in her words, obvious joy radiated on her face.

While it was nice finding out more about her, because she fascinated him, he hated that he'd been pulled away from the investigation. But he wasn't so muzzy that he didn't recall her earlier words.

"You said you found something," he prompted.

Excitement peppered her words as she said, "I think I did."

She released his hand and her absence registered immediately.

She whipped out her laptop, popped it open and pulled up a file with what looked like gibberish to him. Pointing at the characters, she said, "We were expecting some kind of hack and intercepted it. We know how they're trying to break in, and they left some code behind for us. For me, I should say."

"I don't get it," he said and gestured to the laptop, which was making his head hurt even more than it had before, both from the brightness of the screen and the jumble of text.

Seeing his distress, she snapped the laptop shut. "Remember that we said we can identify hackers by how they do what they do?"

He vaguely remembered and nodded. "I do. I guess you see something?"

A slight flush of color erupted on her cheeks. "I do. I see things other people might not, and my parents know that."

She seemed embarrassed by her skill but he pressed her, wanting to know more. Still, to ease her discomfort, he reached for her hand again and cradled it as he asked, "What is it you see, Sophie?"

The blush deepened and she looked away as, in a strangled voice, she said, "I see patterns, and…numbers and words are sometimes in color. It's called synesthesia. I don't normally share that with people because they think it's… Only my family knows." She seemed ashamed and yet…

"It's amazing to see the world with so much color."

His response both surprised and pleased her and put her at ease. With a nod, she said, "I see a pattern and hidden words in my parents' hacking. It may help us find out where they are. Thankfully, they're still alive since this attack is happening right now."

"That's good to hear, but I worry we're running out of time."

Sophie seemed worried. "Hacks take time and that will give us time to find them. Especially with what I'm seeing."

"Hopefully, we'll make the connections we need to build a case against Oliver and his cronies," Ryder said, earning a laugh from Sophie.

"'Cronies.' It's such an old-fashioned word," she said at his puzzled look.

"I'm an old-fashioned kind of guy." He twined his fingers with hers, wanting her to know he wasn't the kind to play around.

With a dip of her head, she said, "I'm good with that."

"Good. That means I'm not just going to lay here while your parents are at risk. Will you help me break out?"

"Break out, as in go AMA?" she said to make sure she understood.

"Yes, as in against medical advice. Are you game?"

"MAYBE THIS WASN'T a good idea," Sophie said, Ryder leaning on her heavily as they struggled up the steps of the police station.

"I'll be okay," he said but grunted in pain as he took the last step up to the front door.

She peered at him. Fine beads of sweat dotted his upper lip and a sickly white-green colored his face and neck.

"Let's get you inside," she said, somehow managing

to open the front door with one hand while helping him stay upright.

As soon as they walked in, Milly eyeballed them uneasily and unlocked the security gate. "Are you sure you should be here, Agent Hunt?" she asked, gazing at him with concern.

"I'm sure, Milly," he answered and pushed ahead with Sophie at his side.

Jackson was standing at a desk beside Officer Diego Rodriguez, the head of Regina's new K-9 unit. As they approached, she noticed Ryder's Delilah cuddled up to a beautiful German shepherd. But as soon as the corgi saw Ryder, she rushed over to jump around his feet excitedly.

"Thanks for taking care of my girl, Diego," Ryder said and wobbly bent to rub Delilah's head.

Diego gestured to the corgi. "I was just going to take her home with Poppy. I didn't think you were being released until the morning."

"I didn't think so either," Jackson said in an accusatory tone and glared at Sophie.

"Don't blame her, Jax. I insisted," Ryder said in her defense as he took Delilah's leash from Diego.

"Why isn't Cromwell at the front desk?" Ryder asked with a jerk of his head in Milly's direction.

Although Jackson knew he was changing the subject, he went with it. "Thought it wasn't wise to have him around in case we brought in Matt."

"Is Matt still on the run?" Sophie asked, using air quotes around "run" in emphasis.

Jackson nodded. "We still haven't tracked him down. I'm hoping he'll decide to go home and that his mother can convince him to cooperate."

"If he is the hacker," Sophie said.

"Do you have any doubt about that?" Diego asked, his dark cocoa gaze shifting from her to the two men.

"What we have so far is circumstantial evidence. We don't have anything concrete to prove that he's the hacker, do we?" Sophie pressed.

Jackson nodded. "All circumstantial unless Robbie has had some success with the videos from the school. If he has, we may be able to get a warrant to access Matt's computers and home."

"I don't know what Robbie has done, but I may have something," Sophie said and, beside her, Ryder wavered a little on his feet.

"I think it's time we got you to sit," she said. That he didn't argue with her confirmed he wasn't feeling quite right.

She guided him in the direction of their conference room and, when they entered, Robbie looked up from where he was hard at work.

"Dude, sit before you pass out," he said and immediately shot up to help Ryder into a nearby chair. Delilah settled in at his feet, her normally smiling face filled with worry as she stared at Ryder.

"Let me get you something to drink," Robbie added and rushed out to the water cooler.

"I must really look awful." Ryder glanced at her.

In the bright light of the conference room, she finally noticed the darkening bruises and scrapes along one side of his face. She winced. "You look a little…rough."

"I must if your brother noticed," he said, which elicited a chuckle from her.

"Robbie and I can be a little dense at times," she admitted because she, like her brother, could often get so involved with her work that the world around her didn't register.

Robbie returned with the promised glass of water and

some aspirin, but Ryder waved him off and took a bottle of pills out of his pocket. "Hospital gave me these, but they dull things, so I'll hold off as long as I can," he explained and set the bottle on the tabletop.

Jackson entered just a second later and closed the door behind him. "Matt's mom called. He still hasn't come home."

"But you have your officers looking for him?" Ryder asked.

Jackson dipped his head to confirm it. "Mark Dillon is cruising around, including by Matt's home. Diego just took Poppy out to patrol the business district. Since Matt was on foot, he likely didn't get far."

"What if Oliver finds him first?" Ryder asked, his worry evident.

"My guess is Oliver is laying low for now," Jackson said as he walked up to the whiteboard and wrote Matt's name above where they had earlier jotted down *cyber mercenary*. Along with the teen's traits, he then added *Needs money for college* and *Reached out to Sophie*.

Tapping the latter two entries, he said, "He never expected it would get this complicated. He's probably scared."

"Of both us and Oliver," Sophie said, thinking of the e-mail he'd sent.

"He should be more worried about Oliver finding him first," Robbie noted as he joined Jackson at the board and added a photo of Matt's driver's license and then a black-and-white photo. Tapping it, he said, "John Wilson and I—"

"Wilson, the tech billionaire?" Ryder interrupted, eyes narrowed as he scrutinized the two photos.

Robbie nodded. "He's married to our cousin Mia Gonzalez. He often helps us with SBS investigations."

"And he's the one with that predictive program?" Ryder asked, likely aware of the software that John was offering in beta form to various police agencies for use in preventing crimes.

"He is," Sophie said and laid a hand on his arm as it rested on the table.

"I'd heard SBS had big guns at their disposal, but I didn't know just how big. NSA operatives. Billionaires. Robbie and you," Ryder said with a side-glance in her direction.

"Can we get back to this?" Robbie said impatiently and tapped the enhanced image. When he had their attention, he ran a finger along the sections of the individual's face not covered by the hoodie in the black-and-white photo. "Look at the similarities in the jawline and nose," he said, running his index finger along those elements in both images.

"Similar," Jackson admitted as he stepped back to likewise scrutinize them.

"John's program says there's a ninety percent certainty it's the same individual," Robbie advised.

"Will that be enough for you to get a warrant?" Sophie asked, skipping her gaze from the board to Jackson.

"It's finally something more than circumstantial evidence, but the program is a new, unproven technology. I'll go to the district attorney first thing in the morning and try to persuade her," Jackson said.

"Why the morning?" Robbie asked, impatient as ever.

"First, I want to hear what Sophie thinks she's found."

Chapter Ten

The hoodie he'd been wearing to unload groceries at the store wasn't enough protection against the damp chill of the spring night.

Matt hunkered into the hoodie and wrapped his arms around himself as he slipped in and out of the narrow service alleys behind the businesses in town, looking for somewhere to hide while he thought about what to do.

He reached the end of one alley and the lights of an oncoming car illuminated the side street.

Stepping back into the shadows and pressing into a small niche in one wall, he held his breath as a vintage red Camaro drove into sight and paused. He couldn't see anyone through the heavily tinted passenger's-side window and hoped that the driver also couldn't see him.

The car moved on, and Matt expelled a breath. He'd seen the Camaro in and around the school and his house. He'd put money that whoever was behind the wheel wasn't a good guy.

Neither are you, chastised the little voice in his head.

He wasn't a bad guy, he told himself. He'd just made a terrible mistake.

I just need to figure out how to get out of this mess, he thought as he started walking again, keeping to the shadows.

His mind whirling with a variety of permutations much like those he might use when he was trying to do a hack.

Over and over, he ran through his options—they all ended up with him either dead or in prison. Neither was a satisfactory outcome and not just for him. For his family.

What would they do without the support he provided? They were barely making ends meet now. What would they do with him either dead or locked up?

He had been so caught up in his thoughts, he hadn't noticed that he was no longer alone in the service alley until he heard a jangle from behind him.

Turning, he caught sight of a large hulking shape in the heavy spring mist, almost like ground fog, it was so thick. He blinked to clear his vision and realized it was a large man with a large dog.

Maybe he is just out for a stroll. Matt started walking again, not sure where to go. He couldn't go home, and he had few friends. None he'd involve in his troubles.

Mr. Snyder came to mind. The IT teacher had always been a great source of support until… It occurred to him that Snyder was the one who'd introduced him to Oliver. He didn't want to think that Snyder was dirty also, but he couldn't take that chance.

The jangle came again, slightly closer, and he peered over his shoulder to see where the man and dog might be.

Not just a man, he realized as a splash of light from one of the business's security lights spilled into the service alley.

A cop.

He picked up his pace while trying not to seem suspicious.

But as he neared the end of the alleyway, a patrol car blocked the mouth to the street.

The driver of the cruiser opened his window and Matt met

the young cop's gaze. A crackle of a radio snapping to life was followed by, "We have eyes on our suspect."

There'd be no escape from either side of the alley, so he whirled and headed for one of the businesses.

"Such," one of the cops shouted. The shepherd barked as if acknowledging the command and took off toward Matt.

Matt barely made it halfway up the alley behind the business, the thud of paws chasing him. He muttered a curse and, a second later, the weight of the shepherd landed on his back and drove him into the ground.

Rolling, he tossed off the dog, but it was immediately on him once again, standing on his chest and growling in warning.

The pounding of feet followed and suddenly a bright light blinded him.

He stilled and the K-9 cop commanded, *"Fuss."*

The weight of the shepherd lifted from his chest but the dog's hulking shadow sitting beside him cautioned him to not run again.

"Hands above your head and get on your stomach," said the cop with the flashlight that was glaring into his face.

Matt did as instructed and the second cop from the car yanked his hands down behind his back and zip-tied them. He hauled Matt to his feet where the flashlight cop shined the light in his face again.

"Matt Clark?" he asked.

Since there was no use denying it, he said, "Yes. I'm Matt Clark."

"We've been looking for you."

"THEY GOT HIM. They're bringing him in," Jackson told the group gathered around the table.

"Good news," Ryder said and stared at the few letters that

Sophie had been able to detect in whatever breadcrumbs her parents had left behind.

He shook his head, which was aching again, and said, "Can you explain what you see?"

"It's tough to simplify," she said but then did just that. "Sometimes the letters are in different colors. Other times they pop out, like those eye tests they make you take to check your depth perception."

He was familiar with the tests but still couldn't wrap his head around the fact that Sophie saw things so differently. A unique gift but also possibly a burden, he imagined.

"What other things pop out?" he said as she glanced at the text on her screen, which only looked black and white to him.

"So we have *J*, *I* and *L* so far. Robbie's running through permutations of words with those letters, but *jail* immediately comes to mind."

"As in that's where Oliver will end up?" Jackson pressed.

She shrugged her fine-boned shoulders. "Maybe. Or where my parents are being held?"

It didn't make any sense to Ryder that the Whitakers would be held in a real jail, but maybe Cromwell wasn't the only dirty cop working for Oliver and his friends.

"Anything else?" he prodded, wishing they were making more progress although he was grateful they'd tracked down the teen.

SOPHIE SCREWED HER EYES half-closed because that sometimes helped with her special gift.

A few letters darted out here and there, a combination of colors and depth.

"I see a couple of *K*s. *S*, *N*, *B*, *U* and another pair of *R*s," she tacked on quickly, and Ryder jotted them down on a pad beside him while Robbie tapped them into his keyboard.

Barely a few seconds later, Robbie said, "Only 77,911 English words have *K* in them and it's not a common letter in the romance languages."

"Only 13,617 English words have both *S* and *K*," Sophie said, working on the next combination based on the letters she had seen.

"Like in *ski*," Ryder offered for consideration, seeing that as Sophie had said earlier, sometimes Robbie and she got too focused on what they were doing and maybe missed the bigger picture.

Sophie's head looked up from her screen, a becoming flush on her cheeks. "Like in the ski resort that's right in front of our faces."

"Oliver's vacation home is near the ski resort," Jackson said and tapped their note on the board.

"But if *jail* is the right word, how does that fit in?" Robbie leaned back in his chair, examining their board.

"Are you familiar with any jails near the ski resort?" Sophie asked as she, too, relaxed into the chair beside him.

"Not recent ones. I can reach out to our local historians as well as Mark Dillon when he comes in with Matt. He's hiked and skied most of the areas in and around the resort and may be aware of something I'm not," Jackson advised just as a knock came on the door.

Jackson walked to the door and opened it. Mark Dillon stood there. "I put Matt in the interview room," he said, a furrow of worry across his brow that cautioned there was more that he wasn't saying.

"What's wrong?" Ryder asked.

Hesitantly, Mark said, "I thought I noticed that red Camaro when we were putting Clark into the cruiser. They took off before I could get a good look."

"Can you ask Diego to do a quick walk past Cromwell's condo and see if he's there?" Jackson said.

"Sure. What about Clark? What should I do with him?" Mark asked with a quick look in the direction of the interrogation room.

"Did you take off the zip ties?" Jackson asked.

Mark nodded. "Also told him to make himself comfortable. I read him his Miranda rights and had him sign the card, but I never told him he was in custody, although any lawyer could argue that's what he believed."

"He could and he's a minor, so I'll have to get his mother here. But we'll let him stew for a little while. When you're done with Diego, please come back since we need your expertise on the nearby trails and hiking areas."

"Got you, jefe. Let me call Diego and then I'll be back," Mark said and rushed off.

"Jefe, huh?" Ryder teased.

"Trey hates it when we call him that," Sophie said with a grin and gleam in her bright aqua eyes.

"I'm not a fan either, but Diego started it and it's stuck," Jackson admitted, his lips in a wry grin.

Mark returned barely a minute later and closed the door behind him.

"What can I do to help?" he asked.

MERCEDES PUSHED AWAY from the worktable, stood and stretched out her back, which ached from the long hours of sitting.

"I'm tired. Everything's starting to blur together," she said as Robert likewise stood and worked out some kinks.

"It is, but we can't rush this. If we do, it'll only make future access that much harder," Robert said and embraced her.

"Good to hear. I thought y'all might only be taking your sweet time," said the disembodied voice over the speaker.

Mercedes glanced at the cameras keeping an eye on them. "Like Robert said, we need to be careful to hide what we're doing. If they can detect how we're getting in, they'll only shore up those vulnerabilities and make it harder for us."

A long pause followed her words before the voice asked, "Do y'all think your children have noticed?"

With a shrug, Robert said, "We taught them well but they're still the students while we're the masters."

Harsh laughter drifted across the speakers. "Y'all are *my* masters for now, but don't push it. I won't be patient for long."

A click like on an old-fashioned phone line signaled that their captor was done.

Mercedes shared a look with her husband. "He might be impatient, but we can't rush this. Plus, I need some food. How about you?"

His stomach growled his answer.

She chuckled and said, "Let's see what we have in the fridge."

JACKSON GAVE A little bob of his head and said, "Thanks for that info, Diego. Keep an eye on the condo and let me know when Cromwell comes back."

"Seems like too much coincidence the Camaro is out cruising while Cromwell isn't at his condo," Mark Dillon said.

The young officer wasn't wrong. "Did we get that list of vintage Camaros from the DMV yet?"

Jackson shook his head. "They've had some kind of system issue that they're working on. Hopefully, we'll have it by the morning."

"Do you think they hacked the DMV as well?" Sophie asked.

Jackson once again shook his head. "They've been having trouble with it off and on for months."

"Plus, it might call too much attention with another hack, and Cromwell is probably too low on the food chain to matter," Ryder pointed out.

"I agree," Jackson said and checked his watch. "I think Matt's stewed long enough. It's time that we call his mom and have her come in."

He left the room and Ryder turned his attention to Robbie. "Did Wilson send those lists of words generated from the letters Sophie saw?"

Robbie nodded and said, "I'll print copies for you and Mark. Sophie was copied on the e-mail."

"Anything pop for you?" he asked as a nearby printer spit out paper, and he wondered if Sophie's synesthesia would work on the lists.

"Just the same letters as before. That's how it works. I tend to see the same letters and numbers in either colors or varying depths. It's probably why my parents buried those particular items in the breadcrumbs they left behind," she said.

He rose slowly, his body a giant ache, and was about to walk to the printer when Mark nearly jumped out of his chair. "I'll get the copies."

"Thanks," he said and plopped back into his chair, stifling a moan as every muscle in his body protested the simple movement.

"Are you okay?" Sophie whispered, not wanting to embarrass him in front of the others.

"Sore," he admitted, hating that he was feeling so feeble, especially as Mark came over with the papers. He was young and fit, making him feel even older. When the officer shot a little grin in Sophie's direction, unexpected jealousy filled Ryder's core.

"Thank you, Officer Dillon," he said, using his most authoritarian voice to dispel any ideas Mark might have about flirting with Sophie.

Mark immediately adopted a more serious demeanor and sat to review the word lists Robbie had just printed.

Jackson returned, ridges of worry deep on his forehead.

"Matt's mom is in the room with him and already pushing for us to let him go. I don't think we have enough to charge and keep him. Luckily, they haven't asked for a lawyer yet."

"Probably because they can't afford one. But I've been watching some of Oliver's campaign videos and this is just the kind of situation he loves. Social injustice. Law enforcement abusing their power," Robbie said and eyed everyone around the table.

"Sophie is law enforcement and Matt reached out to her," Ryder said and focused his attention on her.

With a shrug, she said, "I have no problem chatting with him. Maybe he'll open up to me."

Jackson jammed his hands on his hips and dipped his head from side to side, considering that possibility. With a hesitant nod, he said, "It's worth a try. Especially since I think you're right about Oliver. If he finds out Matt is here, he'll find a way to exploit it."

With a lift of his hand in the direction of the door, Jackson led her out of their workroom and to an interrogation area just a couple of doors down.

Sophie knocked and at the muffled, "Come in," she entered.

Matt was a handsome young man but slight, she noted. Much like the suspect they'd spied the other night and seen in the CCTV footage. He was bouncing up and down in the chair, all nervous energy. His mother sat beside him, fingers twined together, strangling each other to white with pressure.

She is a pretty woman that life seems to have treated roughly, Sophie thought, considering the dark circles under her eyes and the deep lines across her forehead and at the sides of her mouth.

"Matt?" Sophie said, voice soft in question.

Matt nodded and she held out her hand.

"Sophie Whitaker. I think you e-mailed me," she said, her tone inviting him to chat. She also shook his mother's hands, cradling them in hers to reassure the woman.

Matt glanced in his mother's direction and then to Jackson, who stood at the door, arms across his chest, in a negligent pose.

With a lift of his chin in the police chief's direction, he said, "Does he have to be here?"

Peering over her shoulder at her cousin, she silently pleaded for him to leave. With a grimace, he did, closing the door behind him.

A sigh of relief slipped from Matt. "You said 'Sophie Whitaker.' Are you related to the people the news reports say are missing?"

She nodded. "The missing Whitakers are my parents, and the chief is my cousin. That's why I'm here. To help Jax find them before anything else happens to them. But I think you know that already, don't you?"

"I do," he replied quickly, shocking his mother.

"Matt?" she queried, surprise morphing into confusion.

He looked at her, lips locked tight before the words exploded from him. "I didn't mean to cause any trouble, Mom. I just wanted to help you out and maybe have a little extra money for college."

"What did you do, Matt? Does this have to do with Oliver?" she immediately countered.

He dipped his head to stare at his navel, obviously embarrassed, and shrugged. "I worked on his campaign, and he was pleased with what I did. Then he offered me another job for a lot more money."

"How much more money?" his mother pressed.

"Twenty thousand."

"But you didn't deposit it anywhere, did you?" Sophie asked, lying—not that Matt would know that.

He snapped his head up to look at her, shocked, and she said, "You checked me out. I checked you out as well."

"You hacked my info?" he said, eyes narrowing while he examined her.

"Let's call us even since you hacked Jackson and the CBI. Well, even except for the possibility that Oliver may have my parents somewhere."

"I had nothing to do with that," he said, furiously waving his hands in denial.

"I know you didn't, but it's happened, and you can help us," Sophie said, her voice pleading.

"I don't want to go to jail," he said, fear alive in his gaze.

"I can't make any promises, but I'll do whatever I can to help. Jackson will as well," she said without hesitation.

After a quick glance at his mom, who nodded to confirm what he should do, Matt said, "Whatever you need."

WITH SOPHIE'S ASSISTANCE and Jackson's return to the room, Matt detailed the hack Oliver had asked him to do. He also said that when he'd heard about the kidnapping and freaked out, he'd approached Oliver. But the senator had denied any involvement. He'd also warned Matt that if he said anything, he'd make sure Matt took the fall for the hack.

"I promise you that we'll do what we can to make sure that doesn't happen," Jackson said, trying to ease both mother's and son's worries.

"How? Oliver is a powerful man," Ms. Williams challenged.

"The Whitaker and Gonzalez families have influential connections also," Sophie said, certain that with their combined networks they'd be able to keep the young man out of trouble.

"Even with those connections, we need to keep you safe. If it's not Oliver behind this, then whoever took Sophie's parents may take action," Jackson said.

Sophie gave Jackson a withering look since his words had ramped up the fear she'd managed to calm throughout the interrogation.

"What exactly does that mean?" Matt's mom asked, faded blue eyes wide with worry.

"We'll take you home to get some things. I have an officer already there with Danny. After, we'll take you all to a safe house," Jackson advised.

Matt and his mom shared another troubled look but then both reluctantly nodded.

"Great." Jackson shot to his feet. Glancing at Sophie, he said, "I think it's time Robbie, Ryder and you go get some rest."

She couldn't argue. The tension and worry of the day had taken its toll on her. She suspected Ryder was also ready to drop, considering his injuries.

"I'll arrange for the safe house. It won't take long," Jackson said as he opened the door to the interrogation room and stepped outside.

Sophie stood and reached out to lay a hand on Matt's mom's arm. "It is going to work out. Try not to worry," she said even though her heart was filled with concern about her parents.

Sensing that, Matt's mom patted her hand and said, "Your

parents are going to be fine. I'll pray for them to come home safe."

Emotion choking her throat tight, Sophie managed to say, "Gracias."

RYDER STOOD IN the nearby viewing room, watching the interaction between Sophie and Matt and his mother.

That she could be so forgiving and supportive considering what Matt had done spoke volumes about the woman she was. But her use of Spanish at the end warned him that her emotions were on the edge.

She stepped out and he met her in the hallway between the two rooms. He opened his arms and she stepped into them, buried her head against his chest.

"We'll find them," he said and hugged her tight even if it made his bruised ribs ache like all get-out.

A rough breath escaped her before she shifted away slightly, wiping moisture from beneath her eyes. "Just tired."

Jackson returned, carrying several bulletproof vests. "I'm going to get them and us ready for the transfer."

He handed Ryder one and then entered the room to prepare Matt and his mom.

"Is that really necessary?" Sophie asked as Ryder slipped on his vest.

"We can't take any chances. That's also why I want you and Robbie to hang back until we finish the transfer. I'll take you to the inn once everyone is safe and secure."

She smoothed a shaky hand over the center of his vest, directly above his heart. "Please don't do anything stupid."

He laughed roughly and gave a lopsided grin. "Like get hit by a car? I think I'm done with that for today."

As Matt and his mom walked out and caught sight of Ryder also in a vest, she said, "Is that necessary?"

"Just a precaution," Jackson said and, a second later, his radio crackled to life.

"I'm ready," Officer Dillon said.

"We'll be out in a few," Jackson confirmed and then inspected the vests that Matt and his mother had donned.

Ryder did the same, pulling the straps tight to make sure his vest fit snugly. As he turned to follow Jackson, Matt and his mother to the door of the police station, Sophie snagged his hand.

He gave her a puzzled look until she leaned close and dropped a fleeting kiss on his lips. "Stay safe," she whispered before rushing back into their war room.

Quickening his pace, he met Jackson at the front door where his friend had stepped out to inspect the street before taking their witnesses down the steps to the waiting cruiser.

Ryder reached for his waist and undid the clip on his holster so he could draw his weapon if need be.

Jackson pulled open the door of the station and did a "come with me" jerk of his head in the direction of the squad car at the base of the stairs.

It was no more than twenty feet or so from the doors to the vehicle.

Twenty feet that seemed like a mile as a black pickup screeched around a corner and sped in the direction of the police station.

Jackson positioned himself in front of Matt and his mom and Ryder rushed forward to join him, providing a human shield.

But the pickup rushed by and the excited shouts of teens out for the night spiced the night air. A block up, a bottle flew out the window and shattered against the pavement.

Jackson called it in. "Be on the lookout for a black pickup with several teens. Speeding and possible DUI."

Distracted by the teens, they almost missed the red Camaro seemingly moving in slow motion toward the station.

"Jackson!" Ryder called out, whipped out his gun and assumed a shooting position as the streetlamp outside the station illuminated a gun barrel through the open window of the car.

Jackson whirled, gun in hand.

The bright flare of muzzle fire erupted from inside the moving Camaro, but the shots were wild, striking the steps in front of them and a nearby planter.

They opened fire, bullets pinging against metal. One shot shattered the side window of the Camaro before the driver, finding themselves outgunned, hit the gas and flew down the road.

Jackson and Ryder rushed down the steps to the cruiser, worried that Dillon might have been hit, but it was immediately obvious that he was uninjured.

"Follow him," Jackson said, and Dillon whipped out of the space and gave chase while Jackson called in another BOLO to their fellow officers.

"Be on the lookout for a vintage red Camaro. Side window shot out. Driver is armed and dangerous. Approach with caution."

For safety's sake, he radioed the officer taking Matt's brother to the safe house. Luckily, they'd reached the location without incident.

"Roger that," Jackson said and faced him.

"I'm going to take them there in my SUV. But I'm worried the inn may not be secure enough for Sophie and Robbie anymore. Plus, you took a nasty hit to your head. You shouldn't be alone tonight."

He couldn't argue with his friend. "My place has all the latest security features. I'll take them there."

The radio snapped to life again, filled with an assortment of curses before Dillon said, "I lost control on a turn and spun out. He got away, but, jefe, I'm pretty sure it was Cromwell at the wheel."

Ryder and Jackson shared a look. "Are you sure, Dillon?"

"I'm pretty sure," Mark replied.

"Head back to the station. We'll take a look at our CCTV footage to see what's visible," Jackson said and then instantly called over to Diego, who was watching the suspect officer's home. "Any sight of Cromwell yet?"

"Not yet, jefe," Diego confirmed.

With a rough sigh and shake of his head, Jackson said, "Do not approach when he arrives. Consider him armed and dangerous. If it looks like he's making a run for it, follow with caution."

"Roger that," Diego replied.

HER HEART HAD STOPPED at a sound she unfortunately knew all too well.

Gunfire.

Jumping to her feet, Sophie was about to rush out of the workroom when Robbie snagged her arm.

She met his gaze, worry and the bite of fear filling her.

"They would want us to stay here and stay safe," Robbie said calmly, but there was no missing the concern in his features.

"Lo se. Lo se, pero…" She knew that was what they'd want, but it wasn't easy to just wait there, not knowing if her cousin and Ryder were hurt.

Long, torturous moments passed before a knock came at the door.

Her chair flew back, clattering on the tile floor as she raced to the door and opened it.

Ryder stood there, unharmed, until she launched herself into his arms, jerking a pained oomph from him.

"Perdoname. I didn't mean to hurt you," she said in apology and glanced back toward the main area of the police station. "Jackson?" she asked, fear in her voice.

He cradled her face gently and offered a gentle smile. "We're all fine. Jackson is transporting the witnesses to the safe house. Matt's brother, Danny, is already there. Dillon lost sight of the red Camaro with the shooter but he's pretty sure it was Cromwell."

"And if DMV wasn't down, we might know if he owned something like that," Robbie said with a frustrated sigh and dragged a hand through the longish locks of his dark hair.

"We need to stop waiting and start searching," Sophie said and was about to sit back at her laptop when Ryder snagged her hand.

"Later. It's time to go, but with what's happened, we're not sure it's safe for you to stay at the inn. I'm taking you to my place."

Sophie hadn't known what to expect of Ryder's weekend home.

Somehow, she'd pictured something like Jackson's large and rustic place in the foothills just above Regina.

The Craftsman-style home on the banks at the far end of the lake was quaint and welcoming, but her eagle eyes spotted the driveway alarms as well as strategically placed cameras along the wooded edges of the property and on the front porch.

She suspected that he had similar protections at the back of the property that faced the lake.

"It's beautiful," she said as they exited and were greeted by an assortment of spring bulbs rising through the melting snow from the day before. In her mind's eye, she pictured them blooming in a few days, adding to the welcoming feel of the home.

On the front porch, two rocking chairs invited you to sit for a bit alongside Delilah's doggy bed and an assortment of barren pots, which she suspected would be filled with flowers once the weather allowed. But flowers required care, which made her say, "Do you come here often?"

He nodded as he unlocked the door. "Every weekend if I can. Sometimes longer during the summer months."

The beep-beep-beep of an alarm confirmed her earlier observations that his home was well secured and, after they entered, he locked the door and rearmed the security system.

Inside, the place had a homey but masculine feel. A large leather sectional was off to one side of the room in front of a fireplace and large-screen television. To the other side of the open space was a sizeable oak table and kitchen.

He tossed a hand in the direction of a hallway and said, "The bathroom and two bedrooms are down that way. Pick whichever one you want. I'll take the couch."

Sophie shook her head. "You need to rest, and I plan on working for a few more hours. I'll take the couch."

"You two can argue but I'm going to get settled," Robbie said and sauntered down the hall.

"Not too settled. Remember you're going to Denver with Selene tomorrow," Sophie called out. Facing Ryder, she repeated, "Couch for me."

He smiled, took hold of her hand and gave it a playful shake. "How about this? I'll nap on there while you work, but first, some food. We haven't had dinner."

"I can make something—"

"Rhea brought over a big pot of stew early this morning on her way to town. We can reheat that, and I've got some bread in the freezer," he offered and immediately marched to the kitchen.

"I'll set the table."

While she grabbed plates, napkins and cutlery, Ryder took a large pot from a cabinet to the right of the stove and placed it on the cooktop. At the fridge, he pulled out an enormous plastic container and dumped its contents into the pot.

Once he was done with that, he filled a bowl with water for Delilah and scooped out some kibble into a second bowl. The corgi, who had been following Ryder around as he worked, buried her head in the food, making short work of it before waddling away toward her doggy bed in the living room.

In no time, the aromatic flavor of beef stew filled the air, making Sophie's stomach grumble with hunger.

Robbie, ever a bottomless pit when it came to food, must have also smelled the stew since he ambled over to lift the cover and check out the contents of the pot. "Looks great," he said and covered it back up. "What can I do to help?" he asked, surprising her.

"Bread's in the freezer and the oven's warming up. You can toss the rolls in there when it's ready," Ryder said and laid out some cheese and crackers that he put in the center of the table. "To tide us over until dinner," he said, grabbing a piece of cheese and popping it into his mouth.

She didn't doubt that he was hungry. He was a big man who likely had a big appetite, and they hadn't eaten much that day.

A little curl of desire erupted in her core at what else he might be hungry for and as their gazes accidentally met, his mahogany-brown eyes widened and desire flooded in, darkening them to almost black.

The heat of color worked its way up her neck and she

dragged her gaze away, busied herself with prepping a cracker with cheese.

The ding of the oven warned it was ready and Robbie tossed in the cookie sheet where he'd placed the take-and-bake rolls, and their yeasty smell melded with the earthier aroma from the stew.

Robbie's stomach protested loudly as he sat at the table and made himself several servings of cheese and crackers while Ryder brought over bottles of soda.

"Some pop for you, unless you want something stronger. I have wine and beer," he said as he set the bottles on the table.

"Pop, huh?" she teased but quickly added, "Nothing stronger for me. Still have a lot of work to do."

Robbie waved it off as well. "Me too. Too much to do."

RYDER DIDN'T DOUBT that the siblings would be up late to find information that might help free their kidnapped parents. It made him feel a little useless because his energy was flagging from his injuries and he didn't know how much longer he could work, but he'd do what he could for as long as he could.

That meant getting dinner on the table and cleaning up so Sophie and her brother could get to work.

Sophie, he thought with a silent sigh, peeking over his shoulder to where she had finished laying out the place settings.

She caught him looking at her, smiled and walked to stand beside him, so close the side of her breast brushed against his arm, rousing instant desire.

"How's it going?" She leaned forward to inhale the aroma of the stew. "Mmm, smells great," she said, and that simple humming sound sent that desire into overdrive.

He sucked in a breath to control those urges. A mistake.

It made him hyperaware of the clean, flowery scent of her even after a long day at work.

"Almost done," he said with a strangled breath, jerking her attention to him.

She narrowed her gaze, scrutinizing him as she said, "Are you okay?"

"Fine," he said from behind gritted teeth and, a second later, awareness dawned and she created a little distance between them.

Pointing with an index finger tipped in sexy red, she said, "I'll just go sit at the table. Let me know if you need any help."

She joined her brother at the table, but as she sat, Robbie leaned close and said, "Get a room."

Hot color flooded her cheeks and the heat of embarrassment likewise had Ryder unduly focusing on the stew and the bread in the oven, whose toasty smell warned the rolls were ready.

Grabbing oven mitts, he pulled the cookie sheet out of the oven and set it on the granite countertop. Since the stew was bubbling, he removed some deep bowls from a cabinet, filled them with stew and took them over to the table.

Sophie rose and snatched a woven basket from the countertop, placed a paper napkin in it as a doily and plucked hot rolls from the cookie sheet into the basket with what he supposed was a muttered Spanish curse.

He chuckled, filled the last bowl and joined her at the table where they all sat to eat.

Hunger produced silence and grateful sighs since Rhea's stew was delicious.

"Jax is a lucky man," Robbie said and spooned up a big chunk of tender beef.

"He is that. Rhea is a lovely woman," Ryder confirmed with an emphatic nod.

"I guess you spend a lot of time with them since you're down here so often," Sophie said.

With a shrug that caused assorted aches over his still-healing body, he said, "I do, but not too much. They've only been married about two years now so still almost newlyweds. Plus, they've got the baby on the way."

"What about Selene? Does she come down often?" Robbie asked, surprising him. He hadn't thought that Robbie had noticed Rhea's beautiful twin, but then again, he might have run into her during one of the Whitakers' many family reunions.

"Selene visits but not as often as she used to. Her music career is really starting to take off so she spends a lot more time in Denver," Ryder advised.

"It's good to hear she's doing well. I know she had a terrible experience when she was kidnapped and held captive a few years ago," Sophie said, aware of the incident that had brought Rhea and Jackson together.

"She's a strong woman, just like Rhea. Any man would be lucky to have her," he said, which earned a complaint from Robbie.

"I heard her ex-husband didn't treat her the way she deserved," Robbie said.

"He didn't. It's why it'll take a special man to interest her again," Sophie said with a long glance in her brother's direction as if assessing Robbie as interested in being that man.

If Robbie noticed her perusal, he didn't acknowledge it. He just shot out of his chair to get more stew, but Ryder gave him props for politely asking, "Can I get anyone more?"

"I'm good," he said. His appetite was off for many reasons and he was keen to get back to work and help in any way he could to locate the missing Whitakers and stop the threat to Matt Clark and his family.

"No more for me or I'll need a nap," Sophie said as she tipped her chair back slightly and laid a hand on her flat stomach.

He forced himself not to look at the long-sleeved T-shirt that hugged every luscious curve and that flat stomach. Sophie might be a desk jockey but she clearly stayed in shape.

Pushing to his feet, he said, "I'll clean up so you can work."

He grabbed the empty bowls and basket of rolls and took them to the kitchen counter.

Sophie joined him a second later and rummaged through the cupboards and across the countertop to put up a pot of coffee, which they all might need after the belly-filling stew and rolls.

In no time, the sound of coffee dripping like rain into the carafe filled the quiet of the room while the earthy aroma spiced the air.

"I'm heading to my room to work. I'll let you know if I find anything on Cromwell's Camaro," Robbie called out as he snagged his laptop in one hand and rushed down the hall.

Sophie met Ryder's glance and motioned to the kitchen table. "I'll work there, if that's okay?"

Needing distance, Ryder jerked his head in the direction of the sofa. "I'm going to stretch out on the couch. I'm feeling achy from too much sitting," he lied, not wanting to admit that he needed space from her because she was far too tempting and he didn't know how much longer he could keep his passion in check.

Chapter Eleven

Sophie was surprised that Ryder was even mobile thanks to his injuries. It was a testament to his sense of duty and loyalty to Jackson as well as Robbie and her. He knew how important it was to find her parents and end the threats to the many investigations that might be damaged if the databases were hacked.

He stretched out his long lean frame before settling his laptop on the six-pack stomach visible through the cotton T-shirt he wore beneath a brown-and-green flannel shirt.

That curl of desire came again, and she tamped it down.

It wasn't the right time to be attracted to him. There were too many other more important things to think about.

But she couldn't deny that he intrigued her, and it wasn't just because he was handsome with his dark, nearly seal-black hair and mahogany eyes gleaming with intelligence. She'd been around lots of handsome men who worked for her family's South Beach Security Agency.

And, like those men, he was a man of duty and honor who hadn't been challenged by her claim that she could take care of herself. Or by the violent background that he'd managed to escape and had made him want to help others.

That took a strong man. And it was that strength combined with everything else that had her wanting to explore more.

But not now, she thought, sitting at the table to work. Both Robbie and she were trying to track down more info on who might own the vintage Camaro as well as find out more about Cromwell and the reasons for his involvement with Oliver.

They often worked on the same thing but independently because, even though they were alike in so many ways, they also saw things very differently, and it wasn't just because of her synesthesia. That reminded her about the list of words generated from the letters her parents had planted as clues.

She looked in Ryder's direction and asked, "Are you taking a look at the words?"

Ryder nodded. "I am. I'm eliminating any that don't seem to make sense based on what we're dealing with."

Satisfied that part of the investigation was under control, she turned to her tasks, searching for information on Cromwell and the Camaro.

It wasn't hard to find him on Facebook. His profile was public, and she pulled out her portfolio and pen to take notes. She found that, for her, writing things down on paper helped her focus better. Not an uncommon occurrence since studies showed that most people had better reading comprehension with printed materials than with screen text.

As she scrolled through Cromwell's profile, the images provided the picture of a man who seemed quite happy. Cromwell was often smiling in the photos and sharing his adventures hiking the nearby trails in Regina, fishing at the lake, gambling at a Denver area casino and attending an assortment of antique car shows.

The car show photos intrigued her since a car like the vintage Camaro might be displayed at those events. She scanned the images and linked out to the groups and websites connected to the shows. There were multiple photos of similar vehicles, which disheartened her. She'd hoped the vehicle would be more unique. But she jotted down any info available so they could do additional tracking.

Feeling as if she'd exhausted that branch of investigation, she turned to a set of images that had sent up warning signals as she'd come across them.

Although most casinos discouraged taking photos on the casino floor, selfie-snappers often snuck some in, and as long as it wasn't at one of the tables or of the patrons or employees, the casinos didn't normally chase photographers away.

Cromwell had snapped a few selfies and, while she couldn't identify the location from the casino floor itself, he had taken one near the entrance. An image search revealed that it was a casino not far from Denver and a little less than an hour from Regina.

Had Cromwell been unlucky and amassed gambling debts that would have made him vulnerable to underworld types? she wondered.

Sophie jotted down the name of the casino that might be able to provide information on Cromwell's luck, or lack of it.

A soft snore yanked her attention away from her search.

Ryder had fallen asleep on the sofa, the laptop close to falling off his stomach. Delilah lay on her doggy bed beside the couch, looking like a gigantic dead cockroach with her stubby little legs up in the air and her tongue lolling out of her mouth.

She couldn't fault Ryder for falling asleep. He'd been going hard on the investigation even after being struck by the car.

But that also reminded her that since he had a concussion, it would be good to check that his sleep seemed normal without waking him. He'd only had a light concussion and sleep was a good way for him to heal.

Plus, it's late, past midnight, she thought with a glance at her smartphone. Time for her to get some rest so she could be sharp in the morning.

Easing from the table, she tiptoed to his side and snared the laptop midair as it finally slid off his lap.

He jerked away and also reached for it, realizing what had happened.

She offered him an apologetic smile and said, "I'm sorry. I didn't want to wake you."

"No, I'm sorry. I didn't mean to fall asleep, but working on the computer was giving me a massive headache and I closed my eyes for just a second," he said and sat up, the leather creaking loudly with his motion.

Sophie kneeled by the sofa, handed him back his laptop and brushed away a lock of his hair that had slipped down onto his forehead. His hair was silky beneath her fingers, tempting her to brush it back a second time.

When her gaze drifted from that action to his face, she realized he was watching her intently. So intently, it caused a skitter of awareness deep in her core and heat to flood her face.

She jerked her hand away. "I'm sorry. I didn't mean to invade your space."

"Invade at will," he said, his voice husky as he tenderly skimmed his knuckle across the blush on her cheek.

She did, rising to press her lips to his and explore the attraction she'd been feeling since they'd first met.

His lips were hard beneath hers. Warm. Mobile. Tempting her to go back over and over to sample the contours of his mouth and the press of his chest as he wrapped an arm around her and tugged her closer.

When the leather of the sofa creaked loudly again, Robbie called out, "Get a room."

They eased apart slowly, breathing heavily. Embarrassment colored both their faces, but that didn't stop Sophie from saying, "My room is right down the hall."

RYDER KNEW THAT, especially since it was *his* room.

But he didn't want to rush her if she wasn't sure. After all, her emotions had to be a jumble with everything that was going on.

"Are you sure?" he asked softly, well aware of Robbie's apparently acute hearing.

She licked her lips and nodded. "Sí, I am."

With a nod, he swiveled on the sofa to rise, grimacing with pain at the assorted aches in his body. Sophie didn't miss it, offering a hand to help him stand.

He hated the weakness. He hated that it had forced him to stop his research just when he'd thought he'd hit on something.

And he worried how it might hinder him in other ways as Sophie tugged him in the direction of his bedroom.

Delilah was following along, intending to join them, but he gave her a hand command to stay. Like always, she ignored it until he issued a stronger, verbal command. "Stay, Delilah. Stay."

The corgi's grin faded, miffed by his instruction, and she sprawled by the door to his room.

Once they entered, he kicked the door closed with his foot and, with a little pull, urged Sophie to face him.

She did with a puzzled look.

"I don't want to rush," he said. He laid his hands at her waist to draw her close and kissed her again, wanting to give her time to change her mind if she was uncertain.

He moved his mouth on hers, exploring. Tasting the sweetness of her, from the soft sigh of pleasure that escaped her to the first touch of her tongue as she invited him to open to her.

That dance of mouths dragged a moan of pleasure from him and he wrapped his arms around her waist and walked her back toward the bed, needing to feel all of her against him. Needing to see all of her.

As they neared the bed, he turned and sat on its edge, breaking away from their kiss.

He urged her between his legs and skimmed his hands beneath the edge of her T-shirt, slowly dragging it upward to reveal the soft skin of her belly. Upward over her ribs until she flew into action, grabbed the hem of the shirt and ripped it off to reveal the lacy bra beneath.

On her surface, Sophie was all work and casual, but beneath...

Sweet lord, he thought and cupped her breasts, drawing his thumbs over the hard nipples beneath the sinful black lace. Taking them between his thumb and forefinger to tease them into even harder peaks as she laid her hands on his arms and skimmed them up to his shoulders.

"Tell me what you want," he said, not wanting to push her since this was all so new and possibly way too quick.

"*Tu boca...*" she started and then shook her head, as if chastising herself. "Your mouth. I want your mouth on me."

He did as she asked, sucking her through the lace, and she wrapped her arms around his head to keep him close, keening with pleasure at the sharp pull of his mouth.

He needed more and reached around to unsnap her bra and draw it off her breasts.

Now it was only her silky skin against his mouth and he kissed her over and over until it wasn't enough for either of them.

In a rush of action, they undressed, touching and caressing as each little bit of skin was revealed.

Finally naked, Sophie crawled onto the bed but, as he was

about to join her, she laid a hand on the center of his chest to stop him. When her gaze skipped to his side, he tracked her line of sight to the mottled bruises along his ribs and lower.

She gently skimmed her hands across the area. "Does it hurt as bad as it looks?"

In truth, it didn't. "It looks worse than it feels. At least right now. Ask me tomorrow and you might get a different answer."

"I will ask tomorrow," she said and met his gaze as if to tell him that for her this wasn't just going to be a one-night stand.

He liked that. A lot. He wasn't a one-night-stand kind of guy.

SHE SLIPPED HER hand into his and with a soft tug urged him over her on the bed.

His hard weight pressed her down into the firm mattress, forcing every inch of their bodies close.

She welcomed his weight. It was comforting and his touch was gentle at first, exploring the contours of her body. Slipping between her legs to build her passion until she was arching against him, almost pleading for completion.

He shifted to her center, sheathed in the condom he'd slipped on after they'd undressed.

But he paused then and lifted away from her, making sure that she was certain about what they were about to do.

"Sí, por favor, Ryder. Sí," she pleaded, wanting him deep inside. Wanting to join with him in every way she could.

He surged into her, taking her breath away from the force of it and the way he stilled, letting her adjust to his possession. Letting her control their lovemaking as she rolled and buried him ever deeper.

She moved on him, drawing him up with her until passion had her shaking and on the edge, almost undone.

Gazes locked, he gently shifted until she was beneath him again and drove ever harder until the release exploded across her and then took him with her, a rough groan escaping him as he came.

Shakily, he lay on her and said, "I'm not too heavy, am I?"

Smiling, she held him close, soothing her hands across his sweat-slick back. "Not at all. I like the weight of you," she admitted.

AND HE LIKED the feel of her, all soft and yielding beneath him. Hot and wet where they were still joined until he had to leave.

When he came back to bed, she was beneath the covers, her eyes sleepy.

She patted the space beside her and he slipped in, went to her side and drew her tight to his body.

"That was nice," she said in a tired but satisfied tone.

"Ouch, just nice?" he teased, loving how easy it was to be with her.

"I wouldn't want you to get a swelled head," she kidded and playfully crept her hand down his middle, but he snared it to stop the motion.

"We need to rest," he warned even though he wanted nothing more than to make love to her all night long.

"Mmm," she said and shifted her hand to soothe it over the bruises on his side. "I'm sorry you were hurt."

"Part of the job. You must know what with the work you do with your family at South Beach Security," he said.

She nodded and gave a reluctant shrug. "Trey and Mia have both been hurt on the job, which was scary for the family. Robbie and I are usually behind the scenes."

He stroked his fingers down her arm and then back up to cup her face. "I'm glad you don't risk yourself with dangerous assignments."

She made a face of disapproval. "Sometimes I wish we could do more. Like now. My parents are missing and all I can do is type away at my computer."

Her attitude explained last night's secretive walk to meet Matt Clark. "The last thing your parents would want is for you to risk your life for them."

"Like you do to help others?" she challenged and peered at him.

With a wag of his head, he said, "Helping others is a calling. Whether as a Marine or with CBI. Your family understands that more than most." Many members of the Gonzalez and Whitaker families had served in the military and law enforcement.

Her light caress came across his bruised ribs once again. "Doesn't make it any easier to live with."

He tucked this thumb and forefinger beneath her chin and applied gentle pressure to tilt her head up to meet his gaze. "The only promise I can make is to be more careful."

A sad smile drifted across her lips a heartbeat before she shifted to whisper against his lips, "I'll hold you to that."

Her mouth covered his, sealing that promise. Welcoming him to join her to celebrate life once again and drive away the danger and death that was ever present in the work they both did.

After, they lay together, limbs entwined. Arms wrapped around each other as sleep finally claimed them.

Chapter Twelve

To her surprise, both Ryder and Robbie were up and making breakfast as she strolled out of her bedroom after an early morning shower. Delilah wove in and out around their feet, hoping that the men would either provide a treat or maybe drop something she could gobble up.

Sophie ran her fingers through her damp hair, tousling the shoulder-length strands to help it air-dry. She didn't want to waste time blow-drying with all the work she still had to do, but she wanted to look semipresentable, especially after last night with Ryder.

"Nice that you can join us, Sleeping Beauty," Robbie teased with a smile as he laid a plate with eggs, bacon and toast at a spot on the table.

"Not sure she's Sleeping Beauty since she's up without a kiss," Ryder said and, to remedy that, he walked over and laid a hand at her waist. "Do you need that kiss?" he added with a wry smile.

She rose on tiptoe and covered his mouth with hers, providing her answer.

"Mmm, I think I like waking you up like this," he murmured against her lips.

"Not me. It's too early for PDAs," Robbie complained, set another plate on the table and sat. "Coffee's ready if you want," he added and jerked his head in the direction of the counter.

With a quick kiss and stroke of her hand across the spot above Ryder's heart, she hurried to the coffee machine to pour herself a big mug that she doctored with a few tablespoons of sugar and lots of half-and-half.

At the table, Robbie and Ryder had started a discussion about last night's work. Ryder tossed Delilah a piece of bread and she plopped herself by Ryder's chair with a contented sigh.

"I found a few photos of vintage red Camaros on several Facebook groups for car aficionados but nothing connecting them to Cromwell," Robbie said.

"Me too, but I also found out that Cromwell is a gambler," she chimed in and, as the aromas of the breakfast wafted up, hunger awoke.

"Ditto. It's something else to investigate." Robbie glanced at Ryder.

With a shrug, Ryder said, "I worked with all those words created from the letters that Sophie saw. The ones that stuck in my brain were *jail*, *ski* and possibly *bunker*."

"*Ski* seems obvious," Robbie said with a dismissive shake of his shoulders as he focused on gobbling down the eggs and bacon.

"But not *jail* or *bunker*," Sophie offered in Ryder's defense as she broke off a small piece of buttered toast to toss it to Delilah, who gobbled it down in a bite.

"Not *jail* or *bunker*, which got me thinking about where things like that could be located," Ryder said.

"Jackson mentioned that he was reaching out to local historians and Mark Dillon about the jail," Sophie recalled as she also gave her attention to the delicious breakfast both men had prepared.

"And that made me think about Selene's case and how they located where she might be held," Ryder said with a jab of his fork in her direction.

"You mean the light detecting and ranging drones that Robbie and I suggested Jackson use to survey the mountainside?" Sophie asked, just to confirm she understood the direction Ryder was going.

"Yes, the LiDAR. I searched the evidence database for the images and had just started going through them last night, but the headache was just too much for me to finish," Ryder admitted reluctantly.

Sophie shared a look with Robbie. "We can work on that once we update Jackson."

With a shrug, Robbie confirmed it. "We can do that. It's a great idea. Should have thought of it myself."

"When you're too emotionally involved in a case, you sometimes lose sight of the bigger picture," Ryder said and finished the last of the eggs on his plate.

Robbie had likewise cleaned off his dish and glanced at hers, where a good amount of the eggs still sat. He pointed to it and said, "You better hurry up and finish. We should get going."

She nodded and said, "I'll prep it to go so we don't waste more time."

As the men rose to take the dishes to the sink, she quickly made a sandwich with her eggs, bacon and slices of toast. She wrapped it up with her napkin and then went in search of a plastic bag, but Ryder was already there, handing her one. "I'm sorry you were rushed."

"It's okay. I shouldn't have overslept," she replied, and as her gaze met his knowing one, heat flooded her face.

Leaning close, he whispered in her ear, "I'll try to not keep you up so late tonight."

His lips skimmed her cheek before he stepped away to stuff his laptop into his bag and grab Delilah's leash, which he clipped to her collar.

Minutes later, they were all heading to the front door, but as they neared it, Ryder lifted his arm like a tollgate waiting for payment. At her questioning look, he said, "I just want to make sure it's clear. I don't want a repeat of last night at the station."

He handed her Delilah's leash, and she waited while he slipped out but returned barely a minute later.

"All clear," he said and, with that, they all hurried to his SUV for the short drive to downtown Regina.

They hadn't gone more than a mile when Sophie realized Ryder was glancing at his rearview mirror way too often. She spun in her seat and glimpsed a black luxury SUV come around a turn about a football field's distance behind them.

"Are you worried about that car?" she asked and peered back at it again. The vehicle had picked up speed on the straighter length of the road and was gaining on them.

"License plates have those black covers that make them hard to read. Not what you expect on cars around here," he said and checked the mirror again.

She did as well and realized that the windows were so tinted it was impossible to identify the driver.

Not good, she thought just as Ryder said, "Hold on."

Barely several yards ahead was a driveway and Ryder turned into it, the car fishtailing until Ryder righted it onto the narrow lane and jerked to a stop. Delilah whined and shifted uneasily in her seat, clearly sensing the heightened tension in the vehicle.

They all turned as the suspicious SUV shot past the driveway.

Ryder immediately jammed his car into Reverse and, seeing it was clear, whipped out and back onto the road.

The SUV was in sight but pulling away quickly.

"In a rush or escaping?" Sophie asked, trying to read past the dark license plate covers to get the number.

Ryder peeked in her direction and said, "Only one way to find out."

He put the pedal to the metal, making up ground on their suspect car, but the driver increased his speed, trying to outrun them.

"I guess we know," she said and braced her hand against the dash as Ryder made a tight turn, jostling them all and earning a barked rebuke from Delilah.

It was one of the last sharp turns before they'd have to get on the main highway to town, but the final few miles of the road were a tight, curvy, swerving two-lane stretch. She held on tight, one hand against the dash and another on the console as speed and motion moved her to and fro in her seat. The greens and golds of forest and aspens were a blur around them as Ryder sped to catch their suspect.

Delilah fussed in the back where she was harnessed beside Robbie, unhappy as well with the abrupt movements.

Ryder muttered a curse and slowed as they neared the sharp turnoff for the highway.

Ahead of them, the driver of the SUV had no such reservations about making the right at full speed.

A big mistake.

The SUV turned but the back wheels couldn't hold the road. The rear end whipped from side to side and then the car tipped up on two wheels as the driver struggled to control the vehicle.

He lost the battle as his overcompensation made the SUV roll over and over across the pavement until, with a last flip, it hit the side of the road and tipped into a ditch.

The sickening crunch of metal and the shatter of glass echoed through the morning quiet.

They rushed from their car and hurried over to the wrecked SUV lying on its side in the ditch.

At the vehicle, they scanned the inside to check on the driver. The side airbag had deployed, preventing the driver from hitting the window, but his head had struck either the steering wheel or the windshield. Blood covered the driver's face.

Too much blood and a familiar face, she realized.

Roger Cromwell.

Chapter Thirteen

Mercedes woke with a groan and wince. The cot and the spring dampness were wreaking havoc with her back and knees.

Robert was immediately at her side, offering his hand for support. "We're too old for this," he teased.

She smiled, slipped her hand into his and slowly got to her feet. "I'll make some coffee so we can get to work."

The annoying voice snapped across the speaker. "It is time for y'all to wake up and do something. Time's a wasting."

"It's not an easy thing to do right," she fired back, too tired and achy to care about what the punishment might be.

"I'm tired of waiting on y'all. You better do as I asked if you ever want to see your children alive," the voice warned.

"You mean if our children want to see us alive," Robert clarified and shared a confused look with her.

A rough, angry laugh exploded across the speakers. "Twenty-four hours or we take out Josefina and Robert Junior. It wouldn't be all that hard to do, as y'all see from the photos on the computers."

Fear stole her breath, making it impossible for her to reply. Well, that and the click signaling that the speaker had signed off.

They rushed to the computers and, with a touch of the keyboard, the screens jumped to life, displaying a collage of images showing Sophie and Robbie in Regina.

Robert muttered a curse and pounded the worktable with his fist. Glancing at her, he said, "We can't risk this, Mercedes. We have to find a way into that database."

She shook her head. "But if we do as they ask—"

"It's a price I'm willing to pay for our children's lives," he said and muttered a rough expletive.

She laid a hand on his arm and stroked it reassuringly. "You know I would do anything for our children. Anything," she said, but beneath her words was the unspoken plea to not make her do this for her children.

"We have twenty-four hours, my love. We can figure this out." He sat down in front of the computer.

Mercedes wasn't quite as ready to take her spot. She had to think of a plan that wouldn't jeopardize cases and set criminals free.

"I'll make us some coffee. We're going to need it," she said and set off to the small countertop to prep what was a necessary ritual for her whenever she worked.

But as she made their coffees, she thought about the photos that had been taken and how to get another series of messages to her children.

Twenty-four hours, she reminded herself as she walked to the worktable and placed the cups of coffee on its surface.

She sat down and opened the photos of her children. They looked well. Sophie in particular seemed to be glowing in one snapshot.

There was a man with her in that one. *Handsome*. Either ex-military or law enforcement. He had that look about him, which provided some relief.

She didn't doubt that whoever he was, he would protect her daughter.

Armed with that, she got to work.

"I JUST HEARD from the hospital. Cromwell's surgery went well but they've had to place him in a medically induced coma," Jackson said from his spot at the whiteboard.

Even though she knew what that likely meant, she had to confirm it. "Where exactly does that leave us?"

With a disgusted sigh, Jackson said, "It could be a few days before we're able to interview him."

Sophie shook her head and blew out an exasperated breath. "So close and yet so far."

Ryder reached over and laid his hand on hers. "At least we have enough to get search warrants. Something at Cromwell's might lead us to your parents."

"I know," she said and pursed her lips to keep from crying out her frustration.

"Let's look at those LiDAR images," Robbie said, fake enthusiasm filling his tone.

"Yes, review them. Let me call Mark. He's spoken to the local historians," Jackson said and phoned Officer Dillon to join them.

The young man hurried in a couple of minutes later, carrying a portfolio, several pieces of paper haphazardly sticking out.

When he sat, he tried to organize them into some semblance of order as Jackson said, "What do you have for us, Mark?"

"Quite a bit. I spoke to Harry Langford and Muffy Simmons at the Regina Historical Society," he began, which earned a strangled chuckle from Jackson.

"I'm sure they talked your ear off," he said.

"You can say that again," Mark said and peered at Robbie. "I just sent you a topographical map of the area. Could you please put that on the screen?"

With a few keystrokes, Robbie displayed the image, and Mark grabbed some notes and walked up to the screen to explain.

"The Colorado gold rush occurred from 1858 to 1859 around Pike's Peak, but it spilled over to the mountains around Regina. Right here," he said and gestured to an area about three-quarters of the way up one of the mountains.

"An initial discovery of nuggets in the mountain streams led to the building of a fairly large mill and expansion into a nearby mine." He handed Jackson a photo to review that he, in turn, passed to her.

It was an old, grainy black-and-white of several small wooden cabins that climbed to a large wooden structure.

Sophie examined the photo for a long moment before passing it on to Ryder. "Are the mine and mill still around?"

"Most of the mill was destroyed by an avalanche in the early 1900s. By then most of the mining had stopped and the mill had been abandoned. In its heyday, though, a fairly large encampment had grown up around the mill and mine, and where there was gold and miners, there was drink and fighting. The owners of the mill had constructed a jail at the location to deal with the problem miners."

"Is that still there?" Sophie asked, losing patience with Mark's history lesson even though she was sure it had been severely edited from the historian's info.

"Possibly. I don't normally hike this northern slope since the vegetation is denser and there are more established trails on the southern slope."

"Is this spot on the LiDAR images from Selene's case?" Ryder asked.

"Let me overlay that survey on this map," Robbie said and tapped away at his laptop.

The LiDAR survey instantly obscured the topographical map but, with a few adjustments to the transparency and scale, they were soon able to see the stream winding down the northern slope and, about three-quarters of the way up the slope, some kind of structure.

Mark immediately raced over to his notes and, after rummaging through them, held up an old sepia-tone map against the digital images. Jabbing a finger at the survey, he said, "This hit from the LiDAR matches up with what this map says was the location for the mill and mine."

"And what's that other, more defined rectangle that's higher up and to the right of that area?" Sophie asked.

With a shrug, he said, "I don't know. But this is Oliver's home." He gestured to another defined image that was much lower on the slope and then made a little circle with his index finger. "Just past this area on the southern slope is the ski resort where he met the woman he raped."

"Allegedly raped," Jackson clarified, although it obviously pained him to correct his officer.

"How hard would it be to make the climb to those areas?" Ryder asked, brows furrowed as he considered the hike.

"Tough. Like I said, the vegetation will be denser. Incline is about the same but there's also the altitude to consider," Mark said and shot a quick look at Robbie and Sophie. "They're not used to the altitude." He gestured in their direction.

Robbie held his hands up in a surrender gesture. "I'm headed to Denver as soon as Selene gets here."

"I can handle it. I've hiked here before," Sophie said, recalling many a summer trek during one of their family reunions with the Whitaker cousins.

Mark arched a brow in disbelief and Ryder immediately jumped to her defense. "If Sophie says she can do it, I believe her."

She was both pleased and annoyed that he even had to defend her.

Jackson, who had been mostly silent during his officer's report, chimed in. "If we use the ski resort as a base camp, how long do you suppose it would take to reach those two spots on the map?"

Mark turned and considered the images on the maps, hands on his hips and legs outspread. After a long moment, he faced Jackson and said, "I'm guesstimating that it's about four or five miles from the resort to the mill position. If we start on one of the ski trails on the southern slope and then cut across, we'll be able to avoid the thicker forest. But once we do the cut, if there isn't a trail there, we'll face downed trees and thick underbrush."

"Meaning?" Ryder asked, a slightly impatient tone in his voice with Mark's meandering explanation.

Gesturing to the map, Mark said, "About four or so hours to reach what we think is the mine and mill."

"What about the second structure?" Sophie asked, worried about how much time they'd be wasting if it turned out her parents weren't at either of the two locations.

"The incline may be steeper there. I'd say another hour or so," Mark admitted, a frown on his face as he also finally realized how long it would take.

"It's a big risk," Ryder said and glanced at everyone sitting at the table.

"And in that time, our parents could crack into that database." Robbie glanced at her.

"I don't have any warnings yet," she said and opened her laptop to check. They'd set up alerts if anything unusual was happening to the database they'd identified as a target the day before. But as skilled as her parents were, it was possible they could avoid tripping any kind of alarm that Robbie and she had set.

Shock reverberated through her when an activity warning blared to life, alerting everyone in the room at the sound of it. Her parents were at work on a hack and as she watched the attack, she realized they were leaving her another message.

The numbers popped out at her over and over again.

She had no doubt what it meant.

"I don't think we have that much time left," she said and brought up the code over the map and survey to explain.

"What is it, Sophie? What do you see?" Ryder asked as her face lost all color and she shakily got to her feet to point out what was only visible to her.

She shifted her finger across the screen and said, "The number twenty-four. Another one here and here and here."

With her pointing them out, it was obvious there were several twenty-fours all across the code displayed on the monitor.

"It's a warning. We're in a countdown," Sophie said.

Robbie tipped his chair back on two legs and laced his fingers behind his head as he examined the code. Shaking his head, he said, "I don't see anything else besides what you pointed out. Am I missing something?"

Sophie shook her head. "No. Only that, and this code is… weird. It doesn't seem to be directed toward hacking the database, but I don't know what just yet. Maybe only enough activity to trip an alarm to get us this message."

Ryder saw only a jumble of letters and numbers, although the twenty-fours scattered throughout were screaming countdown to him also.

"If it's a countdown, to what?" he tossed out for discussion even though he suspected the answer was obvious.

"It's the time my aunt and uncle have left." Jackson drove a hand through his hair in frustration. Glancing at Mark, he said, "Can you get us ready to hike out in an hour? Diego and Poppy also?"

Mark glanced at his watch. "If we go in the next hour or so, we should be able to reach the mine and mill in late afternoon. It might be getting dark by the time we make it to the higher spot on the mountain."

Jackson nodded. "Selene should be here shortly," he said and then eyed Robbie. "I trust you can continue to work on this while on the trip to Denver?"

"I can. Sophie and I—"

"I'm going with you, Jax," she said.

Ryder shook his head. "I don't doubt you can do the hike, but isn't your time better spent on what your parents are doing?"

"I can't just sit here—"

"He's right, Soph. You're the only one who sees the messages they're sending. You need to stay here and let Ryder and Jax know what you find out," Robbie said and reached across the table to hold her hand. "You need to do this," he pleaded.

SOPHIE HATED THAT they were right.

"Sophie," Ryder said and skimmed a hand across her shoulders, offering comfort.

"You'll all stay safe, right?" she said and met his gaze, fighting back tears of frustration and fear.

"We will, and my gut tells me we're on the right track to find your parents." He skimmed his thumb across her cheek to wipe away her tears.

A knock at the door interrupted and at Jackson's "Come in," Selene and Rhea entered.

She was always shocked by just how identical the two women were, even down to how they dressed in their loose boho-style skirts and blouses. The one main thing that set them apart now was Rhea's large baby belly.

"Sorry to interrupt, but I'm ready for the drive to Denver," Selene said.

Robbie immediately shut down his laptop and jumped to his feet. "I'm ready to go."

Jackson embraced his sister-in-law. "I'm going to have one of my officers follow you. He'll let Denver PD know you're heading there so Robbie can work with them."

"Thanks. I appreciate the police escort since I'm still a little..." Her voice trailed off and Sophie understood. How did you explain the PTSD you might be suffering after being kidnapped and violated by mountain men for nearly a year?

Jackson hugged her again. "Robbie will keep an eye on you as well. Right, Robbie?"

Robbie nodded enthusiastically. "I will. She's safe with me," he said, but Sophie knew her brother well enough to detect that he was interested in Rhea's twin sister and not just as a bodyguard.

"Good. As for you," Jackson said and heartily hugged his very pregnant wife, "I'm going to have to leave you alone tonight. We're going to hike to a spot where my aunt and uncle might be."

Rhea forced a smile and stroked a hand across Jackson's face. "You be careful. We're supposed to get some more snow tonight."

"We'll keep that in mind when we pack for the hike," he said to allay her worry.

Rhea seemed to relax a little bit and set her eyes on Sophie. "If Ryder and Robbie are deserting you, why don't you stay with me tonight?"

"And with Delilah, if it's not a problem? She wouldn't be good on the trail," Ryder said and bent to rub the corgi's stomach as she sprawled at his feet again in that dead cockroach position.

"Delilah will be good with us," Rhea said with a smile, waddled over and bent to also rub the dog's belly.

Delilah immediately flipped her roly-poly body onto her stubby legs and licked Rhea's face, dragging amused laughter from her.

"Down, girl. Down," Ryder insisted, and Delilah complied, earning a head rub from Ryder.

"I'm good with that, although I didn't pack a bag," Sophie said. Unlike Robbie, who had known he was leaving Ryder's, she had expected that they'd be returning to his lake house.

"I have some things you can borrow," Rhea said and, since it all seemed to be settled, the team members flew into action.

Robbie hugged her reassuringly. "If anyone can see what Mami and Papi are doing, it's you," he whispered in her ear and then rushed off to join Selene.

They walked out and Jackson, Rhea and Mark followed, leaving her alone with Ryder.

He stood, took hold of her hand and assisted her to her feet to embrace her.

She buried her head against his chest, anxious. The slopes at the higher elevations could be dangerous and adding snow to the mix just increased the risk.

"¡Cuídate!" she begged, wanting him to stay safe.

"My high school Spanish is rusty, but I guess you want me to take care," he teased, trying to lighten the mood.

"Sí, I want you to take care and make sure that all of you

stay safe as well. Especially Jax. He's got his little son on the way."

"We will, and I need you to do the same. No more nighttime outings or playing Nancy Drew," he said and laid his forehead on hers.

"I promise," she said and tilted her head the slightest bit to kiss him.

He answered her kiss, opening his mouth on hers and bracketing his hands against her back to haul her close.

A faked cough had them slowly drifting apart.

Jackson was at the door and eyed Ryder with some concern. "I think we're about the same size. I have some boots and things you can borrow for the hike."

Ryder nodded but didn't release his hold on her. Peering at Sophie, he said, "You take care of yourself, Rhea and Delilah. We're going to find your parents before the time runs out."

She forced a smile she wasn't feeling and dipped her head in acknowledgment. "Lo se," she said and then quickly translated. "I know, and if I figure out anything else in the meantime, you'll be the first to know."

RYDER DROPPED A last kiss on her lips and hurried out the door, following Jackson to his office to prep whatever gear they might need for the hike.

Once in his office, Jackson closed the door behind them and leaned on it, his face as hard and impenetrable as granite.

Ryder narrowed his gaze to examine his friend. "Is something wrong?"

Jackson's lips thinned into an ugly slash and, with a rough exhale, he said, "Are you sure you're up to this? I mean, you just survived getting hit by a car yesterday."

Ryder couldn't deny that his body was still a mass of

bruises and aches, but he couldn't just sit back while the Whitakers' lives were at stake. Hands held out in pleading, he said, "I need to help, Jax. I can't just sit here and do nothing."

"There's lots you can do. For starters, we should have the warrant to search Cromwell's place shortly. There might be valuable information there."

Ryder hated that his friend might be right. From what Officer Dillon had said, the climb along the northern slope wouldn't be easy. The last thing he wanted was to hold them back in case the Whitakers were being held in either of the two locations they had identified.

With a reluctant nod, he said, "I'll execute the warrant as soon as it comes in."

Almost on cue, Jackson's office phone rang.

He picked up and, after a short conversation with someone, Jackson said, "Thanks, Milly. I'll let CBI Agent Hunt know we got the warrant."

After Jackson hung up, he said, "You can take Officer Longmeadow with you. He's fresh out of the academy but he's got a good eye."

"I guess I've got a job to do," Ryder said, walked over and bro-hugged his friend. "Stay safe and keep me posted."

"You do the same."

Ryder marched to the door and hurried to the front desk. As he neared, Milly smiled at him and waved a piece of paper.

He snagged it from her, opened it to review the specifics of the warrant and, satisfied that it authorized the kind of search he wanted to do, he walked into the bullpen to find the officer Jackson had recommended that he take.

The young man was at his desk, filling out an incident report. "Officer Longmeadow," he said as he approached.

The officer's head snapped up and he pushed to his feet, recognizing him. "CBI Agent Hunt. How may I help?"

"Chief Jackson says you have good eyes. Have you ever executed a search warrant before?" he asked, needing to know who he was dealing with for the operation.

Longmeadow shook his head. "No, Agent Hunt."

With a shrug, Ryder said, "I guess there's a first time for everything."

Chapter Fourteen

Sophie paced across the width of the room, impatience and worry driving her long strides in the small space.

I'm missing something. She was annoyed by her failure to decipher the message her parents had sent.

Over and over, she replayed in her brain the breadcrumbs, frustrated that the twenty-four she'd seen remained the most prominent thing. She didn't doubt the meaning of that: a clock was ticking.

Time was running out for her parents.

Muttering a curse, she rushed back to her laptop and opened the screen again, wanting to see something, anything, of value.

A knock came at the door, startling her from her review.

Barely a second later, Ryder hurried in, surprising her.

"What are you doing here? I thought you were going with Jax," she said, eyeing him in confusion.

A flush of hot color erupted on his neck and raced upward to his cheeks. "Jax wasn't sure I was up for the hike."

And her cousin wouldn't have embarrassed his friend and colleague by mentioning that in front of everyone.

She walked over, cupped his jaw and ran her thumb across the flush of color on his cheeks. "You did just get out of the hospital."

Ryder looked away and expelled a shaky sigh. "Yes, I did. And the last thing I want is to jeopardize your parents' lives." He jerked a thumb in the direction of the door. "I'm headed to Cromwell's house to execute a search warrant."

"Can I come with?" she asked, hoping that a change of location might help her break past her block about the message.

He stared at her hard and then skipped his glance to her laptop. With a flip of his hand toward the computer, he said, "Aren't you working on that?"

"I'm stuck. I'm not seeing what I should." She glared at her laptop and shook her head.

Twining his fingers with hers, he gave a little reassuring squeeze. "Maybe there's nothing else for you to see."

"Maybe. Or maybe this 'gift' I have is failing us," she said, using rabbit ears to emphasize that she didn't consider her ability as something positive.

With a playful swing of their joined hands to lift her negative mood, he said, "Let's go to Cromwell's. Hopefully, we'll find a clue that might help."

She nodded and said, "Let me just grab my laptop and I'm ready to go."

CROMWELL'S HOME WASN'T all that far from Ryder's lake house, but the two houses couldn't look more different.

While his lake house was tidy, neat and reminiscent of an English country cottage, Cromwell's place was a contemporary, with harsh lines, and screamed run-down, sad and slightly scary. Like what you might find as a movie set for a slasher flick.

Off to the left was a large stand-alone garage with doors that hung half off their hinges, making them sag toward the middle, exposing a hint of bright red.

But the proximity to his home meant they would both be

using the same road to come and go from Regina. It had the CBI agent wondering if Cromwell had been following them or just heading to town.

As Officer Longmeadow pulled his cruiser in behind them, Sophie and Ryder slipped from the SUV. He unharnessed Delilah and, with a hand command and a soft "Stay," the corgi sat by the side of the car.

Ryder eased the search warrant from his jacket pocket and reviewed it to confirm what areas they could search, worried it didn't cover the garage.

Sure enough, the warrant was only for the house.

He handed it to Longmeadow. "We stick to the house, but I would say we're good to take a look into that semiopen garage door. Wouldn't you?"

The young officer had been reading the warrant and looked toward the garage. "I would. It's as good as open," he said and gestured with the warrant toward the dilapidated doors.

They walked over, Sophie following behind them.

Ryder peeked through the gaping doors and had no doubt the garage held a vintage red Camaro. "Looks like the car for our BOLO," he said and shifted away so the others could examine the vehicle.

Longmeadow and Sophie confirmed his impression.

"Definitely the car," the young officer said.

Sophie chimed in with, "I think that's the one we saw on the videos of the attack at the station."

With a nod and dip of his head at the house, Ryder said, "Let's head in. Sophie, please hang back in case Cromwell's left us any surprises."

Ryder walked to the front door and found it unlocked.

Not surprising since most people thought the area in and around Regina was relatively safe. He held up his hand, urging Longmeadow and Sophie to stay back as he turned the knob and, with a shove, opened the door.

Nothing except a loud creak and a thud as it hit the wall.

"Police," he called out to identify himself in case anyone else resided in the home besides Cromwell. "We have a search warrant," he said. But no one responded.

Satisfied the home was empty, he walked in and did a quick inspection of the small foyer. No sign of any kind of booby trap so he waved to Longmeadow and Sophie to come in.

Once they were inside, they all paused at the threshold to examine the space.

To the left was a well-kept kitchen. Dishes sat in a dish drain and a nearby table was timeworn but clean.

A parlor to the right seemed better suited to a Regency movie than a single police officer. The surfaces of the mahogany tables and sideboard had a layer of dust that spoke of a lack of care.

They strolled down the hall, which opened into a living room that was clearly where Cromwell spent most of his time since it wasn't anywhere near as clean or orderly.

A leather recliner boasted a sagging cushion and well-worn patches fashioned from silver duct tape on the arms.

A few empty beer cans littered the floor by the recliner.

Faded pink blossoms adorned a chintz-covered sofa better suited to someone's grandmother. Sitting on a side table beside the sofa was a picture of an elderly couple, and Ryder suspected they had been the original occupants of the home as well as the recliner and sofa.

"Do you know much about Cromwell's family?" Ryder asked, looking over his shoulder at Longmeadow.

With a shrug, he said, "He's divorced. No kids that I know of. And I think he lost his parents about six months ago."

"Explains the décor." He pivoted slowly to take in the pictures on the walls of a younger Cromwell, and what were likely his parents, as well as the large mounted bass hanging over a fireplace.

Sophie had whipped out her smartphone and tapped away during his inspection. A second later, she said, "County clerk's office shows a change in ownership about six months ago. He must have inherited this place."

But where had he been before?

"Can you see if Cromwell owned any other property before this one?" he asked.

With a nod, Sophie's fingers flew across her smartphone and barely a minute later, she said, "Townhouse in Regina. Jackson must have thought Cromwell still lived there since he sent Diego to watch it. Bank foreclosed on it about six months ago."

His gut warned him that there was more to that story and faced Longmeadow. "Do you know how his parents died?"

Longmeadow shook his head. "I don't."

Sophie and her smartphone research quickly provided the answer. "Newspaper article says carbon monoxide poisoning. Supposedly from the water heater in this home."

"Too much coincidence. Cromwell's in financial trouble and his parents die and leave him this and I'm assuming some kind of insurance policy," Ryder said.

"I do remember that Cromwell seemed flush for a little bit," Longmeadow advised.

"Hmm," Ryder said as they pushed through to the two smallish bedrooms in the back. One had been Cromwell's childhood space, judging from the posters and pictures on the walls and the twin bed.

Cromwell had taken over his parents' room.

The bed was unmade and on an old mahogany dresser sat

a tank filled with colorful tropical fish. Beside the tank was an assortment of supplies and one of them caught his eye.

He picked up a box of activated charcoal and held it up for the others to see. "Burn this—"

"And you get carbon monoxide. Charcoal burning can be used to attempt suicide, but it's normally done in an enclosed space," Sophie said.

"I wonder where the water heater is." Longmeadow stepped out of the bedroom to a slatted door in the hall they hadn't checked on their way to the bedrooms. He opened it and said, "Here it is. Right next door."

"And six months ago the weather is getting colder and you turn on the heat. They have baseboard heating," Ryder said, gesturing to the units along the floors of the room.

"Everything is sealed up, and as close as this heater is..." Sophie didn't need to finish since they all understood.

"Who would have investigated?" Ryder asked the young officer.

"Regina PD and the fire marshal. We can pull the reports once we finish here, but I suspect they just assumed it was a terrible accident."

Ryder nodded and said, "Let's each take a room. Look for anything out of the ordinary but keep an eye out for any booby traps."

Sophie appreciated that Ryder was treating her as an equal in the investigation since on more than one occasion when SBS had been called in to work with law enforcement, the officers had looked askance at her and assumed she couldn't hold her own.

But she was well-versed in searches, and thanks to her cousin Trey, he'd made a point of training them on the kinds of traps that might be set when they'd had to investigate a serial killer using their new K-9 training facility as a dump site for his victims.

"I'll take the kitchen," she said. She considered herself a good cook with lots of knowledge about the kinds of tools and gadgets you might find in a kitchen.

Armed with that, she carefully examined all the cabinets and drawers, but didn't find much of interest except some promo items from the Denver area casino: a bottle opener, corkscrew and lighter.

She assumed you didn't score all that swag in one visit, which just confirmed that Cromwell had been a regular.

Stepping back, she scrutinized the cabinets again, her gut screaming that she was missing something, just like she was missing the hidden meaning in her parents' messages.

Returning to the first cabinet, she opened it again and stared inside. A set of inexpensive glasses along with a collection of jars from fast-food promotions and jellies.

She closed the door and moved to the next cabinet. Normal dinner-sized plates. Smaller lunch plates and cereal bowls. All were in a dated floral pattern. Probably his mother's choice based on the flowers on the sofa.

Moving to the next cupboard, she encountered a lazy Susan crammed with assorted spices and shelves with several different flours and other baking essentials. Cromwell's mom had been a baker.

But as she closed that cabinet and moved to the next, something called her back to the very first one.

She opened it and noticed the stacks of glasses, about two deep. Only two deep, she realized, and she opened the cabinet with the plates.

A deeper cabinet, which made no sense. Most kitchen cabinets were a standard depth.

Walking to the side of the cabinet, she suddenly noticed

the very thin line about a third of the way from the wall. Running her fingers down the line, she realized it ran the entire length of the cupboard. At the base of it was a lip that allowed for under-cabinet lighting.

She gripped the lip of the smaller section and tugged. It shifted, sliding out slightly. With a stronger yank, she pulled out an entire back section of shelves and then stood in shock at what she had discovered.

Bundles of hundred-dollar bills sat along the top two shelves. The bottom shelf held glass jars filled with what looked like casino gaming chips.

She was reaching for one when the sound of Delilah barking, sharp and insistent, snared her attention.

It had drawn Ryder and Longmeadow as well since they all shifted toward the front parlor and its big picture window to take a look.

"Get down," Ryder shouted and threw himself at her to haul her to the ground, cradling her to lessen the impact.

Above them, the window exploded, sending glass flying, and the rat-a-tat of gunfire peppered the air for long moments as bullets bit into the walls and furniture in the room.

Ryder shielded her from the bits of glass, wood and drywall flying through the air as the pop-pop of the automatic weapon filled the room for what seemed like forever.

The squeal of tires finally signaled their assailants had left and, luckily, Delilah was still vigorously barking, hopefully signaling that she was unharmed.

"Are you okay?" Ryder asked as he helped her to her feet and brushed away debris from her hair and shoulders.

"I'm fine," she said and likewise dusted dirt off him.

"Longmeadow, are you okay?" Ryder said and faced the young officer as he got to his feet.

"I am. It was a black pickup, wasn't it?" Longmeadow

said and was about to call it in but stopped abruptly. "All the Regina officers are busy with the case."

"Right, but the state troopers can be on the lookout and Chief Whitaker needs to know in case they're being followed also. The same goes for the detail with Selene and Robbie," Ryder said, aware that they needed to pull in whatever resources they could to protect their people.

"Got it," Longmeadow said and stepped away to make all the necessary calls.

"They're drive-by happy, aren't they?" Ryder asked with a harsh laugh as Sophie brushed debris from him.

"Maybe because they are worried about what I just found," she said and guided him back to the kitchen and the hidden shelving with the cash and casino chips.

Ryder's eyes widened in surprise. "There's easily a hundred thousand or more in cash."

He grabbed one of the jars with his latex-gloved hand, opened it and spilled out some chips on the counter.

"Hundred-dollar chips from that casino we identified," Sophie said, eyeing the bottles filled with them.

"Easy way to launder dirty money," Ryder said and gestured to the stacks of hundreds. "He cashes the money in for chips, plays at the casino and then gets a check or 'clean' money."

"They use fixed-odds betting terminals to minimize gambling losses, right?" Sophie asked.

Ryder smiled and nodded. "You know your money laundering."

"We recently had a case involving a stable owner that might have involved some money laundering, so I had to do some research," she explained.

"If Cromwell had done badly with his gambling, it made

him a prime mark to assist them with the theft of the evidence as well as the money laundering," Ryder said.

Longmeadow entered the kitchen and, as he did so, his eyes almost bugged out of his head when he saw the stacks of bills and bottles filled with chips.

"Wow," he said, virtually speechless.

"A big wow. I'm going to call the CBI CSI unit to collect additional evidence. I'll need you to secure the scene and also give Chief Jackson a rundown on what we've found," Ryder said.

"Roger that," Longmeadow said.

"What are we going to do in the meantime?" Sophie asked, wishing she still didn't have that niggling worry that she was missing something.

Ryder picked up a chip. "We're going to pay a visit to the casino."

Chapter Fifteen

As Ryder drove, he kept an eye on the road for the black pickup and on Sophie, who had been working on her computer after calling Rhea to tell her of the change in plans and warn her to head to the police station, where she would be safe. They'd left Delilah at the station with Milly once again, certain they wouldn't be able to take the corgi into the casino with them, or if they'd end up staying overnight if it got too late to return to Regina.

Her smartphone chirped to warn of an incoming call from Robbie. After a too-brief discussion, she urged her brother to be cautious with a worried, "¡Cuídate! Por favor, Robbie."

"I got this. Besides, Selene and I are in Denver PD headquarters. It's quite a bit bigger than the Regina station," he reminded her.

"You have to go to her place later," Sophie reminded.

"And, thanks to Ryder, CBI is keeping an eye on that building," Robbie said, drawing Sophie's attention to Ryder.

"Okay, I get it. All is under control," she said, although as their eyes connected for the slightest moment, Ryder sensed she didn't believe that.

She ended the call, and he brushed the back of his hand across her cheek, offering comfort. "He'll be fine."

"He will," she said almost as if to reassure herself, but then blurted out, "But we're running out of time for my parents."

He knew. Boy did he know that—everything around him, from his phone to the heads-up display on his car, reminded him that the minutes were ticking away.

"We're making progress," he said and, before she could object, added, "It's slow, I know. But it's progress."

Her lips thinned into a grimace and to keep from responding, she opened her laptop and resumed the work her brother's phone call had interrupted. As she worked, she mumbled, "There's more here I'm not seeing."

"Besides the twenty-fours?" he asked, hoping that he might trigger an idea with his questions.

"Besides those. It's almost like I see them too well and they're hiding something more important," she admitted as she tapped away.

He snuck a quick look at her screen, where text seemed to be flying by.

"Tunnel vision. It happens to the best of us when we're working on a problem," he admitted.

She regarded him, eyes slit, as she considered his comment. Nodding, she said, "It could be that. Maybe our focus has been wrong. What's the real reason Oliver and whoever is behind him want to hack those databases? Just to avoid prosecution, or is it about more?"

Ryder let that thought percolate but then dipped his head back and forth. "Like the money laundering we just discovered? What if their operation is being threatened by Oliver's actions?"

"We have Oliver dead to rights thanks to Matt Clark. And if Oliver talks, he might reveal what they're doing to get a more lenient sentence," she said.

"So, to find your parents, we find the people behind the money laundering," Ryder said, buying into her theory.

"It would explain why Cromwell is involved and why he has all that money in his kitchen cabinet."

"But we don't have any connections between Oliver and the casino," Ryder said as he shifted toward the exit for the casino.

"Not yet, but Robbie and I can get to work on that. I'll e-mail him about our suspicions," she said.

"Is that the message that you think your parents buried in whatever you're seeing?" he asked.

She immediately and vehemently shook her head. "No, it's just something that came to me. I still think I'm missing the message that they're sending. It's just my gut telling me that," she said and gave her attention to working on her laptop for the last minutes before they reached the casino.

As she did so, he mulled her theory over. If Oliver was somehow connected to the money laundering, Ryder didn't doubt he'd roll over on that kind of operation for a break on his case. But kidnapping the Whitakers as a ruse? That was a major escalation that just didn't make sense. Unless, of course, whatever the Whitakers deleted could also disappear any connections to the casino and possible crimes.

As he parked the car, he faced her and said, "I still think they want your parents to eliminate evidence."

She tipped her head from side to side, contemplating it, and said, "I agree, but only because every person who is facing a trial may roll over on them and end their operation."

"Agreed. I'm going to call Jax and fill him in on what we've found and where we are," he said and dialed his friend.

When Jackson answered, he was winded. "What's…up?"

Ryder quickly explained what they'd found and their plan to investigate the casino connections.

"Sounds...like...a...plan," he puffed out, and it was followed by an oomph and expletive.

"Tough going, huh?" Ryder asked, wishing he had gone while also accepting he possibly wasn't physically up to the task.

"Real...rough. The northern slope is...dense," Jackson admitted.

"I'll let you go then. We'll call later with whatever we have," he said and ended the call.

He faced Sophie, who had tucked her laptop into her knapsack and seemed ready for action. But just to confirm, he said, "Ready to go?"

She nodded. "Ready as I'll ever be."

MERCEDES DRUMMED HER fingers on the table and glanced at the clock on the computer's taskbar.

According to her internet search, sunset wouldn't arrive until about seven thirty, which meant they had another few hours before she could launch her plan.

Beside her, Robert was hard at work, and as she looked at his screen, she realized he was close to writing the final code to hack the CBI database. She recognized the commands from a program they had once written to break into a terror organization's website to collect information.

"You're close," she said in a low whisper and skipped her gaze across the assorted cameras watching them, fearful of discovery.

Robert leaned close and in a barely legible whisper said, "I am. You?"

She sneaked a peek at her screen and hesitantly shrugged. "Hopefully," she said and eyed the cameras once again. "But it's not time yet."

"It's going to take me at least another hour or so before I can try this attack." He gestured to the computer.

She nodded, bit her lip and, in a hushed whisper, said, "I don't think Sophie has seen it."

She had been counting on her daughter to intercept the clues buried in the denial-of-service attack she had launched against the CBI database. It had been her job to weaken the site with the excess traffic so that Robert could perform the final break-in.

Had Sophie and Robbie not noticed the increased network traffic? she wondered.

No, Sophie had to have seen the various clues. Mercedes hoped that help was on the way and that Sophie and Robbie were somewhere safe.

And if help wasn't coming, Robert and she were ready to do what they could to free themselves and stop the hack of the database.

All it would take was a few quick keystrokes.

But not yet. Not until it is time, she thought and went back to check the coding on her hack.

SOPHIE HAD BEEN in several casinos in her life, from those gracing the Jersey Shore in Atlantic City to the huge establishments in Las Vegas to the Native American–owned ones in and around Florida. She'd also visited the other nearby casino in Denver but not this smaller more luxurious casino.

It wasn't that she was a gambler. Just that, on occasion, Robbie and she were called in to check on IT networks to make sure they were safe and secure.

As white hat hackers, they were in demand for investigations like that.

She smoothed the front of her blouse, feeling underdressed

as men and women in designer clothes flitted in and around the various slot machines and gaming tables.

It reeked more of Monte Carlo than Denver. Not that she'd had the opportunity to visit Monaco, although it was on her bucket list.

Ryder was also taking in the clientele, and as their gazes met, he leaned close. "I think we may have to up our game to not stick out like sore thumbs."

"I agree," she said and gestured to a sign directing people to the shops at the casino.

They hurried to the stores and weren't disappointed to find outfits and accessories much like those being flaunted by the casino-goers. Splitting apart, Sophie hurried into the dress shop, and as she skimmed through the outfits, it reminded her of her Miami fashionista cousin, Mia, who would have loved many of the designer outfits.

Channeling her inner Mia, she selected a body-hugging sheath that would work well in the late afternoon as well as evening since she suspected they'd be at the casino for hours. *Maybe even possibly overnight*, she thought, and grabbed a simple but silky nightshirt, lingerie and toiletries. Not wanting to overdo, she selected an elegant linen blouse that would dress up her jeans for the morning.

Hurrying from the store, she nearly crashed into Ryder. He had to grab her arms to keep her from falling, but even after she was steady, his touch lingered, creating fire. Especially as his gaze skimmed up and down her body.

"You look lovely," he said and raised his hand to tenderly stroke her cheek.

She smiled shyly and brushed her hand across the crisp cotton of his shirt. "You don't look bad yourself."

Glancing at his bag, which was almost as full as hers, she

said, "Great minds. Do you think we should get a room and have our things taken there?"

"I do. This place isn't quite what I pictured, and I want to take my time and explore what and who we might be dealing with. Maybe even find a way to get them to come to us," he said and, with a dip of his head, directed her to the lobby area for the hotel section of the building.

Gleaming white marble veined with gold went from floor to ceiling in the lobby. Ornate gold wall sconces and chandeliers dripping with crystal created an ambience of over-the-top Old World elegance. There was nothing minimalist-modern about the space, except maybe the spaceship-looking black slab seemingly floating on more white marble that made up the reception desk.

In no time the very efficient staff had checked them in, taken their bags to be delivered to their room, and they were on their way to the casino.

As they strolled around, watching the action at the slot machines and gaming tables, Ryder said into her ear, "I don't know Cromwell at all but somehow I don't see him fitting in here."

Based on the house they'd visited and what little she knew of the corrupt cop, she didn't see him in these environs either.

It took them a while to find the small section where the fixed-odds betting terminals were located. There were only a dozen or so, making her wonder how Cromwell could have placed so many bets without detection. Especially considering the various CCTV units placed throughout the casino.

"Not many," Ryder commented as he, too, took in the terminal area.

With a shrug, she said, "Those online betting sites have probably eaten into the clientele who might have come here, although my research said Colorado only recently approved fixed-odds betting but only for horse racing."

Ryder nodded. "That's my understanding as well."

After another glance around, he said, "We have enough on Cromwell for a search warrant on that CCTV footage."

"You do, but do you want to tip your hand so soon?" she asked, although she suspected anyone watching them might already know they were investigating the casino.

"No. Let's just keep an eye out for anything out of the ordinary."

"Let's try some gambling to see how they handle that, especially if we're winning too much money," she said, but before they left the FOB terminals, she took a mental picture of the people placing bets at the terminals and watching the live casts of the races. She planned to come back to see if any of the same people were there later and, if so, if they had been lucky and were hitting the row of cashier cages just a few feet away.

Slipping her hand into Ryder's, she guided him toward the gaming tables. Craps, which supposedly had the best odds for bettors. Blackjack and poker. Roulette, which she'd played on occasion when on an assignment.

That reminded her of something she'd learned in one case. Walking over to a roulette table, she motioned to the flat felt surface of green adorned with the red, black and white of the numbers and boxes for bets.

"Maybe Cromwell wasn't just gaming at the FOB terminals. These tables won't issue any kind of tax document even if you win millions," she said, watching how the wheel was running even though a nearby screen kept the bettors alert to the numbers that had recently won as well as what numbers and colors had been common winners at the table.

"But what about when he cashes out at the cage?" Ryder asked, not as familiar with how it worked as she was.

"Normally, if you get chips from a cashier at the cage, they would keep track of that purchase. The same should happen at the table, and if there were cash transactions of ten thousand dollars or more at the cage, they'd have to report it," she explained.

"And suspicious activity reports?" he asked by leaning close, not wanting those at the table to overhear their discussion.

His breath was warm against her neck, rousing awareness of his proximity. The smooth, almost-cool cotton of his shirt brushed across her bare back. As he shifted near, he bracketed her waist with one hand, the gesture both possessive and protective.

She peered up at him, meeting that melty-chocolate gaze that did all kinds of things to her insides. In a breathy voice, she said, "Do you want to test it out for ourselves? Maybe draw someone out?"

With a dip of his head, he said, "Sure."

She was about to reach into the small clutch she had also bought at the store when he laid a big hand on hers to stop her.

At her confused look, he grinned and said, "Let me float you. I hit the ATM after I was done at the store."

He whipped out a money clip and peeled off several hundred-dollar bills. "Buena suerte. Did I say that right?"

Grinning, she said, "Sí. Let's hope I'm lucky."

Chapter Sixteen

Sophie laid the bills in front of an empty seat and cashed them in for chips. Red, like the polish on her perfectly manicured nails.

Ryder stood behind her, watching as she laid chips on the table, her fingers as nimble on the felt as they were on a keyboard. While she readied for play, he scanned the casino, looking for anything out of the ordinary.

Several feet away, a very muscular man in a dark suit, earpiece wire dangling from one ear, appeared to be watching them intently. His hands were crossed before him in that stereotypical bodyguard movie pose that only made him stick out even more.

When Ryder's gaze connected with his, the man quickly half turned, as if to hide his interest.

Ryder returned to Sophie and the roulette game, although he kept watching the security guard from the corner of his eye.

He'd never played roulette. The one thing he understood was that every spin of the wheel was costing the five players around the table twenty-five dollars.

With each spin taking a little over a minute or so, it wouldn't take long for a player on a losing streak to run out of cash quickly, as happened to one player at the end of the table. They had been laying what seemed like dozens of chips on numbers all across the table.

Totally unlike Sophie, who had kept to playing columns and seemed to be winning with every spin.

He bent and whispered, "Do you ever play numbers or the colors?"

"Sometimes if I get a feeling. After all, this is a total game of chance," she said and laid the same bets again.

"That doesn't seem too chancy," he said, pointing to her bets.

"I'd lose by not covering two of the columns or if zero or double zero hits," she explained just as the ball dropped into a slot with a clinky-clink-clank.

The dealer paid Sophie out again and the losing player at the end pushed away from the table and stalked off, all his chips having been lost with his last bet.

"Seems like you have a system," he said, watching her place basically the same bets while also keeping an eye out for what was happening around them.

She shook her head and gave a slight turn of her wrist to check her watch, a silver-and-gold TAG Heuer, which he had noticed days earlier because he had expected her to have a smartwatch.

"It's time to do something big because we're running out of time," she said and crooked a finger to alert the dealer that she wanted to cash out her colored roulette chips for casino tokens.

While she'd left the table with way more money than she had started with, it hadn't been enough to attract any kind of suspicion. She walked toward one of the blackjack tables and, as they headed there, the security guard he had spotted earlier also moved, trailing them from a distance.

When they reached one blackjack table, Sophie leaned

close and breathed into his ear, "Now this isn't so chancy. I think I can make this hurt enough that they'll want to talk to us."

Slipping into an open seat, she exchanged the casino tokens for table chips and waited for the first hand to be dealt.

While that happened, he kept an eye on the guard and realized he'd been joined by another security person, who had his back to them but glanced over his shoulder in their direction fairly regularly. A short conversation ensued between the two men and the newcomer walked away, but Ryder was certain he'd be back.

He returned his attention to Sophie and found that the dealer was paying her out a mound of chips. He'd missed the hand with his attention being diverted by the two men.

The dealer was already tossing out cards to the players, and once he finished, he realized Sophie had been dealt a pair of aces that she was splitting.

A risky move? He was a little more familiar with blackjack than he was with roulette.

The dealer doled out the next round of cards.

Sophie remained cool as a cucumber as the dealer flipped a nine onto one ace and then a ten. Blackjack and a winner for sure on the one bet and twenty would be hard for the dealer to beat.

As the dealer finished with all the players, he revealed his hand: seven and ten cards. Dealer rules forced him to stay at seventeen and made Sophie a double winner.

The dealer paid out another mountain of chips to Sophie and, over the next few hands, her luck continued.

Or was it luck? Her win streak was truly impressive, as was the pile of chips growing in front of her.

Most of the players around her were cheering her on although one man seemed rather put out with her winning.

The cheering had attracted the attention of players at some of the other tables as well as passersby who stopped to gape at the mound of chips and to see if Sophie could pull off another win.

They had wanted to attract attention, preferably of the casino owners, and this was a good start.

The first security guard he'd seen was still to his left and the second man who had walked away was now on their right, like two battalions flanking an enemy during battle.

As Sophie won yet another hand, and excited cheers erupted, the pit boss came over and stood there watching them play. After two more winning hands, the pit boss leaned in to say something in the dealer's ear before walking away. With a nod, the dealer reached beneath the table and set out a sign that the table minimum was going up to a fifty-dollar minimum bet in five minutes.

That announcement was met with groans from the players and lookie-loos getting vicarious excitement from Sophie's play.

The dealer held his hands up in surrender and said, "Sorry. Just doing what the pit boss said."

The five minutes passed quickly, and Sophie finally lost a hand, but the two security guards drifted closer.

Ryder's gut tightened with apprehension. He probably could take one man, even in his current condition. Two would be difficult, until he remembered Robbie's claim that Sophie had a black belt. If that was true, it might even the odds.

He'd also bet on the fact they wouldn't make a scene on the crowded casino floor.

Once the minimum went up, almost all the players left the blackjack table. Only Sophie and the grumpy player remained.

Sophie looked up at Ryder and asked, "One more big bet?"

Fortune favors the brave, he thought and nodded. "Make it big."

With a wry smile, she plunked down one thousand dollars as a bet, but the dealer waved her off.

"Max bet is ten times the minimum. So you can only bet five hundred," he explained.

"Thought a pro like you might know that," grumbled the player beside her.

Sophie laughed and leveled him after his dis. "Thought a pro like you might know how to win," she parried and took back the extra money she had bet.

The pit boss must have noticed that something was up and walked over. The two men had a short sidebar. The pit boss waved at her and said, "You want to bet more than the max?"

Sophie nodded. "At least a thousand."

The pit boss snorted and raised his index finger in the air. "I'll raise the max to ten thousand for this bet. But just this one bet," he said, possibly hoping that the casino could somehow recoup a portion of their losses since Sophie's winning streak had to end.

"Gracias," she said and pushed ten thousand dollars worth of chips toward the dealer.

Spanish meant she was nervous. *Too nervous?* He worried she'd made a bad bet even though she had turned their original hundred into thousands. No matter what happened, they'd walk away as winners.

The dealer dealt the first cards out to Sophie and her grumpy companion and then dealt himself a card.

The second round of cards revealed a five for the man next to Sophie, a seven for Sophie and a six for the dealer.

Ryder held his breath, wondering what she'd do as the man next to her drew a third card and busted.

She slashed her hand to indicate she was staying. If the

dealer had seventeen, it would be a push and Sophie would keep her cash. Less than seventeen...

The dealer had sixteen. Anything from a two to a five and he would win. An ace would make it a push.

Ryder heard Sophie's sharp inhale and laid a hand on her shoulder as the dealer drew another card.

A six. A bust.

Beneath his hand, the tension left Sophie's body.

But from the corner of his eye, he saw the security guards rapidly approaching.

Since they had to wait for the payout and exchange the table chips for casino tokens they could cash out at the cashier's cage, there was no time for them to avoid the advancing security guards.

"MR. BLACKWELL WOULD like to meet you," one of the security guards said as Sophie rose with handfuls of yellow one-thousand-dollar casino tokens that she stuffed into her purse.

"And Mr. Blackwell is?" Sophie said even though her research on the casino had mentioned the owner's name on various occasions.

"He's the boss," the man said in a high-pitched voice that didn't match his stout muscular physique.

Ryder pushed back. "What if we have somewhere to be?"

The taller, skinnier guard responded in a deep, almost-melodic voice. "You don't want to make Mr. Blackwell angry."

Ryder did a dismissive shrug and tilted his chin defiantly, going nearly nose to nose with the taller man.

He was clearly in bad-cop mode. She'd seen her cousin Trey do it more than once. And since she'd seen how his detective wife, Roni, would assist, she jumped in as the good-guy mediator.

Slipping her hand between the two men, she smoothed it

across Ryder's chest and in a sweet-as-honey voice said, "I think we can spare a few minutes and not get these gentlemen into trouble with their boss."

Ryder grunted but played along, stepping in beside her as she followed the muscular guard. He laid a possessive hand at the small of her back, applying gentle pressure while also glaring at the other security guard to keep his distance.

When they walked across the casino floor, Sophie searched for exits and memorized the layout in case they had to leave in a hurry.

As it turned out, the guards led them to the hotel lobby, through a side door and down a long hallway. At the end of the hall, there were two glass doors. The left one had to be to their security area since a peek inside revealed tables where personnel sat viewing monitors with video feeds of the casino floor. The other door led to an office where an older, elegantly dressed man sat behind a massive black lacquer desk.

The man, Mr. Blackwell she assumed, rose and motioned them to sit in the duo leather chairs in front of the desk.

He was a trim man dressed in a bespoke black suit and a white shirt starched to within an inch of its life. His salt-and-pepper hair was wavy and ruthlessly slicked back from a face that was relatively unlined for a man his age. She suspected he was in his late seventies, but he moved smoothly and with confidence.

As they sat as requested, the two guards peeled back to stand close to a bookcase filled with dozens of books, various trophies and pictures of Blackwell with several well-known celebrities and politicians, including State Senator Connell Oliver.

"I understand y'all have been quite lucky today, Ms.…" he began and waited for her to introduce herself.

"Ms. Gonzalez," she said, using her mother's name because Whitaker would be too much of a giveaway if this man was involved in the kidnapping.

He dipped his head to acknowledge it and narrowed his eyes as he sat and considered Ryder. "And this is…?"

"My bodyguard. As you can imagine, I don't like walking around with this much money without protection," she said and patted her bulging purse.

Blackwell's lips tightened with displeasure. "Yes, I can well imagine, although my casino is used to high rollers such as yourself. Card counter?" he asked with the arch of a trimmed eyebrow.

"A very good memory. I don't think that's illegal in Colorado. For that matter, neither is card counting," she responded, a little glibly because she wanted to push this man to see how he would react.

Blackwell sucked in a deep breath and held it as if marshaling control. When he spoke, his voice was tight, his words clipped. "It is not, although if I had my druthers, it would be. You've got gumption, I'll give you that, but you must know it's within my rights to ban you from future play."

Eyes wide in feigned surprise, she laughed lightly. "Afraid I'll win even more?" she challenged, which yanked a chuckle and smile from Ryder that he quickly hid with his hand.

Bright red colored Blackwell's cheeks and his hands tightened on the arms of his chair, turning white from the control he was exerting.

"Y'all don't want to mess with me," he said. Gesturing to the two guards with gnarly fingers, arthritis if she had to guess, he added, "Mr. Smith and Mr. Jones will escort you back to the casino so you can cash out. After that, they'll escort you to the lobby to make sure you don't reenter the casino. If you do, y'all will be treated as trespassers and we'll take whatever steps are necessary."

"No cement shoes or broken legs?" she teased and managed to draw a choked laugh from the angry casino owner.

"You've watched too many Scorsese movies," Blackwell quipped and made a "come here" gesture to his security guards, who approached them.

With a quick glance at Ryder, who nodded to confirm they should comply, she rose, and he slipped his hand into hers and they walked out of the office, the guards following close behind.

She imagined their warm breaths at the back of her neck, the way a fox might feel chased by hounds. Although she'd been calm inside Blackwell's office, certain they wouldn't take any action there, she wasn't feeling quite as safe now.

Ryder must have sensed her apprehension since he bent his head toward hers and said, "Don't worry. We can take these guys."

She laughed, as he'd intended, but the humor was lost on the two guards.

"You wish," the taller one said while Mr. Muscular just grunted in agreement.

Their entrance into the casino was marked by inquisitive stares from many of the patrons walking around the floor and some at the gaming tables.

A good thing, she thought. It would make for lots and lots of witnesses if anything happened.

At the cashier's cage, which was very similar to a teller's window at a bank, she handed the young woman behind the window handfuls of thousand-dollar chips.

"I'll have to take your information for this cash-out," she said, and Sophie provided the necessary details.

Once the formalities were done and the chips counted, the cashier handed over three stacks of hundreds along with another few loose hundreds.

Sophie nervously tucked those into her purse and turned to leave, but bumped into the taller guard, who had positioned himself close by during the transaction.

Ryder jumped between them and, as before, challenged the man. "I believe Mr. Blackwell said you should take us to the lobby."

The man raised his hands in surrender and stepped back. "Just wanted to make sure no one had any ideas. That's a lot of money to carry around."

"Thanks, but we've got this," he said, slipping his arm around her waist and applying soft pressure to guide her from the cashier's cage.

They walked side by side, so close, her hip bumped his as they hurried from the casino floor and out to the lobby.

Once there, they rushed to the elevators to go to their room, the guards following not far behind. The elevator arrived and when they entered and turned, she realized the two men stood just outside the doors, hands braced before them. Menacing glares focused on them until the elevator doors swooshed closed.

She didn't doubt that they'd see them again.

The question was, How soon?

NERVOUS ENERGY ZIPPED through Mercedes's body as the hour approached.

She tapped out a beat with her feet and drummed her fingers on the worktable until Robert reached over and stilled the anxious motion.

"It's going to be okay," he said in a low tone.

"What if it doesn't work?" she asked, suddenly losing the confidence that had had many a colleague calling her a "tough cookie."

Robert offered her a half smile and glance that chided her for her doubts.

"It's you, my love," he added, more sure of her skills than she was.

With a nod, she positioned her index finger over Enter, closed her eyes and hit the key.

Chapter Seventeen

Every light in the room went dark, including the red dots on the security cameras watching them.

The click of a lock hopefully signaled that the electronic dead bolt keeping them in the bunker had also lost power.

Hopefully, its default setting in a power outage was in the open position.

"Let's go," Robert said, grabbed her arm and urged her to the door.

When he turned the knob, it opened wide.

The damp chill of the coming night warned them to be better prepared than during their last escape attempt.

They propped the door open, not wanting to take any chances that Mercedes's hack would be quickly undone and power restored, locking them in again.

Grabbing blankets from the beds, they wrapped them around their bodies and rushed out the door to the road their captors had used to transport them from the old jail.

From their vantage point, the dense foliage of the mountain sloped to more forest, but there was a break created by a stream. Lower down the mountain, along the stream, the remnants of some kind of mill drew her attention. Pointing to it, she said, "That must be where we were first being held."

Robert nodded and raked his gaze across the landscape. "We can't see Regina, so I'm guessing this is the northern slope."

She dipped her head in agreement. "It is, but we could see some ski trails from the jail, so it must not be all that far to work our way across to the southern slope."

"And not too far from Oliver's vacation home. Too much coincidence for me," Robert said.

"Me too. But we need to decide which way to go. However they got us to that mill, they'll probably use this road up the slope because the vegetation is too dense."

"They'll expect us on this road," he said and made a slow turn, once again considering their landscape and their possible avenue for escape.

Mercedes also took another look around and shook her head. "They will, but it will be night soon. And it may take some time for them to figure out what's happening with the power."

"And that we're gone."

She nodded and gestured to the road. "That's our best bet. And we have to somehow get word to Sophie and Robbie that they're in danger."

"We do. Let's go," he said as he grabbed her hand and, with a reassuring squeeze, they rushed down the road together.

THEY HAD BEEN too wired after the wins at the blackjack table and the confrontation with Blackwell to remain in the room. Sophie had wanted to deposit the money she had won to avoid it being a source of temptation for anyone who had been watching her win and for Blackwell. But the local branch for her bank chain had been closed for a few hours.

Needing a break, they'd opted for a bite to eat before returning to the hotel to work and wait for word from Jackson on the outing on the mountainside.

"What do you plan on doing with the money?" he asked as they exited the hotel, vigilant for any signs that they were being followed.

"I suspect Matt Clark might need it to hire a good lawyer if we can't make arrangements with the DA to be lenient," she said and likewise quickly peeked around, uncomfortable with carrying so much cash because they couldn't leave it at the hotel.

"That's very generous of you," he said. He was aware Sophie's family and their agency often undertook cases that others wouldn't at little or no charge.

With a careless shrug, she said, "I get Matt. And our families know what it's like to have it hard. It wasn't always easy for us."

Her unexpected answer made him want to know more. "I never pictured either of the two families struggling."

Another shrug, almost hesitant, warned that it might not be easy to talk about, so he tried to ease her discomfort. "I get Matt also, remember. My family had similar problems," he said as they strolled along the picturesque main street where the casino was located.

The town reminded him of Regina with its quaint downtown, so different from the casino, although the casino's opulence and over-the-top décor weren't obvious from the street.

Sophie stopped walking, forcing him to likewise pause and face her. "It couldn't have been easy for you," she said and laid her hand over his heart.

He covered her hand with his and pressed it close. "I survived and Matt will as well with all of us in his corner."

"We will help him," she said with a determined nod and

was about to walk away, but he took hold of her hand to stop her.

"What's troubling you, Sophie? Besides this investigation?" he asked, sensing the undercurrents darkening her normally blue eyes to the turbulent gray of a stormy sea.

She huffed out a breath and threw her hands up in frustration. "Besides the investigation? My missing parents, who might be dead now for all I know."

He gently took hold of her hands as she waved them and brought them close to his heart again. "We're closer to finding them. Believe that, Sophie."

She lowered her head and shook it. Drawing in a shaky breath, she raised her eyes to his again, tears glistening in their depths. "I'm trying to believe that, Ryder. It's just hard to do with all that's going on."

Releasing her hands, he swept his arms around her and drew her close. He hugged her, rocking her the way a father might comfort a child, but Sophie was no child and his comfort…

She likely would better appreciate his helping her find her parents.

That became obvious as she stepped from his embrace and wiped the tears from her face. "We really should get that bite and go back to work," she said, voice husky with emotion.

With a nod, he took hold of her hand and they strolled down the street and crossed to a small bistro that seemed to have a nice number of customers. Hopefully, a sign that the food was good.

Despite the crowd, they were instantly seated at a table near the windows, allowing them to watch for any signs of Blackwell's two goons or any other suspicious types.

Luckily, all appeared quiet, and as the waitress brought over the menus, he turned his attention to dinner.

SOPHIE WASN'T REALLY HUNGRY. She was too anxious about way too many things. Her parents. The money. Blackwell. Ryder.

She wanted to believe that they'd find her parents soon. She really did. After all, they'd made so much progress. But was it quick enough?

The twenty-four hours were speeding away. Too rapidly. By her estimate, they only had about another ten hours.

"Sophie? Sophie," Ryder said, snapping her attention back to the present.

The waitress was there, pen poised over her pad. "Would you like a drink?"

"House red is fine," she said, thinking that a glass of wine might help her relax.

The waitress nodded and rushed off, but Ryder leaned close over the narrow width of the table and said, "I'm here if you want to chat."

She avoided his gaze, feeling the warmth of tears rising again. "What's there to say?"

He laid his hand on hers as it rested on the table. "I've never been to Miami. What's your life there like?"

She chuckled and wagged her head, aware of his ploy and yet going along with it because it might clear her mind so she could find the hidden message her parents had sent.

"What's it like? I work a lot with my cousins at the agency," she said and grabbed a piece of crusty French bread from the basket in the center of the table.

"All work and no play—"

"I play with my cousins, especially Mia and Carolina. They used to be important lifestyle influencers, so they still have an in at all the big events," she said while applying butter to the bread although, with as much as she liked, it might be better to say butter with bread.

"Is it as glamorous as you see on all those shows?" he asked and popped a piece of buttered bread into his mouth.

"It is, and dangerous as well at times. But I suspect you may face much of the same in Denver since it's gotten so popular."

"Sometimes," he began but stopped as the waitress placed their drinks on the table and took their food orders before walking away.

He'd ordered a soda, which almost made her reconsider her glass of wine. *Almost*, she thought as she took a sip. Fruity, slightly sweet, and light, with little alcohol.

"You said it hadn't always been easy for your family," he said and buttered another piece of bread for himself.

"It wasn't. Miami wasn't as welcoming of Cubans when my grandparents first arrived in the 1960s and both the Whitaker and Gonzalez families served in the military. That presented the issues of moving around and finances," she admitted, recalling the stories she'd heard over the years from the various family members.

"I get that about the military, but I don't regret serving. I protected my country, and I met Jackson and Diego."

"My cousin Trey met many of his friends in the Marines and quite a few of them work for SBS now, especially with the addition of our new K-9 unit. Trey is still looking for more agents."

A wry grin erupted across his features. "Any room for a corgi with an attitude?" he teased.

She couldn't picture Delilah chasing after criminals even if some Asian police department had decided to try it out. But she could definitely picture Ryder working with SBS.

Delilah would make a good...photo op, she thought, picturing the corgi with her happy grin and a guard dog harness. Come to think of it, Ryder would be pretty appealing in the photo as well.

He raised his glass as if in a toast and said, "Here's to whatever put that smile on your face and twinkle in your eye."

"If I tell you, we might not finish dinner," she teased, voice husky with desire.

His eyes widened and then grew darker as passion flared.

Fate spared them as the waitress arrived at that moment with their meals.

She placed the thick hunk of filet sitting beside potatoes and peas in front of Ryder. She'd noticed that about him in the short couple of days since they'd met. He was a meat-and-potatoes kind of man and that had her thinking of how he might acclimate to Miami. Not that there weren't plenty of steakhouses, or Cuban foods for that matter, to satisfy him.

The aroma of her pulled pork over mac and cheese awoke hunger, and she picked up her fork and dug into her meal. The bite of green chilies in the pork surprised her at first but mellowed as the buttery and creamy flavors of the cheese sauce joined in.

Silence and appreciative murmurs filled the air as they ate, driven by hunger. But as that need was sated, reality reminded her that a clock was ticking and not just for her parents, she realized.

For them.

Once her parents were back home safe and sound, because she had to believe that would happen, she'd be headed home. To Miami.

And Ryder would be back here. In Denver and Regina.

The ache that erupted in the middle of her chest stole her breath for a hot second and drew Ryder's attention.

"Everything okay?" he asked, his gaze intense as it roamed her features.

"A little spicy," she lied. It was too soon to admit what she was feeling.

"Maybe some milk?" He was about to wave the waitress over but she stilled the motion of his hand.

"I'm good. Just not used to the green chilies in so many foods," she said and pulled a chuckle from him.

"Cuban food isn't as spicy, I guess."

"It isn't. Maybe you'll visit Miami and find out for yourself," she said in that sex-husky voice that she didn't recognize since it was so unlike her regular self.

His gaze warmed again and an enticing half smile erupted. "I'd like that," he said and motioned the waitress for the check. "We should get going."

"Yes, I need to work," she said, reminding herself of what needed to happen once they returned to the room.

The waitress was efficient, the walk short, and in no time they were hurrying off the elevator on the way to their room.

But as they neared the door, she slowed, tension building inside her as that ticking clock inside warned again that time was running out.

For her parents.

For her time with him.

She turned, leaned against the door and stared up at him, wanting to memorize every detail. His seal-black hair, the longer strands at the top either tousled from the way he shifted his hand through it to tame the wavy locks or in frustration. The dark shadow of his evening beard. It would be rough against her skin as it had been when they'd made love the night before. The mahogany brown of his eyes, darker now, almost black, as passion rose. His lips…

She wanted to remember it all. Remember him for when she left.

Rising on tiptoes, she kissed him, pressing her body to his. Feeling every inch of him as he wrapped an arm around her waist and hauled her close.

The sharp, insistent ring of a phone registered, shattering the moment.

She whipped it out of her pocket.

"Robbie," she whispered and shook her head, certain she'd kill her brother the next time she saw him.

Ryder scowled, opened the door, and they stepped in, distracted by passion and the phone call.

The men came at them, tasing Ryder first as the second man wrapped her in his arms and squeezed, driving the air from her.

Black circles danced before her gaze, and she struggled. *Not like this. It's not going to end like this.*

Chapter Eighteen

His ears were ringing and ringing, his body shuddering, as Ryder fought for control.

His knees weakened and he hit the ground, battling to remain conscious.

He rolled and rolled, trying to disengage the wires to the Taser and, as the shock stopped, he realized he had succeeded.

But the relief would be temporary, he knew, if his attacker decided to drive-stun him with the weapon.

Eyesight clearing, he managed a leg swipe to take down his attacker as the man came at him with the Taser.

Lurching to his feet, he steadied himself for an attack as his assailant likewise rose and charged, driving him against the wall.

Drywall crumbled behind him, dampening the force of the blow.

He brought his elbow down sharply on the back of the man's neck, stunning him and letting him break free.

Ryder's first thought as he stumbled away from his attacker was, *Sophie*.

He had only a second to search for her before his assailant recovered and came at him again.

She was fighting off the taller security guard from the casino.

Shaking his head to clear his vision some more, he recognized the shorter, squatter guard rushing at him.

Like a matador dodging a bull, he sidestepped the man and gave him a shove that sent him reeling into a nearby console table.

The weight of the man sent the table tumbling down, glasses and bottles hitting the floor and shattering with a loud crash.

Loud enough, he hoped, to draw someone's attention and have them calling for help.

His one hope was that it wouldn't be more of Blackwell's goons.

As the man untangled himself from the shattered wood of the table, Ryder punched him in the side of the head, stunning him. A second blow rendered him unconscious.

Ryder rushed to help Sophie, not that she needed the help as, with a roundhouse kick, she sent the security guard bouncing against the wall. Stunned, the man stood there for an unsteady second before slowly sliding down the wall, unconscious.

Sophie grabbed the zip ties sticking out of the man's pocket and secured his hands and feet.

A groan drew their attention to the second guard.

Ryder accepted the zip ties that Sophie handed him, hurried over and restrained the man before he could attack them again.

The loud pounding of footsteps coming down the hall blended with the harsh ringing of Sophie's phone again.

A duo of security guards came to the door just as Sophie walked away to answer the phone.

The men seemed shocked to see their two colleagues in restraints until Ryder quickly explained what had happened.

One of the men got on the phone with someone. Blackwell,

he supposed, but was surprised when the man said, "Yes, roger that. We'll wait for the police to arrive."

The police? He was surprised for quite a few reasons. He didn't think Blackwell would want that kind of publicity associated with the casino. He also couldn't believe that Blackwell would turn on his men so speedily.

Almost as if he'd heard, Blackwell suddenly appeared at the door, a worried look on his face before it flipped to one of surprise.

"Heavens to Betsy," he said and wrung his hands as he walked into the room. "I don't know what to say. I trusted these men."

Yep, he's throwing his men under the bus. Ryder wasn't going to let Blackwell off so easily.

"I suppose you knew nothing about them coming here," he challenged.

"You think I told them to do this?" he said and elegantly splayed a hand across his chest. "My only instructions were to keep you out of the casino. Nothing else. I guess the thought of all that money gave them other ideas."

Ryder laughed harshly and shook his head. "If you think I believe that, I've got a bridge to sell you."

Sophie walked over at that moment and laid a hand on his arm. "I need to talk to you."

RYDER NODDED AND they stepped off to one side of the room for privacy. As they did so, Ryder cradled her cheek. "Are you okay? Did he hurt you?"

They'd been so busy securing the men, they hadn't had a chance to recover. "I'm fine. A few bruises but okay. What about you?"

He glanced down at his side and the tears and blood from

the Taser barbs. "Aching, again, and I'll need to have these taken out."

She muttered a curse in Spanish and tenderly skimmed her fingers near his wound. "¡Lo siento tanto!"

"No need for you to apologize. You didn't do this," he said as tears filled her gaze, making his face shimmer.

She looked away, feeling guilty at all he'd suffered on her behalf and because she had failed. "I didn't see the message but Robbie finally did. The countdown wasn't for my parents, it was for us. Whoever is behind this warned we'd be dead in twenty-four hours."

"Is he safe? Selene?" Ryder asked, worried furrows across his brow.

"He fought off an attack and they're both fine. They're heading back to Rhea's condo for the night."

Ryder nodded and shot a look over his shoulder at Blackwell, who seemed to be leaning toward them as if to overhear.

"It isn't just about the money," she said, certain that the two men had been instructed to take them to pressure her parents.

"It isn't, and we need to put some pressure on Blackwell, but not now," he said as two police officers came to the door and signaled to them.

What followed was nearly an hour of questioning about what had happened, with Blackwell profusely apologizing for his men and denying any involvement. The police officers seemed undecided by his entreaties and inclined to take him in as well for questioning.

Sophie waved them off. "It seems clear to us these men acted alone," she said, keeping her attention on the bigger picture of stopping the threat to her parents now that the danger to her and Robbie had been neutralized for the moment.

The female officer's eyes widened in disbelief and focused on Ryder. "Are you sure, CBI Agent Hunt? I'd rather be on the safe side and take everyone in for questioning."

Ryder nodded to confirm Sophie's instructions. "I'm sure, but I'd appreciate any update on what happens with their interview," he said and tossed a hand in the direction of their two attackers.

The officer nodded. "Will do."

Sophie glanced at Blackwell, who was still standing there, feigning ignorance and innocence as he gawked at her and said, "Again, I'm so sorry. We'll move you to another room, at no charge, of course. And if you need anything, my number is on this card."

"Of course. We appreciate that," Sophie said pleasantly. Or as Blackwell might say, so sweetly that butter wouldn't melt in her mouth. Southern expressions one and all, it occurred to her.

Blackwell motioned to two replacement security guards, who followed him into the hallway. His innocent demeanor vanished as he almost berated the guards with his instructions.

After, he stalked off down the hall, his pronounced posture and bouncing gait reminding her of an illustration she'd once seen of Ichabod Crane in a *Sleepy Hollow* book.

"He won't try again tonight," Ryder said in a whisper.

"He won't, but who knows what he might do to my parents now," she replied but didn't get to consider it further as the new security guards flew into action, helping them gather their things and moving them to a luxurious penthouse suite.

The door had barely closed on the two guards when room service staff wheeled in a cart covered with pastries, cheeses, crackers and a bottle of champagne.

"Compliments of Mr. Blackwell," the man said, as if that could possibly make up for all that had happened.

But Sophie wasn't about to blame the staff and opened her purse to hand him a tip. "Please thank him for us."

The man's eyes widened at the sight of all the hundreds, but he quickly scurried away, leaving them alone in the immense suite.

Too alone, she thought and then remembered Ryder's injuries. Gesturing to his side, she said, "We should take care of those barbs."

"And call Jackson while we're at it."

IN THE BATHROOM, Ryder handed her the shaving kit he'd picked up in the casino's store. Besides his shaving needs, he'd luckily added some basic first-aid supplies.

"You should have all you need in there," he said as he opened the buttons on his shirt and carefully removed it to not drive the barbs deeper.

Sophie bent to examine them and winced. "They're not in deep but..."

"It'll hurt. I understand," he said and eased his phone from his front pocket.

Waving it in the air, he said, "Let's call Jackson while you do it." He hoped the call might distract him from the pain.

Jackson answered immediately and he turned on the speaker and set the phone on the bathroom vanity so that Sophie could hear as she worked. "Are you okay? I just heard from Robbie that you were both attacked."

Ryder's gaze met Sophie's as he said, "We're okay. Minor injuries."

"Glad to hear. We've had some surprises here as well," Jackson said.

"I hope you're all okay," he said.

"No attacks, just something unexpected," Jackson said and then continued his report. "Mark, Diego and I got part of the way up the northern slope and realized someone had cut a new trail across the slope. We backtracked to get an ATV and accessed the new trail. Turns out that trail took us to the mill, where we could spot one of the ski trails."

"So it isn't as hard to get to from the resort or Oliver's vacation home?" Ryder asked, just to confirm he was understanding correctly.

"It isn't, because someone has razed a trail to the mill and then up the mountain," Jackson reported.

Ryder and Sophie shared a look and Sophie said, "A road that didn't show up on the LiDAR images from Selene's investigation?"

"It looks to be too new," Jackson advised, and in the background they could hear Mark and Diego echoing their agreement to his observation.

"We're at the mill right now. There's evidence that someone's been inside what looks like a small jail. Dirt and dust are disturbed. There are some scratches on the lock," Jackson added.

"As if someone broke out. Do you think it was the Whitakers?" Ryder pressed.

"Who else?" Jackson replied and quickly added, "It's getting dark but we're not stopping. We're following this road up since it might lead to that other image on the LiDAR survey."

"Keep us posted and, more importantly, stay safe," Ryder said and ended the call.

As he met Sophie's glance, she gestured to his side and said, "All done."

He glanced at the white gauze and tape that was stark against his skin and the darker bruises from his earlier injuries.

"Thank you," he said and met her teary gaze. Unexpected in the warrior he'd come to love.

That thought shocked him so much that he did a little jump on the toilet seat.

Her eyes narrowed and she laid a hand on his bare shoulder. "Are you okay?"

He shook his head, rose and held her gaze. "I'm not sure," he admitted.

Her eyes widened in surprise and she jerked a thumb in the direction of the bathroom door. "Should we go to the hospital?"

Grabbing hold of her thumb, he pulled her close to his hardening body, making it clear what it was that he needed.

Chapter Nineteen

"O-o-oh," Sophie stammered, eyes wide at his scrutiny, so dark and compelling it made her heart trip in anticipation.

"I want you, Sophie. I think I love you," he said and shook his head ruefully, almost as if he didn't believe that he'd finally said the words out loud.

"I think I love you too," she said with a hint of surprise that turned to joy as she repeated it. "I love you too."

He wrapped his arms around her and, smiling, kissed her.

She felt that smile, that happiness, against her lips and welcomed it, meeting his kiss over and over.

They backed out of the bathroom and rushed into the nearby bedroom, leaving a trail of clothes along the journey to coming together. Blissful laughter and kisses celebrated that they'd survived and found something special because of it.

The rush to passion slowed, embraced that celebration as they explored each other, learning even more about one another. About what pleasured and pleased. About what united them as she arched against him, nearing completion. Wanting to join with him as she fell over the edge.

He entered her, so slowly she almost begged him to go faster.

Deeper, she thought, tilting her hips up to welcome his possession.

Ryder stilled then and braced his arms on the bed, rising slightly to peer down at her as he answered her plea, shifting inside her. Watching her as he drew her ever higher until, with one sharp thrust, they tumbled over together.

She wrapped her arms around him, keeping him close as they shifted to their sides.

"Te quiero, mi amor," she said, pledging her love.

"Te quiero," he repeated and sealed his promise with a kiss.

Long moments passed in satisfying silence until he slipped from her, prompting groans of complaint.

"I'll be back," he said, hurried to the bathroom and returned quickly to join her under the covers.

He cradled her in his arms, offering comfort she held on to since she knew that at any moment, her smartphone could ring and destroy their joy.

MERCEDES HEARD THE ROAR of the ATV before spotting the bouncing headlights racing up the road.

Robert swept his arm across her and hauled her back into the protective embrace of the boughs of a stand of pines.

Their scent wrapped around her, so alive and fresh, reminding her that Robert and she were still alive. That they could survive this.

She held her breath as the noise of the ATV grew ever closer, the lights ever brighter.

It was less than ten yards away when, through the boughs of the pines, she detected something different this time.

Three men, not two. Unmasked. Two dogs tucked into a cargo area.

Another bounce and shift allowed the moonlight to drift over the driver.

A white Stetson and the gleam of a badge.

"It's Jackson," she said and grabbed hold of Robert's arm.

"Are you sure?" he said, but she didn't wait to rush out from the pines to the middle of the road where she waved her arms to alert them to her presence.

The engine noise quieted as the ATV jolted to a stop.

A tall figure slipped from behind the wheel and stepped toward her.

"Tia Mercedes?" Jackson called out, almost as if he didn't believe what he was seeing.

"Dios mio, Jax. It's us. We're here," she babbled as Robert wrapped his arms around her, and Jackson and his officers approached, their canines leashed at their sides.

Jackson embraced them in a bear hug. "I can't believe you're here."

Mercedes pointed up the road. "They were holding us in some kind of bunker up the mountain."

He nodded and glanced at his two officers. "We need to secure that location until we can get CBI's CSI to gather evidence."

Mercedes laid a hand on his arm and warned, "We broke out by taking down all the power to the bunker, Jax. I'm not sure if they know we're gone or if they'll come back for us."

"If they're coming to investigate what's happening, they'll be coming up this trail," he said and examined the road in both directions. Facing her, he said, "I need to get you somewhere safe—"

"It's more important that you catch these men," she said, understanding that there was no way to move them to safety without possibly encountering their kidnappers.

"Diego, take point and head to that bunker in case they

beat us there somehow. We'll head up behind you, but wait until you say it's clear," Jackson said, taking command.

"Roger that," Diego said and took off at a jog up the road, Poppy loping beside him.

Jackson walked them to the ATV. "Mark, watch our six while I drive to the bunker."

Mark nodded, commanded his dog into the cargo bin and climbed up into it, rifle at the ready.

Jackson helped them into the back seat, hopped into the driver's seat and slowly advanced up the road, waiting for Diego's all clear before proceeding.

When that permission came, Jackson hurried to the bunker, the ATV bouncing to and fro, forcing Mercedes to grab hold of one of the roll bar supports and Robert.

At the bunker, Jackson drove the ATV a distance away and tucked it deep into a stand of pines. He hopped out, faced them and said, "You wait here until it's clear."

"Mark, you're with me," he said, and they rushed off to join Diego.

Her heart pounded in her chest as she watched them go, fearing for her nephew and his officers. She worried that their two kidnappers wouldn't give up without a fight. She also worried that even if they did capture the two minions, they'd be unable to find the mastermind behind the plot and keep Sophie and Robbie safe.

Robert must have sensed her fear. He took hold of her hand and said, "It'll be over soon, my love. Believe that."

Mercedes only wished she could.

THE CALL CAME shortly after ten, just as Sophie and Ryder were working on locating possible connections from the money laundering to State Senator Oliver.

"We've got Mercedes and Robert. They're safe," Jackson

said, but Ryder heard past those words to what his friend wasn't saying.

"Are you safe? Where are you?" he asked and met Sophie's gaze over the phone sitting on the tabletop.

"At the bunker they escaped from. We've called CSI and backups from CBI, but we're holding down the fort on our own for now," Jackson said.

Since he knew that the situation was fluid and could get dangerous at any moment, he said, "Stay safe, Jax. Remember you have a baby who'll be here soon and a wife who's waiting for you."

"Roger that," Jackson said and ended the call.

Sophie blew out a frustrated sigh and dragged her fingers through her hair. "I feel so useless just sitting here."

Ryder reached out and tucked back a lock of hair that had fallen forward with her action. "Not useless. You and Robbie are going to find a link between the money laundering and Oliver."

With a nod and pained smile, she said, "You're right. What are you going to do?"

It took Ryder only a second to know how he could help. "Blackwell gave you his business card, right?"

Sophie opened a side pocket on her purse, pulled it out and slid it across the table to him.

He examined it and said, "There's a phone number here. Any way to tell if it's a landline without alerting him?"

"SBS has access to a service that lets us verify that." She took the card back from him and typed away on her laptop. With a dip of her head, she said, "Cell phone."

"Any way I can track it?"

She wiggled her fingers in a give-it-to-me gesture and said, "Your cell phone, please."

He handed it over and waited as she danced her nimble

fingers across the surface. Patient, he waited until she gave a satisfied little nod and laid the phone on the table. Pointing to it, she explained, "I've got a program that's tracking that number. Right now, it appears he's stationary, probably in his office. As soon as he moves, you'll see this blip shift on the screen."

"I'll monitor this while you work. Any idea on how to tie Oliver to all this?" he asked as he motioned to everything around them.

She tipped her head to one side, thoughtful, before snapping her fingers. "Dark money."

He narrowed his gaze as she went to work on the computer. "Dark money?"

With a quick nod, she said, "Wealthy donors who want to fly under the radar funnel money into a super PAC to support a politician. Sometimes the donors hide behind shell companies so the public doesn't know who's influencing the elections. Especially if the super PAC doesn't reveal their donors until after the polls have closed."

"Seems like dangerous interference in our elections," he said, brow furrowed as he considered the bad actors who might be manipulating naïve voters unaware of the dark money flow.

"It is, but it has me thinking," she said and peered upward as if searching for an answer in the heavens.

"What if a super PAC was being used to launder money? Shell company with dirty money donates. The politician gets the money and pays it out to another shell company as supposed campaign expenses," she said after a short pause.

"Do you think you can find that connection from Blackwell to a PAC and then to Oliver?" he asked just as a beep on the phone warned that the cell phone had moved.

"I think so. I'll get Robbie working on it while we see where Blackwell is going," she said and shot to her feet.

"Where do you think you're going?" He also rose and reached for his holster and jacket.

"I'm not going to just sit here, especially if Blackwell is going to rabbit now that my parents are free," she said.

He couldn't argue. "I'll have my SUV brought around. I get the feeling we might need it," he said and called the hotel valet.

Sophie packed her laptop and purse into her knapsack and slipped on a jacket.

Slinging one knapsack strap over her shoulder, she followed Ryder out the door as he rushed to the elevator.

Once on the elevator, he blew out a frustrated breath. "If this is right, Blackwell is on his way out of the lobby."

Sophie glanced at the cell phone screen. "Hopefully we can catch up to him."

They hit the ground level almost running and noticed a familiar silhouette rushing through the entrance to the casino. He wheeled a small carry-on behind him, clearly intending to travel.

Halfway through the lobby, two of Blackwell's security guards barred their path.

"You're not permitted into the casino," the one said, glaring at Sophie, his legs and arms spread wide to block their way.

With a glance at Ryder from the corner of her eye, she held her hand out and said, "I'll get the car. You go after him."

There was the barest hesitation before he handed her the valet ticket. "Wait for me."

He rushed off, trying to make up for the ground lost by the security guard's interference.

RYDER'S GUT WAS in a knot about leaving Sophie alone, but she had told him early on that she could handle herself and she'd proven it to him more than once.

That didn't stop his worry as he nearly jogged across the casino floor, trying to catch up to Blackwell.

The older man wasn't that quick on his feet, and he'd been wheeling a suitcase, so the odds were in his favor.

But Blackwell likely knew every nook and crevice of this casino and where to make his escape.

Ryder bet on it being out a side entrance by the FOB terminals they'd investigated earlier.

Luck was on his side as he arrived and noticed the exit door slowly closing.

He ran there and jerked the door open only to be greeted by the slam of a car door and a screech of wheels as a big black SUV sped down the street.

But it had to go right past where his SUV sat in the driveway for the casino, Sophie at the wheel.

Running to his vehicle, he held his one side as the pounding reawakened pain from his injuries.

He yanked open the door, hopped in and said, "Go, go, go."

SOPHIE DIDN'T NEED him to say another word.

She hit the gas, almost fishtailing out of the driveway to eat up the distance to Blackwell's SUV.

Beside her, Ryder, buckling up, let out a pained grunt as they hit a big dip in the road that almost made her lose control of the wheel.

Luckily, her cousin Trey had insisted that all South Beach Security personnel take a course on defensive and security driving that had honed her skills behind the wheel.

She righted the nose of the SUV and was now barely a few

yards behind their fleeing suspect's vehicle, which had lost some speed when its front end bottomed out after the dip.

"We've got a 10-80, pursuit in progress. Black Porsche SUV. License plate 666888. Heading south on the main street. Suspects may be armed and dangerous. We need backup," he advised the local PD dispatcher while also digging a police light out of his glove compartment to slap on the roof.

"Sixes and eights are hopefully not going to be lucky for them today," she said, referring to the lucky Chinese numbers on the SUV's license plate.

A second later, the flash of red, blue and white reflected on the back window of Blackwell's SUV. It was immediately joined by other flashing lights as a police cruiser blocked the street in front of them.

Blackwell's driver turned sharply onto a side street, metal crunching and shrieking as the SUV clipped the side of a parked car.

Sophie followed, fighting the wheel to keep control as Ryder called in their current heading.

As before, it wasn't long before a second cruiser appeared yards ahead, hindering escape down the side street. Another police cruiser was on their tail, providing backup.

Bright brake lights had Sophie pumping her brakes, trying to avoid a collision as Blackwell's SUV attempted another turn.

Attempted because they hadn't counted on the oncoming traffic.

A large tractor trailer slammed into the passenger side of the SUV, driving it across several lanes before coming to a sickening stop.

Carefully, she inched onto the street and, once it was clear, moved as close as she could to the site of the accident where two other police cruisers had blocked any avenue of escape. The officers from those vehicles were already on the ground, guns drawn.

"Police. Come out with your hands up," the one officer called out as the driver's-side door slowly opened.

Hands became visible over the edge of the door. A large body in a black suit followed and the armed officers approached.

"Where's Blackwell?" she queried aloud as Ryder and she exited their vehicle and neared the scene, Ryder flashing his badge to alert the officers.

They reached the vehicle just as the officers had secured the driver's hands with a zip tie.

The driver looked toward the SUV and said, "It doesn't look good."

Ryder swept an arm to hold her back, went to the rear driver's-side door and opened it. Bending to look inside, he reached in and then shook his head.

"He's dead. Call in the coroner," he said, stepped back and returned to her side.

Sadness filled his features as he told her, "Blackwell's side took the brunt of the blow. It's over."

But was it?

Chapter Twenty

The police had kept them at the accident scene for well over an hour. By the time they returned to the casino and made a brief call to Jackson to advise him on what had happened, the midnight hour had come and gone.

Sophie stood at the wall of windows on the suite's penthouse floor, arms wrapped around herself as if she were trying to hold herself together.

He walked over and slipped his arm around her waist, and she sank against his chest, the action filled with weariness.

"We should get some rest. It'll be a busy day tomorrow," he said, bending and whispering a kiss along the underside of her jaw.

She turned into his arms and embraced him. Peering upward, she said, "It will be busy, but… I can't believe it's over just like that."

He tipped his head to the side, wondering if it meant they were also over just like that. But he saw something in her eyes that gave him hope and so he took the risk.

"It may take months to sort things out with Oliver and Matt Clark. Any others that were involved. Will you be able to stay that long?"

A wry smile crept across her lips and she ran her hand up

his body to splay it over his heart. "Is that the only reason I should stay, Ryder?"

Covering her hand with his, he pressed it tight, as if willing her to feel the way his heart beat when she was near. "What do you think, Sophie?"

SOPHIE HADN'T COME to Regina expecting this man and what she was feeling for him.

But she knew that she wasn't ready to leave until she'd had a chance to explore him and the love they had declared for each other.

"I think I'd like that. I think I'd like to see if what we're feeling is…forever," she said and rose on tiptoes to skim her lips against his.

He tightened his hold on her, hauling her tight against him. Every dip and hollow of his body, the hard length of him, had her body throbbing for the pleasure he could bring.

As she rubbed her body along his, he groaned, bent and lifted her into his arms, dragging a happy laugh from her as she wrapped her arms around his neck and rained kisses along the strong line of his jaw and sensitive skin beneath.

He scrunched his neck and groused, "Stop, that tickles."

"Does it?" she teased and, for good measure, gave a little love bite at that sensitive spot.

Payback came quickly as he dropped her into the center of the bed and immediately began a slow and seductive attack on her senses, dropping kisses against the skin he revealed as he undressed her.

She was shaking, her fingers digging into the mattress as he reached her center.

"Ryder, por favor," she pleaded and, with a shove, had him on his back on the mattress.

Straddling him, she met his gaze and it nearly undid her at the sight of the love there and she had to say it.

"Te quiero, Ryder. I don't know how it happened, but I love you," she said, bent and kissed him with all that she was. With all that she had to give.

He answered, his mouth meeting hers over and over until it wasn't enough for either of them.

Without breaking the kiss, she somehow got his shirt and pants off and then they were rolling on the bed, laughing and kissing. Celebrating that they'd found each other amid so much danger and death.

As it got serious, she opened for him, her hands on his shoulders, guiding him to her center. Joined with him as passion overwhelmed and drew them up, ever higher, until with their rough shouts of completion they fell over together.

Cradled in each other's arms, they finally let sleep pull their tired minds and bodies to rest, knowing that the next day would be a busy one.

But one they would face together.

THE THUD OF FEET on wood sounded in the morning air as Delilah raced down the police station steps and then launched herself at him.

An oomph escaped him at the force of the impact against his thighs, but he picked up the corgi and hugged her close before setting her on the ground and rubbing her head and body affectionately.

"I've missed you too," he said.

From beside him, he heard, "Dios mio. Dios mio."

Sophie raced up the steps and into the arms of her parents. They embraced each other and rocked with happiness.

He waited, not wanting to interrupt the moment, his heart filled with joy.

As the trio separated, Sophie swiveled to hug Jackson, who had been standing off to one side, giving the Whitaker family the moment for their reunion.

Ryder figured it was as good a time as any and walked up the steps to finally meet the Whitakers in person.

He held his hand out to Mercedes but she immediately enveloped him in her arms and hugged him tight.

When she released him, he took a minute to examine her and realized this was what Sophie would look like as she grew older. Still beautiful but with the graceful lines of age and happiness at the edges of her lips and bright blue-green eyes. The barest threads of silver marred the long strands of her chocolate-brown hair.

He faced Robert and held out his hand. The man grabbed it with both of his hands and shook it enthusiastically. "Nice to finally meet you, Ryder."

"I'm happy to see you both happy and healthy."

"We should get inside. I've got Oliver and his lawyer in the box," Jackson said and gestured for them to enter.

At the front desk, Milly greeted them and said, "Do I have the pleasure of a visit from Delilah again?"

Ryder hated passing off the corgi again, especially since they'd been apart for so long and his fur baby wasn't used to being without him for such a long time.

"If you don't mind, I'll take her with us," he said and walked with her back toward the interrogation room and their war room.

Once they were safely ensconced there, Jackson took a spot at the front of the room while Sophie sat beside him and opened up her laptop. Robert and Mercedes sat opposite them.

Delilah hopped into Ryder's lap, clearly determined to

make up for his absence as she dropped doggy kisses all along his face.

"Easy, girl," he said and, after rubbing her barrel-like body playfully, let her slip to the floor where she took a spot close to his legs.

Jackson turned on the monitor on the far wall, pointed at Sophie's computer and said, "Robbie should be calling you in a few."

No sooner had he said that, Sophie's laptop rang out with a warning that a video call was incoming. With a few keystrokes, she answered and popped Robbie's video feed to the monitor.

That prompted a chorus of surprised gasps as Robbie's black eye and bruised face filled the screen. Selene sat beside him, worry marring her beautiful features.

Although Robbie had mentioned an attack the night before, he'd given the impression that it hadn't been anything serious. His face said otherwise.

"Someone came at us. He got away and honestly..." Robbie hesitated and glanced at Selene. "I'm not sure it has to do with this case, but this does," he said and immediately broadcast a website for a political super PAC.

"You were so right, Sophie. This PAC donated a ton of money to Oliver, and guess who made the donations?"

"Let me guess?" Sophie said facetiously.

"About a dozen shell companies created by the law firm representing Blackwell," Robbie said.

"Robert and I did some more digging on Blackwell once Jackson brought us to his home. It turns out that he was originally from Georgia, and the man who spoke to us in that bunker used many Southern idioms," Mercedes advised.

"You think it was Blackwell directing you?" Ryder asked just to confirm.

"We do," Robert immediately said and added, "Plus, the records we were being asked to delete were connected to a money laundering case the FBI had brought against someone with connections to Blackwell."

"It seems as if we have all the connections we need to make a case against Oliver," Sophie said and glanced around the table to judge the others' thoughts.

Her parents were nodding, almost in unison. Jackson tipped his head from side to side before dipping his head in agreement.

"We do, and I've got the district attorney coming in shortly with one of the FBI agents on that money laundering case. I've also talked to the DA and pressed for leniency for Matt Clark based on his age and cooperation with us," Jackson advised.

"Do you think she'll agree to that?" Ryder asked.

Jackson nodded. "I think she will, especially since John Wilson has offered to take on Matt as an intern while he's serving a probationary term. Wilson has also offered to move the Clark family to the Miami area so they can start new lives away from Oliver or any of Blackwell's associates."

"You've been busy while Sophie and I were at the casino," Ryder said, feeling as if the investigation had zoomed past them in just the course of a few hours.

"I have, and I'm sorry we couldn't keep you posted, but since you were busy with the police about Blackwell's death and then driving home, there wasn't time," Jackson said by way of apology.

He understood. Anticipation about returning to Regina had hauled them from bed early. Too early for them to share any morning intimacies, but they would have time for more now that Sophie planned on staying in Colorado for a few more months at least.

That had him reaching beneath the edge of the table to slip his hand into Sophie's and twine his fingers with hers as he anticipated spending more time together.

Sophie took comfort from the weight of Ryder's hand in hers.

Glancing around the table and at the screen at Robbie's bruised face, she figured it was as good a time as any to let her family know of her plans.

"It seems as if everything is under control right now," she said, and all around the table offered words or nods in agreement.

Glancing at Ryder, who smiled and nodded, she pushed on. "It's going to take a few months to finish up everything on this case and I thought I'd stay in Colorado, with Ryder, while that's all going on."

She'd expected surprise but instead received words of encouragement and congratulations from all around the table.

"I'm happy to hear that. Rhea and I will love having you around once the baby arrives," Jackson said. With a jab of his finger at Ryder, however, he said, "Remember what I told you."

Ryder laughed. "She's your cuz and, believe me, I'm going to take real good care of her," he said and, as if to prove it, dropped a kiss on her cheek.

"That's wonderful, Sophie," her mother said with a side-eye at her husband.

Robert immediately piped in with, "Mercedes and I had a lot of time to think while we were captive, and we're going to retire from the NSA. If your parents don't mind, Jax, we'd like to borrow their lake cottage for a few weeks while we decide what to do next."

"I think they'd love that. They won't be back from Florida for at least another month or more," Jackson said.

"Wow, that's so...weird," Robbie said, pulling their attention to the screen where Robbie and Selene seemed to be sharing more than a friendly glance.

"What's so weird, Robbie?" Sophie asked, although she could guess from her brother's bruised face.

"I thought I'd hang out a little more in Denver. Selene's offered to let me use the spare room and I'd feel better once I know that last night's attack was related to Oliver."

A worried look swept across Jackson's face. "If you need help—"

"I got you and also Ryder and Sophie since I assume they'll be coming back to Denver," Robbie said without hesitation.

"Will your staying here be a problem for SBS?" Jackson asked, peering between Robbie and her.

She shook her head. "We've worked remotely before, and I think Trey will be happy to know we're happy."

The phone rang, interrupting their family announcements.

Jackson answered and listened for only a few seconds before hanging up. "The DA and FBI agent are here. I get the feeling the Feds are going to snatch this case from us and I'm okay with that. I want to reopen the investigation into Cromwell's parents' deaths, get this station secured better and ramp up our new K-9 division," he said.

"We can help with the security, and I'm sure Trey can offer some advice on the K-9s since we just started our division," Sophie said.

"Great. I'll go meet with the DA and FBI agent." Jackson then glanced toward Mercedes and Robert. "Milly can get you the keys to the lake cottage and arrange for a rental car."

"If they'll even give us one after the last rental," Robert said with a laugh now that the danger was over.

Jackson chuckled and shook his head. "You always were a bad driver," he teased and skipped his gaze between Sophie and Ryder.

"You're welcome to stay for the interrogation."

Ryder clasped her hand a little tighter and said, "We will sit in just to confirm that the Feds are going to take credit for all the hard work we did."

That prompted laughter all around the table and as they started to rise, Robbie signed off with, "See you two in Denver."

Jackson hurried from the room first, but Sophie and Ryder waited to heartily hug and e*f*mbrace her parents.

"I'll be back to visit once I'm settled in Denver," Sophie promised, earning a tight hug from her mother, who looked intensely at Ryder.

"Take care of mija," she said before grabbing him for a hug.

"I will take care of your daughter. I love her," he admitted, provoking another tight hug and handshake from Robert.

After her parents left, they stood in the room, staring at each other until Ryder held his hand out to her.

"Are you ready?" he asked, eyes gleaming with joy and an inviting smile on his face.

Was she ready for forever with him?

She wondered for only a millisecond.

Slipping her hand into his, she said, "I'm ready."

* * * * *